EVERYMAN'S LIBRARY

EVERYMAN,
I WILL GO WITH THEE,
AND BE THY GUIDE,
IN THY MOST NEED
TO GO BY THY SIDE

V. S. NAIPAUL

COLLECTED
SHORT
FICTION

WITH AN INTRODUCTION
BY THE AUTHOR

EVERYMAN'S LIBRARY
Alfred A. Knopf New York Toronto

334

THIS IS A BORZOI BOOK

PUBLISHED BY ALFRED A. KNOPF

First included in Everyman's Library, 2011

Miguel Street:
Copyright © 1959, copyright renewed 1987 by V. S. Naipaul
A Flag on the Island:
Copyright © 1967, copyright renewed 1995 by V. S. Naipaul
In a Free State:
Copyright © 1971 by V. S. Naipaul

Miguel Street originally published in Great Britain by André Deutsch
Limited, London, in 1959. First published in the United States by
The Vanguard Press, New York, in 1960.
A Flag on the Island originally published in Great Britain by André
Deutsch Limited, London, in 1967.
In a Free State originally published in Great Britain by André Deutsch
Limited, London, in 1971 and in the United States by Alfred A.
Knopf, New York, in 1973.

Introduction Copyright © 2010 by V. S. Naipaul.
Select Bibliography and Chronology Copyright © 2011 by
Everyman's Library
Typography by Peter B. Willberg

All rights reserved. Published in the United States by Alfred A.
Knopf, a division of Random House, Inc., New York, and in Canada
by Random House of Canada Limited, Toronto. Distributed by
Random House, Inc., New York.

www.randomhouse.com/everymans

ISBN: 978-0-307-59402-0

A CIP catalogue reference for this book is available from the
British Library

Book design by Barbara de Wilde and Carol Devine Carson

Typeset in the UK by AccComputing, North Barrow, Somerset

Printed and bound in Germany by GGP Media GmbH, Pössneck

CONTENTS

INTRODUCTION

The stories in *Miguel Street* were begun by a man who had everything to learn about writing and himself. The writing ambition had come very early to me, but it had always been only a kind of warm glow inside me, giving me the vaguest idea of what I might do. The writing ambition had come without the wish to do a particular kind of book, and so it stayed for years. I didn't even know in the beginning what kind of writer I might be. Was my gift a comic one or was it profounder? I wrote many stories in this blank period, but nothing like a book announced itself to me. I did attempt a book; I attempted two books; but the creative fog refused to lift. The first book I attempted was a version of *Black Mischief*, giving it a Trinidadian setting. I managed, with a kind of self-induced blindness, to take this to the end in the long vacation, writing very fast when the end was in sight. One man said it was 'phoney Waugh'. I suffered at that, and marked this man down both for his wit and the soundness of his judgement. I believe the book was actually presented, by a very kind friend, to a London publisher, but fortunately for everyone it was turned down.

It seemed to me as a result that farce or comedy was not what I was meant for, and the next book I attempted three or four years later was extremely serious. I had no story; I thought I should do an account of a day in the life of someone such as I had been. The book lumbered on and on. When I left Oxford I took this dreadful half-book with me to London. I had had the good fortune to land a little editorial job at the BBC. This job not only saved me from destitution; it also put me in touch with real writers and real critics, and I had the folly or the vanity to send my manuscript to one of those people. He sent it back almost by return post and said that I should forget this work. It was very wounding to me; especially as it was so close to what I had begun to feel about the book. And it was with this great depression, of rejection and general hopelessness, that one afternoon, in the freelancers' room in the Langham Hotel, then a part of the BBC, I sat before one of the big typewriters and started the first story of *Miguel Street*. I had no idea where I was going, but somehow the idea had come to me that I should not leave the freelancers' room until I had finished the story. My life as a writer until then had been full of beginnings, and it would have added to my gloom to make yet another false start.

The next day I began and finished a second story, and the day after that I did a third. These stories had the same imaginative setting, were written in the same tone of voice, in the same spare language, and were in fact part of a vision I didn't know I possessed as a writer until the moment of writing. After a few days – of immense excitement – the stories became too long to be completed at a sitting. The stories had to be carried in my head until the following day, and sometimes for days. It was new to me to carry work with me for many days; and without my knowing it, without understanding what I had let myself in for I in this way learnt something about the nature of writing. The reader of this book can follow this process of learning and discovery in the stories of the *Miguel Street* sequence. He may think I claim too much for the stories, but I am speaking here of something very personal, something that tipped me over from despair into beginning to be a writer.

This is a process that happened in my own mind and will not be easy to explain. Until I had begun *Miguel Street* I had been obsessed with style and language, and had worked very hard to master that aspect of the craft. I had read and tried to learn from many of the approved masters, Defoe, Swift, Dryden and even a few of the moderns who had come my way – the now-forgotten H. M. Tomlinson among them. I suppose they all helped in a way, but they didn't take me nearer to becoming a writer. They didn't take me nearer into understanding what my material was going to be. In fact they made it harder for me to have an idea of the value of my own material; their metropolitan glamour was too great.

The *Miguel Street* stories seemed to write themselves. I didn't step back to consider myself writing, and it was hard for me to understand where I had got that tone of voice. Many years later I thought the voice came from the Castilian, and especially from the sixteenth-century picaresque novel *Lazarillo de Tormes*. I had studied and greatly admired this book in the sixth form. Later I was to translate it. I was hoping that the Penguin Classics might want to do it; but after a little initial encouragement it was not to be. But the effect of all this was that the tone of the old Spanish book sang in my head, and I am sure it helped me to get started.

The stories I was writing in this dreamlike way were of the life of a Port of Spain street. I had no idea where the stories would lead me, and the theme of the street and its life was part of the luck of that occasion in the freelancers' room in the BBC. I had worried a great deal about arriving at my material. This luck undid that worry. To write about the street, which I of course knew, was to be flooded with material, an embarrassment of riches, folk myths, folk songs, newspaper stories, all worked on now by transforming memory. My concern when I began had been with language, a wish to raise my language above the language of the school essay, and to turn it into something closer to the writing one might come upon in a book. Yet, miraculously this concern with language led to narrative, to writing at length. It led me very close to having an idea of the book. I had begun, as I said, to carry the material in my head, and insensibly the stories became longer. I didn't know where I was going. The story of 'The Enemy', published here in a later section, was written as a part of *Miguel Street*. At this stage I was sufficiently in control of my material to understand that it was wrong for the *Street*. I kept it apart, then and later, and I was glad that I did so because three years later it led me to one of the stronger scenes of a much more important book, *A House for Mr Biswas*. To have used the material in another way would have been to lose it. So I was given a sense of what I was doing and was no longer as keen as I might have been earlier to bulk out a book. Inevitably the stories of *Miguel Street* came to an end; it became important to look for a publisher.

In a better-ordered world the stories of *Miguel Street* would have excited a publisher. The publisher I was dealing with was indeed excited; he wanted to publish me, but he had the publisher's wisdom about short stories. He said that they never sold. He wanted a novel before anything else and so I spent the rest of the year trying to write a novel. It was four years before *Miguel Street* was published, and – alas for the publisher's wisdom – it has never been out of print, earning its regular fifty percent for the publisher. The stories that were done later need no apology; I consider them part of my work.

Three or four of these stories, however, deserve a special word. I was in India at the time, writing *Mr Stone and the Knights Companion* in a small lake hotel in Kashmir. I had an arrangement with my London bank whereby they regularly sent me money. It occurred to me one day – out of an abundance of caution, as the lawyers say – to write to the bank to find out how my money was holding up. They replied in a frightening and unexpected way that my money had almost run out.

'The Baker's Story' and 'A Christmas Story' were written out of that ensuing panic. They were written on the typewriter at a great rate, and almost nothing was corrected. I have written nothing else in this way, and I suppose it was possible because I had trained myself to write carefully during the writing of *Miguel Street*.

People who think I exaggerate the importance of *Miguel Street* in my development as a writer should consider some of the stories from *A Flag on the Island*. 'The Mourners' and 'My Aunt Gold Teeth' would be among the earlier things I wrote, 'The Mourners' done when I was eighteen and 'My Aunt Gold Teeth' when I was twenty-two. People were kind about 'The Mourners' in Oxford. It was read out to small groups and it flattered me to hear distinguished voices reading my words. But as the years passed I began to have doubts about 'The Mourners' and I pass these doubts to the reader. What was the basis of the narrator's knowingness in 'The Mourners'? How much did he know about grief or birth? How much of this knowingness was pretence, to go with the satirical tone of the narration? I got to feel in the end that that story and one or two others like it had got away by the skin of their teeth. I saw very clearly that skill with the language is no substitute for true experience. I leave these stories in this compilation because they are among the earlier work I wrote.

Day by day, as I wrote *Miguel Street*, I seemed to see the faces on the street. I saw their fences, the pavements outside their houses, and many of the other things that went to create their characters in my eyes. They were like a revelation, bringing back to life. Respectable old black women lived in tightly fenced jalousied houses, and one never saw what they looked like. Some houses, not of the best kind, had no fences; these were dwelt in for some reason by Indians. The shop at the end of the street was of course a Chinese shop, and the older people there still had trouble with English. As the street came near to me in this writing recall, I moved away from what was close to my house. I went near the sea, the area we knew as Docksite. This area of the harbour had been dredged and deepened before the war and the dredged-up mud of the Gulf had slowly dried into black saucers cracked at the edges. This area became the American military base. They ran up their attractive timber buildings very fast and their building talent, their elegance, put our houses to shame. The men were always neatly dressed, khaki trousers and shirt freshly ironed, the khaki tie tucked in between the third and fourth button of the shirt. Jeeps appeared on the street, driven by soldiers apparently indifferent to the wear of tyres; our own poor folk had to be more careful with their smooth, shiny, irreplaceable tyres. Every evening the American flag on the base was lowered, and the bugle sounded: an extra drama added to the life of the street.

In this section 'The Nightwatchman's Occurrence Book' deserves a special mention. It is my most anthologised piece of short fiction, and deservedly so. It is very funny. The idea came to me from a boarding-house where I had stayed when I was doing the travel for *The Middle Passage*. I carried the idea for ten years and then, when I was in India, gathering material for *An Area of Darkness*, and being shocked out of my life as I have said earlier by a letter from a London bank, I wrote it all at once on the typewriter. Some of the sentences are still with me.

'... he pelt a box of matches at me, matches scatter all over the place ...'

'Mr Wills complained bitterly to me this morning that last night he was denied entry to the bar by you. I wonder if you know exactly what the purpose of this hotel is ...'

V. S. NAIPAUL

'Mr Manager, remarks noted. I sorry I didnt get the chance to take some education sir. *Chas. Ethelbert Hillyard*'

'This morning I received a report from a guest that there were screams in the hotel during the night. You wrote All Quiet. Kindly explain in writing. *W. A. G. Inskip*'

'Sir, nothing unusual means everything usual. I dont know, nothing I writing you liking . . .'

The stories in the last section of this compilation are quite different from what has gone before. They are the work of a liberated man, and the reader may like to see how far he can link the stories of *Miguel Street* with the stories of this final section. Its theme is displacement in the modern world, an idea which would have been beyond the imagining of the people of *Miguel Street*. The main fiction of this segment has been left out here. It is now published as an independent novel in another place, and in that place I have written about the origin and inspiration of the work. The idea of displacement did not come out of the air; I had sold my London house, and was living and trying to write – not unhappily, but with a daily sense of wrongness – in someone else's house. It was a far cry from that to the plight of two English expatriates caught in tribal conflict in East Africa; but that is the way literary inspiration sometimes works. The expatriates in this fiction are working for the local African government. They're reasonably secure, and for them, besides, in the good times the country is a kind of resort, with every sort of amenity. The whole protected thing begins to break down at a time of local tribal conflict, and reaches a climax during a long drive from a place like Nairobi to a place like Kampala. I made these characters English because I wished to make the point that displacement doesn't concern colonised people alone.

The managing of that narration, of the increasingly dangerous long drive, would have been taxing enough for an experienced writer. But I added to it two unrelated stories. These stories were meant to support, to add weight to, the main fiction and also indirectly to bring the writer into the picture, to link the writer to the material he was presenting to the reader. The first of these supporting stories was about an

Indian servant in Washington, the second about a West Indian Asian in London. And, as though that wasn't complexity enough, there was a non-fiction prologue, and a non-fiction epilogue. The prologue began in Greece and was played out on a Greek ship going to Alexandria; the epilogue was about Chinese communist sightseers in Egypt (the reader should bear in mind that the Egyptian piece was written in 1969–70).

The superstructure was too great. Perhaps the central fiction by itself (about the expatriates caught up in a tribal bloodletting) would have been enough to make my point; but this was the first time that I had ventured out into what I saw as metropolitan territory and I wished to leave nothing to chance. Later, when I had shed my nerves about the metropolis, I was to wonder why I had burdened myself with all the extra labour. The subsidiary pieces of *In a Free State* were not easy to write, they each required to be 'set'. This slowed me at a time when I would have liked to move more quickly but the book brought me reward of a sort. It won the Booker Prize, then in its second or third year, and still at that stage dedicated to the idea of giving recognition to the unrecognised. So the book gave me a kind of reputation.

V. S. Naipaul

SELECT BIBLIOGRAPHY

The Adventures of Gurudeva, André Deutsch, 1976, a collection of stories by Naipaul's father Seepersad, with a foreword by Naipaul, is indispensable reading for anyone interested in this writer's work, besides possessing its own considerable interest. The books of his brother Shiva are also recommended. They include the novels *Fireflies*, André Deutsch, 1970, and *The Chip-Chip Gatherers*, André Deutsch, 1973.

V. S. Naipaul: A Critical Introduction, Macmillan, 1975, by Landeg White, is valuable for its sensitive readings of the earlier work by a critic inward with West Indian life. Another critic of West Indian background is Selwyn Cudjoe, whose *V. S. Naipaul: A Materialist Reading*, University of Massachusetts, 1988, has an appreciative discussion of *Biswas*; the later work is discussed from an adversarial standpoint. A similar approach, concerned mainly with Naipaul's non-fiction, can be found in *London Calling: V. S. Naipaul, Postcolonial Mandarin*, Oxford University Press, 1992, by Rob Nixon. An earlier account is William Walsh's *V. S. Naipaul*, Oliver and Boyd, 1973. John Thieme's *The Web of Tradition*, Hansib Publishing, 1987, deals with 'the uses of allusion' in the fiction. A short study by Peter Hughes, *V. S. Naipaul*, Routledge, appeared in 1988. Naipaul's books have attracted a large amount of periodical criticism: a selection of such material is presented in *Critical Perspectives on V. S. Naipaul*, Heinemann Educational, ed. Robert Hamner, 1979.

CHRONOLOGY

DATE	AUTHOR'S LIFE	LITERARY CONTEXT
1932	Birth of Vidiadhar Surajprasad Naipaul in Trinidad (August 17).	1932 Huxley: *Brave New World.* Faulkner: *Light in August.*
		1934 Fitzgerald: *Tender is the Night.* Miller: *Tropic of Cancer.* Waugh: *A Handful of Dust.* 1935 Lewis: *It Can't Happen Here.* Steinbeck: *Tortilla Flat.* 1936 Faulkner: *Absalom, Absalom!* Eliot: *Collected Poems.* 1937 Dos Passos: *USA.* Steinbeck: *Of Mice and Men.* Hemingway: *To Have and Have not.* 1938 Greene: *Brighton Rock.* Waugh: *Scoop.* 1939 Steinbeck: *The Grapes of Wrath.* Joyce: *Finnegans Wake.* Miller: *Tropic of Capricorn.* 1940 Hemingway: *For Whom the Bell Tolls.* Greene: *The Power and the Glory.* 1941 Fitzgerald: *The Last Tycoon.* 1942 Eliot: *Four Quartets.* Camus: *The Stranger.*
1943–8	Attends Queen's Royal College, Port of Spain.	
		1945 Orwell: *Animal Farm.* Waugh: *Brideshead Revisited.* Borges: *Fictions.* 1948 Greene: *The Heart of the Matter.* Paton: *Cry, the Beloved Country.* 1949 Orwell: *Nineteen Eighty-Four.*

1932 Election of Roosevelt in US. Nazis become largest party in German Reichstag.
1933 Roosevelt announces 'New Deal'; Hitler becomes German Chancellor.

1935 Nuremberg Laws depriving Jews of citizenship and rights.

1936 Outbreak of Spanish Civil War (to 1939). Hitler and Mussolini form Rome–Berlin Axis. Stalin's 'Great Purge' (to 1938).

1937 Japanese invasion of China.

1938 Germany annexes Austria; Munich crisis.

1939 World War II.

1940 Fall of France; Battle of Britain.

1941 Japanese attack Pearl Harbor; USA enters war. Hitler invades USSR.

1942 Rommel defeated at El Alamein.

1943 Allied invasion of Italy.
1944 Allied landings in Normandy.
1945 Defeat of Germany. Atomic bombs dropped on Hiroshima and Nagasaki. End of World War II. Foundation of the United Nations.
1947 Indian independence. Cold War develops.
1948 Jewish state of Israel comes into existence. Apartheid introduced in South Africa. Gandhi assassinated in India.

1949 Chinese Revolution. Foundation of NATO.

DATE	AUTHOR'S LIFE	LITERARY CONTEXT
1950–54	University College, Oxford; settles in England.	1951 Frost: *Complete Poems.* Salinger: *The Catcher in the Rye.* 1952 Beckett: *Waiting for Godot.* Steinbeck: *East of Eden.* 1953 Bellow: *The Adventures of Augie March.*
1954–6	Editor, 'Caribbean Voices' for the BBC, England.	1954 Amis: *Lucky Jim.* Golding: *Lord of the Flies.*
1955	Marries Patricia Anna Hale.	1955 Nabokov: *Lolita.* Williams: *Cat on a Hot Tin Roof.* 1956 Osborne: *Look Back in Anger.*
1957–61	Fiction reviewer for the *New Statesman*. *The Mystic Masseur* (1957, wins John Llewellyn Rhys Prize); *The Suffrage of Elvira* (1958); *Miguel Street* (1959, wins Somerset Maugham Award).	1957 Kerouac: *On the Road.* 1958 Pasternak: *Doctor Zhivago.* Achebe: *Things Fall Apart.* 1959 Burroughs: *Naked Lunch.* Bellow: *Henderson the Rain King.* 1960 Updike: *Rabbit, Run.*
1961	*A House for Mr Biswas.*	Heller: *Catch-22.*
1962	*The Middle Passage.*	1962 Nabokov: *Pale Fire.* Solzhenitsyn: *One Day in the Life of Ivan Denisovich.*
1963	*Mr Stone and the Knights Companion.*	
1964	*An Area of Darkness.*	
		1966 Rhys: *Wide Sargasso Sea.*
1967	*A Flag on the Island*; *The Mimic Men.*	1967 Márquez: *One Hundred Years of Solitude.* 1968 Solzhenitsyn: *Cancer Ward.*
1969	*The Loss of El Dorado.*	
1971	*In a Free State.* (Wins Booker Prize.)	1971 Updike: *Rabbit Redux.*

CHRONOLOGY

1950 Korean War (to 1953)

1952 Eisenhower elected US President. Accession of Elizabeth II.

1953 Death of Stalin. European Court of Human Rights set up in Strasbourg.
1954 Vietnam War begins.

1956 Suez crisis. British and French begin process of decolonization in Africa. Khrushchev reveals to the Twentieth Party Congress the truth about Stalinist purges. Soviet troops crush Hungarian uprising.
1957 Civil Rights Act in US. European Economic Community founded.

1959 Castro seizes power in Cuba.

1960 Sixty-seven demonstrators killed at Sharpeville, South Africa. Belgian Congo becomes independent.
1961 John F. Kennedy elected US President. Erection of Berlin Wall. South Africa excluded from Commonwealth. ANC banned. Yuri Gagarin becomes first man in space.
1962 Cuban missile crisis. Trinidad and Tobago become independent within the British Commonwealth. Commonwealth Immigrants Act. Algeria granted independence by France.
1963 Assassination of John F. Kennedy.

1964 Khrushchev deposed and replaced by Brezhnev.
1965 India–Pakistan war.
1966 Mao launches Cultural Revolution in China. Indira Gandhi becomes Prime Minster of India.
1967 Arab–Israeli Six-Day War. Civil war in Nigeria (Biafra).

1968 Student unrest in US and throughout Europe. Russian invasion of Czechoslovakia. Assassination of Martin Luther King. Nixon US President.
1969 Resignation of de Gaulle in France. Americans land first man on the moon.
1970 Black Power revolt in Trinidad.
1971 Formation of Bangladesh.

V. S. NAIPAUL

DATE	AUTHOR'S LIFE	LITERARY CONTEXT
1972	*The Overcrowded Barracoon.*	
		1973 Pynchon: *Gravity's Rainbow.*
		Greene: *The Honorary Consul.*
1975	*Guerrillas.*	1975 Levi: *The Periodic Table.*
1977	*India: A Wounded Civilization.*	1977 Morrison: *Song of Solomon.*
1979	*A Bend in the River.*	1979 Calvino: *If on a winter's night a traveler.*
1980	*The Return of Eva Perón* (with *The Killings in Trinidad*).	1980 Burgess: *Earthly Powers.*
1981	*Among the Believers.*	1981 Rushdie: *Midnight's Children.*
1983	Honorary Fellow, University College, Oxford.	1983 Narayan: *A Tiger for Malgudi.*
1984	*Finding the Centre.*	
		1985 Márquez: *Love in the Time of Cholera.*
		1986 Walcott: *Collected Poems.*
1987	*The Enigma of Arrival.*	1987 Morrison: *Beloved.* Levi: *The Drowned and the Saved.*
		1988 Rushdie: *The Satanic Verses.*
1989	*A Turn in the South.*	1989 Márquez: *The General in his Labyrinth.*
1990	*India: A Million Mutinies Now.* Knighthood for Services to Literature.	1990 Updike: *Rabbit at Rest.* Walcott: *Omeros.*
		1991 M. Amis: *Time's Arrow.* Okri: *The Famished Road.*
1993	Wins the first David Cohen Prize for Literature.	
1994	*A Way in the World.*	1994 Heller: *Closing Time.*
1996	Wife Patricia Naipaul dies (3 February); marries Nadira Khannum Alvi (15 April).	1996 Márquez: *News of a Kidnapping.*
1997	*Letters.*	1997 Bellow: *The Actual.* Roth: *American Pastoral.* Roy: *The God of Small Things.*

CHRONOLOGY

1972 President Amin expels Asians from Uganda. First Strategic Arms Limitation Treaty.

1973 Arab–Israeli War.

1974 Resignation of Nixon following Watergate scandal.

1975 End of Vietnam War; exodus of the 'Boat People' begins. State of Emergency declared in India (to 1977). Guerrilla armies come to power in Angola and Mozambique. USSR and Western powers sign Helsinki Agreement.

1976 Trinidad and Tobago become an independent republic.

1979 Margaret Thatcher first woman Prime Minister in UK. Carter and Brezhnev sign SALT-2 arms limitation treaty. Soviet occupation of Afghanistan. Iranian revolution; American hostage crisis.

1980 An independent Zimbabwe formed.

1982 Falklands War.

1983 Reagan proposes 'Star Wars'.

1984 Famine in Ethiopia. Indira Gandhi assassinated.

1985 Riots in South Africa. Gorbachev General Secretary in USSR.

1986 Gorbachev–Reagan summit.

1988 Gorbachev announces big troop reductions. Benazir Bhutto Prime Minister of Pakistan.

1989 Collapse of Communism in Eastern Europe. Fall of the Berlin Wall. Tiananmen Square massacre in China.

1990 Nelson Mandela released from jail after 27 years' imprisonment. German reunification. John Major becomes Prime Minister in UK. Attempted coup by Islamic fundamentalists in Trinidad.

1991 Gulf War. Yeltsin President of Russia. USSR disbanded.

1992 Bill Clinton elected US President. Civil war in former Yugoslavia.

1993 Israel hands over West Bank and Jericho to Palestinians. Storming of White House, Moscow.

1994 Mandela and ANC sweep to victory in South African elections. Rwandan massacres. Russian military action against Chechen republic.

1997 Tony Blair elected Prime Minister in UK (first Labour government since 1979). Princess Diana is killed in a car accident in Paris.

DATE	AUTHOR'S LIFE	LITERARY CONTEXT
1998	*Beyond Belief.*	1998 Morrison: *Paradise.* Pamuk: *My Name is Red.*
1999	*Between Father and Son: Family Letters.*	1999 Coetzee: *Disgrace.*
2000	*Reading and Writing: A Personal Account.*	2000 Ishiguro: *When We Were Orphans.* Smith: *White Teeth.*
2001	*Half a Life*; Nobel Prize.	2001 McEwan: *Atonement.* Franzen: *The Corrections.*
2002	*The Writer and the World: Essays.*	2002 Martel: *Life of Pi.*
2003	*Literary Occasions: Essays.*	2003 Atwood: *Oryx and Crake.* Adichie: *Purple Hibiscus.*
2004	*Magic Seeds.*	2004 Munro: *Runaway.*
2005		2005 Banville: *The Sea.*
2006		2006 Kiran Desai: *The Inheritance of Loss.* Murakami: *Blind Willow, Sleeping Woman.*
2007	*A Writer's People: Ways of Looking and Feeling.*	2007 Hosseini: *A Thousand Splendid Suns.*
2008		2008 Pamuk: *The Museum of Innocence.*
2009		2009 Mantel: *Wolf Hall.* Byatt: *The Children's Book.*
2010	*The Masque of Africa: Glimpses of African Belief.*	

CHRONOLOGY

1998 Northern Ireland Referendum accepts the Good Friday Agreement. Clinton orders air strikes against Iraq.

1999 Serbs attack ethnic Albanians in Kosovo; US leads NATO in bombing of Belgrade.

2000 Milosevic's regime in the former Yugoslavia collapses. George W. Bush is elected President of the US. Putin becomes Russian President. Palestinian *intifadah*.

2001 Al-Qaeda terrorist attacks of 9/11. US and allied military action against the Taliban in Afghanistan.

2002 Guantanamo Bay detention camps established by Bush administration.

2003 Iraq weapons crisis. American and British troops invade Iraq. Civil war in Dafur.

2004 Terrorist bombings in Madrid. Beslan school hostage crisis. Ten countries join the European Union. Indian Ocean tsunami.

2005 Terrorist bombings of 7/7 in London. Major earthquake in Pakistan. Death of Pope John Paul II.

2006 Iran announces that it has joined the nuclear club. Conflict between Israeli and Hezbollah forces in South Lebanon. Saddam Hussein hanged.

2007 Gordon Brown succeeds Tony Blair as Labour Prime Minister in UK. Benazir Bhutto assassinated. Anti-government demonstrations in Burma.

2008 Largest global recession since Great Depression begins. Barack Obama becomes first African-American to be elected US President.

2009 Israel invades Gaza. Defeat of Tamil Tigers ends 26 years of civil war in Sri Lanka.

2010 Earthquake in Haiti. Major oil spill in Mexican Gulf. David Cameron becomes Conservative Prime Minister in UK, leading coalition government.

MIGUEL STREET

For my Mother and Kamla

CONTENTS

1 BOGART

EVERY MORNING WHEN he got up Hat would sit on the banister of his back verandah and shout across, 'What happening there, Bogart?'

Bogart would turn in his bed and mumble softly, so that no one heard, 'What happening there, Hat?'

It was something of a mystery why he was called Bogart; but I suspect that it was Hat who gave him the name. I don't know if you remember the year the film *Casablanca* was made. That was the year when Bogart's fame spread like fire through Port of Spain and hundreds of young men began adopting the hardboiled Bogartian attitude.

Before they called him Bogart they called him Patience, because he played that game from morn till night. Yet he never liked cards.

Whenever you went over to Bogart's little room you found him sitting on his bed with the cards in seven lines on a small table in front of him.

'What happening there, man?' he would ask quietly, and then he would say nothing for ten or fifteen minutes. And somehow you felt you couldn't really talk to Bogart, he looked so bored and superior. His eyes were small and sleepy. His face was fat and his hair was gleaming black. His arms were plump. Yet he was not a funny man. He did everything with a captivating languor. Even when he licked his thumb to deal out the cards there was grace in it.

He was the most bored man I ever knew.

He made a pretence of making a living by tailoring, and he had even paid me some money to write a sign for him:

TAILOR AND CUTTER
Suits made to Order
Popular and Competitive Prices

He bought a sewing machine and some blue and white and brown chalks. But I never could imagine him competing with anyone; and I cannot remember him making a suit. He was a little bit like Popo, the carpenter next door, who never made a stick of furniture and was always planing and chiselling and making what I think he called mortises. Whenever I asked him, 'Mr Popo, what you making?' he would reply, 'Ha, boy! That's the question. I making the thing without a name.' Bogart was never even making anything like this.

Being a child, I never wondered how Bogart came by any money. I assumed that grown-ups had money as a matter of course. Popo had a wife who worked at a variety of jobs; and ended up by becoming the friend of many men. I could never think of Bogart as having mother or father; and he never brought a woman to his little room. This little room of his was called the servant-room but no servant to the people in the main house ever lived there. It was just an architectural convention.

It is still something of a miracle to me that Bogart managed to make friends. Yet he did make many friends; he was at one time quite the most popular man in the street. I used to see him squatting on the pavement with all the big men of the street. And while Hat or Edward or Eddoes was talking, Bogart would just look down and draw rings with his fingers on the pavement. He never laughed audibly. He never told a story. Yet whenever there was a fête or something like that, everybody would say, 'We must have Bogart. He smart like hell, that man.' In a way he gave them great solace and comfort, I suppose.

And so every morning, as I told you, Hat would shout, very loudly, 'What happening there, Bogart?'

And he would wait for the indeterminate grumble which was Bogart saying, 'What happening there, Hat?'

But one morning, when Hat shouted, there was no reply. Something which had appeared unalterable was missing.

Bogart had vanished; had left us without a word.

The men in the street were silent and sorrowful for two whole days. They assembled in Bogart's little room. Hat lifted up the deck of cards that lay on Bogart's table and dropped two or three cards at a time reflectively.

Hat said, 'You think he gone Venezuela?'

But no one knew. Bogart told them so little.

And the next morning Hat got up and lit a cigarette and went to his back verandah and was on the point of shouting, when he remembered. He milked the cows earlier than usual that morning, and the cows didn't like it.

A month passed; then another month. Bogart didn't return.

Hat and his friends began using Bogart's room as their club house. They played *wappee* and drank rum and smoked, and sometimes brought the odd stray woman to the room. Hat was presently involved with the police for gambling and sponsoring cock-fighting; and he had to spend a lot of money to bribe his way out of trouble.

It was as if Bogart had never come to Miguel Street. And after all Bogart had been living in the street only for four years or so. He had come one day with a single suitcase, looking for a room, and he had spoken to Hat who was squatting outside his gate, smoking a cigarette and reading the cricket scores in the evening paper. Even then he hadn't said much. All he said – that was Hat's story – was, 'You know any rooms?' and Hat had led him to the next yard where there was this furnished servant-room going for eight dollars a month. He had installed himself there immediately, brought out a pack of cards, and begun playing patience.

This impressed Hat.

For the rest he had always remained a man of mystery. He became Patience.

When Hat and everybody else had forgotten or nearly forgotten Bogart, he returned. He turned up one morning just about seven and found Eddoes and a woman on his bed. The woman jumped up and screamed. Eddoes jumped up, not so much afraid as embarrassed.

Bogart said, 'Move over. I tired and I want to sleep.'

He slept until five that afternoon, and when he woke up he found his room full of the old gang. Eddoes was being very loud and noisy to cover up his embarrassment. Hat had brought a bottle of rum.

Hat said, 'What happening there, Bogart?'

And he rejoiced when he found his cue taken up. 'What happening there, Hat?'

Hat opened the bottle of rum, and shouted to Boyee to go buy a bottle of soda water.

Bogart asked, 'How the cows, Hat?'

'They all right.'

'And Boyee?'

'He all right too. Ain't you just hear me call him?'

'And Errol?'

'He all right too. But what happening, Bogart? *You* all right?'

Bogart nodded, and drank a long Madrassi shot of rum. Then another, and another; and they had presently finished the bottle.

'Don't worry,' Bogart said. 'I go buy another.'

They had never seen Bogart drink so much; they had never heard him talk so much; and they were alarmed. No one dared to ask Bogart where he had been.

Bogart said, 'You boys been keeping my room hot all the time?'

'It wasn't the same without you,' Hat replied.

But they were all worried. Bogart was hardly opening his lips when he spoke. His mouth was twisted a little, and his accent was getting slightly American.

'Sure, sure,' Bogart said, and he had got it right. He was just like an actor.

Hat wasn't sure that Bogart was drunk.

In appearance, you must know, Hat recalled Rex Harrison, and he had done his best to strengthen the resemblance. He combed his hair backwards, screwed up his eyes, and he spoke very nearly like Harrison.

'Damn it, Bogart,' Hat said, and he became very like Rex Harrison. 'You may as well tell us everything right away.'

Bogart showed his teeth and laughed in a twisted, cynical way.

'Sure I'll tell,' he said, and got up and stuck his thumbs inside his waistband. 'Sure, I'll tell everything.'

He lit a cigarette, leaned back in such a way that the smoke got into his eyes; and, squinting, he drawled out his story.

He had got a job on a ship and had gone to British Guiana. There he had deserted, and gone into the interior. He became a cowboy on the Rupununi, smuggled things (he didn't say what) into Brazil, and had gathered some girls from Brazil and taken them to Georgetown. He was running the best brothel in the town when the police treacherously took his bribes and arrested him.

'It was a high-class place,' he said, 'no bums. Judges and doctors and big shot civil servants.'

'What happen?' Eddoes asked. 'Jail?'

'How you so stupid?' Hat said. 'Jail, when the man here with we. But why you people so stupid? Why you don't let the man talk?'

But Bogart was offended, and refused to speak another word.

From then on the relationship between these men changed. Bogart became the Bogart of the films. Hat became Harrison. And the morning exchange became this:

'Bogart!'

'Shaddup, Hat!'

Bogart now became the most feared man in the street. Even Big Foot was said to be afraid of him. Bogart drank and swore and gambled with the best. He shouted rude remarks at girls walking by themselves in the street. He bought a hat, and pulled down the brim over his eyes. He became a regular sight, standing against the high concrete fence of his yard, hands in his pockets, one foot jammed against the wall, and an eternal cigarette in his mouth.

Then he disappeared again. He was playing cards with the gang in his room, and he got up and said, 'I'm going to the latrine.'

They didn't see him for four months.

When he returned, he had grown a little fatter but he had become a little more aggressive. His accent was now pure American. To complete the imitation, he began being expansive towards children. He called out to them in the streets, and gave them money to buy gum and chocolate. He loved stroking their heads, and giving them good advice.

The third time he went away and came back he gave a great party in his room for all the children or kids, as he called them. He bought cases of Solo and Coca-Cola and Pepsi-Cola and about a bushel of cakes.

Then Sergeant Charles, the policeman who lived up Miguel Street at number forty-five, came and arrested Bogart.

'Don't act tough, Bogart,' Sergeant Charles said.

But Bogart failed to take the cue.

'What happening, man? I ain't do anything.'

Sergeant Charles told him.

There was a little stir in the papers. The charge was bigamy; but it was up to Hat to find out all the inside details that the newspapers never mention.

'You see,' Hat said on the pavement that evening, 'the man leave his first wife in Tunapuna and come to Port of Spain. They couldn't have children. He remain here feeling sad and small. He go away, find a girl in Caroni and he give she a baby. In Caroni they don't make joke about that sort of thing and Bogart had to get married to the girl.'

'But why he leave she?' Eddoes asked.

'To be a man, among we men.'

2 THE THING WITHOUT A NAME

THE ONLY THING that Popo, who called himself a carpenter, ever built was the little galvanized-iron workshop under the mango tree at the back of his yard. And even that he didn't quite finish. He couldn't be bothered to nail on the sheets of galvanized iron for the roof, and kept them weighted down with huge stones. Whenever there was a high wind the roof made a frightening banging noise and seemed ready to fly away.

And yet Popo was never idle. He was always busy hammering and sawing and planing. I liked watching him work. I liked the smell of the woods – cyp and cedar and crapaud. I liked the colour of the shavings, and I liked the way the sawdust powdered Popo's kinky hair.

'What you making, Mr Popo?' I asked.

Popo would always say, 'Ha, boy! That's the question. I making the thing without a name.'

I liked Popo for that. I thought he was a poetic man.

One day I said to Popo, 'Give me something to make.'

'What you want to make?' he said.

It was hard to think of something I really wanted.

'You see,' Popo said. 'You thinking about the thing without a name.'

Eventually I decided on an egg-stand.

'Who you making it for?' Popo asked.

'Ma.'

He laughed. 'Think she going use it?'

My mother was pleased with the egg-stand, and used it for about a week. Then she seemed to forget all about it, and began putting the eggs in bowls or plates, just as she did before.

And Popo laughed when I told him. He said, 'Boy, the only thing to make is the thing without a name.'

After I painted the tailoring sign for Bogart, Popo made me do one for him as well.

He took the little red stump of a pencil he had stuck over his ear and puzzled over the words. At first he wanted to announce himself as an architect; but I managed to dissuade him. He wasn't sure about the spelling. The finished sign said:

BUILDER AND CONTRACTOR
Carpenter
And Cabinet-Maker

And I signed my name, as sign-writer, in the bottom right-hand corner.

Popo liked standing up in front of the sign. But he had a little panic when people who didn't know about him came to inquire.

'The carpenter fellow?' Popo would say. 'He don't live here again.'

I thought Popo was a much nicer man than Bogart. Bogart said little to me, but Popo was always ready to talk. He talked about serious things, like life and death and work, and I felt he really liked talking to me.

Yet Popo was not a popular man in the street. They didn't think he was mad or stupid. Hat used to say, 'Popo too conceited, you hear.'

It was an unreasonable thing to say. Popo had the habit of taking a glass of rum to the pavement every morning. He never sipped the rum. But whenever he saw someone he knew he dipped his middle finger in the rum, licked it, and then waved to the man.

'We could buy rum too,' Hat used to say. 'But we don't show off like Popo.'

I myself never thought about it in that way, and one day I asked Popo about it.

Popo said, 'Boy, in the morning, when the sun shining and it still cool, and you just get up, it make you feel good to know that you could go out and stand up in the sun and have some rum.'

Popo never made any money. His wife used to go out and work, and this was easy, because they had no children. Popo said, 'Women and them like work. Man not make for work.'

Hat said, 'Popo is a man-woman. Not a proper man.'

Popo's wife had a job as a cook in a big house near my school. She used to wait for me in the afternoons and take me into the big kitchen and give me a lot of nice things to eat. The only thing I didn't like was the way she sat and watched me while I ate. It was as though I was eating for her. She asked me to call her Auntie.

She introduced me to the gardener of the big house. He was a good-looking brown man, and he loved his flowers. I liked the gardens he looked after. The flower-beds were always black and wet; and the grass green and damp and always cut. Sometimes he let me water the flower-beds. And he used to gather the cut grass into little bags which he gave me to take home to my mother. Grass was good for the hens.

One day I missed Popo's wife. She wasn't waiting for me.

Next morning I didn't see Popo dipping his finger in the glass of rum on the pavement.

And that evening I didn't see Popo's wife.

I found Popo sad in his workshop. He was sitting on a plank and twisting a bit of shaving around his fingers.

Popo said, 'Your auntie gone, boy.'

'Where, Mr Popo?'

'Ha, boy! That's the question,' and he pulled himself up there.

Popo found himself then a popular man. The news got around very quickly. And when Eddoes said one day, 'I wonder what happen to Popo. Like he got no more rum,' Hat jumped up and almost cuffed him. And then all the men began to gather in Popo's workshop, and they would talk about cricket and football and pictures – everything except women – just to try to cheer Popo up.

Popo's workshop no longer sounded with hammering and sawing. The sawdust no longer smelled fresh, and became black, almost like dirt. Popo began drinking a lot, and I didn't like him when he was drunk. He smelled of rum, and he used to cry and then grow angry and want to beat up everybody. That made him an accepted member of the gang.

Hat said, 'We was wrong about Popo. He is a man, like any of we.'

Popo liked the new companionship. He was at heart a loquacious man, and always wanted to be friendly with the men of the street and he was always surprised that he was not liked. So it looked as though he had got what he wanted. But Popo was not really happy. The friendship had come a little too late, and he found he didn't like it as much as he'd expected. Hat tried to get Popo interested in other women, but Popo wasn't interested.

Popo didn't think I was too young to be told anything.

'Boy, when you grow old as me,' he said once, 'you find that you don't care for the things you thought you woulda like if you coulda afford them.'

That was his way of talking, in riddles.

Then one day Popo left us.

Hat said, 'He don't have to tell me where he gone. He gone looking for he wife.'

Edward said, 'Think she going come back with he?'

Hat said, 'Let we wait and see.'

We didn't have to wait long. It came out in the papers. Hat said it was just what he expected. Popo had beaten up a man in Arima, the man had taken his wife away. It was the gardener who used to give me bags of grass.

Nothing much happened to Popo. He had to pay a fine, but they let him off otherwise. The magistrate said that Popo had better not molest his wife again.

They made a calypso about Popo that was the rage that year. It was the road-march for the Carnival, and the Andrews Sisters sang it for an American recording company:

> *A certain carpenter feller went to Arima*
> *Looking for a mopsy called Emelda.*

It was a great thing for the street.

At school, I used to say, 'The carpenter feller was a good, good friend of mine.'

And, at cricket matches, and at the races, Hat used to say, 'Know him? God, I used to drink with that man night and day. Boy, he could carry his liquor.'

Popo wasn't the same man when he came back to us. He growled at me when I tried to talk to him, and he drove out Hat and the others when they brought a bottle of rum to the workshop.

Hat said, 'Woman send that man mad, you hear.'

But the old noises began to be heard once more from Popo's workshop. He was working hard, and I wondered whether he was still making the thing without a name. But I was too afraid to ask.

He ran an electric light to the workshop and began working in the night-time. Vans stopped outside his house and were always depositing and taking away things. Then Popo began painting his house. He used a bright green, and he painted the roof a bright red. Hat said, 'The man really mad.'

And added, 'Like he getting married again.'

Hat wasn't too far wrong. One day, about two weeks later, Popo returned, and he brought a woman with him. It was his wife. My auntie.

'You see the sort of thing woman is,' Hat commented. 'You see the sort of thing they like. Not the man. But the new house paint up, and all the new furniture inside it. I bet you if the man in Arima had a new house and new furnitures, she wouldnta come back with Popo.'

But I didn't mind. I was glad. It was good to see Popo standing outside with his glass of rum in the mornings and dipping his finger into the rum and waving at his friends; and it was good to ask him again, 'What you making, Mr Popo?' and to get the old answer, 'Ha, boy! That's the question. I making the thing without a name.'

Popo returned very quickly to his old way of living, and he was still devoting his time to making the thing without a name. He had stopped working, and his wife got her job with the same people near my school.

People in the street were almost angry with Popo when his wife came back. They felt that all their sympathy had been mocked and wasted. And again Hat was saying, 'That blasted Popo too conceited, you hear.'

But this time Popo didn't mind.

He used to tell me, 'Boy, go home and pray tonight that you get happy like me.'

What happened afterwards happened so suddenly that we didn't even know it had happened. Even Hat didn't know about it until he read it in the papers. Hat always read the papers. He read them from about ten in the morning until about six in the evening.

Hat shouted out, 'But what is this I seeing?' and he showed us the headlines: CALYPSO CARPENTER JAILED.

It was a fantastic story. Popo had been stealing things left and right. All the new furnitures, as Hat called them, hadn't been made by Popo. He had stolen things and simply remodelled them. He had stolen too much, as a matter of fact, and had had to sell the things he didn't want. That was how he had been caught. And we understand now why the vans were always outside

Popo's house. Even the paint and the brushes with which he had redecorated the house had been stolen.

Hat spoke for all of us when he said, 'That man too foolish. Why he had to sell what he thief? Just tell me that. Why?'

We agreed it was a stupid thing to do. But we felt deep inside ourselves that Popo was really a man, perhaps a bigger man than any of us.

And as for my auntie . . .

Hat said, 'How much jail he get? A year? With three months off for good behaviour, that's nine months in all. And I give she three months good behaviour too. And after that, it ain't going have no more Emelda in Miguel Street, you hear.'

But Emelda never left Miguel Street. She not only kept her job as cook, but she started taking in washing and ironing as well. No one in the street felt sorry that Popo had gone to jail because of the shame; after all, that was a thing that could happen to any of us. They felt sorry only that Emelda was going to be left alone for so long.

He came back as a hero. He was one of the boys. He was a better man than either Hat or Bogart.

But for me, he had changed. And the change made me sad.

For Popo began working.

He began making Morris chairs and tables and wardrobes for people.

And when I asked him, 'Mr Popo, when you going start making the thing without a name again?' he growled at me.

'You too troublesome,' he said. 'Go away quick, before I lay my hand on you.'

I WAS MUCH MORE afraid of George than I was of Big Foot, although Big Foot was the biggest and the strongest man in the street. George was short and fat. He had a grey moustache and a big belly. He looked harmless enough but he was always muttering to himself and cursing and I never tried to become friendly with him.

He was like the donkey he had tied in the front of his yard, grey and old and silent except when it brayed loudly. You felt that George was never really in touch with what was going on around him all the time, and I found it strange that no one should have said that George was mad, while everybody said that Man-man, whom I liked, was mad.

George's house also made me feel afraid. It was a broken-down wooden building, painted pink on the outside, and the galvanized-iron roof was brown from rust. One door, the one to the right, was always left open. The inside walls had never been painted, and were grey and black with age. There was a dirty bed in one corner and in another there was a table and a stool. That was all. No curtains, no pictures on the wall. And even Bogart had a picture of Lauren Bacall in his room.

I found it hard to believe that George had a wife and a son and a daughter.

Like Popo, George was happy to let his wife do all the work in the house and yard. They kept cows, and again I hated George for that. Because the water from his pens made the gutters stink, and when we were playing cricket on the pavement the ball often got wet in the gutter. Boyee and Errol used to wet the ball deliberately in the stinking gutter. They wanted to make it shoot.

George's wife was never a proper person. I always thought of her just as George's wife, and that was all. And I always thought, too, that George's wife was nearly always in the cow-pen.

And while George sat on the front concrete step outside the open door of his house, his wife was busy.

George never became one of the gang in Miguel Street. He didn't seem to mind. He had his wife and his daughter and his son. He beat them all. And when the boy Elias grew too big, George beat his daughter and his wife more than ever. The blows didn't appear to do the mother any good. She just grew thinner and thinner; but the daughter, Dolly, thrived on it. She grew fatter and fatter, and giggled more and more every year. Elias, the son, grew more and more stern, but he never spoke a hard word to his father.

Hat said, 'That boy Elias have too much good mind.'

One day Bogart, of all people, said, 'Ha! I mad to break old George tail up, you hear.'

And the few times when Elias joined the crowd, Hat would say, 'Boy, I too sorry for you. Why you don't fix the old man up good?'

Elias would say, 'It is all God work.'

Elias was only fourteen or so at the time. But that was the sort of boy he was. He was serious and he had big ambitions.

I began to be terrified of George, particularly when he bought two great Alsatian dogs and tied them to pickets at the foot of the concrete steps.

Every morning and afternoon when I passed his house, he would say to the dogs, 'Shook him!'

And the dogs would bound and leap and bark; and I could see their ropes stretched tight and I always felt that the ropes would break at the next leap. Now, when Hat had an Alsatian, he made it like me. And Hat had said to me then, 'Never fraid dog. Go brave. Don't run.'

And so I used to walk slowly past George's house, lengthening out my torture.

I don't know whether George disliked me personally, or whether he simply had no use for people in general. I never discussed it with the other boys in the street, because I was too ashamed to say I was afraid of barking dogs.

Presently, though, I grew used to the dogs. And even George's laughter when I passed the house didn't worry me very much.

One day George was on the pavement as I was passing and I heard him mumbling. I heard him mumble again that afternoon and again the following day. He was saying, 'Horse-face!'

Sometimes he said, 'Like it only have horse-face people living in this place.'

Sometimes he said, 'Short-arse!'

And, 'But how it have people so short-arse in the world?'

I pretended not to hear, of course, but after a week or so I was almost in tears whenever George mumbled these things.

One evening, when we had stopped playing cricket on the pavement because Boyee had hit the ball into Miss Hilton's yard, and that was a lost ball (it counted six and out) – that evening I asked Elias, 'But what your father have with me so? Why he does keep on calling me names?'

Hat laughed, and Elias looked a little solemn.

Hat said, 'What sort of names?'

I said, 'The fat old man does call me horse-face.' I couldn't bring myself to say the other name.

Hat began laughing.

Elias said, 'Boy, my father is a funny man. But you must forgive him. What he say don't matter. He old. He have life hard. He not educated like we here. He have a soul just like any of we, too besides.'

And he was so serious that Hat didn't laugh, and whenever I walked past George's house I kept on saying to myself, 'I must forgive him. He ain't know what he doing.'

And then Elias's mother died, and had the shabbiest and the saddest and the loneliest funeral Miguel Street had ever seen.

That empty front room became sadder and more frightening for me.

The strange thing was that I felt a little sorry for George. The Miguel Street men held a post-mortem outside Hat's house. Hat said, 'He did beat she too bad.'

Bogart nodded and drew a circle on the pavement with his right index finger.

Edward said, 'I think he kill she, you know. Boyee tell me that the evening before she dead he hear George giving the woman licks like fire.'

Hat said, 'What you think they have doctors and magistrates in this place for? For fun?'

'But I telling you,' Edward said. 'It really true. Boyee wouldn't lie about a thing like that. The woman dead from blows. I telling you. London can take it; but not George wife.'

Not one of the men said a word for George.

Boyee said something I didn't expect him to say. He said, 'The person I really feel sorry for is Dolly. You suppose he going to beat she still?'

Hat said wisely, 'Let we wait and see.'

Elias dropped out of our circle.

George was very sad for the first few days after the funeral. He drank a lot of rum and went about crying in the streets, beating his chest and asking everybody to forgive him and to take pity on him, a poor widower.

He kept up the drinking into the following weeks, and he was still running up and down the street, making everyone feel foolish when he asked for forgiveness. 'My son Elias,' George used to say, 'my son Elias forgive me, and he is a educated boy.'

When he came to Hat, Hat said, 'What happening to your cows? You milking them? You feeding them? You want to kill your cows now too?'

George sold all his cows to Hat.

'God will say is robbery,' Hat laughed. 'I say is a bargain.'

Edward said, 'It good for George. He beginning to pay for his sins.'

'Well, I look at it this way,' Hat said. 'I give him enough money to remain drunk for two whole months.'

George was away from Miguel Street for a week. During that time we saw more of Dolly. She swept out the front room and begged flowers of the neighbours and put them in the room. She giggled more than ever.

Someone in the street (not me) poisoned the two Alsatians.

We hoped that George had gone away for good.

He did come back, however, still drunk, but no longer crying or helpless, and he had a woman with him. She was a very Indian woman, a little old, but she looked strong enough to handle George.

'She look like a drinker sheself,' Hat said.

This woman took control of George's house, and once more Dolly retreated into the back, where the empty cow-pens were.

We heard stories of beatings and everybody said he was sorry for Dolly and the new woman.

My heart went out to the woman and Dolly. I couldn't understand how anybody in the world would want to live with George, and I wasn't surprised when one day, about two weeks later, Popo told me, 'George new wife leave him, you ain't hear?'

Hat said, 'I wonder what he going do when the money I give him finish.'

We soon saw.

The pink house, almost overnight, became a full and noisy place. There were many women about, talking loudly and not paying too much attention to the way they dressed. And whenever I passed the pink house, these women shouted abusive remarks at me; and some of them did things with their mouths, inviting me to 'come to mooma'. And there were not only these new women. Many American soldiers drove up in jeeps, and Miguel Street became full of laughter and shrieks.

Hat said, 'That man George giving the street a bad name, you know.'

It was as though Miguel Street belonged to these new people. Hat and the rest of the boys were no longer assured of privacy when they sat down to talk things over on the pavement.

But Bogart became friendly with the new people and spent two or three evenings a week with them. He pretended he was disgusted at what he saw, but I didn't believe him because he was always going back.

'What happening to Dolly?' Hat asked him one day.

'She dey,' Bogart said, meaning that she was all right.

'Ah know she dey,' Hat said. 'But how she dey?'

'Well, she cleaning and cooking.'

'For everybody?'

'Everybody.'

Elias had a room of his own which he never left whenever he came home. He ate his meals outside. He was trying to study for some important exam. He had lost interest in his family, Bogart said, or rather, implied.

George was still drinking a lot; but he was prospering. He was wearing a suit now, and a tie.

Hat said, 'He must be making a lot of money, if he have to bribe all the policemen and them.'

What I couldn't understand at all, though, was the way these new women behaved to George. They all appeared to like him as well as respect him. And George wasn't attempting to be nice in return either. He remained himself.

*   *   *

One day he said to everyone, 'Dolly ain't have no mooma now. I have to be father and mother to the child. And I say is high time Dolly get married.'

His choice fell on a man called Razor. It was hard to think of a more suitable name for this man. He was small. He was thin. He had a neat, sharp moustache above neat, tiny lips. The creases on his trousers were always sharp and clean and straight. And he was supposed to carry a knife.

Hat didn't like Dolly marrying Razor. 'He too sharp for we,' he said. 'He is the sort of man who wouldn't think anything about forgetting a knife in your back, you know.'

But Dolly still giggled.

Razor and Dolly were married at church and they came back to a reception in the pink house. The women were all dressed up, and there were lots of American soldiers and sailors drinking and laughing and congratulating George. The women and the Americans made Dolly and Razor kiss and kiss, and they cheered. Dolly giggled.

Hat said, 'She ain't giggling, you know. She crying really.'

Elias wasn't at home that day.

The women and the Americans sang *Sweet Sixteen* and *As Time Goes By*. Then they made Dolly and Razor kiss again. Someone shouted, 'Speech!' and everybody laughed and shouted, 'Speech! Speech!'

Razor left Dolly standing by herself, giggling.

'Speech! Speech!' the wedding guests called.

Dolly only giggled more.

Then George spoke out. 'Dolly, you married, it true. But don't think you too big for me to put you across my lap and cut your tail.' He said it in a jocular manner, and the guests laughed.

Then Dolly stopped giggling and looked stupidly at the people.

For a moment so brief you could scarcely measure it there was absolute silence; then an American sailor waved his hands drunkenly and shouted, 'You could put this girl to better work, George.' And everybody laughed.

Dolly picked up a handful of gravel from the yard and was making as if to throw it at the sailor. But she stopped suddenly, and burst into tears.

There was much laughing and cheering and shouting.

I never knew what happened to Dolly. Edward said one day that she was living in Sangre Grande. Hat said he saw her selling in the George Street Market. But she had left the street, left it for good.

As the months went by, the women began to disappear and the numbers of jeeps that stopped outside George's house grew smaller.

'You gotta be organized,' Hat said.

Bogart nodded.

Hat added, 'And they have lots of nice places all over the place in Port of Spain these days. The trouble with George is that he too stupid for a big man.'

Hat was a prophet. Within six months George was living alone in his pink house. I used to see him then, sitting on the steps, but he never looked at me any more. He looked old and weary and very sad.

He died soon afterwards. Hat and the boys got some money together and we buried him at Lapeyrouse Cemetery. Elias turned up for the funeral.

4 HIS CHOSEN CALLING

AFTER MIDNIGHT THERE were two regular noises in the street. At about two o'clock you heard the sweepers; and then, just before dawn, the scavenging-carts came and you heard the men scraping off the rubbish the sweepers had gathered into heaps.

No boy in the street particularly wished to be a sweeper. But if you asked any boy what he would like to be, he would say, 'I going be a cart-driver.'

There was certainly a glamour to driving the blue carts. The men were aristocrats. They worked early in the morning and had the rest of the day free. And then they were always going on strike. They didn't strike for much. They struck for things like a cent more a day; they struck if someone was laid off. They struck when the war began; they struck when the war ended. They struck when India got independence. They struck when Gandhi died.

Eddoes, who was a driver, was admired by most of the boys. He said his father was the best cart-driver of his day, and he told us great stories of the old man's skill. Eddoes came from a low Hindu caste, and there was a lot of truth in what he said. His skill was a sort of family skill, passing from father to son.

One day I was sweeping the pavement in front of the house where I lived, and Eddoes came and wanted to take away the broom from me. I liked sweeping and I didn't want to give him the broom.

'Boy, what you know about sweeping?' Eddoes asked, laughing.

I said, 'What, it have so much to know?'

Eddoes said, 'This is my job, boy. I have experience. Wait until you big like me.'

I gave him the broom.

I was sad for a long time afterwards. It seemed that I would never never grow as big as Eddoes, never have that thing he called experience. I began to admire Eddoes more than ever; and more than ever I wanted to be a cart-driver.

But Elias was not that sort of boy.

When we who formed the Junior Miguel Street Club squatted on the pavement, talking, like Hat and Bogart and the others, about things like life and cricket and football, I said to Elias, 'So you don't want to be a cart-driver? What you want to be then? A sweeper?'

Elias spat neatly into the gutter and looked down. He said very earnestly, 'I think I going be a doctor, you hear.'

If Boyee or Errol had said something like that, we would all have laughed. But we recognized that Elias was different, that Elias had brains.

We all felt sorry for Elias. His father George brutalized the boy with blows, but Elias never cried, never spoke a word against his father.

One day I was going to Chin's shop to buy three cents' worth of butter, and I asked Elias to come with me. I didn't see George about, and I thought it was safe.

We were just about two houses away when we saw George. Elias grew scared. George came up and said sharply, 'Where you going?' And at the same time he landed a powerful cuff on Elias's jaw.

George liked beating Elias. He used to tie him with rope, and then beat him with rope he had soaked in the gutters of his cow-pen. Elias didn't cry even then. And shortly after, I would see George laughing with Elias, and George used to say to me, 'I know what you thinking. You wondering how me and he get so friendly so quick.'

The more I disliked George, the more I liked Elias.

I was prepared to believe that he would become a doctor some day.

Errol said, 'I bet you when he come doctor and thing he go forget the rest of we. Eh, Elias?'

A small smile appeared on Elias's lips.

'Nah,' he said. 'I wouldn't be like that. I go give a lot of money and thing to you and Boyee and the rest of you fellows.' And Elias waved his small hands, and we thought we could see the Cadillac and the black bag and the tube-thing that Elias was going to have when he became a doctor.

Elias began going to the school at the other end of Miguel Street. It didn't really look like a school at all. It looked just like any house to me, but there was a sign outside that said:

TITUS HOYT, I.A. (London, External)
*Passes in the Cambridge
School Certificate Guaranteed*

The odd thing was that although George beat Elias at the slightest opportunity, he was very proud that his son was getting an education. 'The boy learning a hell of a lot, you know. He reading Spanish, French and Latin, and he writing Spanish, French and Latin.'

The year before his mother died, Elias sat for the Cambridge Senior School Certificate.

Titus Hoyt came down to our end of the street.

'That boy going pass with honours,' Titus Hoyt said. 'With honours.'

We saw Elias dressed in neat khaki trousers and white shirt, going to the examination room, and we looked at him with awe.

Errol said, 'Everything Elias write not remaining here, you know. Every word that boy write going to England.'

It didn't sound true.

'What you think it is at all?' Errol said. 'Elias have brains, you know.'

Elias's mother died in January, and the results came out in March.

Elias hadn't passed.

Hat looked through the list in the *Guardian* over and over again, looking for Elias's name, saying, 'You never know. People always making mistake, especially when it have so much names.'

Elias's name wasn't in the paper.

Boyee said, 'What else you expect? Who correct the papers? Englishman, not so? You expect them to give Elias a pass?'

Elias was with us, looking sad and not saying a word.

Hat said, 'Is a damn shame. If they know what hell the boy have to put up with, they woulda pass him quick quick.'

Titus Hoyt said, 'Don't worry. Rome wasn't built in a day. This year! This year, things going be much much better. We go show those Englishmen and them.'

Elias left us and he began living with Titus Hoyt. We saw next to nothing of him. He was working night and day.

One day in the following March, Titus Hoyt rode up to us and said, 'You hear what happen?'

'What happen?' Hat asked.

'The boy is a genius,' Titus Hoyt said.

'Which boy?' Errol asked.

'Elias.'

'What Elias do?'

'The boy gone and pass the Cambridge Senior School Certificate.'

Hat whistled. 'The Cambridge Senior School Certificate?'

Titus Hoyt smiled. 'That self. He get a third grade. His name going to be in the papers tomorrow. I always say it, and I saying it again now, this boy Elias have too much brains.'

Hat said later, 'Is too bad that Elias father dead. He was a good-for-nothing, but he wanted to see his son a educated man.'

Elias came that evening, and everybody, boys and men, gathered around him. They talked about everything but books, and Elias, too, was talking about things like pictures and girls and cricket. He was looking very solemn, too.

There was a pause once, and Hat said, 'What you going to do now, Elias? Look for work?'

Elias spat. 'Nah, I think I will write the exam again.'

I said, 'But why?'

'I want a second grade.'

We understood. He wanted to be a doctor.

Elias sat down on the pavement and said, 'Yes, boy. I think I going to take that exam again, and this year I going to be so good that this Mr Cambridge go bawl when he read what I write for him.'

We were silent, in wonder.

'Is the English and litritcher that does beat me.'

In Elias's mouth litritcher was the most beautiful word I heard. It sounded like something to eat, something rich like chocolate.

Hat said, 'You mean you have to read a lot of poultry and thing?'

Elias nodded. We felt it wasn't fair, making a boy like Elias do litritcher and poultry.

Elias moved back into the pink house which had been empty since his father died. He was studying and working. He went back to Titus Hoyt's school, not as pupil, but as a teacher, and Titus Hoyt said he was giving him forty dollars a month.

Titus Hoyt added, 'He worth it, too. He is one of the brightest boys in Port of Spain.'

Now that Elias was back with us, we noticed him better. He was the cleanest boy in the street. He bathed twice a day and scrubbed his teeth twice a day. He did all this standing up at the tap in front of the house. He swept the house every morning before going to school. He was the opposite of his father. His father was short and fat and dirty. He was tall and thin and clean. His father drank and swore. He never drank and no one ever heard him use a bad word.

My mother used to say to me, 'Why you don't take after Elias? I really don't know what sort of son God give me, you hear.'

And whenever Hat or Edward beat Boyee and Errol, they always said, 'Why you beating we for? Not everybody could be like Elias, you know.'

Hat used to say, 'And it ain't only that he got brains. The boy Elias have nice *ways* too.'

So I think I was a little glad when Elias sat the examination for the third time, and failed.

Hat said, 'You see how we catch these Englishmen and them. Nobody here can tell me that the boy didn't pass the exam, but you think they go want to give him a better grade? Ha!'

And everybody said, 'Is a real shame.'

And when Hat asked Elias, 'What you going to do now, boy?' Elias said, 'You know, I think I go take up a job. I think I go be a sanitary inspector.'

We saw him in khaki uniform and khaki topee, going from house to house with a little notebook.

'Yes,' Elias said. 'Sanitary inspector, that's what I going to be.'

Hat said, 'It have a lot of money in that, I think. I hear your father George uses to pay the sanitary inspector five dollars a month to keep his mouth shut. Let we say you get about ten or even eight people like that. That's – let me see . . . ten fives is fifty, eight fives is forty. There, fifty, forty dollars straight. And mark you, that ain't counting your salary.'

Elias said, 'Is not the money I thinking about. I really like the work.'

It was easy to understand that.

Elias said, 'But it have a exam, you know.'

Hat said, 'But they don't send the papers to England for that?'

Elias said, 'Nah, but still, I fraid exams and things, you know. I ain't have any luck with them.'

Boyee said, 'But I thought you was thinking of taking up doctoring.'

Hat said, 'Boyee, I going to cut your little tail if you don't shut up.'

But Boyee didn't mean anything bad.

Elias said, 'I change my mind. I think I want to be a sanitary inspector. I really like the work.'

For three years Elias sat the sanitary inspectors' examination, and he failed every time.

Elias began saying, 'But what the hell you expect in Trinidad? You got to bribe everybody if you want to get your toenail cut.'

Hat said, 'I meet a man from a boat the other day, and he tell me that the sanitary inspector exams in British Guiana much easier. You could go to B.G. and take the exams there and come back and work here.'

Elias flew to B.G., wrote the exam, failed it, and flew back.

Hat said, 'I meet a man from Barbados. He tell me that the exams easier in Barbados. It easy, easy, he say.'

Elias flew to Barbados, wrote the exam, failed it, and flew back.

Hat said, 'I meet a man from Grenada the other day—'

Elias said, 'Shut your arse up, before it have trouble between we in this street.'

A few years later I sat the Cambridge Senior School Certificate Examination myself, and Mr Cambridge gave me a second grade. I applied for a job in the Customs, and it didn't cost me much to get it. I got a khaki uniform with brass buttons, and a cap. Very much like the sanitary inspector's uniform.

Elias wanted to beat me up the first day I wore the uniform.

'What your mother do to get you that?' he shouted, and I was going for him when Eddoes put a stop to it.

Eddoes said, 'He just sad and jealous. He don't mean anything.'

For Elias had become one of the street aristocrats. He was driving the scavenging carts.

'No theory here,' Elias used to say. 'This is the practical. I really like the work.'

5 MAN-MAN

EVERYBODY IN MIGUEL STREET said that Man-man was mad, and so they left him alone. But I am not so sure now that he was mad, and I can think of many people much madder than Man-man ever was.

He didn't look mad. He was a man of medium height, thin; and he wasn't bad-looking, either. He never stared at you the way I expected a mad man to do; and when you spoke to him you were sure of getting a very reasonable reply.

But he did have some curious habits.

He went up for every election, city council or legislative council, and then he stuck posters everywhere in the district. These posters were well printed. They just had the word 'Vote' and below that, Man-man's picture.

At every election he got exactly three votes. That I couldn't understand. Man-man voted for himself, but who were the other two?

I asked Hat.

Hat said, 'I really can't say, boy. Is a real mystery. Perhaps is two jokers. But they is funny sort of jokers if they do the same thing so many times. They must be mad just like he.'

And for a long time the thought of these two mad men who voted for Man-man haunted me. Every time I saw someone doing anything just a little bit odd, I wondered, 'Is he who vote for Man-man?'

At large in the city were these two men of mystery.

Man-man never worked. But he was never idle. He was hypnotized by the word, particularly the written word, and he would spend a whole day writing a single word.

One day I met Man-man at the corner of Miguel Street.

'Boy, where you going?' Man-man asked.

'I going to school,' I said.

And Man-man, looking at me solemnly, said in a mocking way, 'So you goes to school, eh?'

I said automatically, 'Yes, I goes to school.' And I found that without intending it I had imitated Man-man's correct and very English accent.

That again was another mystery about Man-man. His accent. If you shut your eyes while he spoke, you would believe an Englishman – a good-class Englishman who wasn't particular about grammar – was talking to you.

Man-man said, as though speaking to himself, 'So the little man is going to school.'

Then he forgot me, and took out a long stick of chalk from his pocket and began writing on the pavement. He drew a very big s in outline and then filled it in, and then the c and the h and the o. But then he started making several o's, each smaller than the last, until he was writing in cursive, o after flowing o.

When I came home for lunch, he had got to French Street, and he was still writing o's, rubbing off mistakes with a rag.

In the afternoon he had gone round the block and was practically back in Miguel Street.

I went home, changed from my school-clothes into my home-clothes and went out to the street.

He was now halfway up Miguel Street.

He said, 'So the little man gone to school today?'

I said, 'Yes.'

He stood up and straightened his back.

Then he squatted again and drew the outline of a massive l and filled that in slowly and lovingly.

When it was finished, he stood up and said, 'You finish your work. I finish mine.'

Or it was like this. If you told Man-man you were going to the cricket, he would write CRICK and then concentrate on the E's until he saw you again.

One day Man-man went to the big café at the top of Miguel Street and began barking and growling at the customers on the stools as though he were a dog. The owner, a big Portuguese man with hairy hands, said, 'Man-man, get out of this shop before I tangle with you.'

Man-man just laughed.

They threw Man-man out.

Next day, the owner found that someone had entered his café during the night and had left all the doors open. But nothing was missing.

Hat said, 'One thing you must never do is trouble Man-man. He remember everything.'

That night the café was entered again and the doors again left open.

The following night the café was entered and this time little blobs of excrement were left on the centre of every stool and on top of every table and at regular intervals along the counter.

The owner of the café was the laughing-stock of the street for several weeks, and it was only after a long time that people began going to the café again.

Hat said, 'Is just like I say. Boy, I don't like meddling with that man. These people really bad-mind, you know. God make them that way.'

It was things like this that made people leave Man-man alone. The only friend he had was a little mongrel dog, white with black spots on the ears. The dog was like Man-man in a way, too. It was a curious dog. It never barked, never looked at you, and if you looked at it, it looked away. It never made friends with any other dog, and if some dog tried either to get friendly or aggressive, Man-man's dog gave it a brief look of disdain and ambled away, without looking back.

Man-man loved his dog, and the dog loved Man-man. They were made for each other, and Man-man couldn't have made a living without his dog.

Man-man appeared to exercise a great control over the movements of his dog's bowels.

Hat said, 'That does really beat me. I can't make that one out.'

It all began in Miguel Street.

One morning, several women got up to find that the clothes they had left to bleach overnight had been sullied by the droppings of a dog. No one wanted to use the sheets and the shirts after that, and when Man-man called, everyone was willing to give him the dirty clothes.

Man-man used to sell these clothes.

Hat said, 'Is things like this that make me wonder whether the man really mad.'

From Miguel Street Man-man's activities spread, and all the people who had suffered from Man-man's dog were anxious to get other people to suffer the same thing.

We in Miguel Street became a little proud of him.

*   *   *

I don't know what it was that caused Man-man to turn good. Perhaps the death of his dog had something to do with it. The dog was run over by a car, and it gave, Hat said, just one short squeak, and then it was silent.

Man-man wandered about for days, looking dazed and lost.

He no longer wrote words on the pavement; no longer spoke to me or to any of the other boys in the street. He began talking to himself, clasping his hands and shaking as though he had ague.

Then one day he said he had seen God after having a bath.

This didn't surprise many of us. Seeing God was quite common in Port of Spain and, indeed, in Trinidad at that time. Ganesh Pundit, the mystic masseur from Fuente Grove, had started it. He had seen God, too, and had published a little book-let called *What God Told Me.* Many rival mystics and not a few masseurs had announced the same thing, and I suppose it was natural that since God was in the area Man-man should see Him.

Man-man began preaching at the corner of Miguel Street, under the awning of Mary's shop. He did this every Saturday night. He let his beard grow and he dressed in a long white robe. He got a Bible and other holy things and stood in the white light of an acetylene lamp and preached. He was an impressive preacher, and he preached in an odd way. He made women cry, and he made people like Hat really worried.

He used to hold the Bible in his right hand and slap it with his left and say in his perfect English accent, 'I have been talking to God these few days, and what he tell me about you people wasn't really nice to hear. These days you hear all the politicians and them talking about making the island self-sufficient. You know what God tell me last night? Last night self, just after I finish eating? God say, "Man-man, come and have a look at these people." He show me husband eating wife and wife eating husband. He show me father eating son and mother eating daughter. He show me brother eating sister and sister eating brother. That is what these politicians and them mean by saying that the island going to become self-sufficient. But, brethren, it not too late now to turn to God.'

I used to get nightmares every Saturday night after hearing Man-man preach. But the odd thing was that the more he fright-ened people the more they came to hear him preach. And when the collection was made they gave him more than ever.

In the week-days he just walked about, in his white robe, and he begged for food. He said he had done what Jesus ordered and he had given away all his goods. With his long black beard and his bright deep eyes, you couldn't refuse him anything. He noticed me no longer, and never asked me, 'So you goes to school?'

The people in Miguel didn't know what to make of the change. They tried to comfort themselves by saying that Man-man was really mad, but, like me, I think they weren't sure that Man-man wasn't really right.

What happened afterwards wasn't really unexpected.

Man-man announced that he was a new Messiah.

Hat said one day, 'You ain't hear the latest?'

We said, 'What?'

'Is about Man-man. He say he going to be crucified one of these days.'

'Nobody go touch him,' Edward said. 'Everybody fraid of him now.'

Hat explained. 'No, it ain't that. He going to crucify hisself. One of these Fridays he going to Blue Basin and tie hisself to a cross and let people stone him.'

Somebody – Errol, I think – laughed, but finding that no one laughed with him, fell silent again.

But on top of our wonder and worry, we had this great pride in knowing that Man-man came from Miguel Street.

Little hand-written notices began appearing in the shops and cafés and on the gates of some houses, announcing Man-man's forthcoming crucifixion.

'They going to have a big crowd in Blue Basin,' Hat announced, and added with pride, 'and I hear they sending some police, too.'

That day, early in the morning, before the shops opened and the trolley-buses began running in Ariapita Avenue, the big crowd assembled at the corner of Miguel Street. There were lots of men dressed in black and even more women dressed in white. They were singing hymns. There were also about twenty policemen, but they were not singing hymns.

When Man-man appeared, looking very thin and very holy, women cried and rushed to touch his gown. The police stood by, prepared to handle anything.

A van came with a great wooden cross.

Hat, looking unhappy in his serge suit, said, 'They tell me it make from match-wood. It ain't heavy. It light light.'

Edward said, in a snapping sort of way, 'That matter? Is the heart and the spirit that matter.'

Hat said, 'I ain't saying nothing.'

Some men began taking the cross from the van to give it to Man-man, but he stopped them. His English accent sounded impressive in the early morning. 'Not here. Leave it for Blue Basin.'

Hat was disappointed.

We walked to Blue Basin, the waterfall in the mountains to the northwest of Port of Spain, and we got there in two hours. Man-man began carrying the cross from the road, up the rocky path and then down to the Basin.

Some men put up the cross, and tied Man-man to it.

Man-man said, 'Stone me, brethren.'

The women wept and flung bits of sand and gravel at his feet.

Man-man groaned and said, 'Father, forgive them. They ain't know what they doing.' Then he screamed out, 'Stone me, brethren!'

A pebble the size of an egg struck him on the chest.

Man-man cried, 'Stone, *stone*, STONE me, brethren! I forgive you.'

Edward said, 'The man really brave.'

People began flinging really big stones at Man-man, aiming at his face and chest.

Man-man looked hurt and surprised. He shouted, 'What the hell is this? What the hell you people think you doing? Look, get me down from this thing quick, let me down quick, and I go settle with that son of a bitch who pelt a stone at me.'

From where Edward and Hat and the rest of us stood, it sounded like a cry of agony.

A bigger stone struck Man-man; the women flung the sand and gravel at him.

We heard Man-man's shout, clear and loud, 'Cut this stupidness out. Cut it out, I tell you. I finish with this arseness, you hear.' And then he began cursing so loudly and coarsely that the people stopped in surprise.

The police took away Man-man.

The authorities kept him for observation. Then for good.

THREE BEGGARS CALLED punctually every day at the hospitable houses in Miguel Street. At about ten an Indian came in his dhoti and white jacket, and we poured a tin of rice into the sack he carried on his back. At twelve an old woman smoking a clay pipe came and she got a cent. At two a blind man led by a boy called for his penny.

Sometimes we had a rogue. One day a man called and said he was hungry. We gave him a meal. He asked for a cigarette and wouldn't go until we had lit it for him. That man never came again.

The strangest caller came one afternoon at about four o'clock. I had come back from school and was in my home-clothes. The man said to me, 'Sonny, may I come inside your yard?'

He was a small man and he was tidily dressed. He wore a hat, a white shirt and black trousers.

I asked, 'What you want?'

He said, 'I want to watch your bees.'

We had four small gru-gru palm trees and they were full of uninvited bees.

I ran up the steps and shouted, 'Ma, it have a man outside here. He say he want to watch the bees.'

My mother came out, looked at the man and asked in an unfriendly way, 'What you want?'

The man said, 'I want to watch your bees.'

His English was so good it didn't sound natural, and I could see my mother was worried.

She said to me, 'Stay here and watch him while he watch the bees.'

The man said, 'Thank you, Madam. You have done a good deed today.'

He spoke very slowly and very correctly, as though every word was costing him money.

We watched the bees, this man and I, for about an hour, squatting near the palm trees.

The man said, 'I like watching bees. Sonny, do you like watching bees?'

I said, 'I ain't have the time.'

He shook his head sadly. He said, 'That's what I do, I just watch. I can watch ants for days. Have you ever watched ants? And scorpions, and centipedes, and *congorees* – have you watched those?'

I shook my head.

I said, 'What you does do, mister?'

He got up and said, 'I am a poet.'

I said, 'A good poet?'

He said, 'The greatest in the world.'

'What your name, mister?'

'B. Wordsworth.'

'B for Bill?'

'Black. Black Wordsworth. White Wordsworth was my brother. We share one heart. I can watch a small flower like the morning glory and cry.'

I said, 'Why you does cry?'

'Why, boy? Why? You will know when you grow up. You're a poet, too, you know. And when you're a poet you can cry for everything.'

I couldn't laugh.

He said, 'You like your mother?'

'When she not beating me.'

He pulled out a printed sheet from his hip pocket and said, 'On this paper is the greatest poem about mothers and I'm going to sell it to you at a bargain price. For four cents.'

I went inside and I said, 'Ma, you want to buy a poetry for four cents?'

My mother said, 'Tell that blasted man to haul his tail away from my yard, you hear.'

I said to B. Wordsworth, 'My mother say she ain't have four cents.'

B. Wordsworth said, 'It is the poet's tragedy.'

And he put the paper back in his pocket. He didn't seem to mind.

I said, 'Is a funny way to go round selling poetry like that. Only calypsonians do that sort of thing. A lot of people does buy?'

He said, 'No one has yet bought a single copy.'

'But why you does keep on going round, then?'

He said, 'In this way I watch many things, and I always hope to meet poets.'

I said, 'You really think I is a poet?'

'You're as good as me,' he said.

And when B. Wordsworth left, I prayed I would see him again.

About a week later, coming back from school one afternoon, I met him at the corner of Miguel Street.

He said, 'I have been waiting for you for a long time.'

I said, 'You sell any poetry yet?'

He shook his head.

He said, 'In my yard I have the best mango tree in Port of Spain. And now the mangoes are ripe and red and very sweet and juicy. I have waited here for you to tell you this and to invite you to come and eat some of my mangoes.'

He lived in Alberto Street in a one-roomed hut placed right in the centre of the lot. The yard seemed all green. There was the big mango tree. There was a coconut tree and there was a plum tree. The place looked wild, as though it wasn't in the city at all. You couldn't see all the big concrete houses in the street.

He was right. The mangoes were sweet and juicy. I ate about six, and the yellow mango juice ran down my arms to my elbows and down my mouth to my chin and my shirt was stained.

My mother said when I got home, 'Where you was? You think you is a man now and could go all over the place? Go cut a whip for me.'

She beat me rather badly, and I ran out of the house swearing that I would never come back. I went to B. Wordsworth's house. I was so angry, my nose was bleeding.

B. Wordsworth said, 'Stop crying, and we will go for a walk.'

I stopped crying, but I was breathing short. We went for a walk. We walked down St Clair Avenue to the Savannah and we walked to the race-course.

B. Wordsworth said, 'Now, let us lie on the grass and look up at the sky, and I want you to think how far those stars are from us.'

I did as he told me, and I saw what he meant. I felt like nothing, and at the same time I had never felt so big and great in all my life. I forgot all my anger and all my tears and all the blows.

When I said I was better, he began telling me the names of the stars, and I particularly remembered the constellation of

Orion the Hunter, though I don't really know why. I can
spot Orion even today, but I have forgotten the rest.

Then a light was flashed into our faces, and we saw a policeman. We got up from the grass.

The policeman said, 'What you doing here?'

B. Wordsworth said, 'I have been asking myself the same
question for forty years.'

We became friends, B. Wordsworth and I. He told me, 'You
must never tell anybody about me and about the mango tree and
the coconut tree and the plum tree. You must keep that a secret.
If you tell anybody, I will know, because I am a poet.'

I gave him my word and I kept it.

I liked his little room. It had no more furniture than George's
front room, but it looked cleaner and healthier. But it also looked
lonely.

One day I asked him, 'Mister Wordsworth, why you does keep
all this bush in your yard? Ain't it does make the place damp?'

He said, 'Listen, and I will tell you a story. Once upon a time
a boy and girl met each other and they fell in love. They loved
each other so much they got married. They were both poets. He
loved words. She loved grass and flowers and trees. They lived
happily in a single room, and then one day the girl poet said to
the boy poet, "We are going to have another poet in the family."
But this poet was never born, because the girl died, and the
young poet died with her, inside her. And the girl's husband was
very sad, and he said he would never touch a thing in the girl's
garden. And so the garden remained, and grew high and wild.'

I looked at B. Wordsworth, and as he told me this lovely story,
he seemed to grow older. I understood his story.

We went for long walks together. We went to the Botanical
Gardens and the Rock Gardens. We climbed Chancellor Hill in
the late afternoon and watched the darkness fall on Port of Spain,
and watched the lights go on in the city and on the ships in the
harbour.

He did everything as though he were doing it for the first time
in his life. He did everything as though he were doing some
church rite.

He would say to me, 'Now, how about having some ice-
cream?'

And when I said yes, he would grow very serious and say,
'Now, which café shall we patronize?' As though it were a very

important thing. He would think for some time about it and finally say, 'I think I will go and negotiate the purchase with that shop.'

The world became a most exciting place.

One day, when I was in his yard, he said to me, 'I have a great secret which I am now going to tell you.'

I said, 'It really secret?'

'At the moment, yes.'

I looked at him, and he looked at me. He said, 'This is just between you and me, remember. I am writing a poem.'

'Oh.' I was disappointed.

He said, 'But this is a different sort of poem. This is the greatest poem in the world.'

I whistled.

He said, 'I have been working on it for more than five years now. I will finish it in about twenty-two years from now, that is, if I keep on writing at the present rate.'

'You does write a lot, then?'

He said, 'Not any more. I just write one line a month. But I make sure it is a good line.'

I asked, 'What was last month's good line?'

He looked up at the sky and said, '*The past is deep.*'

I said, 'It is a beautiful line.'

B. Wordsworth said, 'I hope to distil the experiences of a whole month into that single line of poetry. So, in twenty-two years, I shall have written a poem that will sing to all humanity.'

I was filled with wonder.

Our walks continued. We walked along the sea-wall at Docksite one day, and I said, 'Mr Wordsworth, if I drop this pin in the water, you think it will float?'

He said, 'This is a strange world. Drop your pin, and let us see what will happen.'

The pin sank.

I said, 'How is the poem this month?'

But he never told me any other line. He merely said, 'Oh, it comes, you know. It comes.'

Or we would sit on the sea-wall and watch the liners come into the harbour.

But of the greatest poem in the world I heard no more.

*   *   *

I felt he was growing older.

'How you does live, Mr Wordsworth?' I asked him one day.

He said, 'You mean how I get money?'

When I nodded, he laughed in a crooked way.

He said, 'I sing calypsoes in the calypso season.'

'And that last you the rest of the year?'

'It is enough.'

'But you will be the richest man in the world when you write the greatest poem?'

He didn't reply.

One day when I went to see him in his little house I found him lying on his little bed. He looked so old and so weak that I found myself wanting to cry.

He said, 'The poem is not going well.'

He wasn't looking at me. He was looking through the window at the coconut tree, and he was speaking as though I wasn't there. He said, 'When I was twenty I felt the power within myself.' Then, almost in front of my eyes, I could see his face growing older and more tired. He said, 'But that – that was a long time ago.'

And then – I felt it so keenly, it was as though I had been slapped by my mother. I could see it clearly on his face. It was there for everyone to see. Death on the shrinking face.

He looked at me, and saw my tears and sat up.

He said, 'Come.' I went and sat on his knees.

He looked into my eyes, and he said, 'Oh, you can see it, too. I always knew you had the poet's eye.'

He didn't even look sad, and that made me burst out crying loudly.

He pulled me to his thin chest and said, 'Do you want me to tell you a funny story?' and he smiled encouragingly at me.

But I couldn't reply.

He said, 'When I have finished this story, I want you to promise that you will go away and never come back to see me. Do you promise?'

I nodded.

He said, 'Good. Well, listen. That story I told you about the boy poet and the girl poet, do you remember that? That wasn't true. It was something I just made up. All this talk about poetry and the greatest poem in the world, that wasn't true, either. Isn't that the funniest thing you have heard?'

But his voice broke.

I left the house and ran home crying, like a poet, for everything I saw.

I walked along Alberto Street a year later, but I could find no sign of the poet's house. It hadn't vanished, just like that. It had been pulled down, and a big, two-storeyed building had taken its place. The mango tree and the plum tree and the coconut tree had all been cut down, and there was brick and concrete everywhere.

It was just as though B. Wordsworth had never existed.

BIG FOOT WAS really big and really black, and everybody in Miguel Street was afraid of him. It wasn't his bigness or his blackness that people feared, for there were blacker and bigger people about. People were afraid of him because he was so silent and sulky; he *looked* dangerous, like those terrible dogs that never bark but just look at you from the corner of their eyes.

Hat used to say, 'Is only a form of showing off, you know, all this quietness he does give us. He quiet just because he ain't have anything to say, that's all.'

Yet you could hear Hat telling all sorts of people at the races and cricket, 'Big Foot and me? We is bosom pals, man. We grow up together.'

And at school I myself used to say, 'Big Foot does live in my street, you hear. I know him good good, and if any one of all you touch me, I go tell Big Foot.'

At that time I had never spoken a single word to Big Foot.

We in Miguel Street were proud to claim him because he was something of a character in Port of Spain, and had quite a reputation. It was Big Foot who flung the stone at the Radio Trinidad building one day and broke a window. When the magistrate asked why he did it, Big Foot just said, 'To wake them up.'

A well-wisher paid the fine for him.

Then there was the time he got a job driving one of the diesel-buses. He drove the bus out of the city to Carenage, five miles away, and told the passengers to get out and bathe. He stood by to see that they did.

After that he got a job as a postman, and he had a great time misplacing people's letters. They found him at Docksite, with the bag half full of letters, soaking his big feet in the Gulf of Paria.

He said, 'Is hard work, walking all over the place, delivering people letters. You come like a postage stamp, man.'

All Trinidad thought of him as a comedian, but we who knew him thought otherwise.

It was people like Big Foot who gave the steel-bands a bad name. Big Foot was always ready to start a fight with another band, but he looked so big and dangerous that he himself was never involved in any fight, and he never went to jail for more than three months or so at a time.

Hat, especially, was afraid of Big Foot. Hat often said, 'I don't know why they don't lose Big Foot in jail, you know.'

You would have thought that when he was beating his pans and dancing in the street at Carnival, Big Foot would at least smile and look happy. But no. It was on occasions like this that he prepared his sulkiest and grimmest face; and when you saw him beating a pan, you felt, to judge by his earnestness, that he was doing some sacred act.

One day a big crowd of us – Hat, Edward, Eddoes, Boyee, Errol and myself – went to the cinema. We were sitting in a row, laughing and talking all during the film, having a good time.

A voice from behind said, very quietly, 'Shut up.'

We turned and saw Big Foot.

He lazily pulled out a knife from his trouser pocket, flicked the blade open, and stuck it in the back of my chair.

He looked up at the screen and said in a frightening friendly way, 'Talk.'

We didn't say a word for the rest of the film.

Afterwards Hat said, 'You does only get policeman son behaving in that way. Policeman son and priest son.'

Boyee said, 'You mean Big Foot is priest son?'

Hat said, 'You too stupid. Priests and them does have children?'

We heard a lot about Big Foot's father from Hat. It seemed he was as much a terror as Big Foot. Sometimes when Boyee and Errol and I were comparing notes about beatings, Boyee said, 'The blows we get is nothing to what Big Foot uses to get from his father. That is how he get so big, you know. I meet a boy from Belmont the other day in the savannah, and this boy tell me that blows does make you grow.'

Errol said, 'You is a blasted fool, man. How you does let people give you stupidness like that?'

And once Hat said, 'Every day Big Foot father, the policeman, giving Big Foot blows. Like medicine. Three times a day after meals. And hear Big Foot talk afterwards. He used to say, "When I get big and have children, I go beat them, beat them." '

I didn't say it then, because I was ashamed; but I had often felt the same way when my mother beat me.

I asked Hat, 'And Big Foot mother? She used to beat him too?'

Hat, said, 'Oh, God! That woulda kill him. Big Foot didn't have any mother. His father didn't married, thank God.'

The Americans were crawling all over Port of Spain in those days, making the city really hot. Children didn't take long to find out that they were easy people, always ready to give with both hands. Hat began working a small racket. He had five of us going all over the district begging for chewing gum and chocolate. For every packet of chewing gum we gave him we got a cent. Sometimes I made as much as twelve cents in a day. Some boy told me later that Hat was selling the chewing gum for six cents a packet, but I didn't believe it.

One afternoon, standing on the pavement outside my house, I saw an American soldier down the street, coming towards me. It was about two o'clock in the afternoon, very hot, and the street was practically empty.

The American behaved in a very surprising way when I sprinted down to ask, 'Got any gum, Joe?'

He mumbled something about begging kids and I think he was going to slap me or cuff me. He wasn't very big, but I was afraid. I think he was drunk.

He set his mouth.

A gruff voice said, 'Look, leave the boy alone, you hear.'

It was Big Foot.

Not another word was said. The American, suddenly humble, walked away, making a great pretence of not being in a hurry.

Big Foot didn't even look at me.

I never said again, 'Got any gum, Joe?'

Yet this did not make me like Big Foot. I was, I believe, a little more afraid of him.

I told Hat about the American and Big Foot.

Hat said, 'All the Americans not like that. You can't throw away twelve cents a day like that.'

But I refused to beg any more.

I said, 'If it wasn't for Big Foot, the man woulda kill me.'

Hat said, 'You know, is a good thing Big Foot father dead before Big Foot really get big.'

I said, 'What happen to Big Foot father, then?'

Hat said, 'You ain't hear? It was a famous thing. A crowd of black people beat him up and kill him in 1937 when they was having the riots in the oilfields. Big Foot father was playing hero, just like Big Foot playing hero now.'

I said, 'Hat, why you don't like Big Foot?'

Hat said, 'I ain't have anything against him.'

I said, 'Why you fraid him so, then?'

Hat said, 'Ain't you fraid him too?'

I nodded. 'But I feel you do him something and you worried.'

Hat said, 'Nothing really. It just funny. The rest of we boys use to give Big Foot hell too. He was thin thin when he was small, you know, and we use to have a helluva time chasing him all over the place. He couldn't run at all.'

I felt sorry for Big Foot.

I said, 'How that funny?'

Hat said, 'You go hear. You know the upshot? Big Foot come the best runner out of all of we. In the school sports he run the hundred yards in ten point four seconds. That is what they say, but you know how Trinidad people can't count time. Anyway, then we all want to come friendly with him. But he don't want we at all at all.'

And I wondered then why Big Foot held himself back from beating Hat and the rest of the people who had bullied him when he was a boy.

But still I didn't like him.

Big Foot became a carpenter for a while, and actually built two or three enormous wardrobes, rough, ugly things. But he sold them. And then he became a mason. There is no stupid pride among Trinidad craftsmen. No one is a specialist.

He came to our yard one day to do a job.

I stood by and watched him. I didn't speak to him, and he didn't speak to me. I noticed that he used his feet as a trowel. He mumbled, 'Is hard work, bending down all the time.'

He did the job well enough. His feet were not big for nothing.

About four o'clock he knocked off, and spoke to me.

He said, 'Boy, let we go for a walk. I hot and I want to cool off.'

I didn't want to go, but I felt I had to.

We went to the sea-wall at Docksite and watched the sea. Soon it began to grow dark. The lights came on in the harbour. The world seemed very big, dark, and silent. We stood up without speaking a word.

Then a sudden sharp yap very near us tore the silence.

The suddenness and strangeness of the noise paralysed me for a moment.

It was only a dog; a small white and black dog with large flapping ears. It was dripping wet, and was wagging its tail out of pure friendliness.

I said, 'Come, boy,' and the dog shook off the water from its coat on me and then jumped all over me, yapping and squirming.

I had forgotten Big Foot, and when I looked for him I saw him about twenty yards away running for all he was worth.

I shouted, 'Is all right, Big Foot.'

But he stopped before he heard my shout.

He cried out loudly, 'Oh God, I dead, I dead. A big big bottle cut up my foot.'

I and the dog ran to him.

But when the dog came to him he seemed to forget his foot which was bleeding badly. He began hugging and stroking the wet dog, and laughing in a crazy way.

He had cut his foot very badly, and next day I saw it wrapped up. He couldn't come to finish the work he had begun in our yard.

I felt I knew more about Big Foot than any man in Miguel Street, and I was afraid that I knew so much. I felt like one of those small men in gangster films who know too much and get killed.

And thereafter I was always conscious that Big Foot knew what I was thinking. I felt his fear that I would tell.

But although I was bursting with Big Foot's secret I told no one. I would have liked to reassure him but there was no means.

His presence in the street became something that haunted me. And it was all I could do to stop myself telling Hat, 'I not fraid of Big Foot. I don't know why you fraid him so.'

Errol, Boyee, and myself sat on the pavement discussing the war.

Errol said, 'If they just make Lord Anthony Eden Prime Minister, we go beat up the Germans and them bad bad.'

Boyee said, 'What Lord Eden go do so?'

Errol just haaed, in a very knowing way.

I said, 'Yes, I always think that if they make Lord Anthony Eden Prime Minister, the war go end quick quick.'

Boyee said, 'You people just don't know the Germans. The Germans strong like hell, you know. A boy was telling me that these Germans and them could eat a nail with their teeth alone.'

Errol said, 'But we have Americans on we side now.'

Boyee said, 'But they not big like the Germans. All the Germans and them big big and strong like Big Foot, you know, and they braver than Big Foot.'

Errol said, 'Shh! Look, he coming.'

Big Foot was very near, and I felt he could hear the conversation. He was looking at me, and there was a curious look in his eyes.

Boyee said, 'Why you shhhing me so for? I ain't saying anything bad. I just saying that the Germans brave as Big Foot.'

Just for a moment, I saw the begging look in Big Foot's eyes. I looked away.

When Big Foot had passed, Errol said to me, 'Like Big Foot have something with you, boy.'

One afternoon Hat was reading the morning paper. He shouted to us, 'But look at what I reading here, man.'

We asked, 'What happening now?'

Hat said, 'Is about Big Foot.'

Boyee said, 'What, they throw him in jail again?'

Hat said, 'Big Foot taking up boxing.'

I understood more than I could say.

Hat said, 'He go get his tail mash up. If he think that boxing is just throwing yourself around, he go find out his mistake.'

The newspapers made a big thing out of it. The most popular headline was PRANKSTER TURNS PUGILIST.

And when I next saw Big Foot, I felt I could look him in the eyes.

And now I wasn't afraid of him, I was afraid for him.

But I had no need. Big Foot had what the sports-writers all called a 'phenomenal success'. He knocked out fighter after fighter, and Miguel Street grew more afraid of him and more proud of him.

Hat said, 'Is only because he only fighting stupid little people. He ain't meet anybody yet that have real class.'

Big Foot seemed to have forgotten me. His eyes no longer sought mine whenever we met, and he no longer stopped to talk to me.

He was the terror of the street. I, like everybody else, was frightened of him. As before, I preferred it that way.

He even began showing off more.

We used to see him running up and down Miguel Street in stupid-looking maroon shorts and he resolutely refused to notice anybody.

Hat was terrified.

He said, 'They shouldn't let a man who go to jail box.'

An Englishman came to Trinidad one day and the papers to interview him. The man said he was a boxer and a champion of the Royal Air Force. Next morning his picture appeared.

Two days later another picture of him appeared. This time he was dressed only in black shorts, and he had squared up towards the cameraman with his boxing gloves on.

The headline said, '*Who will fight this man?*'

And Trinidad answered, 'Big Foot will fight this man.'

The excitement was intense when Big Foot agreed. Miguel Street was in the news, and even Hat was pleased.

Hat said, 'I know is stupid to say, but I hope Big Foot beat him.' And he went around the district placing bets with everyone who had money to throw away.

We turned up in strength at the stadium on the night.

Hat rushed madly here and there, waving a twenty-dollar bill, shouting, 'Twenty to five, Big Foot beat him.'

I bet Boyee six cents that Big Foot would lose.

And, in truth, when Big Foot came out to the ring, dancing disdainfully in the ring, without looking at anybody in the crowd, we felt pleased.

Hat shouted, 'That is man!'

I couldn't bear to look at the fight. I looked all the time at the only woman in the crowd. She was an American or a Canadian woman and she was nibbling at peanuts. She was so blonde, her hair looked like straw. Whenever a blow was landed, the crowd roared, and the woman pulled in her lips as though she had given the blow, and then she nibbled furiously at her peanuts. She never shouted or got up or waved her hands. I hated that woman.

The roars grew louder and more frequent.

I could hear Hat shouting, 'Come on, Big Foot. Beat him up. Beat him up, man.' Then, with panic in his voice, 'Remember your father.'

But Hat's shouts died away.

Big Foot had lost the fight, on points.

Hat paid out about a hundred dollars in five minutes.

He said, 'I go have to sell the brown and white cow, the one I buy from George.'

Edward said, 'Is God work.'

Boyee said to me, 'I go give you your six cents tomorrow.'

I said, 'Six cents *tomorrow*? But what you think I is? A millionaire? Look, man, give me money now now, you hear.'

He paid up.

But the crowd was laughing, laughing.

I looked at the ring.

Big Foot was in tears. He was like a boy, and the more he cried, the louder he cried, and the more painful it sounded.

The secret I had held for Big Foot was now shown to everybody.

Hat said, 'What, he crying?' And Hat laughed.

He seemed to forget all about the cow. He said, 'Well, well, look at man, eh!'

And all of us from Miguel Street laughed at Big Foot.

All except me. For I knew how he felt, although he was a big man and I was a boy. I wished I had never betted that six cents with Boyee.

The papers next morning said, 'PUGILIST SOBS IN RING.'

Trinidad thought it was Big Foot, the comedian, doing something funny again.

But we knew otherwise.

Big Foot left Miguel Street, and the last I heard of him was that he was a labourer in a quarry in Laventille.

About six months later a little scandal was rippling through Trinidad, making everybody feel silly.

The R.A.F. champion, it turned out, had never been in the R.A.F., and as a boxer he was completely unknown.

Hat said, 'Well, what you expect in a place like this?'

A STRANGER COULD DRIVE through Miguel Street and just say 'Slum!' because he could see no more. But we who lived there saw our street as a world, where everybody was quite different from everybody else. Man-man was mad; George was stupid; Big Foot was a bully; Hat was an adventurer; Popo was a philosopher; and Morgan was our comedian.

Or that was how we looked upon him. But, looking back now after so many years, I think he deserved a lot more respect than we gave him. It was his own fault, of course. He was one of those men who deliberately set out to clown and wasn't happy unless people were laughing at him, and he was always thinking of new crazinesses which he hoped would amuse us. He was the sort of man who, having once created a laugh by sticking the match in his mouth and trying to light it with his cigarette, having once done that, does it over and over again.

Hat used to say, 'Is a damn nuisance, having that man trying to be funny all the time, when all of we well know that he not so happy at all.'

I felt that sometimes Morgan knew his jokes were not coming off, and that made him so miserable that we all felt unkind and nasty.

Morgan was the first artist I ever met in my life. He spent nearly all his time, even when he was playing the fool, thinking about beauty. Morgan made fireworks. He loved fireworks, and he was full of theories about fireworks. Something about the Cosmic Dance or the Dance of Life. But this was the sort of talk that went clean over our heads in Miguel Street. And when Morgan saw this, he would begin using even bigger words. Just for the joke. One of the big words I learnt from Morgan is the title of this sketch.

But very few people in Trinidad used Morgan's fireworks. All the big fêtes in the island passed – Races, Carnival, Discovery Day, the Indian Centenary – and while the rest of the island was going crazy with rum and music and pretty women by the sea, Morgan was just going crazy with rage.

Morgan used to go to the Savannah and watch the fireworks of his rivals, and hear the cheers of the crowd as the fireworks spattered and spangled the sky. He would come in a great temper and beat all his children. He had ten of them. His wife was too big for him to beat.

Hat would say, 'We better send for the fire brigade.'

And for the next two or three hours Morgan would prowl in a stupid sort of way around his back yard, letting off fireworks so crazily that we used to hear his wife shouting, 'Morgan, stop playing the ass. You make ten children and you have a wife, and you can't afford to go and dead now.'

Morgan would roar like a bull and beat on the galvanized-iron fence.

He would shout, 'Everybody want to beat me. Everybody.'

Hat said, 'You know we hearing the real Morgan now.'

These fits of craziness made Morgan a real terror. When the fits were on him, he had the idea that Bhakcu, the mechanical genius who was my uncle, was always ready to beat him, and at about eleven o'clock in the evenings the idea just seemed to explode in his head.

He would beat on the fence and shout, 'Bhakcu, you fat-belly good-for-nothing son-of-a-bitch, come out and fight like a man.'

Bhakcu would keep on reading the *Ramayana* in his doleful singing voice, lying flat on his belly on his bed.

Bhakcu was a big man, and Morgan was a very small man, with the smallest hands and the thinnest wrists in Miguel Street.

Mrs Bhakcu would say, 'Morgan, why you don't shut up and go to sleep?'

Mrs Morgan would reply, 'Hey, you thin-foot woman! You better leave my husband alone, you hear. Why you don't look after your own?'

Mrs Bhakcu would say, 'You better mind your mouth. Otherwise I come up and turn your face with one slap, you hear.'

Mrs Bhakcu was four feet high, three feet wide, and three feet deep. Mrs Morgan was a little over six foot tall and built like a weight-lifter.

Mrs Morgan said, 'Why you don't get your big-belly husband to go and fix some more motor-car, and stop reading that damn stupid sing-song he always sing-songing?'

By this time Morgan would be on the pavement with us,

laughing in a funny sort of way, saying, 'Hear them women and them!' He would drink some rum from a hip-flask and say, 'Just watch and see. You know the calypso?

> *"The more they try to do me bad*
> *Is the better I live in Trinidad"*

time so next year, I go have the King of England and the King of America paying me millions to make fireworks for them. The most beautiful fireworks anybody ever see.'

And Hat or somebody else would ask, 'You go make the fireworks for them?'

Morgan would say, 'Make *what*? Make nothing. By this time so next year, I go have the King of England the King of America paying me millions to make fireworks for them. The most beautiful fireworks anybody ever see.'

And, in the meantime, in the back of the yard, Mrs Bhakcu was saying, '*He* have big belly. But what yours have? I don't know what yours going to sit on next year this time, you hear.'

And next morning Morgan was as straight and sober as ever, talking about his experiments.

This Morgan was more like a bird than a man. It was not only that he was as thin as a match-stick. He had a long neck that could swivel like a bird's. His eyes were bright and restless. And when he spoke it was in a pecking sort of way, as though he was not throwing out words, but picking up corn. He walked with a quick, tripping step, looking back over his shoulder at somebody following who wasn't there.

Hat said, 'You know how he get so? Is his wife, you know. He fraid she too bad. Spanish woman, you know. Full of blood and fire.'

Boyee said, 'You suppose that is why he want to make fireworks so?'

Hat said, 'People funny like hell. You never know with them.'

But Morgan used to make a joke of even his appearance, flinging out his arms and feet when he knew people were looking at him.

Morgan also made fun of his wife and his ten children. 'Is a miracle to me,' he said, 'that a man like me have ten children. I don't know how I manage it.'

Edward said, 'How you sure is your children?'

Morgan laughed and said, 'I have my doubts.'

* * *

Hat didn't like Morgan. He said, 'Is hard to say. But it have something about him I can't really take. I always feel he overdoing everything. I always feel the man lying about everything. I feel that he even lying to hisself.'

I don't think any of us understood what Hat meant. Morgan was becoming a little too troublesome, and it was hard for all of us to begin smiling as soon as we saw him, which was what he wanted.

Still his firework experiments continued; and every now and then we heard an explosion from Morgan's house, and we saw the puffs of coloured smoke. This was one of the standing amusements of the street.

But as time went by and Morgan found that no one was willing to buy his fireworks, he began to make fun even of his fireworks. He was not content with the laughter of the street when there was an explosion in his house.

Hat said, 'When a man start laughing at something he fight for all the time, you don't know whether to laugh or cry.' And Hat decided that Morgan was just a fool.

I suppose it was because of Hat that we decided not to laugh at Morgan any more.

Hat said, 'It go make him stop playing the fool.'

But it didn't.

Morgan grew wilder than ever, and began challenging Bhakcu to fight about two or three times a week. He began beating his children more than ever.

And he made one last attempt to make us laugh.

I heard about it from Chris, Morgan's fourth son. We were in the café at the corner of Miguel Street.

Chris said, 'Is a crime to talk to you now, you know.'

I said, 'Don't tell me. Is the old man again?'

Chris nodded and he showed me a sheet of paper, headed CRIME AND PUNISHMENT.

Chris said with pride, 'Look at it.'

It was a long list, with entries like this:

For fighting	(i) at home	Five strokes
	(ii) in the street	Seven strokes
	(iii) at school	Eight strokes

Chris looked at me and said in a very worried way, 'It funny like hell, eh? This sort of thing make blows a joke.'

I said yes, and asked, 'But you say is a crime to talk to me. Where it is?'

Chris showed me:

| For talking to street rabs | Four strokes |
| For playing with street rabs | Eight strokes |

I said, 'But your father don't mind talking to us. What wrong if you talk to us?'

Chris said, 'But this ain't nothing at all. You must come on Sunday and see what happen.'

I could see that Chris was pleased as anything.

About six of us went that Sunday. Morgan was there to meet us and he took us into his drawing room. Then he disappeared. There were many chairs and benches, as though there was going to be a concert. Morgan's eldest son was standing at a little table in the corner.

Suddenly this boy said, 'Stand!'

We all stood up, and Morgan appeared, smiling all round.

I asked Hat, 'Why he smiling so?'

Hat said, 'That is how the magistrates and them does smile when they come in court.'

Morgan's eldest son shouted, 'Andrew Morgan!'

Andrew Morgan came and stood before his father.

The eldest boy read very loudly, 'Andrew Morgan, you are charged with stoning the tamarind tree in Miss Dorothy's yard; you are charged with ripping off three buttons for the purpose of purchasing some marbles; you are charged with fighting Dorothy Morgan; you are charged with stealing two *tolums* and three sugar-cakes. Do you plead guilty or not guilty?'

Andrew said, 'Guilty.'

Morgan, scribbling on a sheet of paper, looked up.

'Have you anything to say?'

Andrew said, 'I sorry, sir.'

Morgan said, 'We will let the sentences run concurrently. Twelve strokes.'

One by one, the Morgan children were judged and sentenced. Even the eldest boy had to receive some punishment.

Morgan then rose and said, 'These sentences will be carried out this afternoon.'

He smiled all round and left the room.

The joke misfired completely.

Hat said, 'Nah, nah, man, you can't make fun of your own self and your own children that way, and invite all the street to see. Nah, it ain't right.'

I felt the joke was somehow terrible and frightening.

And when Morgan came out on the pavement that evening, his face fixed in a smile, he got none of the laughter he had expected. Nobody ran up to him and clapped him on the back, saying, 'But this man Morgan really mad, you hear. You hear how he beating his children these days . . . ?' No one said anything like that. No one said anything to him.

It was easy to see he was shattered.

Morgan got really drunk that night and challenged everybody to fight. He even challenged me.

Mrs Morgan had padlocked the front gate, so Morgan could only run about in his yard. He was as mad as a mad bull, bellowing and butting at the fence. He kept saying over and over again, 'You people think I not a man, eh? My father had eight children. I is his son. I have ten. I better than all of you put together.'

Hat said, 'He soon go start crying and then he go sleep.'

But I spent a lot of time that night before going to sleep thinking about Morgan, feeling sorry for him because of that little devil he had inside him. For that was what I thought was wrong with him. I fancied that inside him was a red, grinning devil pricking Morgan with his fork.

Mrs Morgan and the children went to the country.

Morgan no longer came out to the pavement, seeking our company. He was busy with his experiments. There were a series of minor explosions and lots of smoke.

Apart from that, peace reigned in our end of Miguel Street.

I wondered what Morgan was doing and thinking in all that solitude.

The following Sunday it rained heavily, and everyone was forced to go to bed early. The street was wet and glistening, and by eleven there was no noise save for the patter of the rain on the corrugated-iron roofs.

A short, sharp shout cracked through the street and got us up.

I could hear windows being flung open, and I heard people saying, 'What happen? What happen?'

'Is Morgan. Is Morgan. Something happening by Morgan.'

I was already out in the street and in front of Morgan's house. I never slept in pyjamas. I wasn't in that class.

The first thing I saw in the darkness of Morgan's yard was the figure of a woman hurrying away from the house to the back gate that opened on to the sewage trace between Miguel Street and Alfonso Street.

It was drizzling now, not very hard, and in no time at all quite a crowd had joined me.

It was all a bit mysterious – the shout, the woman disappearing, the dark house.

Then we heard Mrs Morgan shouting, 'Teresa Blake, Teresa Blake, what you doing with my man?' It was a cry of great pain.

Mrs Bhakcu was at my side. 'I always know about this Teresa, but I keep my mouth shut.'

Bhakcu said, 'Yes, you know everything, like your mother.'

A light came on in the house.

Then it went off again.

We heard Mrs Morgan saying, 'Why you fraid the light so for? Ain't you is man? Put the light on, let we see the great big man you is.'

The light went on; then off again.

We heard Morgan's voice, but it was so low we couldn't make out what he was saying.

Mrs Morgan said, 'Yes, hero.' And the light came on again.

We heard Morgan mumbling again.

Mrs Morgan said, 'No, hero.'

The light went off; then it went on.

Mrs Morgan was saying, 'Leave the light on. Come, let we show the big big hero to the people in the street. Come, let we show them what man really make like. You is not a anti-man, you is real man. You ain't only make ten children with me, you going to make more with somebody else.'

We heard Morgan's voice, a fluting unhappy thing.

Mrs Morgan said, 'But what you fraid now for? Ain't you is the funny man? The clown? Come, let them see see the clown and the big man you is. Let them see what man really make like.'

Morgan was wailing by this time, and trying to talk.

Mrs Morgan was saying, 'If you try to put that light off, I break up your little thin tail like a match-stick here, you hear.'

Then the front door was flung open, and we saw.

Mrs Morgan was holding up Morgan by his waist. He was practically naked, and he looked so thin, he was like a boy with an old man's face. He wasn't looking at us, but at Mrs Morgan's face, and he was squirming in her grasp, trying to get away. But Mrs Morgan was a strong woman.

Mrs Morgan was looking not at us, but at the man in her arm.

She was saying, 'But this is the big man I have, eh? So this is the man I married and slaving all my life for?' And then she began laughing in a croaking, nasty way.

She looked at us for a moment and said, 'Well, laugh now. He don't mind. He always want people to laugh at him.'

And the sight was so comic, the thin man held up so easily by the fat woman, that we did laugh. It was the sort of laugh that begins gently and then builds up into a bellowing belly laugh.

For the first time since he came to Miguel Street, Morgan was really being laughed at by the people.

And it broke him completely.

All the next day we waited for him to come out to the pavement, to congratulate him with our laughter. But we didn't see him.

Hat said, 'When I was little, my mother used to tell me, "Boy, you laughing all day. I bet you you go cry tonight." '

That night my sleep was again disturbed. By shouts and sirens.

I looked through the window and saw a red sky and red smoke.

Morgan's house was on fire.

And what a fire! Photographers from the papers were climbing up into other people's houses to get their pictures, and people were looking at them and not at the fire. Next morning there was a first-class picture with me part of the crowd in the top right-hand corner.

But what a fire it was! It was the most beautiful fire in Port of Spain since 1933 when the Treasury (of all places) burnt down, and the calypsonian sang:

> *It was a glorious and a beautiful scenery*
> *Was the burning of the Treasury.*

What really made the fire beautiful was Morgan's fireworks going off. Then for the first time everybody saw the astonishing splendour of Morgan's fireworks. People who used to scoff at Morgan felt a little silly. I have travelled in many countries since, but I have seen nothing to beat the fireworks show in Morgan's house that night.

But Morgan made no more fireworks.

Hat said, 'When I was a little boy, my mother used to say, "If a man want something, and he want it really bad, he does get it, but when he get it he don't like it."'

Both of Morgan's ambitions were fulfilled. People laughed at him, and they still do. And he made the most beautiful fireworks in the world. But as Hat said, when a man gets something he wants badly, he doesn't like it.

As we expected, the thing came out in court. Morgan was charged with arson. The newspaper people had a lot of fun with Morgan, within the libel laws. One headline I remember: PYROTECHNIST ALLEGED PYROMANIAC.

But I was glad, though, that Morgan got off.

They said Morgan went to Venezuela. They said he went mad. They said he became a jockey in Colombia. They said all sorts of things, but the people of Miguel Street were always romancers.

9 TITUS HOYT, I.A.

THIS MAN WAS born to be an active and important member of a local road board in the country. An unkind fate had placed him in the city. He was a natural guide, philosopher and friend to anyone who stopped to listen.

Titus Hoyt was the first man I met when I came to Port of Spain, a year or two before the war.

My mother had fetched me from Chaguanas after my father died. We travelled up by train and took a bus to Miguel Street. It was the first time I had travelled in a city bus.

I said to my mother, 'Ma, look, they forget to ring the bell here.'

My mother said, 'If you ring the bell you damn well going to get off and walk home by yourself, you hear.'

And then a little later I said, 'Ma, look, the sea.'

People in the bus began to laugh.

My mother was really furious.

Early next morning my mother said, 'Look now, I giving you four cents. Go to the shop on the corner of this road, Miguel Street, and buy two hops bread for a cent apiece, and buy a penny butter. And come back quick.'

I found the shop and I bought the bread and the butter – the red, salty type of butter.

Then I couldn't find my way back.

I found about six Miguel Streets, but none seemed to have my house. After a long time walking up and down I began to cry. I sat down on the pavement and got my shoes wet in the gutter.

Some little white girls were playing in a yard behind me. I looked at them, still crying. A girl wearing a pink frock came out and said, 'Why you crying?'

I said, 'I lost.'

She put her hands on my shoulder and said, 'Don't cry. You know where you live?'

I pulled out a piece of paper from my shirt pocket and showed her. Then a man came up. He was wearing white shorts and a white shirt, and he looked funny.

The man said, 'Why he crying?' in a gruff, but interested way.
The girl told him.
The man said, 'I will take him home.'
I asked the girl to come too.
The man said, 'Yes, you better come to explain to his mother.'
The girl said, 'All right, Mr Titus Hoyt.'
That was one of the first things about Titus Hoyt that I found interesting. The girl calling him 'Mr Titus Hoyt'. Not Titus, or Mr Hoyt, but Mr Titus Hoyt. I later realized that everyone who knew him called him that.
When we got home the girl explained to my mother what had happened, and my mother was ashamed of me.
Then the girl left.
Mr Titus Hoyt looked at me and said, 'He look like a intelligent little boy.'
My mother said in a sarcastic way, 'Like his father.'
Titus Hoyt said, 'Now, young man, if a herring and a half cost a penny and a half, what's the cost of three herrings?'
Even in the country, in Chaguanas, we had heard about that.
Without waiting, I said, 'Three pennies.'
Titus Hoyt regarded me with wonder.
He told my mother, 'This boy bright like anything, ma'am. You must take care of him and send him to a good school and feed him good food so he could study well.'
My mother didn't say anything.
When Titus Hoyt left, he said, 'Cheerio!'
That was the second interesting thing about him.
My mother beat me for getting my shoes wet in the gutter but she said she wouldn't beat me for getting lost.
For the rest of that day I ran about the yard saying, 'Cheerio! Cheerio!' to a tune of my own.
That evening Titus Hoyt came again.
My mother didn't seem to mind.
To me Titus Hoyt said, 'You can read?'
I said yes.
'And write?'
I said yes.
'Well, look,' he said, 'get some paper and a pencil and write what I tell you.'
I said, 'Paper and pencil?'
He nodded.

I ran to the kitchen and said, 'Ma, you got any paper and pencil?'

My mother said, 'What you think I is? A shopkeeper?'

Titus Hoyt shouted, 'Is for me, ma'am.'

My mother said, 'Oh,' in a disappointed way.

She said, 'In the bottom drawer of the bureau you go find my purse. It have a pencil in it.'

And she gave me a copy-book from the kitchen shelf.

Mr Titus Hoyt said, 'Now, young man, write. Write the address of this house in the top right-hand corner, and below that, the date.' Then he asked, 'You know who we writing this letter to, boy?'

I shook my head.

He said, 'Ha, boy! Ha! We writing to the *Guardian*, boy.'

I said, 'The *Trinidad Guardian*? The paper? What, *me* writing to the *Guardian*! But only big big man does write to the *Guardian*.'

Titus Hoyt smiled. 'That's why you writing. It go surprise them.'

I said, 'What I go write to them about?'

He said, 'You go write it now. Write. To the Editor, *Trinidad Guardian*. Dear Sir, I am but a child of eight (How old you is? Well, it don't matter anyway) and yesterday my mother sent me to make a purchase in the city. This, dear Mr Editor, was my first peregrination (p-e-r-e-g-r-i-n-a-t-i-o-n) in this metropolis, and I had the misfortune to wander from the path my mother had indicated—'

I said, 'Oh God, Mr Titus Hoyt, where you learn all these big words and them? You sure you spelling them right?'

Titus Hoyt smiled. 'I spend all afternoon making up this letter,' he said.

I wrote: '. . . and in this state of despair I was rescued by a Mr Titus Hoyt, of Miguel Street. This only goes to show, dear Mr Editor, that human kindness is a quality not yet extinct in this world.'

The *Guardian* never printed the letter.

When I next saw Titus Hoyt he said, 'Well, never mind. One day, boy, one day, I go make them sit up and take notice of every word I say. Just wait and see.'

And before he left he said, 'Drinking your milk?'

He had persuaded my mother to give me half a pint of milk every day. Milk was good for the brains.

It is one of the sadnesses of my life that I never fulfilled Titus Hoyt's hopes for my academic success.

I still remember with tenderness the interest he took in me. Sometimes his views clashed with my mother's. There was the business of the cobwebs, for instance.

Boyee, with whom I had become friendly very quickly, was teaching me to ride. I had fallen and cut myself nastily on the shin.

My mother was attempting to cure this with sooty cobwebs soaked in rum.

Titus Hoyt was horrified. 'You ain't know what you doing,' he shouted.

My mother said, 'Mr Titus Hoyt, I will kindly ask you to mind your own business. The day you make a baby yourself I go listen to what you have to say.'

Titus Hoyt refused to be ridiculed. He said, 'Take the boy to the doctor, man.'

I was watching them argue, not caring greatly either way.

In the end I went to the doctor.

Titus Hoyt reappeared in a new role.

He told my mother, 'For the last two three months I been taking the first-aid course with the Red Cross. I go dress the boy foot for you.'

That really terrified me.

For about a month or so afterwards, people in Miguel Street could tell when it was nine o'clock in the morning. By my shrieks. Titus Hoyt loved his work.

All this gives some clue to the real nature of the man.

The next step followed naturally.

Titus Hoyt began to teach.

It began in a small way, after the fashion of all great enterprises.

He had decided to sit for the external arts degree of London University. He began to learn Latin, teaching himself, and as fast as he learned, he taught us.

He rounded up three or four of us and taught us in the verandah of his house. He kept chickens in his yard and the place stank.

That Latin stage didn't last very long. We got as far as the fourth declension, and then Boyee and Errol and myself began asking questions. They were not the sort of questions Titus Hoyt liked.

Boyee said, 'Mr Titus Hoyt, I think you making up all this, you know, making it up as you go on.'

Titus Hoyt said, 'But I telling you, I not making it up. Look, here it is in black and white.'

Errol said, 'I feel, Mr Titus Hoyt, that one man sit down one day and make all this up and have everybody else learning it.'

Titus Hoyt asked me, 'What is the accusative singular of *bellum*?'

Feeling wicked, because I was betraying him, I said to Titus Hoyt, 'Mr Titus Hoyt, when you was my age, how you woulda feel if somebody did ask you that question?'

And then Boyee asked, 'Mr Titus Hoyt, what is the meaning of the ablative case?'

So the Latin lessons ended.

But however much we laughed at him, we couldn't deny that Titus Hoyt was a deep man.

Hat used to say, 'He is a thinker, that man.'

Titus Hoyt thought about all sorts of things, and he thought dangerous things sometimes.

Hat said, 'I don't think Titus Hoyt like God, you know.'

Titus Hoyt would say, 'The thing that really matter is faith. Look, I believe that if I pull out this bicycle-lamp from my pocket here, and set it up somewhere, and really really believe in it and pray to it, what I pray for go come. That is what I believe.'

And so saying he would rise and leave, not forgetting to say, 'Cheerio!'

He had the habit of rushing up to us and saying, 'Silence, everybody. I just been thinking. Listen to what I just been thinking.'

One day he rushed up and said, 'I been thinking how this war could end. If Europe could just sink for five minutes all the Germans go drown—'

Eddoes said, 'But England go drown too.'

Titus Hoyt agreed and looked sad. 'I lose my head, man,' he said. 'I lose my head.'

And he wandered away, muttering to himself and shaking his head.

One day he cycled right up to us when we were talking about the Barbados–Trinidad cricket match. Things were not going well for Trinidad and we were worried.

Titus Hoyt rushed up and said, 'Silence. I just been thinking. Look, boys, it ever strike you that the world not real at all? It ever strike you that we have the only mind in the world and you just thinking up everything else? Like me here, having the only mind in the world, and thinking up you people here, thinking up the war and all the houses and the ships and them in the harbour. That ever cross your mind?'

His interest in teaching didn't die.

We often saw him going about with big books. These books were about teaching.

Titus Hoyt used to say, 'Is a science, man. The trouble with Trinidad is that the teachers don't have this science of teaching.'

And, 'Is the biggest thing in the world, man. Having the minds of the young to train. Think of that. Think.'

It soon became clear that whatever we thought about it, Titus Hoyt was bent on training our minds.

He formed the Miguel Street Literary and Social Youth Club, and had it affiliated to the Trinidad and Tobago Youth Association.

We used to meet in his house, which was well supplied with things to eat and drink. The walls of his house were now hung with improving quotations, some typed, some cut out of magazines and pasted on bits of cardboard.

I also noticed a big thing called 'Time-table'.

From this I gathered that Titus Hoyt was to rise at five-thirty, read Something from Greek philosophers until six, spend fifteen minutes bathing and exercising, another five reading the morning paper, and ten on breakfast. It was a formidable thing altogether.

Titus Hoyt said, 'If I follow the time-table I will be a educated man in about three four years.'

The Miguel Street Club didn't last very long.

It was Titus Hoyt's fault.

No man in his proper senses would have made Boyee secretary. Most of Boyee's minutes consisted of the names of people present.

And then we all had to write and read something.

The Miguel Street Literary and Social Club became nothing more than a gathering of film critics.

Titus Hoyt said, 'No, man. We just can't have all you boys

talking about pictures all the time. I will have to get some propaganda for you boys.'

Boyee said, 'Mr Titus Hoyt, what we want with propaganda?
Is a German thing.'

Titus Hoyt smiled. 'That is not the proper meaning of the
word, boy. I am using the word in it proper meaning. Is education, boy, that make me know things like that.'

Boyee was sent as our delegate to the Youth Association annual
conference.

When he came back Boyee said, 'Is a helluva thing at that
youth conference. Is only a pack of old, old people it have there.'

The attraction of the Coca-Cola and the cakes and the ice-
cream began to fade. Some of us began staying away from
meetings.

Titus Hoyt made one last effort to keep the club together.

One day he said, 'Next Sunday the club will go on a visit to
Fort George.'

There were cries of disapproval.

Titus Hoyt said, 'You see, you people don't care about your
country. How many of you know about Fort George? Not one
of you here know about the place. But is history, man, your
history, and you must learn about things like that. You must
remember that the boys and girls of today are the men and
women of tomorrow. The old Romans had a saying, you know.
Mens sana in corpore sano. I think we will make the walk to Fort
George.'

Still no one wanted to go.

Titus Hoyt said, 'At the top of Fort George it have a stream,
and it cool cool and the water crystal clear. You could bathe there
when we get to the top.'

We couldn't resist that.

The next Sunday a whole group of us took the trolley-bus to
Mucurapo.

When the conductor came round to collect the fares, Titus
Hoyt said, 'Come back a little later.' And he paid the conductor
only when we got off the bus. The fare for everybody came up to
about two shillings. But Titus Hoyt gave the conductor a shilling,
saying, 'We don't want any ticket, man!' The conductor and
Titus Hoyt laughed.

It was a long walk up the hill, red and dusty, and hot.

Titus Hoyt told us, 'This fort was built at a time when the French and them was planning to invade Trinidad.'

We gasped.

We had never realized that anyone considered us so important.

Titus Hoyt said, 'That was in 1803, when we was fighting Napoleon.'

We saw a few old rusty guns at the side of the path and heaps of rusty cannon-balls.

I asked, 'The French invade Trinidad, Mr Titus Hoyt?'

Titus Hoyt shook his head in a disappointed way. 'No, they didn't attack. But we was ready, man. Ready for them.'

Boyee said, 'You sure it have this stream up there you tell us about, Mr Titus Hoyt?'

Titus Hoyt said, 'What you think I is? A liar?'

Boyee said, 'I ain't saying nothing.'

We walked and sweated. Boyee took off his shoes.

Errol said, 'If it ain't have that stream up there, somebody going to catch hell.'

We got to the top, had a quick look at the graveyard where there were a few tombstones of British soldiers dead long ago; and we looked through the telescope at the city of Port of Spain, large and sprawling beneath us. We could see the people walking in the streets as large as life.

Then we went looking for the stream.

We couldn't find it.

Titus Hoyt said, 'It must be here somewhere. When I was a boy I use to bathe in it.'

Boyee said, 'And what happen now? It dry up?'

Titus Hoyt said, 'It look so.'

Boyee got really mad, and you couldn't blame him. It was hard work coming up that hill, and we were all hot and thirsty.

He insulted Titus Hoyt in a very crude way.

Titus Hoyt said, 'Remember, Boyee, you are the secretary of the Miguel Street Literary and Social Club. Remember that you have just attended a meeting of the Youth Association as our delegate. Remember these things.'

Boyee said, 'Go to hell, Hoyt.'

We were aghast.

So the Literary Club broke up.

* * *

It wasn't long after that Titus Hoyt got his Inter Arts degree and
set up a school of his own. He had a big sign placed in his garden:

TITUS HOYT, I.A. (London, External)
Passes in the Cambridge
School Certificate Guaranteed

One year the *Guardian* had a brilliant idea. They started the
Needy Cases Fund to help needy cases at Christmas. It was popular and after a few years was called the Neediest Cases Fund. At
the beginning of November the *Guardian* announced the target
for the fund and it was a daily excitement until Christmas Eve to
see how the fund rose. It was always front page news and everybody who gave got his name in the papers.

In the middle of December one year, when the excitement
was high, Miguel Street was in the news.

Hat showed us the paper and we read:

'FOLLOW THE EXAMPLE OF THIS TINYMITE!

'The smallest and most touching response to our appeal to
bring Yuletide cheer to the unfortunate has come in a letter
from Mr Titus Hoyt, I.A., a headmaster of Miguel Street, Port
of Spain. The letter was sent to Mr Hoyt by one of his pupils
who wishes to remain anonymous. We have Mr Hoyt's permission to print the letter in full.

' "Dear Mr Hoyt, I am only eight and, as you doubtless
know, I am a member of the GUARDIAN Tinymites League.
I read Aunt Juanita every Sunday. You, dear Mr Hoyt, have
always extolled the virtue of charity and you have spoken
repeatedly of the fine work the GUARDIAN Neediest Cases
Fund is doing to bring Yuletide cheer to the unfortunate.
I have decided to yield to your earnest entreaty. I have very
little money to offer – a mere six cents, in fact, but take it, Mr
Hoyt, and send it to the GUARDIAN Neediest Cases Fund.
May it bring Yuletide cheer to some poor unfortunate! I know
it is not much. But, like the widow, I give my mite. I remain,
dear Mr Hoyt, One of Your Pupils." '

And there was a large photograph of Titus Hoyt, smiling and
pop-eyed in the flash of the camera.

I SUPPOSE LAURA holds a world record.

Laura had eight children.

There is nothing surprising in that.

These eight children had seven fathers.

Beat that!

It was Laura who gave me my first lesson in biology. She lived just next door to us, and I found myself observing her closely.

I would notice her belly rising for months.

Then I would miss her for a short time.

And the next time I saw her she would be quite flat.

And the leavening process would begin again in a few months.

To me this was one of the wonders of the world in which I lived, and I always observed Laura. She herself was quite gay about what was happening to her. She used to point to it and say, 'This thing happening again, but you get use to it after the first three four times. Is a damn nuisance, though.'

She used to blame God, and speak about the wickedness of men.

For her first six children she tried six different men.

Hat used to say, 'Some people hard to please.'

But I don't want to give you the impression that Laura spent all her time having babies and decrying men, and generally feeling sorry for herself. If Bogart was the most bored person in the street, Laura was the most vivacious. She was always gay, and she liked me.

She would give me plums and mangoes when she had them; and whenever she made sugar-cakes she would give me some.

Even my mother, who had a great dislike of laughter, especially in me, even my mother used to laugh at Laura.

She often said to me, 'I don't know why Laura muching you up so for. Like she ain't have enough children to mind.'

I think my mother was right. I don't think a woman like Laura could have ever had too many children. She loved all her children, though you wouldn't have believed it from the language she used when she spoke to them. Some of Laura's shouts and curses were the richest things I have ever heard, and I shall never forget them.

Hat said once, 'Man, she like Shakespeare when it come to using words.'

Laura used to shout, 'Alwyn, you broad-mouth brute, come here.'

And, 'Gavin, if you don't come here this minute, I make you fart fire, you hear.'

And, 'Lorna, you black bow-leg bitch, why you can't look what you doing?'

Now, to compare Laura, the mother of eight, with Mary the Chinese, also mother of eight, doesn't seem fair. Because Mary took really good care of her children and never spoke harshly to them. But Mary, mark you, had a husband who owned a shop, and Mary could afford to be polite and nice to her children, after stuffing them full of chop-suey and chow-min and chow-fan, and things with names like that. But who could Laura look to for money to keep her children?

The men who cycled slowly past Laura's house in the evening, whistling for Laura, were not going to give any of their money to Laura's children. They just wanted Laura.

I asked my mother, 'How Laura does live?'

My mother slapped me, saying, 'You know, you too fast for a little boy.'

I suspected the worst.

But I wouldn't have liked that to be true.

So I asked Hat. Hat said, 'She have a lot of friends who does sell in the market. They does give she things free, and sometimes one or two or three of she husbands does give she something too, but that not much.'

The oddest part of the whole business was Laura herself. Laura was no beauty. As Boyee said one day, 'She have a face like the top of a motor-car battery.' And she was a little more than plump.

I am talking now of the time when she had had only six children.

One day Hat said, 'Laura have a new man.'

Everybody laughed, 'Stale news. If Laura have she way, she go try every man once.'

But Hat said, 'No, is serious. He come to live with she for

good now. I see him this morning when I was taking out the
cows.'

We watched and waited for this man.

We later learned that he was watching and waiting for us.

In no time at all this man, Nathaniel, had become one of the
gang in Miguel Street. But it was clear that he was not really one
of us. He came from the east end of Port of Spain, which we
considered dirtier; and his language was really coarse.

He made out that he was a kind of terror in the east end around
Piccadilly Street. He told many stories about gang-fights, and he
let it be known that he had disfigured two or three people.

Hat said, 'I think he lying like hell, you know.'

I distrusted him myself. He was a small man, and I always felt
that small men were more likely to be wicked and violent.

But what really sickened us was his attitude to women. We
were none of us chivalrous, but Nathaniel had a contempt for
women which we couldn't like. He would make rude remarks
when women passed.

Nathaniel would say, 'Women just like cows. Cow and they is
the same thing.'

And when Miss Ricaud, the welfare woman, passed, Nathaniel
would say, 'Look at that big cow.'

Which wasn't in good taste, for we all thought that Miss
Ricaud was too fat to be laughed at, and ought instead to be
pitied.

Nathaniel, in the early stages, tried to make us believe that he
knew how to keep Laura in her place. He hinted that he used to
beat her. He used to say, 'Woman and them like a good dose of
blows, you know. You know the calypso:

> *Every now and then just knock them down.*
> *Every now and then just throw them down.*
> *Black up their eye and bruise up their knee*
> *And then they love you eternally.*

Is gospel truth about woman.'

Hat said, 'Woman is a funny thing, for truth, though. I don't
know what a woman like Laura see in Nathaniel.'

Eddoes said, 'I know a helluva lot about woman. I think
Nathaniel lying like hell. I think when he with Laura he got his
tail between his legs all the time.'

We used to hear fights and hear the children screaming all over the place, and when we saw Nathaniel, he would just say, 'Just been beating some sense into that woman.'

Hat said, 'Is a funny thing. Laura don't look any sadder.'

Nathaniel said, 'Is only blows she really want to keep she happy.'

Nathaniel was lying, of course. It wasn't he who was giving the blows, it was Laura. That came out the day when Nathaniel tried to wear a hat to cover up a beaten eye.

Eddoes said, 'It look like they make up that calypso about men, not women.'

Nathaniel tried to get at Eddoes, who was small and thin. But Hat said, 'Go try that on Laura. I know Laura. Laura just trying not to beat you up too bad just to keep you with she, but the day she start getting tired of you, you better run, boy.'

We prayed for something to happen to make Nathaniel leave Miguel Street.

Hat said, 'We ain't have to wait long. Laura making baby eight months now. Another month, and Nathaniel gone.'

Eddoes said, 'That would be a real record. Seven children with seven different man.'

The baby came.

It was on a Saturday. Just the evening before I had seen Laura standing in her yard leaning on the fence.

The baby came at eight o'clock in the morning. And, like a miracle, just two hours later, Laura was calling across to my mother.

I hid and looked.

Laura was leaning on her window-sill. She was eating a mango, and the yellow juice was smeared all over her face.

She was saying to my mother, 'The baby come this morning.'

And my mother only said, 'Boy or girl?'

Laura said, 'What sort of luck you think I have? It looks like I really blight. Is another girl. I just thought I would let you know, that's all. Well, I got to go now. I have to do some sewing.'

And that very evening it looked as though what Hat said was going to come true. For that evening Laura came out to the pavement and shouted to Nathaniel, 'Hey, Nathaniel, come here.'

Hat said, 'But what the hell is this? Ain't it this morning she make baby?'

Nathaniel tried to show off to us. He said to Laura, 'I busy. I ain't coming.'

Laura advanced, and I could see fight in her manner. She said, 'You ain't coming? Ain't coming? But what is this I hearing?'

Nathaniel was worried. He tried to talk to us, but he wasn't talking in a sensible way.

Laura said, 'You think you is a man. But don't try playing man with me, you hear. Yes, Nathaniel, is you I talking to, you with your bottom like two stale bread in your pants.'

This was one of Laura's best, and we all began laughing. When she saw us laughing, Laura burst out too.

Hat said, 'This woman is a real case.'

But even after the birth of his baby Nathaniel didn't leave Miguel Street. We were a little worried.

Hat said, 'If she don't look out she go have another baby with the same man, you know.'

It wasn't Laura's fault that Nathaniel didn't go. She knocked him about a lot, and did so quite openly now. Sometimes she locked him out, and then we would hear Nathaniel crying and coaxing from the pavement, 'Laura, darling, Laura, *doux-doux*, just let me come in tonight. Laura, *doux-doux*, let me come in.'

He had dropped all pretence now of keeping Laura in her place. He no longer sought our company, and we were glad of that.

Hat used to say, 'I don't know why he don't go back to the Dry River where he come from. They ain't have any culture there, and he would be happier.'

I couldn't understand why he stayed.

Hat said, 'It have some man like that. They like woman to kick them around.'

And Laura was getting angrier with Nathaniel.

One day we heard her tell him, 'You think because you give me one baby, you own me. That baby only come by accident, you hear.'

She threatened to get the police.

Nathaniel said, 'But who go mind your children?'

Laura said, 'That is my worry. I don't want you here. You is only another mouth to feed. And if you don't leave me right right now I go go and call Sergeant Charles for you.'

It was this threat of the police that made Nathaniel leave.

He was in tears.

But Laura was swelling out again.

Hat said, 'Oh, God! Two babies by the same man!'

One of the miracles of life in Miguel Street was that no one starved. If you sit down at a table with pencil and paper and try to work it out, you will find it impossible. But I lived in Miguel Street, and can assure you that no one starved. Perhaps they did go hungry, but you never heard about it.

Laura's children grew.

The eldest daughter, Lorna, began working as a servant in a house in St Clair and took typing lessons from a man in Sackville Street.

Laura used to say, 'It have nothing like education in the world. I don't want my children to grow like me.'

In time, Laura delivered her eighth baby, as effortlessly as usual.

That baby was her last.

It wasn't that she was tired or that she had lost her love of the human race or lost her passion for adding to it. As a matter of fact, Laura never seemed to grow any older or less cheerful. I always felt that, given the opportunity, she could just go on and on having babies.

The eldest daughter, Lorna, came home from her typing lessons late one night and said, 'Ma, I going to make a baby.'

I heard the shriek that Laura gave.

And for the first time I heard Laura crying. It wasn't ordinary crying. She seemed to be crying all the cry she had saved up since she was born, all the cry she had tried to cover up with her laughter. I have heard people cry at funerals, but there is a lot of showing-off in their crying. Laura's crying that night was the most terrible thing I had heard. It made me feel that the world was a stupid, sad place, and I almost began crying with Laura.

All the street heard Laura crying.

Next day Boyee said, 'I don't see why she so mad about that. She does do the same.'

Hat got so annoyed that he took off his leather belt and beat Boyee.

I didn't know who I felt sorrier for – Laura or her daughter.

I felt that Laura was ashamed now to show herself in the street.

When I did see her I found it hard to believe that she was the same woman who used to laugh with me and give me sugar-cakes.

She was an old woman now.

She no longer shouted at her children, no longer beat them. I don't know whether she was taking especial care of them or whether she had lost interest in them.

But we never heard Laura say a word of reproach to Lorna.

That was terrible.

Lorna brought her baby home. There were no jokes about it in the street.

Laura's house was a dead, silent house.

Hat said, 'Life is helluva thing. You can see trouble coming and you can't do a damn thing to prevent it coming. You just got to sit and watch and wait.'

According to the papers, it was just another week-end tragedy, one of many.

Lorna was drowned at Carenage.

Hat said, 'Is what they always do, swim out and out until they tired and can't swim no more.'

And when the police came to tell Laura about it, she had said very little.

Laura said, 'It good. It good. It better that way.'

11 THE BLUE CART

THERE WERE MANY reasons why I wanted to be like Eddoes when I grew up.

He was one of the aristocrats of the street. He drove a scavenging cart and so worked only in the mornings.

Then, as everybody said, Eddoes was a real 'saga-boy'. This didn't mean that he wrote epic poetry. It meant that he was a 'sweet-man', a man of leisure, well-dressed, and keen on women.

Hat used to say, 'For a man who does drive a scavenging cart, this Eddoes too clean, you hear.'

Eddoes was crazy about cleanliness.

He used to brush his teeth for hours.

If fact, if you were telling a stranger about Eddoes you would say, 'You know – the little fellow with a tooth-brush always in his mouth.'

This was one thing in Eddoes I really admired. Once I stuck a tooth-brush in my mouth and walked about our yard in the middle of the day.

My mother said, 'You playing man? But why you don't wait until your pee make froth?'

That made me miserable for days.

But it didn't prevent me taking the tooth-brush to school and wearing it there. It caused quite a stir. But I quickly realized that only a man like Eddoes could have worn a tooth-brush and carried it off.

Eddoes was always well-dressed. His khaki trousers were always creased and his shoes always shone. He wore his shirts with three buttons undone so you could see his hairy chest. His shirt cuffs were turned up just above the wrist and you could see his gold wrist-watch.

Even when Eddoes wore a coat you saw the watch. From the way he wore the coat you thought that Eddoes hadn't realized that the end of the coat sleeve had been caught in the watch strap.

It was only when I grew up I realized how small and how thin Eddoes really was.

BOOKS INC.
601 Van Ness Ave.
San Francisco, Ca. 94102
(415) 776-1111
returns with receipt within 14 days

524841 Reg 1 ID 79 5:00 pm 09/12/15

S COLL SHORT FICTIO	1 @	8.98	8.98
S 9787777556565			
S MAGAZINES	1 @	6.95	6.95
S X2			
S MAGAZI	1 @	5.95	5.95
S X2			
SUBTOTA			21.88
SALES			1.91
TOTA			23.79
CASH			
CHA			

Ask your Fri

SALE

Publishers Price
$25.00

Books Inc. Price
$8.98

I asked Hat, 'You think is true all this talk Eddoes giving us about how woman running after him?'

Hat said, 'Well, boy, woman these days funny like hell. They go run after a dwarf if he got money.'

I said, 'I don't believe you.'

I was very young at the time.

But I always thought, 'If it have one man in this world woman bound to like, that man is Eddoes.'

He sat on his blue cart with so much grace. And how smart that tooth-brush was in his mouth!

But you couldn't talk to him when he was on his cart. Then he was quite different from the Eddoes we knew on the ground; then he never laughed, but was always serious. And if we tried to ride on the back of his cart, as we used to on the back of the ice-cart, Eddoes would crack his whip at us in a nasty way and shout, 'What sort of cart you think this is? Your father can't buy cart like this, you hear?'

Every year Eddoes won the City Council's award for the cleanest scavenging cart.

And to hear Eddoes talk about his job was to make yourself feel sad and inferior.

He said he knew everybody important in Port of Spain, from the Governor down.

He would say, 'Collected two three tins of rubbish from the Director of Medical Services yesterday. I know him good, you know. Been collecting his rubbish for years, ever since he was a little doctor in Woodbrook, catching hell. So I see him yesterday and he say, "Eddoes (that is how he does always call me, you know) Eddoes," he say, "Come and have a drink." Well, when I working I don't like drinking because it does keep you back. But he nearly drag me off the cart, man. In the end I had to drink with him. He tell me all his troubles.'

There were also stories of rich women waiting for him behind rubbish tins, women begging Eddoes to take away their rubbish.

But you should have seen Eddoes on those days when the scavengers struck. As I have told you already, these scavengers were proud people and stood for no nonsense from anybody.

They knew they had power. They could make Port of Spain stink in twenty-four hours if they struck.

On these important days Eddoes would walk slowly and

thoughtfully up and down Miguel Street. He looked grim then, and fierce, and he wouldn't speak to a soul.

He wore a red scarf and a tooth-brush with a red handle on these days.

Sometimes we went to Woodford Square to the strike meeting, to gaze at these exciting people.

It amazed me to see Eddoes singing. The songs were violent, but Eddoes looked so sad.

Hat told me, 'It have detectives here, you know. They taking down every word Eddoes and them saying.'

It was easy to recognize the detectives. They were wearing a sort of plain-clothes uniform – brown hats, white shirts, and brown trousers. They were writing in big notebooks with red pencils.

And Eddoes didn't look scared!

We all knew that Eddoes wasn't a man to be played with.

You couldn't blame Eddoes then for being proud.

One day Eddoes brought home a pair of shoes and showed it to us in a quiet way, as though he wasn't really interested whether we looked at the shoes or not.

He said, brushing his teeth, and looking away from us, 'Got these shoes today from the *labasse*, the dump, you know. They was just lying there and I pick them up.'

We whistled. The shoes were practically new.

'The things people does throw away,' Eddoes said.

And he added, 'This is a helluva sort of job, you know. You could get anything if you really look. I know a man who get a whole bed the other day. And when I was picking up some rubbish from St Clair the other day this stupid woman rush out, begging me to come inside. She say she was going to give me a radio.'

Boyee said, 'You mean these rich people does just throw away things like that?'

Eddoes laughed and looked away, pitying our simplicity.

The news about Eddoes and the shoes travelled round the street pretty quickly. My mother was annoyed. She said, 'You see what sort of thing life is. Here I is, working my finger to the bone. Nobody flinging me a pair of shoes just like that, you know. And there you got that thin-arse little man, doing next to nothing, and look at all the things he does get.'

Eddoes presently began getting more things. He brought home a bedstead, he brought home dozens of cups and saucers only slightly cracked, lengths and lengths of wood, all sorts of bolts and screws, and sometimes even money.

Eddoes said, 'I was talking to one of the old boys today. He tell me the thing is to never throw away shoes. Always look in shoes that people throw away, and you go find all sort of thing.'

The time came when we couldn't say if Eddoes was prouder of his job or of his collection of junk.

He spent half an hour a day unloading the junk from his cart.

And if anybody wanted a few nails, or a little piece of corrugated iron, the first person they asked was Eddoes.

He made a tremendous fuss when people asked him, though I feel he was pleased.

He would say, 'I working hard all day, getting all these materials and them, and people think they could just come running over and say, "Give me this, give me that." '

In time, the street referred to Eddoes's collection of junk as Eddoes's 'materials'.

One day, after he opened his school, Titus Hoyt was telling us that he had to spend a lot of money to buy books.

He said, 'It go cost me at least sixty dollars.'

Eddoes asked, 'How much book you getting for that?'

Titus Hoyt said, 'Oh, about seven or eight.'

Eddoes laughed in a scornful way.

Eddoes said, 'I could get a whole handful for you for about twelve cents. Why you want to go and spend so much money on eight books for?'

Eddoes sold a lot of books.

Hat bought twenty cents' worth of book.

It just shows how Titus Hoyt was making everybody educated.

And there was this business about pictures.

Eddoes said one day, 'Today I pick up two nice pictures, two nice nice sceneries, done frame and everything.'

I went home and I said, 'Ma, Eddoes say he go sell us some sceneries for twelve cents.'

My mother behaved in an unexpected way.

She wiped her hand on her dress and came outside.

Eddoes brought the sceneries over. He said, 'The glass a little dirty, but you could always clean that. But they is nice sceneries.'

They were engravings of ships in stormy seas. I could see my mother almost ready to cry from joy. She repeated, 'I always always want to have some nice sceneries.' Then, pointing at me, she said to Eddoes, 'This boy father was always painting sceneries, you know.'

Eddoes looked properly impressed.

He asked, 'Sceneries nice as this?'

My mother didn't reply.

After a little talk my mother paid Eddoes ten cents.

And if Eddoes had something that nobody wanted to buy, he always went to my uncle Bhakcu, who was ready to buy anything.

He used to say, 'You never know when these things could come in handy.'

Hat began saying, 'I think all this materials getting on Eddoes mind, you know. It have some men like that.'

I wasn't worried until Eddoes came to me one day and said, 'You ever think of collecting old bus ticket?'

The idea had never crossed my mind.

Eddoes said, 'Look, there's something for a little boy like you to start with. For every thousand you collect I go give you a penny.'

I said, 'Why you want bus ticket?' He laughed as though I were a fool.

I didn't collect any bus tickets, but I noticed a lot of other boys doing so. Eddoes had told them that for every hundred they collected they got a free ride.

Hat said, 'Is to start getting worried when he begin collecting pins.'

But something happened that made Eddoes sober as a judge again.

He said one day, 'I in trouble!'

Hat said, 'Don't tell us that is thief you been thiefing all this materials and them?'

Eddoes shook his head.

He said, 'A girl making baby for me.'

Hat said, 'You sure is for you?'

Eddoes said, 'She say so.'

It was hard to see why this should get Eddoes so worried. Hat said, 'But don't be stupid, man. Is the sort of thing that does happen to anybody.'

But Eddoes refused to be consoled.

He collected junk in a listless way.

Then he stopped altogether.

Hat said, 'Eddoes behaving as though he invent the idea of making baby.'

Hat asked again, 'You sure this baby is for you, and not for nobody else? It have some woman making a living this way, you know.'

Eddoes said, 'Is true she have other baby, but I in trouble.'

Hat said, 'She is like Laura?'

Eddoes said, 'Nah, Laura does only have one baby for one man. This girl does have two three.'

Hat said, 'Look, you mustn't worry. You don't know is your baby. Wait and see. Wait and see.'

Eddoes said sadly, 'She say if I don't take the baby she go make me lose my job.'

We gasped.

Eddoes said, 'She know lots of people. She say she go make them take me away from St Clair and put me in Dry River, where the people so damn poor they don't throw away nothing.'

I said, 'You mean you not going to find any materials there?'

Eddoes nodded, and we understood.

Hat said, 'The calypsonian was right, you hear.

> *Man centipede bad.*
> *Woman centipede more than bad.*

I know the sort of woman. She have a lot of baby, take the baby by the fathers, and get the fathers to pay money. By the time she thirty thirty-five, she getting so much money from so much man, and she ain't got no baby to look after and no responsibility. I know the thing.'

Boyee said, 'Don't worry, Eddoes. Wait and see if it is your baby. Wait and see.'

Hat said, 'Boyee, ain't you too damn small to be meddling with talk like this?'

The months dragged by.

One day Eddoes announced, 'She drop the baby yesterday.'

Hat said, 'Boy or girl?'

'Girl.'

We felt very sorry for Eddoes.

Hat asked, 'You think is yours?'

'Yes.'

'You bringing it home?'

'In about a year or so.'

'Then you ain't got nothing now to worry about. If is your child, bring she home, man. And you still going round St Clair, getting your materials.'

Eddoes agreed, but he didn't look any happier.

Hat gave the baby a nickname long before she arrived in Miguel Street. He called her Pleasure, and that was how she was called until she became a big girl.

The baby's mother brought Pleasure one night, but she didn't stay long. And Eddoes's stock rose when we saw how beautiful the mother was. She was a wild, Spanish-looking woman.

But one glance at Pleasure made us know that she couldn't be Eddoes's baby.

Boyee began whistling the calypso:

> *Chinese children calling me Daddy!*
> *I black like jet,*
> *My wife like tar-baby,*
> *And still –*
> *Chinese children calling me Daddy!*
> *Oh God, somebody putting milk in my coffee.*

Hat gave Boyee a pinch, and Hat said to Eddoes, 'She is a good-looking child, Eddoes. Like you.'

Eddoes said, 'You think so, Hat?'

Hat said, 'Yes, man. I think she go grow up to be a sweet-girl just as how she father is a sweet-man.'

I said, 'You have a nice daughter, Eddoes.'

The baby was asleep and pink and beautiful.

Errol said, 'I could wait sixteen years until she come big enough.'

Eddoes by this time was smiling and for no reason at all was bursting out into laughter.

Hat said, 'Shut up, Eddoes. You go wake the baby up.'

And Eddoes asked, 'You really think she take after me, Hat?'

Hat said, 'Yes, man. I think you do right, you know, Eddoes. If I wasn't so careful myself and if I did have children outside I woulda bring them all home put them down. Bring them all home and put them down, man. Nothing to shame about.'

Eddoes said, 'Hat, it have a bird-cage I pick up long time now. Tomorrow I go bring it for you.'

Hat said, 'Is a long long time now I want a good bird-cage.'

And in no time at all Eddoes became the old Eddoes we knew, proud of his job, his junk; and now proud, too, of Pleasure.

She became the street baby and all the women, Mrs Morgan, Mrs Bhakcu, Laura, and my mother, helped to look after her.

And if there was anyone in Miguel Street who wanted to laugh, he kept his mouth shut when Pleasure got the first prize in the Cow and Gate Baby competition, and her picture came out in the papers.

12 LOVE, LOVE, LOVE, ALONE

ABOUT NINE O'CLOCK one morning a hearse and a motor-car stopped outside Miss Hilton's house. A man and a woman got out of the car. They were both middle-aged and dressed in black. While the man whispered to the two men in the hearse, the woman was crying in a controlled and respectable way.

So I suppose Miss Hilton got the swiftest and most private funeral in Miguel Street. It was nothing like the funeral we had for the other old widow, Miss Ricaud, the M.B.E. and social worker, who lived in a nicer part of the street. At that funeral I counted seventy-nine cars and a bicycle.

The man and the woman returned at midday and there was a bonfire in the yard. Mattresses and pillows and sheets and blankets were burned.

Then all the windows of the grey wooden house were thrown open, a thing I had never seen before.

At the end of the week a sign was nailed on the mango tree: FOR SALE.

Nobody in the street knew Miss Hilton. While she lived, her front gate was always padlocked and no one ever saw her leave or saw anybody go in. So even if you wanted to, you couldn't feel sorry and say that you missed Miss Hilton.

When I think of her house I see just two colours. Grey and green. The green of the mango tree, the grey of the house and the grey of the high galvanized-iron fence that prevented you from getting at the mangoes.

If your cricket ball fell in Miss Hilton's yard you never got it back.

It wasn't the mango season when Miss Hilton died. But we got back about ten or twelve of our cricket balls.

We were prepared to dislike the new people even before they came. I think we were a little worried. Already we had one man who kept on complaining about us to the police. He complained that we played cricket on the pavement; and if we weren't playing cricket he complained that we were making too much noise anyway.

Sergeant Charles would come and say, 'Boys, the Super send me. That blasted man ring up again. Take it a little easier.'

One afternoon when I came back from school Hat said, 'Is a man and a woman. She pretty pretty, but he ugly like hell, man. Portuguese, they look like.'

I didn't see much. The front gate was open, but the windows were shut again.

I heard a dog barking in an angry way.

One thing was settled pretty quickly. Whoever these people were they would never be the sort to ring up the police and say we were making noise and disturbing their sleep.

A lot of noise came from the house that night. The radio was going full blast until midnight when Trinidad Radio closed down. The dog was barking and the man was shouting. I didn't hear the woman.

There was a great peace next morning.

I waited until I saw the woman before going to school.

Boyee said, 'You know, Hat, I think I see that woman somewhere else. I see she when I was delivering milk up Mucurapo way.'

This lady didn't fit in with the rest of us in Miguel Street. She was too well-dressed. She was a little too pretty and a little too refined, and it was funny to see how she tried to jostle with the other women at Mary's shop trying to get scarce things like flour and rice.

I thought Boyee was right. It was easier to see this woman hopping about in shorts in the garden of one of the nice Mucurapo houses, with a uniformed servant fussing around in the background.

After the first few days I began to see more of the man. He was tall and thin. His face was ugly and had pink blotches.

Hat said, 'God, he is a first-class drinking man, you hear.'

It took me some time to realize that the tall man was drunk practically all the time. He gave off a sickening smell of bad rum, and I was afraid of him. Whenever I saw him I crossed the road.

If his wife, or whoever she was, dressed better than any woman in the street, he dressed worse than any of us. He was even dirtier than George.

He never appeared to do any work.

I asked Hat, 'How a pretty nice woman like that come to get mix up with a man like that?'

Hat said, 'Boy, you wouldn't understand. If I tell you you wouldn't believe me.'

Then I saw the dog.

It looked as big as a ram-goat and as vicious as a bull. It had the same sort of thin face its master had. I used to see them together.

Hat said, 'If that dog ever get away it go have big trouble here in this street.'

A few days later Hat said, 'You know, it just strike me. I ain't see those people bring in any furnitures at all. It look like all they have is that radio.'

Eddoes said, 'It have a lot of things I could sell them.'

I used to think of the man and the dog and the woman in that house, and I felt sorry and afraid for the woman. I liked her, too, for the way she went about trying to make out that everything was all right for her, trying to make out that she was just another woman in the street, with nothing odd for people to notice.

Then the beatings began.

The woman used to run out screaming. We would hear the terrible dog barking and we would hear the man shouting and cursing and using language so coarse that we were all shocked.

Hat said to the bigger men, 'Is easy to put two and two and see what happening there.'

And Edward and Eddoes laughed.

I said, 'What happening, Hat?'

Hat laughed.

He said, 'You too small to know, boy. Wait until you in long pants.'

So I thought the worst.

The woman behaved as though she had suddenly lost all shame. She ran crying to anybody in the street, saying, 'Help me! Help me! He will kill me if he catches me.'

One day she rushed to our house.

She didn't make any apology for coming unexpectedly or anything like that. She was too wild and frightened even to cry.

I never saw my mother so anxious to help anyone. She gave the woman tea and biscuits. The woman said, 'I can't understand what has come over Toni these days. But it is only in the nights he is like this, you know. He is so kind in the mornings. But about midday something happens and he just goes mad.'

At first my mother was being excessively refined with the woman, bringing out all her fancy words and fancy pronunciations, pronouncing comfortable as cum-fought-able, and making war rhyme with bar, and promising that everything was deffy-nightly going to be all right. Normally my mother referred to males as man, but with this woman she began speaking about the ways of mens and them, citing my dead father as a typical example.

My mother said, 'The onliest thing with this boy father was that it was the other way round. Whenever I uses to go to the room where he was he uses to jump out of the bed and run away bawling – run away screaming.'

But after the woman had come to us about three or four times my mother relapsed into her normal self, and began treating the woman as though she were like Laura or like Mrs Bhakcu.

My mother would say, 'Now, tell me, Mrs Hereira, why you don't leave this good-for-nothing man?'

Mrs Hereira said, 'It is a stupid thing to say to you or anybody else, but I like Toni. I love him.'

My mother said, 'Is a damn funny sort of love.'

Mrs Hereira began to speak about Toni as though he were a little boy she liked.

She said, 'He has many good qualities, you know. His heart is in the right place, really.'

My mother said, 'I wouldn't know about heart, but what I know is that he want a good clout on his backside to make him see sense. How you could let a man like that disgrace you so?'

Mrs Hereira said, 'No, I know Toni. I looked after him when he was sick. It is the war, you know. He was a sailor and they torpedoed him twice.'

My mother said, 'They shoulda try again.'

'You mustn't talk like this,' Mrs Hereira said.

My mother said, 'Look, I just talking my mind, you hear. You come here asking me advice.'

'I didn't ask for advice.'

'You come here asking me for help, and I just trying to help you. That's all.'

'I don't want your help or advice,' Mrs Hereira said.

My mother remained calm. She said, 'All right, then. Go back

to the great man. Is my own fault, you hear. Meddling in white
people business. You know what the calypso say:

> *Is love, love, love, alone*
> *That cause King Edward to leave the throne.*

Well, let me tell you. You not King Edward, you hear. Go back
to your great love.'

Mrs Hereira would be out of the door, saying, 'I hope I never
come back here again.'

But next evening she would be back.

One day my mother said, 'Mrs Hereira, everybody fraid that
dog you have there. That thing too wild to be in a place like this.'

Mrs Hereira said, 'It isn't my dog. It's Toni's, and not even
I can touch it.'

We despised Toni.

Hat said, 'Is a good thing for a man to beat his woman every
now and then, but this man does do it like exercise, man.'

And he was also despised because he couldn't carry his liquor.

People used to find him sleeping in all sorts of places, dead
drunk.

He made a few attempts to get friendly with us, making us feel
uncomfortable more than anything else.

He used to say, 'Hello there, boys.'

And that appeared to be all the conversation he could make.
And when Hat and the other big men tried to talk to him, as a
kindness, I felt that Toni wasn't really listening.

He would get up and walk away from us suddenly, without a
word, when somebody was in the middle of a sentence.

Hat said, 'Is a good thing too. I feel that if I look at him long
enough I go vomit. You see what a dirty thing a white skin does
be sometimes?'

And, in truth, he had a nasty skin. It was yellow and pink and
white, with brown and black spots. The skin above his left eye
had the raw pink look of scalded flesh.

But the strange thing I noticed was that if you just looked at
Toni's hands and saw how thin and wrinkled they were, you felt
sorry for him, not disgusted.

But I looked at his hands only when I was with Hat and
the rest.

I suppose Mrs Hereira saw only his hands.

Hat said, 'I wonder how long this thing go last.'

Mrs Hereira obviously intended it to last a long time.

She and my mother became good friends after all, and I used to hear Mrs Hereira talking about her plans. She said one day she wanted some furniture, and I think she did get some in.

But most of the time she talked about Toni; and from the way she talked, anybody would believe that Toni was just an ordinary man.

She said, 'Toni is thinking about leaving Trinidad. We could start a hotel in Barbados.'

Or, 'As soon as Toni gets well again, we will go for a long cruise.'

And again, 'Toni is really a disciplined man, you know. Great will-power, really. We'll be all right when he gets his strength back.'

Toni still behaved as though he didn't know about all these plans for himself. He refused to settle down. He got wilder and more unpleasant.

Hat said, 'He behaving like some of those uncultured people from John John. Like he forget that latrines make for some purpose.'

And that wasn't all. He appeared to develop an extraordinary dislike for the human race. One look at a perfect stranger was enough to start Toni cursing.

Hat said, 'We have to do something about Toni.'

I was there the evening they beat him up.

For a long time afterwards the beating-up was on Hat's mind.

It was a terrible thing, really. Hat and the rest of them were not angry. And Toni himself wasn't angry. He wasn't anything. He made no effort to return the blows. And the blows he got made no impression on him. He didn't look frightened. He didn't cry. He didn't plead. He just stood up and took it.

He wasn't being brave.

Hat said, 'He just too damn drunk.'

In the end Hat was angry with himself. He said, 'Is taking advantage. We shouldnta do it. The man ain't have feelings, that's all.'

And from the way Mrs Hereira talked, it was clear that she didn't know what had happened.

Hat said, 'That's a relief, anyway.'

And through all these weeks, one question was always uppermost in our minds. How did a woman like Mrs Hereira get mixed up with Toni?

Hat said he knew. But he wanted to know who Mrs Hereira was, and so did we all. Even my mother wondered aloud about this.

Boyee had an idea.

He said, 'Hat, you know the advertisements people does put out when their wife or their husband leave them?'

Hat said, 'Boyee, you know you getting too damn big too damn fast. How the hell a little boy like you know about a thing like that?'

Boyee took this as a compliment.

Hat said, 'How you know anyway that Mrs Hereira leave she husband? How you know that she ain't married to Toni?'

Boyee said, 'I telling you, Hat. I used to see that woman up Mucurapo way when I was delivering milk. I telling you so, man.'

Hat said, 'White people don't do that sort of thing, putting advertisement in the paper and thing like that.'

Eddoes said, 'You ain't know what you talking about, Hat. How much white people you know?'

In the end Hat promised to read the paper more carefully.

Then big trouble started.

Mrs Hereira ran out of her house screaming one day, 'He's going mad! He's going mad, I tell you. He will kill me this time sure.'

She told my mother, 'He grabbed a knife and began chasing me. He was saying, "I will kill you, I will kill you." Talking in a very quiet way.'

'You do him something?' my mother asked.

Mrs Hereira shook her head.

She said, 'It is the first time he threatened to kill me. And he was serious, I tell you.'

Up till then Mrs Hereira hadn't been crying, but now she broke down and cried like a girl.

She was saying, 'Toni has forgotten all I did for him. He has forgotten how I took care of him when he was sick. Tell me, you think that's right? I did everything for him. Everything. I gave up everything. Money and family. All for him. Tell me, is it right for him to treat me like this? Oh, God! What did I do to deserve all this?'

And so she wept and talked and wept.

We left her to herself for some time.

Then my mother said, 'Toni look like the sort of man who could kill easy, easy, without feeling that he really murdering. You want to sleep here tonight? You could sleep on the boy bed. He could sleep on the floor.'

Mrs Hereira wasn't listening.

My mother shook her and repeated her offer.

Mrs Hereira said, 'I am all right now, really. I will go back and talk to Toni. I think I did something to offend him. I must go back and find out what it is.'

'Well, I really give up,' my mother said. 'I think you taking this love business a little too far, you hear.'

So Mrs Hereira went back to her house. My mother and I waited for a long time, waiting for a scream.

But we heard nothing.

And the next morning Mrs Hereira was composed and refined as ever.

But day by day you could see her losing her freshness and saddening her beauty. Her face was getting lined. Her eyes were red and swollen, and the dark patches under them were ugly to look at.

Hat jumped up and said, 'I know it! I know it! I know it a long time now.'

He showed us the Personal column in the classified advertisements. Seven people had decided to leave their spouses. We followed Hat's finger and read:

> *I, Henry Hubert Christiani, declare that my wife, Angela Mary Christiani, is no longer under my care and protection, and I am not responsible for any debt or debts contracted by her.*

Boyee said, 'Is the selfsame woman.'

Eddoes said, 'Yes, Christiani. Doctor fellow. Know him good good. Used to pick up rubbish for him.'

Hat said, 'Now I ask you, why, why a woman want to leave a man like that for this Toni?'

Eddoes said, 'Yes, know Christiani good good. Good house, nice car. Full of money, you know. It have a long time now I see him. Know him from the days when I used to work Mucurapo way.'

And in about half an hour the news had spread through Miguel Street.

My mother said to Mrs Hereira, 'You better call the police.'

Mrs Hereira said, 'No, no. Not the police.'

My mother said, 'Like you fraid police more than you fraid Toni.'

Mrs Hereira said, 'The scandal—'

'Scandal hell!' my mother said. 'Your life in trouble and you thinking about scandal. Like if this man ain't disgrace you enough already.'

My mother said, 'Why you don't go back to your husband?'

She said it as though she expected Mrs Hereira to jump up in surprise.

But Mrs Hereira remained very calm.

She said, 'I don't feel anything about him. And I just can't stand that clean doctor's smell he has. It chokes me.'

I understood her perfectly, and tried to get my mother's eye.

Toni was growing really wild.

He used to sit on his front steps with a half bottle of rum in his hand. The dog was with him.

He appeared to have lost touch with the world completely. He seemed to be without feeling. It was hard enough to imagine Mrs Hereira, or Mrs Christiani, in love with him. But it was impossible to imagine him being in love with anybody.

I thought he was like an animal, like his dog.

One morning Mrs Hereira came over and said, very calmly, 'I have decided to leave Toni.'

She was so calm I could see my mother getting worried.

My mother said, 'What happen now?'

Mrs Hereira said, 'Nothing. Last night he made the dog jump at me. He didn't look as if he knew what he was doing. He didn't laugh or anything. I think he is going mad, and if I don't get out I think he will kill me.'

My mother said, 'Who you going back to?'

'My husband.'

'Even after what he print in the papers?'

Mrs Hereira said, 'Henry is like a boy, you know, and he thinks he can frighten me. If I go back today, he will be glad to have me back.'

And saying that, she looked different, and hard.

My mother said, 'Don't be so sure. He know Toni?'

Mrs Hereira laughed in a crazy sort of way. 'Toni was Henry's friend, not mine. Henry brought him home one day. Toni was sick like anything. Henry was like that, you know. I never met a man who liked doing good works so much as Henry. He was all for good works and sanitation.'

My mother said, 'You know, Mrs Hereira, I really wish you was like me. If somebody did marry you off when you was fifteen, we wouldnta been hearing all this nonsense, you hear. Making all this damn fuss about your heart and love and all that rubbish.'

Mrs Hereira began to cry.

My mother said, 'Look, I didn't want to make you cry like this. I sorry.'

Mrs Hereira sobbed, 'No, it isn't you, it isn't you.'

My mother looked disappointed.

We watched Mrs Hereira cry.

Mrs Hereira said, 'I have left about a week's food with Toni.'

My mother said, 'Toni is a big man. You mustn't worry about him.'

He made terrible noises when he discovered that she had left him. He bayed like a dog and bawled like a baby.

Then he got drunk. Not drunk in the ordinary fashion; it got to the stage where the rum was keeping him going.

He forgot all about the dog, and it starved for days.

He stumbled drunk and crying from house to house, looking for Mrs Hereira.

And when he got back he took it out on the dog. We used to hear the dog yelping and growling.

In the end even the dog turned on him.

Somehow it managed to get itself free and it rushed at Toni.

Toni was shocked into sense.

The dog ran out of the house, and Toni ran after it. Toni

squatted and whistled. The dog stopped, pricked up its ears, and turned round to look. It was funny seeing this drunk crazy man smiling and whistling at his dog, trying to get him back.

The dog stood still, staring at Toni.

Its tail wagged twice, then fell.

Toni got up and began walking towards the dog. The dog turned and ran.

We saw him sprawling on a mattress in one of the rooms. The room was perfectly empty. Nothing but the mattress and the empty rum bottles and the cigarette ends.

He was drunk and sleeping, and his face was strangely reposed.

The thin and wrinkled hands looked so frail and sad.

Another FOR SALE sign was nailed to the mango tree. A man with about five little children bought the house.

From time to time Toni came around to terrify the new people.

He would ask for money, for rum, and he had the habit of asking for the radio. He would say, 'You have Angela's radio there. I charging rent for that, you know. Two dollars a month. Give me two dollars now.'

The new owner was a small man, and he was afraid of Toni. He never answered.

Toni would look at us and laugh and say, 'You know about Angela's radio, eh, boys? You know about the radio? Now, what this man playing at?'

Hat said, 'Who will tell me why they ever have people like Toni in this world!'

After two or three months he stopped coming to Miguel Street.

I saw Toni many years later.

I was travelling to Arima, and just near the quarry at Laventille I saw him driving a lorry.

He was smoking a cigarette.

That and his thin arms are all I remember.

And riding to Carenage one Sunday morning, I passed the Christianis' house, which I had avoided for a long time.

Mrs Christiani, or Mrs Hereira, was in shorts. She was reading the paper in an easy chair in the garden. Through the open doors of the house I saw a uniformed servant laying the table for lunch.

There was a black car, a new, big car, in the garage.

13 THE MECHANICAL GENIUS

MY UNCLE BHAKCU was very nearly a mechanical genius. I cannot remember a time when he was not the owner of a motor vehicle of some sort. I don't think he always approved of the manufacturers' designs, however, for he was always pulling engines to bits. Titus Hoyt said that this was also a habit of the Eskimos. It was something he had got out of a geography book.

If I try to think of Bhakcu I never see his face. I can see only the soles of his feet as he worms his way under a car. I was worried when Bhakcu was under a car because it looked so easy for the car to slip off the jack and fall on him.

One day it did.

He gave a faint groan that reached the ears of only his wife.

She bawled, 'Oh God!' and burst into tears right away. 'I know something wrong. Something happen to *he*.'

Mrs Bhakcu always used this pronoun when she spoke of her husband.

She hurried to the side of the yard and heard Bhakcu groaning.

'Man,' she whispered, 'you all right?'

He groaned a little more loudly.

He said, 'How the hell I all right? You mean you so blind you ain't see the whole motor-car break up my arse?'

Mrs Bhakcu, dutiful wife, began to cry afresh.

She beat on the galvanized-iron fence.

'Hat,' Mrs Bhakcu called, 'Hat, come quick. A whole motor-car fall on *he*.'

Hat was cleaning out the cow-pen. When he heard Mrs Bhakcu he laughed. 'You know what I always does say,' Hat said. 'When you play the ass you bound to catch hell. The blasted car brand-new. What the hell he was tinkering with so?'

'*He* say the crank-shaft wasn't working nice.'

'And is there he looking for the crank-shaft?'

'Hat,' Bhakcu shouted from under the car, 'the moment you get this car from off me, I going to break up your tail.'

'Man,' Mrs Bhakcu said to her husband, 'how you so advantageous? The man come round with his good good mind to help you and now you want to beat him up?'

Hat began to look hurt and misunderstood.

Hat said, 'It ain't nothing new. Is just what I expect. Is just what I does always get for interfering in other people business. You know I mad to leave you and your husband here and go back to the cow-pen.'

'No, Hat. You mustn't mind *he*. Think what you would say if a whole big new motor-car fall on you.'

Hat said, 'All right, all right. I have to go and get some of the boys.'

We heard Hat shouting in the street. 'Boyee and Errol!'

No answer.

'Bo-yee and Ehhroll!'

'Co-ming, Hat.'

'Where the hell you boys been, eh? You think you is man now and you could just stick your hands in your pocket and walk out like man? You was smoking, eh?'

'Smoking, Hat?'

'But what happen now? You turn deaf all of a sudden?'

'Was Boyee was smoking, Hat.'

'Is a lie, Hat. Was Errol really. I just stand up watching him.'

'Somebody make you policeman now, eh? Is cut-arse for both of you. Errol, go cut a whip for Boyee. Boyee, go cut a whip for Errol.'

We heard the boys whimpering.

From under the car Bhakcu called, 'Hat, why you don't leave the boys alone? You go bless them bad one of these days, you know, and then they go lose you in jail. Why you don't leave the boys alone? They big now.'

Hat shouted back, 'You mind your own business, you hear. Otherwise I leave you under that car until you rotten, you hear.'

Mrs Bhakcu said to her husband, 'Take it easy, man.'

But it was nothing serious after all. The jack had slipped but the axle rested on a pile of wooden blocks, pinning Bhakcu to ground without injuring him.

When Bhakcu came out he looked at his clothes. These were a pair of khaki trousers and a sleeveless vest, both black and stiff with engine grease.

Bhakcu said to his wife, 'They really dirty now, eh?'

She regarded her husband with pride. 'Yes, man,' she said. 'They really dirty.'

Bhakcu smiled.

Hat said, 'Look, I just sick of lifting up motor-car from off you, you hear. If you want my advice, you better send for a proper mechanic.'

Bhakcu wasn't listening.

He said to his wife, 'The crank-shaft was all right. Is something else.'

Mrs Bhakcu said, 'Well, you must eat first.'

She looked at Hat and said, '*He* don't eat when *he* working on the car unless I remind *he*.'

Hat said, 'What you want me do with that? Write it down with a pencil on a piece of paper and send it to the papers?'

I wanted to watch Bhakcu working on the car that evening, so I said to him, 'Uncle Bhakcu, your clothes looking really dirty and greasy. I wonder how you could bear to wear them.'

He turned and smiled at me. 'What you expect, boy?' he said. 'Mechanic people like me ain't have time for clean clothes.'

'What happen to the car, Uncle Bhakcu?' I asked.

He didn't reply.

'The tappet knocking?' I suggested.

One thing Bhakcu had taught me about cars was that tappets were always knocking. Give Bhakcu any car in the world, and the first thing he would tell you about it was, 'The tappet knocking, you know. Hear. Hear it?'

'The tappet knocking?' I asked.

He came right up to me and asked eagerly, 'What, you hear it knocking?'

And before I had time to say, 'Well, *something* did knocking,' Mrs Bhakcu pulled him away, saying, 'Come and eat now, man. God, you get your clothes really dirty today.'

The car that fell on Bhakcu wasn't really a new car, although Bhakcu boasted that it very nearly was.

'It only do two hundred miles,' he used to say.

Hat said, 'Well, I know Trinidad small, but I didn't know it was so small.'

I remember the day it was bought. It was a Saturday. And that morning Mrs Bhakcu came to my mother and they talked about the cost of rice and flour and the black market. As she was leaving, Mrs Bhakcu said, '*He* gone to town today. *He* say *he* got to buy a new car.'

So we waited for the new car.

Midday came, but Bhakcu didn't.

Hat said, 'Two to one, that man taking down the engine right this minute.'

About four o'clock we heard a banging and a clattering, and looking down Miguel Street towards Docksite we saw the car. It was a blue Chevrolet, one of the 1939 models. It looked rich and new. We began to wave and cheer, and I saw Bhakcu waving his left hand.

We danced into the road in front of Bhakcu's house, waving and cheering.

The car came nearer and Hat said, 'Jump, boys! Run for your life. Like he get mad.'

It was a near thing. The car just raced past the house and we stopped cheering.

Hat said, 'The car out of control. It go have a accident if something don't happen quick.'

Mrs Bhakcu laughed. 'What you think it is at all?' she said.

But we raced after the car, crying after Bhakcu.

He wasn't waving with his left hand. He was trying to warn people off.

By a miracle, it stopped just before Ariapita Avenue.

Bhakcu said, 'I did mashing down the brakes since I turn Miguel Street, but the brakes ain't working. Is a funny thing. I overhaul the brakes just this morning.'

Hat said, 'It have two things for you to do. Overhaul your head or haul your arse away before you get people in trouble.'

Bhakcu said, 'You boys go have to give me a hand to push the car back home.'

As we were pushing it past the house of Morgan, the pyrotechnicist, Mrs Morgan shouted, 'Ah, Mrs Bhakcu, I see you buy a new car today, man.'

Mrs Bhakcu didn't reply.

Mrs Morgan said, 'Ah, Mrs Bhakcu, you think your husband go give me a ride in his new car?'

Mrs Bhakcu said, 'Yes, *he* go give you a ride, but first *your* husband must give *me* a ride on his donkey-cart when he buy it.'

Bhakcu said to Mrs Bhakcu, 'Why you don't shut your mouth up?'

Mrs Bhakcu said, 'But how you want me to shut my mouth up? You is my husband, and I have to stand up for you.'

Bhakcu said very sternly, 'You only stand up for me when I tell you, you hear.'

We left the car in front of Bhakcu's house, and we left Mr and Mrs Bhakcu to their quarrel. It wasn't a very interesting one. Mrs Bhakcu kept on claiming her right to stand up for her husband, and Mr Bhakcu kept on rejecting the claim. In the end Bhakcu had to beat his wife.

This wasn't as easy as it sounds. If you want to get a proper picture of Mrs Bhakcu you must consider a pear as a scale-model. Mrs Bhakcu had so much flesh, in fact, that when she held her arms at her sides they looked like marks of parenthesis.

And as for her quarrelling voice . . .

Hat used to say, 'It sound as though it coming from a gramo-phone record turning fast fast backwards.'

For a long time I think Bhakcu experimented with rods for beating his wife, and I wouldn't swear that it wasn't Hat who suggested a cricket bat. But whoever suggested it, a second-hand cricket bat was bought from one of the groundsmen at the Queen's Park Oval, and oiled, and used on Mrs Bhakcu.

Hat said, 'Is the only thing she really could feel, I think.'

The strangest thing about this was that Mrs Bhakcu herself kept the bat clean and well-oiled. Boyee tried many times to borrow the bat, but Mrs Bhakcu never lent it.

So on the evening of the day when the car fell on Bhakcu I went to see him at work.

'What you did saying about the tappet knocking?' he said.

'I didn't say nothing,' I said. 'I was asking you.'

'Oh.'

Bhakcu worked late into the night, taking down the engine. He worked all the next day, Sunday, and all Sunday night. On Monday morning the mechanic came.

Mrs Bhakcu told my mother, 'The company send the mech-anic man. The trouble with these Trinidad mechanics is that they is just piss-in-tail little boys who don't know the first thing about cars and things.'

I went round to Bhakcu's house and saw the mechanic with his head inside the bonnet. Bhakcu was sitting on the running-board, rubbing grease over everything the mechanic handed him. He looked so happy dipping his fingers in the grease that I asked, 'Let me rub some grease, Uncle Bhakcu.'

'Go away, boy. You too small.'

I sat and watched him.

He said, 'The tappet was knocking, but I fix it.'

I said, 'Good.'

The mechanic was cursing.

I asked Bhakcu, 'How the points?'

He said, 'I have to check them up.'

I got up and walked around the car and sat on the running-board next to Bhakcu.

I looked at him and I said, 'You know something?'

'What?'

'When I did hear the engine on Saturday, I didn't think it was beating nice.'

Bhakcu said, 'You getting to be a real smart man, you know. You learning fast.'

I said, 'Is what you teach me.'

It was, as a matter of fact, pretty nearly the limit of my knowledge. The knocking tappet, the points, the beat of the engine and – yes, I had forgotten one thing.

'You know, Uncle Bhakcu,' I said.

'What, boy?'

'Uncle Bhakcu, I think is the carburettor.'

'You really think so, boy?'

'I sure, Uncle Bhakcu.'

'Well, I go tell you, boy. Is the first thing I ask the mechanic. He don't think so.'

The mechanic lifted a dirty and angry face from the engine and said, 'When you have all sort of ignorant people messing about with a engine the white people build with their own own hands, what the hell else you expect?'

Bhakcu winked at me.

He said, '*I* think is the carburettor.'

Of all the drills, I liked the carburettor drill the best. Sometimes Bhakcu raced the engine while I put my palm over the carburettor and off again. Bhakcu never told me why we did this and I never asked. Sometimes we had to siphon petrol from the tank, and I would pour this petrol into the carburettor while Bhakcu raced the engine. I often asked him to let me race the engine, but he wouldn't agree.

One day the engine caught fire, but I jumped away in time. The fire didn't last.

Bhakcu came out of the car and looked at the engine in a puzzled way. I thought he was annoyed with it, and I was prepared to see him dismantle it there and then.

That was the last time we did that drill with the carburettor.

At last the mechanic tested the engine and the brakes, and said, 'Look, the car good good now, you hear. It cost me more work than if I was to build over a new car. Leave the damn thing alone.'

After the mechanic left, Bhakcu and I walked very thoughtfully two or three times around the car. Bhakcu was stroking his chin, not talking to me.

Suddenly he jumped into the driver's seat and pressed the horn-button a few times.

He said, 'What you think about the horn, boy?'

I said, 'Blow it again, let me hear.'

He pressed the button again.

Hat pushed his head through a window and shouted, 'Bhakcu, keep the damn car quiet, you hear, man. You making the place sound as though it have a wedding going on.'

We ignored Hat.

I said, 'Uncle Bhakcu, I don't think the horn blowing nice.'

He said, 'You really don't think so?'

I made a face and spat.

So we began to work on the horn.

When we were finished there was a bit of flex wound round the steering-column.

Bhakcu looked at me and said, 'You see, you could just take this wire now and touch it on any part of the metalwork, and the horn blow.'

It looked unlikely, but it did work.

I said, 'Uncle Bhak, how you know about all these things?'

He said, 'You just keep on learning all the time.'

The men in the street didn't like Bhakcu because they considered him a nuisance. But I liked him for the same reason that I liked Popo, the carpenter. For, thinking about it now, Bhakcu was also an artist. He interfered with motor-cars for the joy of the thing, and he never seemed worried about money.

But his wife was worried. She, like my mother, thought that she was born to be a clever handler of money, born to make money sprout from nothing at all.

She talked over the matter with my mother one day.

My mother said, 'Taxi making a lot of money these days, taking Americans and their girl friends all over the place.'

So Mrs Bhakcu made her husband buy a lorry.

This lorry was really the pride of Miguel Street. It was a big new Bedford and we all turned out to welcome it when Bhakcu brought it home for the first time.

Even Hat was impressed. 'If is one thing the English people could build,' he said, 'is a lorry. This is not like your Ford and your Dodge, you know.'

Bhakcu began working on it that very afternoon, and Mrs Bhakcu went around telling people, 'Why not come and see how *he* working on the Bedford?'

From time to time Bhakcu would crawl out from under the lorry and polish the wings and the bonnet. Then he would crawl under the lorry again. But he didn't look happy.

The next day the people who had lent the money to buy the Bedford formed a deputation and came to Bhakcu's house, begging him to desist.

Bhakcu remained under the lorry all the time, refusing to reply. The money-lenders grew angry, and some of the women among them began to cry. Even that failed to move Bhakcu, and in the end the deputation just had to go away.

When the deputation left, Bhakcu began to take it out of his wife. He beat her and he said, 'Is you who want me to buy lorry. Is you. Is *you*. All you thinking about is money, money. Just like your mother.'

But the real reason for his temper was that he couldn't put back the engine as he had found it. Two or three pieces remained outside and they puzzled him.

The agents sent a mechanic.

He looked at the lorry and asked Bhakcu, very calmly, 'Why you buy a Bedford?'

Bhakcu said, 'I like the Bedford.'

The mechanic shouted, 'Why the arse you didn't buy a Rolls-Royce? They does sell those with the engine sealed down.'

Then he went to work, saying sadly, 'Is enough to make you want to cry. A nice, new new lorry like this.'

The starter never worked again. And Bhakcu always had to use the crank.

Hat said, 'Is a blasted shame. Lorry looking new, smelling new, everything still shining, all sort of chalk-mark still on the chassis, and this man cranking it up like some old Ford pram.'

But Mrs Bhakcu boasted, 'Fust crank, the engine does start.'

One morning – it was a Saturday, market day – Mrs Bhakcu came crying to my mother. She said, '*He* in hospital.'

My mother said, 'Accident?'

Mrs Bhakcu said, '*He* was cranking up the lorry just outside the Market. Fust crank, the engine start. But it was in gear and it roll *he* up against another lorry.'

Bhakcu spent a week in hospital.

All the time he had the lorry, he hated his wife, and he beat her regularly with the cricket bat. But she was beating him too, with her tongue, and I think Bhakcu was really the loser in these quarrels.

It was hard to back the lorry into the yard and it was Mrs Bhakcu's duty and joy to direct her husband.

One day she said, 'All right, man, back back, turn a little to the right, all right, all clear. Oh God! No, no, no, man! Stop! You go knock the fence down.'

Bhakcu suddenly went mad. He reversed so fiercely he cracked the concrete fence. Then he shot forward again, ignoring Mrs Bhakcu's screams, and reversed again, knocking down the fence altogether.

He was in a great temper, and while his wife remained outside crying he went to his little room, stripped to his pants, flung himself belly down on the bed, and began reading the *Ramayana*.

The lorry wasn't making money. But to make any at all, Bhakcu had to have loaders. He got two of those big black Grenadian small-islanders who were just beginning to pour into Port of Spain. They called Bhakcu 'Boss' and Mrs Bhakcu 'Madam', and this was nice. But when I looked at these men sprawling happily in the back of the lorry in their ragged dusty clothes and their squashed-up felt hats, I used to wonder whether they knew how much worry they caused, and how uncertain their own position was.

Mrs Bhakcu's talk was now all about these two men.

She would tell my mother, mournfully, 'Day after tomorrow we have to pay the loaders.' Two days later she would say, as though the world had come to an end, 'Today we pay the loaders.' And in no time at all she would be coming around to my mother in distress again, saying, 'Day after tomorrow we have to pay the loaders.'

Paying the loaders – for months I seemed to hear about nothing else. The words were well known in the street, and became an idiom.

Boyee would say to Errol on a Saturday, 'Come, let we go to the one-thirty show at Roxy.'

And Errol would turn out his pockets and say, 'I can't go, man. I pay the loaders.'

Hat said, 'It look as though Bhakcu buy the lorry just to pay the loaders.'

The lorry went in the end. And the loaders too. I don't know what happened to them. Mrs Bhakcu had the lorry sold just at a time when lorries began making money. They bought a taxi. By now the competition was fierce and taxis were running eight miles for twelve cents, just enough to pay for oil and petrol.

Mrs Bhakcu told my mother, 'The taxi ain't making money.'

So she bought another taxi, and hired a man to drive it. She said, 'Two better than one.'

Bhakcu was reading the *Ramayana* more and more.

And even that began to annoy the people in the street.

Hat said, 'Hear the two of them now. She with that voice she got, and he singing that damn sing-song Hindu song.'

Picture then the following scene. Mrs Bhakcu, very short, very fat, standing at the pipe in her yard, and shrilling at her husband. He is in his pants, lying on his belly, dolefully intoning the *Ramayana*. Suddenly he springs up and snatches the cricket bat in the corner of the room. He runs outside and begins to beat Mrs Bhakcu with the bat.

The silence that follows lasts a few minutes.

And then only Bhakcu's voice is heard, as he does a solo from the *Ramayana*.

But don't think that Mrs Bhakcu lost any pride in her husband. Whenever you listened to the rows between Mrs Bhakcu and Mrs Morgan, you realized that Bhakcu was still his wife's lord and master.

Mrs Morgan would say, 'I hear your husband talking in his sleep last night, loud loud.'

'He wasn't talking,' Mrs Bhakcu said, 'he was singing.'

'Singing? Hahahahaaah! You know something, Mrs Bhakcu?'

'What, Mrs Morgan?'

'If your husband sing for his supper, both of all you starve like hell.'

'*He* know a damn lot more than any of the ignorant man it have in this street, you hear. *He* could read and write, you know. English *and* Hindi. How you so ignorant you don't know that the *Ramayana* is a holy book? If you coulda understand all the good thing *he* singing, you wouldn't be talking all this nonsense you talking now, you hear.'

'How your husband this morning, anyway? He fix any new cars lately?'

'I not going to dirty my mouth arguing with you here, you hear. *He* know how to fix his car. Is a wonder nobody ain't tell your husband where he can fix all his so-call fireworks.'

Mrs Bhakcu used to boast that Bhakcu read the *Ramayana* two or three times a month. 'It have some parts he know by heart,' she said.

But that was little consolation, for money wasn't coming in. The man she had hired to drive the second taxi was playing the fool. She said, 'He robbing me like hell. He say that the taxi making so little money I owe him now.' She sacked the driver and sold the car.

She used all her financial flair. She began rearing hens. That failed because a lot of the hens were stolen, the rest attacked by street dogs, and Bhakcu hated the smell anyway. She began selling bananas and oranges, but she did that more for her own enjoyment than for the little money it brought in.

My mother said, 'Why Bhakcu don't go out and get a work?'

Mrs Bhakcu said, 'But how you want that?'

My mother said, '*I* don't want it. I was thinking about you.'

Mrs Bhakcu said, 'You could see *he* working with all the rude and crude people it have here in Port of Spain?'

My mother said, 'Well, he have to do something. People don't pay to see a man crawling under a motor-car or singing *Ramayana*.'

Mrs Bhakcu nodded and looked sad.

My mother said, 'But what I saying at all? You sure Bhakcu know the *Ramayana*?'

'I sure sure.'

My mother said, 'Well, it easy easy. He is a Brahmin, he know the *Ramayana*, and he have a car. Is easy for him to become a pundit, a real proper pundit.'

Mrs Bhakcu clapped her hands. 'Is a first-class idea. Hindu pundits making a lot of money these days.'

So Bhakcu became a pundit.

He still tinkered with his car. He had to stop beating Mrs Bhakcu with the cricket bat, but he was happy.

I was haunted by thoughts of the *dhoti*-clad Pundit Bhakcu, crawling under a car, attending to a crank-shaft, while poor Hindus waited for him to attend to their souls.

IT WAS NOT UNTIL 1947 that Bolo believed that the war was over. Up till then he used to say, 'Is only a lot of propaganda. Just lies for black people.'

In 1947 the Americans began pulling down their camp in the George V Park and many people were getting sad.

I went to see Bolo one Sunday and while he was cutting my hair he said, 'I hear the war over.'

I said, 'So I hear too. But I still have my doubts.'

Bolo said, 'I know what you mean. These people is master of propaganda, but the way I look at it is this. If they was still fighting they woulda want to keep the camp.'

'But they not keeping the camp,' I said.

Bolo said, 'Exactly. Put two and two together and what you get? Tell me, what you get?'

I said, 'Four.'

He clipped my hair thoughtfully for a few moments.

He said, 'Well, I glad the war over.'

When I paid for my trim I said, 'What you think we should do now, Mr Bolo? You think we should celebrate?'

He said, 'Gimme time, man. Gimme time. This is a big thing. I have to think it over.'

And there the matter rested.

I remember the night when the news of peace reached Port of Spain. People just went wild and there was a carnival in the streets. A new calypso sprang out of nothing and everybody was dancing in the streets to the tune of:

> *All day and all night Miss Mary Ann*
> *Down by the river-side she taking man.*

Bolo looked at the dancers and said, 'Stupidness! Stupidness! How black people so stupid?'

I said, 'But you ain't hear, Mr Bolo? The war over.'

He spat. 'How you know? You was fighting it?'

'But it come over on the radio and I read it in the papers.'

Bolo laughed. He said, 'Anybody would think you was still a little boy. You mean you come so big and you still does believe anything you read in the papers?'

I had heard this often before. Bolo was sixty and the only truth he had discovered seemed to be, 'You mustn't believe anything you read in the papers.'

It was his whole philosophy, and it didn't make him happy. He was the saddest man in the street.

I think Bolo was born sad. Certainly I never saw him laugh except in a sarcastic way, and I saw him at least once a week for eleven years. He was a tall man, not thin, with a face that was a caricature of sadness, the mouth curling downwards, the eyebrows curving downwards, the eyes big and empty of expression.

It was an amazement to me that Bolo made a living at all after he had stopped barbering. I suppose he would be described in a census as a carrier. His cart was the smallest thing of its kind I knew.

It was a little box on two wheels and he pushed it himself, pushed with his long body in such an attitude of resignation and futility you wondered why he pushed it at all. On this cart he could take just about two or three sacks of flour or sugar.

On Sundays Bolo became a barber again, and if he was proud of anything he was proud of his barbering.

Often Bolo said to me, 'You know Samuel?'

Samuel was the most successful barber in the district. He was so rich he took a week's holiday every year, and he liked everybody to know it.

I said, 'Yes, I know Samuel. But I don't like him to touch my hair at all at all. He can't cut hair. He does zog up my head.'

Bolo said, 'You know who teach Samuel all he know about cutting hair? You know?'

I shook my head.

'I. I teach Samuel. He couldn't even shave hisself when he start barbering. He come crying and begging, "Mr Bolo, Mr Bolo, teach me how to cut people hair, I beg you." Well, I teach him, and look what happen, eh. Samuel rich rich, and I still living in one room in this break-down old house. Samuel have a room where he does cut hair, I have to cut hair in the open under this mango tree.'

I said, 'But it nice outside, it better than sitting down in a hot room. But why you stop cutting hair regular, Mr Bolo?'

'Ha, boy, that is asking a big big question. The fact is, I just can't trust myself.'

'Is not true. You does cut hair good good, better than Samuel.'

'It ain't that I mean. Boy, when it have a man sitting down in front of you in a chair, and you don't like this man, and you have a razor in your hand, a lot of funny things could happen. I does only cut people hair these days when I like them. I can't cut any-and–everybody hair.'

Although in 1945 Bolo didn't believe that the war was over, in 1939 he was one of the great alarmists. In those days he bought all three Port of Spain newspapers, the *Trinidad Guardian*, the *Port of Spain Gazette*, and the *Evening News*. When the war broke out and the *Evening News* began issuing special bulletins, Bolo bought those too.

Those were the days when Bolo said, 'It have a lot of people who think they could kick people around. They think because we poor we don't know anything. But I ain't in that, you hear. Every day I sit down and read my papers regular regular.'

More particularly, Bolo was interested in the *Trinidad Guardian*. At one stage Bolo bought about twenty copies of that paper every day.

The *Guardian* was running a Missing Ball Competition. They printed a photograph of a football match in progress, but they had rubbed the ball out. All you had to do to win a lot of money was to mark the position of the ball with an X.

Spotting the missing ball became one of Bolo's passions.

In the early stages Bolo was happy enough to send in one X a week to the *Guardian*.

It was a weekly excitement for all of us.

Hat used to say, 'Bolo, I bet you forget all of us when you win the money. You leaving Miguel Street, man, and buying a big house in St Clair, eh?'

Bolo said, 'No, I don't want to stay in Trinidad. I think I go go to the States.'

Bolo began marking two X's. Then three, four, six. He never won a penny. He was getting almost constantly angry.

He would say, 'Is just a big bacchanal, you hear. The paper people done make up their mind long long time now who going to win the week prize. They only want to get all the black people money.'

Hat said, 'You mustn't get discouraged. You got to try really hard again.'

Bolo bought sheets of squared paper and fitted them over the Missing Ball photograph. Wherever the lines crossed he marked an X. To do this properly Bolo had to buy something like a hundred to a hundred and fifty *Guardian*s every week.

Sometimes Bolo would call Boyee and Errol and me and say, 'Now, boys, where you think this missing ball is? Look, I want you to shut your eyes and mark a spot with this pencil.'

And sometimes again Bolo would ask us, 'What sort of things you been dreaming this week?'

If you said you didn't dream at all, Bolo looked disappointed. I used to make up dreams and Bolo would work them out in relation to the missing ball.

People began calling Bolo 'Missing Ball'.

Hat used to say, 'Look the man with the missing ball.'

One day Bolo went up to the offices of the *Guardian* and beat up a sub-editor before the police could be called.

In court Bolo said, 'The ball not missing, you hear. It wasn't there in the first place.'

Bolo was fined twenty-five dollars.

The *Gazette* ran a story:

THE CASE OF THE MISSING BALL
Penalty for a foul

Altogether Bolo spent about three hundred dollars trying to spot the missing ball, and he didn't even get a consolation prize.

It was shortly after the court case that Bolo stopped barbering regularly and also stopped reading the *Guardian*.

I can't remember now why Bolo stopped reading the *Evening News*, but I know why he stopped reading the *Gazette*.

A great housing shortage arose in Port of Spain during the war, and in 1942 a philanthropist came to the rescue of the unhoused. He said he was starting a co-operative housing scheme. People who wished to take part in this venture had to deposit some two hundred dollars, and after a year or so they would get brand-new houses for next to nothing. Several important men blessed the new scheme, and lots of dinners were eaten to give the project a good start.

The project was heavily advertised and about five or six houses were built and handed over to some of the people who had eaten the dinners. The papers carried photographs of people putting keys into locks and stepping over thresholds.

Bolo saw the photographs and the advertisements in the *Gazette*, and he paid in his two hundred dollars.

In 1943 the Director of the Co-operative Housing Society disappeared and with him disappeared two or three thousand dream houses.

Bolo stopped reading the *Gazette*.

It was on a Sunday in November that year that Bolo made his announcement to those of us who were sitting under the mango tree, waiting for Bolo to cut our hair.

He said, 'I saying something now. And so help me God, if I ever break my word, it go be better if I lose my two eyes. Listen. I stop reading papers. If even I learn Chinese I ain't go read Chinese papers, you hearing. You mustn't believe anything you read in the papers.'

Bolo was cutting Hat's hair at the moment, and Hat hurriedly got up and left.

Later Hat said, 'You know what I think. We will have to stop getting trim from Bolo. The man get me really frighten now, you hear.'

We didn't have to think a lot about Hat's decision because a few days later Bolo came to us and said, 'I coming round to see you people one by one because is the last time you go see me.'

He looked so sad I thought he was going to cry.

Hat said, 'What you thinking of doing now?'

Bolo said, 'I leaving this island for good. Is only a lot of damn crooks here.'

Eddoes said, 'Bolo, you taking your box-cart with you?'

Bolo said, 'No. Why, you like it?'

Eddoes said, 'I was thinking. It look like good materials to me.'

Bolo said, 'Eddoes, take my box-cart.'

Hat said, 'Where you going, Bolo?'

Bolo said, 'You go hear.'

And so he left us that evening.

Eddoes said, 'You think Bolo going mad?'

Hat said, 'No. He going Venezuela. That is why he keeping so secret. The Venezuelan police don't like Trinidad people going over.'

Eddoes said, 'Bolo is a nice man and I sorry he leaving. You know, it have some people I know who go be glad to have that box-cart Bolo leave behind.'

We went to Bolo's little room that very evening and we cleaned it of all the useful stuff he had left behind. There wasn't much. A bit of oil-cloth, two or three old combs, a cutlass, and a bench. We were all sad.

Hat said, 'People really treat poor Bolo bad in this country. I don't blame him for leaving.'

Eddoes was looking over the room in a practical way. He said, 'But Bolo take away everything, man.'

Next afternoon Eddoes announced, 'You know how much I pick up for that box-cart? Two dollars!'

Hat said, 'You does work damn fast, you know, Eddoes.'

Then we saw Bolo himself walking down Miguel Street.

Hat said, 'Eddoes, you in trouble.'

Eddoes said, 'But he give it to me. I didn't thief it.'

Bolo looked tired and sadder than ever.

Hat said, 'What happen, Bolo? You make a record, man. Don't tell me you go to Venezuela and you come back already.'

Bolo said, 'Trinidad people! Trinidad people! I don't know why Hitler don't come here and bomb all the sons of bitches it have in this island. He bombing the wrong people, you know.'

Hat said, 'Sit down, Bolo, and tell we what happen.'

Bolo said, 'Not yet. It have something I have to settle first. Eddoes, where my box-cart?'

Hat laughed.

Bolo said, 'You laughing, but I don't see the joke. Where my box-cart, Eddoes? You think you could make box-cart like that?'

Eddoes said, 'Your box-cart, Bolo? But you give it to me.'

Bolo said, 'I asking you to give it back to me.'

Eddoes said, 'I sell it, Bolo. Look the two dollars I get for it.'

Bolo said, 'But you quick, man.'

Eddoes was getting up.

Bolo said, 'Eddoes, it have one thing I begging you not to do. I begging you, Eddoes, not to come for trim by me again, you hear. I can't trust myself. And go and buy back my box-cart.'

Eddoes went away, muttering, 'Is a funny sort of world where people think their little box-cart so good. It like my big blue cart?'

Bolo said, 'When I get my hand on the good-for-nothing thief who take my money and say he taking me Venezuela, I go let him know something. You know what the man do? He drive around all night in the motor-launch and then put we down in a swamp, saying we reach Venezuela. I see some people. I begin talking to them in Spanish, they shake their head and laugh. You know is what? He put me down in Trinidad self, three four miles from La Brea.'

Hat said, 'Bolo, you don't know how lucky you is. Some of these people woulda kill you and throw you overboard, man. They say they don't like getting into trouble with the Venezuelan police. Is illegal going over to Venezuela, you know.'

We saw very little of Bolo after this. Eddoes managed to get the box-cart back, and he asked me to take it to Bolo.

Eddoes said, 'You see why black people can't get on in this world. You was there when he give it to me with his own two hands, and now he want it back. Take it back to him and tell him Eddoes say he could go to hell.'

I told Bolo, 'Eddoes say he sorry and he send back the box-cart.'

Bolo said, 'You see how black people is. They only quick to take, take. They don't want to give. That is why black people never get on.'

I said, 'Mr Bolo, it have something I take too, but I bring it back. Is the oil-cloth. I did take it and give it to my mother, but she ask me to bring it back.'

Bolo said, 'Is all right. But, boy, who trimming you these days? You head look as though fowl sitting on it.'

I said, 'Is Samuel trim me, Mr Bolo. But I tell you he can't trim. You see how he zog up my head.'

Bolo said, 'Come Sunday, I go trim you.'

I hesitated.

Bolo said, 'You fraid? Don't be stupid. I like you.'

So I went on Sunday.

Bolo said, 'How you getting on with your lessons?'

I didn't want to boast.

Bolo said, 'It have something I want you to do for me. But I not sure whether I should ask you.'

I said, 'But ask me, Mr Bolo. I go do anything for you.'

He said, 'No, don't worry. I go tell you next time you come.'

A month later I went again and Bolo said, 'You could read?'

I reassured him.

He said, 'Well, is a secret thing I doing. I don't want nobody to know. You could keep a secret?'

I said, 'Yes, I could keep secret.'

'A old man like me ain't have much to live for,' Bolo said. 'A old man like me living by hisself have to have something to live for. Is why I doing this thing I tell you about.'

'What is this thing, Mr Bolo?'

He stopped clipping my hair and pulled out a printed sheet from his trouser pocket.

He said, 'You know what this is?'

I said, 'Is a sweepstake ticket.'

'Right. You smart, man. Is really a sweepstake ticket.'

I said, 'But what you want me do, Mr Bolo?'

He said, 'First you must promise not to tell anybody.'

I gave my word.

He said, 'I want you to find out if the number draw.'

The draw was made about six weeks later and I looked for Bolo's number. I told him, 'You number ain't draw, Mr Bolo.'

He said, 'Not even a proxime accessit?'

I shook my head.

But Bolo didn't look disappointed. 'Is just what I expect,' he said.

For nearly three years this was our secret. And all during those years Bolo bought sweepstake tickets, and never won. Nobody knew and even when Hat or somebody else said to him, 'Bolo, I know a thing you could try. Why you don't try sweepstake?' Bolo would say, 'I done with that sort of thing, man.'

At the Christmas meeting of 1948 Bolo's number was drawn. It wasn't much, just about three hundred dollars.

I ran to Bolo's room and said, 'Mr Bolo, the number draw.'

Bolo's reaction wasn't what I expected. He said, 'Look, boy, you in long pants now. But don't get me mad, or I go have to beat you bad.'

I said, 'But it really draw, Mr Bolo.'

He said, 'How the hell you know it draw?'

I said, 'I see it in the papers.'

At this Bolo got really angry and he seized me by the collar. He screamed, 'How often I have to tell you, you little good-for-nothing son of a bitch, that you mustn't believe all that you read in the papers?'

So I checked up with the Trinidad Turf Club.

I said to Bolo, 'Is really true.' Bolo refused to believe.

He said, 'These Trinidad people does only lie, lie. Lie is all they know. They could fool you, boy, but they can't fool me.'

I told the men of the street, 'Bolo mad like hell. The man win three hundred dollars and he don't want to believe.'

One day Boyee said to Bolo, 'Ay, Bolo, you win a sweepstake then.'

Bolo chased Boyee, shouting, 'You playing the ass, eh. You making joke with a man old enough to be your grandfather.'

And when Bolo saw me, he said, 'Is so you does keep secret? Is so you does keep secret? But why all you Trinidad people so, eh?'

And he pushed his box-cart down to Eddoes's house, saying, 'Eddoes, you want box-cart, eh? Here, take the box-cart.'

And he began hacking the cart to bits with his cutlass.

To me he shouted, 'People think they could fool me.'

And he took out the sweepstake ticket and tore it. He rushed up to me and forced the pieces into my shirt pocket.

Afterwards he lived to himself in his little room, seldom came out to the street, never spoke to anybody. Once a month he went to draw his old-age pension.

EDWARD, HAT'S BROTHER, was a man of many parts, and I always thought it a sad thing that he drifted away from us. He used to help Hat with the cows when I first knew him and, like Hat, he looked settled and happy enough. He said he had given up women for good, and he concentrated on cricket, football, boxing, horse-racing, and cockfighting. In this way he was never bored, and he had no big ambition to make him unhappy.

Like Hat, Edward had a high regard for beauty. But Edward didn't collect birds of beautiful plumage, as Hat did. Edward painted.

His favourite subject was a brown hand clasping a black one. And when Edward painted a brown hand, it was a brown hand. No nonsense about light and shades. And the sea was a blue sea, and mountains were green.

Edward mounted his pictures himself and framed them in red passe-partout. The big department stores, Salvatori's, Fogarty's, and Johnson's, distributed Edward's work on commission.

To the street, however, Edward was something of a menace.

He would see Mrs Morgan wearing a new dress and say, 'Ah, Mrs Morgan, is a nice nice dress you wearing there, but I think it could do with some sort of decoration.'

Or he would see Eddoes wearing a new shirt and say, 'Eh, eh, Eddoes, you wearing a new shirt, man. You write your name in it, you know, otherwise somebody pick it up brisk brisk one of these days. Tell you what, I go write it for you.'

He ruined many garments in this way.

He also had the habit of giving away ties he had decorated himself. He would say, 'I have something for you. Take it and wear it. I giving it to you because I like you.'

And if the tie wasn't worn, Edward would get angry and begin shouting, 'But you see how ungrateful black people is. Listen to this. I see this man not wearing tie. I take a bus and I go to town. I walk to Johnson's and I look for the gents' department. I meet a girl and I buy a tie. I take a bus back home. I go inside my room and take up my brush and unscrew my paint. I dip my brush in paint and I put the brush on the tie. I spend two three hours doing that, and after all this, the man ain't wearing my tie.'

But Edward did a lot more than just paint.

One day, not many months after I had come to the street, Edward said, 'Coming back on the bus from Cocorite last night I only hearing the bus wheel cracking over crab back. You know the place by the coconut trees and the swamp? There it just crawling with crab. People say they even climbing up the coconut trees.'

Hat said, 'They does come out a lot at full moon. Let we go tonight and catch some of the crabs that Edward see.'

Edward said, 'Is just what I was going to say. We will have to take the boys because it have so much crab even they could pick up a lot.'

So we boys were invited.

Edward said, 'Hat, I was thinking. It go be a lot easier to catch the crab if we take a shovel. It have so much you could just shovel them up.'

Hat said, 'All right. We go take the cow-pen shovel.'

Edward said, 'That settle. But look, all you have strong shoes? You better get strong shoes, you know, because these crab and them ain't playing big and if you don't look out they start walking away with your big toe before you know what is what.'

Hat said, 'I go use the leggings I does wear when I cleaning out the cow-pen.'

Edward said, 'And we better wear gloves. I know a man was catching crab one day and suddenly he see his right hand walking away from him. He look again and see four five crab carrying it away. This man jump up and begin one bawling. So we have to be careful. If you boys ain't have gloves just wrap some cloth over your hands. That go be all right.'

So late that night we all climbed into the Cocorite bus, Hat in his leggings, Edward in his, and the rest of us carrying cutlasses and big brown sacks.

The shovel Hat carried still stank from the cow-pen and people began squinging up their noses.

Hat said, 'Let them smell it. They does all want milk when the cow give it.'

People looked at the leggings and the cutlasses and the shovel and the sacks and looked away quickly. They stopped talking.

The conductor didn't ask for our fares. The bus was silent until Edward began to talk.

Edward said, 'We must try and not use the cutlass. It ain't nice to kill. Try and get them live and put them in the bag.'

Many people got off at the next stop. By the time the bus got to Mucurapo Road it was carrying only us. The conductor stood right at the front talking to the driver.

Just before we got to the Cocorite terminus Edward said, 'Oh God, I know I was forgetting something. We can't bring back all the crab in a bus. I go have to go and telephone for a van.'

He got off one stop before the terminus.

We walked a little way in the bright moonlight, left the road and climbed down into the swamp. A tired wind blew from the sea, and the smell of stale sea-water was everywhere. Under the coconut trees it was dark. We walked a bit further in. A cloud covered the moon and the wind fell.

Hat called out, 'You boys all right? Be careful with your foot. I don't want any of you going home with only three toes.'

Boyee said, 'But I ain't seeing any crab.'

Ten minutes later Edward joined us.

He said, 'How many bags you full?'

Hat said, 'It look like a lot of people had the same idea and come and take away all the crab.'

Edward said, 'Rubbish. You don't see the moon ain't showing. We got to wait until the moon come out before the crab come out. Sit down, boys, let we wait.'

The moon remained clouded for half an hour.

Boyee said, 'It making cold and I want to go home. I don't think it have any crab.'

Errol said, 'Don't mind Boyee. I know him. He just frighten of the dark and he fraid the crab bite him.'

At this point we heard a rumbling in the distance.

Hat said, 'It look like the van come.'

Edward said, 'It ain't a van really. I order a big truck from Sam.'

We sat in silence waiting for the moon to clear. Then about a dozen torch-lights flashed all around us. Someone shouted, 'We ain't want any trouble. But if any one of you play the fool you going to get beat up bad.'

We saw what looked like a squad of policemen surrounding us.

Boyee began to cry.

Edward said, 'It have man beating their wife. It have people

Edward stopped working in the cow-pen and got a job with the Americans at Chaguaramas.

Hat said, 'Edward, I think you foolish to do that. The Americans ain't here forever and ever. It ain't have no sense in going off and working for big money and then not having nothing to eat after three four years.'

Edward said, 'This war look as though it go last a long long time. And the Americans not like the British, you know. They does make you work hard, but they does pay for it.'

Edward sold his share of the cows to Hat, and that marked the beginning of his drift away from us.

Edward surrendered completely to the Americans. He began wearing clothes in the American style, he began chewing gum, and he tried to talk with an American accent. We didn't see much of him except on Sundays, and then he made us feel small and inferior. He grew fussy about his dress, and he began wearing a gold chain around his neck. He began wearing straps around his wrists, after the fashion of tennis-players. These straps were just becoming fashionable among smart young men in Port of Spain.

Edward didn't give up painting, but he no longer offered to paint things for us, and I think most people were relieved. He entered some poster competition, and when his design didn't win even a consolation prize, he grew really angry with Trinidad.

One Sunday he said, 'I was stupid to send in anything I paint with my own two hands for Trinidad people to judge. What they know about anything? Now, if I was in America, it woulda be different. The Americans is people. They know about things.'

To hear Edward talk, you felt that America was a gigantic country inhabited by giants. They lived in enormous houses and they drove in the biggest cars of the world.

Edward used to say, 'Look at Miguel Street. In America you think they have streets so narrow? In America this street could pass for a sidewalk.'

One night I walked down with Edward to Docksite, the American army camp. Through the barbed wire you could see the huge screen of an open-air cinema.

Edward said, 'You see the sort of theatre they come and build in a stupid little place like Trinidad. Imagine the sort of thing they have in the States.'

And we walked down a little further until we came to a sentry in his box.

Edward used his best American accent and said, 'What's cooking, Joe?'

To my surprise the sentry, looking fierce under his helmet, replied, and in no time at all Edward and the sentry were talking away, each trying to use more swear words than the other.

When Edward came back to Miguel Street he began swaggering along and he said to me, 'Tell them. Tell them how good I does get on with the Americans.'

And when he was with Hat he said, 'Was talking the other night with a American – damn good friend – and he was telling me that as soon as the Americans enter the war the war go end.'

Errol said, 'It ain't *that* we want to win the war. As soon as they make Lord Anthony Eden Prime Minister the war go end quick quick.'

Edward said, 'Shut up, kid.'

But the biggest change of all was the way Edward began talking of women. Up till then he used to say that he was finished with them for good. He made out that his heart had been broken a long time ago and he had made a vow. It was a vague and tragic story.

But now on Sundays Edward said, 'You should see the sort of craft they have at the base. Nothing like these stupid Trinidad girls, you know. No, partner. Girls with style, girls with real class.'

I think it was Eddoes who said, 'I shouldn't let it worry you. They wouldn't tangle with you, those girls. They want big big American men. You safe.'

Edward called Eddoes a shrimp and walked away in a huff.

He began lifting weights, and in this, too, Edward was running right at the head of fashion. I don't know what happened in Trinidad about that time, but every young man became suddenly obsessed with the Body Beautiful ideal, and there were physique competitions practically every month. Hat used to console himself by saying, 'Don't worry. Is just a lot of old flash, you hear. They say they building muscle muscle. Just let them cool off and see what happen. All that thing they call muscle turn fat, you know.'

Eddoes said, 'Is the funniest sight you could see. At the Dairies in Philip Street all you seeing these days is a long line of black black men sitting at the counter and drinking quart bottles of white milk. All of them wearing sleeveless jersey to show off their big arm.'

In about three months Edward made his appearance among us in a sleeveless jersey. He had become a really big man.

Presently he began talking about the women at the base who were chasing him.

He said, 'I don't know what they see in me.'

Somebody had the idea of organizing a Local Talent on Parade show and Edward said, 'Don't make me laugh. What sort of talent they think Trinidad have?'

The first show was broadcast and we all listened to it in Eddoes's house. Edward kept on laughing all the time.

Hat said, 'Why you don't try singing yourself, then?'

Edward said, 'Sing for who? Trinidad people?'

Hat said, 'Do them a favour.'

To everybody's surprise Edward began singing, and the time came when Hat had to say, 'I just can't live in the same house with Edward. I think he go have to move.'

Edward moved, but he didn't move very far. He remained on our side of Miguel Street.

He said, 'Is a good thing. I was getting tired of the cow smell.'

Edward went up for one of the Local Talent shows and in spite of everything we all hoped that he would win a prize of some sort. The show was sponsored by a biscuit company and I think the winner got some money.

'They does give the others a thirty-one-cent pack of biscuits,' Hat said.

Edward got a package of biscuits.

He didn't bring it home, though. He threw it away.

He said, 'Throw it away. Why I shouldn't throw it away? You see, is just what I does tell you. Trinidad people don't know good thing. They just born stupid. Down at the base it have Americans *begging* me to sing. They know what is what. The other day, working and singing at the base, the colonel come up and tell me I had a nice voice. He was begging me to go to the States.'

Hat said, 'Why you don't go then?'

Edward said fiercely, 'Gimme time. Wait and see if I don't go.'

Eddoes said, 'What about all those woman and them who was chasing you? They catch up with you yet or they pass you?'

Edward said, 'Listen, Joe, I don't want to start getting tough with you. Do me a favour and shut up.'

When Edward brought any American friends to his house he pretended that he didn't know us, and it was funny to see him walking with them, holding his arms in the American way, hanging loosely, like a gorilla's.

Hat said, 'All the money he making he spending it on rum and ginger, curryfavouring with them Americans.'

In a way, I suppose, we were all jealous of him.

Hat began saying, 'It ain't hard to get a work with the Americans. I just don't want to have boss, that's all. I like being my own boss.'

Edward didn't mix much with us now.

One day he came to us with a sad face and said, 'Hat, it look like if I have to get married.'

He spoke with his Trinidad accent.

Hat looked worried. He said, 'Why? Why? Why you have to get married?'

'She making baby.'

'Is a damn funny thing to say. If everybody married because woman making baby for them it go be a hell of a thing. What happen that you want to be different now from everybody else in Trinidad? You come so American?'

Edward hitched up his tight American-style trousers and made a face like an American film actor. He said, 'You know all the answers, don't you? This girl is different. Sure I fall in love maybe once maybe twice before, but this kid's different.'

Hat said, 'She's got what it takes?'

Edward said, 'Yes.'

Hat said, 'Edward, you is a big man. It clear that you make up your mind to married this girl. Why you come round trying to make me force you to married her? You is a big man. You ain't have to come to me to get permission to do this to do that.'

When Edward left, Hat said, 'Whenever Edward come to me with a lie, he like a little boy. He can't lie to me. But if he married this girl, although I ain't see she, I feel he go live to regret it.'

Edward's wife was a tall and thin white-skinned woman. She looked very pale and perpetually unwell. She moved as though every step cost her effort. Edward made a great fuss about her and never introduced us.

The women of the street lost no time in passing judgment.

Mrs Morgan said, 'She is a born trouble-maker, that woman. I feel sorry for Edward. He get hisself in one mess.'

Mrs Bhakcu said, 'She is one of these modern girls. They want their husband to work all day and come home and cook and wash and clean up. All they know is to put powder and rouge on their face and walk out swinging their backside.'

And Hat said, 'But how she making baby? I can't see anything.'

Edward dropped out of our circle completely.

Hat said, 'She giving him good hell.'

And one day Hat shouted across the road to Edward, 'Joe, come across here for a moment.'

Edward looked very surly. He asked in Trinidadian, 'What you want?'

Hat smiled and said, 'What about the baby? When it coming?'

Edward said, 'What the hell you want to know for?'

Hat said, 'I go be a funny sort of uncle if I wasn't interested in my nephew.'

Edward said, 'She ain't making no more baby.'

Eddoes said, 'So it was just a line she was shooting then?'

Hat said, 'Edward, you lying. You make up all that in the first place. She wasn't making no baby, and you know that. She didn't tell you she was making baby, and you know that too. If you want to married the woman why you making all this thing about it?'

Edward looked very sad. 'If you want to know the truth, I don't think she could make baby.'

And when this news filtered through to the women of the street, they all said what my mother said.

She said, 'How you could see pink and pale people ever making baby?'

And although we had no evidence, and although Edward's house was still noisy with Americans, we felt that all was not well with Edward and his wife.

One Friday, just as it was getting dark, Edward ran up to me and said, 'Put down that stupidness you reading and go and get a policeman.'

I said, 'Policeman? But how I go go and get policeman just like that.'

Edward said, 'You could ride?'

I said, 'Yes.'

Edward said, 'You have a bicycle lamp?'

I said, 'No.'

Edward said, 'Take the bike and ride without lamp. You bound to get policeman.'

I said, 'And when I get this policeman, what I go tell him?'

Edward said, 'She try to kill sheself again.'

Before I had cycled to Ariapita Avenue I had met not one but two policemen. One of them was a sergeant. He said, 'You thinking of going far, eh?'

I said, 'Is you I was coming to find.'

The other policeman laughed.

The sergeant said to him, 'He smart, eh? I feel the magistrate go like that excuse. Is a new one and even me like it.'

I said, 'Come quick, Edward wife try to kill sheself again.'

The sergeant said, 'Oh, Edward wife always killing sheself, eh?' And he laughed. He added, 'And where this Edward wife try to kill sheself again, eh?'

I said, 'Just a little bit down Miguel Street.'

The constable said, 'He really smart, you know.'

The sergeant said, 'Yes. We leave him here and go and find somebody who try to kill sheself. Cut out this nonsense, boy. Where your bicycle licence?'

I said, 'Is true what I telling you. I go come back with you and show you the house.'

Edward was waiting for us. He said, 'You take a damn long time getting just two policemen.'

The policemen went inside the house with Edward and a little crowd gathered on the pavement.

Mrs Bhakcu said, 'Is just what I expect. I know from the first it was going to end up like this.'

Mrs Morgan said, 'Life is a funny thing. I wish I was like she and couldn't make baby. And it have a woman now trying to kill sheself because she can't make baby.'

Eddoes said, 'How you know is that she want to kill sheself for?'

Mrs Morgan shook a fat shoulder. 'What else?'

From then on I began to feel sorry for Edward because the men in the street and the women didn't give him a chance. And no matter how many big parties Edward gave at his house for Americans, I could see that he was affected when Eddoes shouted, 'Why you don't take your wife to America, boy? Those

American doctors smart like hell, you know. They could do any-thing.' Or when Mrs Bhakcu suggested that she should have a blood test at the Caribbean Medical Commission at the end of Ariapita Avenue.

The parties at Edward's house grew wilder and more extrava-gant. Hat said, 'Every party does have a end and people have to go home. Edward only making hisself more miserable.'

The parties certainly were not making Edward's wife any happier. She still looked frail and cantankerous, and now we sometimes heard Edward's voice raised in argument with her. It was not the usual sort of man-and-wife argument we had in the street. Edward sounded exasperated, but anxious to please.

Eddoes said, 'I wish any woman I married try behaving like that. Man, I give she one good beating and I make she straight straight like bamboo.'

Hat said, 'Edward ask for what he get. And the stupid thing is that I believe Edward really love the woman.'

Edward would talk to Hat and Eddoes and the other big men when they spoke to him, but when we boys tried talking to him, he had no patience. He would threaten to beat us and so we left him alone.

But whenever Edward passed, Boyee, brave and stupid as ever, would say in an American accent, 'What's up, Joe?'

Edward would stop and look angrily at Boyee and then lunge at him, shouting and swearing. He used to say, 'You see the sort of way Trinidad children does behave? What else this boy want but a good cut-arse?'

One day Edward caught Boyee and began flogging him.

At every stroke Boyee shouted, 'No, Edward.'

And Edward got madder and madder.

Then Hat ran up and said, 'Edward, put down that boy this minute or else it have big big trouble in this street. Put him down, I tell you. I ain't fraid of your big arms, you know.'

The men in the street had to break up the fight.

And when Boyee was freed, he shouted to Edward, 'Why you don't make child yourself and then beat it?'

Hat said, 'Boyee, I going to cut your tail this minute. Errol, go break a good whip for me.'

It was Edward himself who broke the news.

He said, 'She leave me.' He spoke in a very casual way.

Eddoes said, 'I sorry too bad, Edward.'

Hat said, 'Edward, boy, the things that not to be don't be.'

Edward didn't seem to be paying too much attention.

So Eddoes went on, 'I didn't like she from the first and I don't think a man should married a woman who can't make baby—'

Edward said, 'Eddoes, shut your thin little mouth up. And you, too, Hat, giving me all this make-up sympathy. I know how sad all-you is, all-you so sad all-you laughing.'

Hat said, 'But who laughing? Look, Edward, go and give any-body else all this temper, you hear, but leave me out. After all, it ain't nothing strange for a man wife to run away. Is like the calypso Invader sing:

> *"I was living with my decent and contented wife*
> *Until the soldiers came and broke up my life."*

It ain't your fault, is the Americans' fault.'

Eddoes said, 'You know who she run away with?'

Edward said, 'You hear me say she run away with anybody?'

Eddoes said, 'No, you didn't say that, but is what I feel.'

Edward said sadly, 'Yes, she run away. With a American soldier. And I give the man so much of my rum to drink.'

But after a few days Edward was running around telling people what had happened and saying, 'Is a damn good thing. I don't want a wife that can't make baby.'

And now nobody made fun of Edward's Americanism, and I think we were all ready to welcome him back to us. But he wasn't really interested. We hardly saw him in the street. When he wasn't working he was out on some excursion.

Hat said, 'Is love he really love she. He looking for she.'

In the calypso by Lord Invader the singer loses his wife to the Americans and when he begs her to come back to him, she says:

> *'Invader, I change my mind,*
> *I living with my Yankee soldier.'*

This was exactly what happened to Edward.

He came back in a great temper. He was miserable. He said, 'I leaving Trinidad.'

Eddoes said, 'Where you going? America?'

Edward almost cuffed Eddoes.

Hat said, 'But how you want to let one woman break up your life so? You behaving as if you is the first man this thing happen to.'

But Edward didn't listen.

At the end of the month he sold his house and left Trinidad. I think he went to Aruba or Curaçao, working with the big Dutch oil company.

And some months later Hat said, 'You know what I hear? Edward wife have a baby for she American.'

HAT LOVED TO MAKE a mystery of the smallest things. His relationship to Boyee and Errol, for instance. He told strangers they
were illegitimate children of his. Sometimes he said he wasn't
sure whether they were his at all, and he would spin a fantastic
story about some woman both he and Edward lived with at the
same time. Sometimes, again, he would make out that they were
his sons by an early marriage, and you felt you could cry when
you heard Hat tell how the boys' mother had gathered them
around her deathbed and made them promise to be good.

It took me some time to find out that Boyee and Errol were
really Hat's nephews. Their mother, who lived up in the bush
near Sangre Grande, died soon after her husband died, and the
boys came to live with Hat.

The boys showed Hat little respect. They never called him
Uncle, only Hat; and for their part they didn't mind when Hat
said they were illegitimate. They were, in fact, willing to support
any story Hat told about their birth.

I first got to know Hat when he offered to take me to the
cricket at the Oval. I soon found out that he had picked up eleven
other boys from four or five streets around, and was taking them
as well.

We lined up at the ticket office and Hat counted us loudly.
He said, 'One and twelve half.'

Many people stopped minding their business and looked up.

The man selling tickets said, 'Twelve half?'

Hat looked down at his shoes and said, 'Twelve half.'

We created a lot of excitement when all thirteen of us, Hat at
the head, filed around the ground, looking for a place to sit.

People shouted, 'They is all yours, mister?'

Hat smiled, weakly, and made people believe it was so. When
we sat down he made a point of counting us loudly again. He
said, 'I don't want your mother raising hell when I get home,
saying one missing.'

It was the last day of the last match between Trinidad and
Jamaica. Gerry Gomez and Len Harbin were making a great

stand for Trinidad, and when Gomez reached his 150 Hat went crazy and danced up and down, shouting, 'White people is God, you hear!'

A woman selling soft drinks passed in front of us.

Hat said, 'How you selling this thing you have in the glass and them?'

The woman said, 'Six cents a glass.'

Hat said, 'I want the wholesale price. I want thirteen.'

The woman said, 'These children is all yours?'

Hat said, 'What wrong with that?'

The woman sold the drinks at five cents a glass.

When Len Harbin was 89, he was out lbw, and Trinidad declared.

Hat was angry. 'Lbw? Lbw? How he lbw? Is only a lot of robbery. And is a Trinidad umpire, too. God, even umpires taking bribe now.'

Hat taught me many things that afternoon. From the way he pronounced them, I learned about the beauty of cricketers' names, and he gave me all his own excitement at watching a cricket match.

I asked him to explain the scoreboard.

He said, 'On the left-hand side they have the names of the batsman who finish batting.'

I remember that because I thought it such a nice way of saying that a batsman was out: to say that he had finished batting.

All during the tea interval Hat was as excited as ever. He tried to get all sorts of people to take all sorts of crazy bets. He ran about waving a dollar-note and shouting, 'A dollar to a shilling, Headley don't reach double figures.' Or, 'A dollar, Stollmeyer field the first ball.'

The umpires were walking out when one of the boys began crying.

Hat said, 'What you crying for?'

The boy cried and mumbled.

Hat said, 'But what you crying for?'

A man shouted, 'He want a bottle.'

Hat turned to the man and said, 'Two dollars, five Jamaican wickets fall this afternoon.'

The man said, 'Is all right by me, if is hurry you is to lose your money.'

A third man held the stakes.

The boy was still crying.

Hat said, 'But you see how you shaming me in front of all these people? Tell me quick what you want.'

The boy only cried. Another boy came up to Hat and whispered in his ear.

Hat said, 'Oh, God! How? Just when they coming out.'

He made us all stand. He marched us away from the grounds and made us line up against the galvanized-iron paling of the Oval.

He said, 'All right now, pee. Pee quick, all of all-you.'

The cricket that afternoon was fantastic. The Jamaican team, which included the great Headley, lost six wickets for thirty-one runs. In the fading light the Trinidad fast bowler, Tyrell Johnson, was unplayable, and his success seemed to increase his speed.

A fat old woman on our left began screaming at Tyrell Johnson, and whenever she stopped screaming she turned to us and said very quietly, 'I know Tyrell since he was a boy so high. We use to pitch marble together.' Then she turned away and began screaming again.

Hat collected his bet.

This, I discovered presently, was one of Hat's weaknesses – his passion for impossible bets. At the races particularly, he lost a lot of money, but sometimes he won, and then he made so much he could afford to treat all of us in Miguel Street.

I never knew a man who enjoyed life as much as Hat did. He did nothing new or spectacular – in fact, he did practically the same things every day – but he always enjoyed what he did. And every now and then he managed to give a fantastic twist to some very ordinary thing.

He was a bit like his dog. This was the tamest Alsatian I have ever known. One of the things I noticed in Miguel Street was the way dogs resembled their owners. George had a surly, mean mongrel. Toni's dog was a terrible savage. Hat's dog was the only Alsatian I knew with a sense of humour.

In the first place it behaved oddly, for an Alsatian. You could make it the happiest dog on earth if you flung things for it to retrieve. One day, in the Savannah, I flung a guava into some thick bushes. He couldn't get at the guava, and he whined and complained. He suddenly turned and ran back past me, barking loudly. While I turned to see what was wrong, he ran back to the bushes. I saw nothing strange, and when I looked back I was just in time to see him taking another guava behind the bushes.

I called him and he rushed up whining and barking.

I said, 'Go on, boy. Go on and get the guava.'

He ran back to the bushes and poked and sniffed a bit and then dashed behind the bushes to get the guava he had himself placed there.

I only wish the beautiful birds Hat collected were as tame as the Alsatian. The macaws and the parrots looked like angry and quarrelsome old women and they attacked anybody. Sometimes Hat's house became a dangerous place with all these birds around. You would be talking quietly when you would suddenly feel a prick and a tug on your calf. The macaw or the parrot. Hat tried to make us believe they didn't bite him, but I know that they did.

Strange that both Hat and Edward became dangerous when they tried meddling with beauty. There was Edward with his painting, and Hat with his sharp-beaked macaws.

Hat was always getting into trouble with the police. Nothing serious, though. A little cockfighting here, some gambling there, a little drinking somewhere else, and so on.

But it never soured him against the law. In fact, every Christmas Sergeant Charles, with the postman and the sanitary inspector, came to Hat's place for a drink.

Sergeant Charles would say, 'Is only a living I have to make, you know, Hat. Nobody ain't have to tell me. I know I ain't going to get any more promotion, but still.'

Hat would say, 'Is all right, Sergeant. None of we don't mind. How your children these days? How Elijah?'

Elijah was a bright boy.

'Elijah? Oh, I think he go get a exhibition this year. Is all we could do, eh, Hat? All we could do is try. We can't do no more.'

And they always separated as good friends.

But once Hat got into serious trouble for watering his milk.

He said, 'The police and them come round asking me how the water get in the milk. As if I know. I ain't know how the water get there. You know I does put the pan in water to keep the milk cool and prevent it from turning. I suppose the pan did have a hole, that's all. A tiny little hole.'

Edward said, 'It better to be frank and tell the magistrate that.'

Hat said, 'Edward, you talking as if Trinidad is England. You ever hear that people tell the truth in Trinidad and get away? In Trinidad the more you innocent, the more they throw you in jail, and the more bribe you got to hand out. You got to bribe the magistrate. You got to give them fowl, big big Leghorn hen, and you got to give them money. You got to bribe the inspectors. By the time you finish bribing it would be better if you did take your jail quiet quiet.'

Edward said, 'It is the truth. But you can't plead guilty. You have to make up some new story.'

Hat was fined two hundred dollars and the magistrate preached a long sermon at him.

He was in a real temper when he came back from court. He tore off his tie and coat and said, 'Is a damn funny world. You bathe, you put on a clean shirt, you put on tie and you put on jacket, you shine up your shoe. And all for what? Is only to go in front of some stupid magistrate for him to abuse you.'

It rankled for days.

Hat said, 'Hitler was right, man. Burn all the law books. Burn all of them up. Make a big pile and set fire to the whole damn thing. Burn them up and watch them burn. Hitler was right, man. I don't know why we fighting him for.'

Eddoes said, 'You talking a lot of nonsense, you know, Hat.'

Hat said, 'I don't want to talk about it. Don't want to talk about it. Hitler was right. Burn the law books. Burn all of them up. Don't want to talk about it.'

For three months Hat and Sergeant Charles were not on speaking terms. Sergeant Charles was hurt, and he was always sending messages of goodwill to Hat.

One day he called me and said, 'You go be seeing Hat this evening?'

I said, 'Yes.'

'You did see him yesterday?'

'Yes.'

'How he is?'

'How?'

'Well, I mean, how he looking? He looking well? Happy?'

I said, 'He looking damn vex.'

Sergeant Charles said, 'Oh.'

I said, 'All right.'

'Look, before you go away—'

'What?'

'Nothing. No, no. Wait before you go. Tell Hat how for me, you hear.'

I told Hat, 'Sergeant Charles call me to his house today and begin one crying and begging. He keep on asking me to tell you that he not vex with you, that it wasn't he who tell the police about the milk and the water.'

Hat said, '*Which* water in *which* milk?'

I didn't know what to say.

Hat said, 'You see the sort of place Trinidad coming now. Somebody say it had water in my milk. Nobody see me put water in the milk, but everybody talking now as if they see me. Everybody talking about *the* water in *the* milk.'

Hat, I saw, was enjoying even this.

I always looked upon Hat as a man of settled habits, and it was hard to think of him looking otherwise than he did. I suppose he was thirty-five when he took me to that cricket-match, and forty-three when he went to jail. Yet he always looked the same to me.

In appearance, as I have said, he was dark-brown in complexion, of medium height and medium build. He had a slightly bow-legged walk and he had flat feet.

I was prepared to see him do the same things for the rest of his life. Cricket, football, horse-racing; read the paper in the mornings and afternoons; sit on the pavement and talk; get noisily drunk on Christmas Eve and New Year's Eve.

He didn't appear to need anything else. He was self-sufficient, and I didn't believe he even needed women. I knew, of course, that he visited certain places in the city from time to time, but I thought he did this more for the vicious thrill than for the women.

And then this thing happened. It broke up the Miguel Street Club, and Hat himself was never the same afterwards.

In a way, I suppose, it was Edward's fault. I don't think any of us realized how much Hat loved Edward and how heartbroken he was when Edward got married. He couldn't hide his delight when Edward's wife ran away with the American soldier, and he was greatly disappointed when Edward went to Aruba.

Once he said, 'Everybody growing up or they leaving.'

Another time he said, 'I think I was a damn fool not go and work with the Americans, like Edward and so much other people.'

Eddoes said, 'Hat going to town a lot these nights.'

Boyee said, 'Well, he is a big man. Why he shouldn't do what he want to do?'

Eddoes said, 'It have some men like that. As a matter of fact, it does happen to all man. They getting old and they get frighten and they want to remain young.'

I got angry with Eddoes because I didn't want to think of Hat in that way and the worst thing was that I was ashamed because I felt Eddoes was right.

I said, 'Eddoes, why you don't take your dirty mind somewhere else, eh? Why you don't leave all your dirtiness in the rubbish-dump?'

And then one day Hat brought home a woman.

I felt a little uneasy now in Hat's company. He had become a man with responsibility and obligations, and he could no longer give us all his time and attention. To make matters worse, everybody pretended that the woman wasn't there. Even Hat. He never spoke about her and he behaved as though he wanted us to believe that everything was just the same.

She was a pale-brown woman, about thirty, somewhat plump, and her favourite colour was blue. She called herself Dolly. We used to see her looking blankly out of the windows of Hat's house. She never spoke to any of us. In fact, I hardly heard her speak at all, except to call Hat inside.

But Boyee and Edward were pleased with the changes she brought.

Boyee said, 'Is the first time I remember living with a woman in the house, and it make a lot of difference. Is hard to explain, but I find it nicer.'

My mother said, 'You see how man stupid. Hat see what happen to Edward and you mean to say that Hat still get hisself mix up with this woman?'

Mrs Morgan and Mrs Bhakcu saw so little of Dolly they had little to dislike in her, but they agreed that she was a lazy good-for-nothing.

Mrs Morgan said, 'This Dolly look like a old *madame* to me, you hear.'

It was easy enough for us to forget that Dolly was there, because Hat continued living as before. We still went to all the sports and we still sat on the pavement and talked.

Whenever Dolly piped, 'Hat, you coming?' Hat wouldn't reply.

About half an hour later Dolly would say, 'Hat, you coming or you ain't coming?'

And Hat would say then, 'I coming.'

I wondered what life was like for Dolly. She was nearly always inside the house and Hat was nearly always outside. She seemed to spend a great deal of her time at the front window looking out.

They were really the queerest couple in the street. They never went out together. We never heard them laughing. They never even quarrelled.

Eddoes said, 'They like two strangers.'

Errol said, 'Don't mind that, you hear. All you seeing Hat sitting quiet quiet here, but is different when he get inside. He ain't the same man when he talking with Dolly. He buy she a lot of joolry, you know.'

Eddoes said, 'I have a feeling she a little bit like Matilda. You know, the woman in the calypso:

> "Matilda, Matilda,
> Matilda, you thief my money
> And gone Venezuela."

Buying joolry! But what happening to Hat? He behaving as though he is a old man. Woman don't want joolry from a man like Hat, they want something else.'

Looking on from the outside, though, one could see only two changes in Hat's household. All the birds were caged, and the Alsatian was chained and miserable.

But no one spoke about Dolly to Hat. I suppose the whole business had come as too much of a surprise.

What followed was an even bigger surprise, and it was some time before we could get all the details. At first I noticed Hat was missing, and then I heard rumours.

This was the story, as it later came out in court. Dolly had run away from Hat, taking all his gifts, of course. Hat had chased her and found her with another man. There was a great quarrel, the man had fled, and Hat had taken it out on Dolly. Afterwards, the police statement said, he had gone, in tears, to the police station to give himself up. He said, 'I kill a woman.'

But Dolly wasn't dead.

We received the news as though it was news of a death. We couldn't believe it for a day or two.

And then a great hush fell on Miguel Street. No boys and men gathered under the lamp-post outside Hat's house, talking about this and that and the other. No one played cricket and disturbed people taking afternoon naps. The Club was dead.

Cruelly, we forgot all about Dolly and thought only about Hat. We couldn't find it in our hearts to find fault with him. We suffered with him.

We saw a changed man in court. He had grown older, and when he smiled at us he smiled only with his mouth. Still, he put on a show for us and even while we laughed we were ready to cry.

The prosecutor asked Hat, 'Was it a dark night?'

Hat said, 'All night dark.'

Hat's lawyer was a short fat man called Chittaranjan who wore a smelly brown suit.

Chittaranjan began reeling off Portia's speech about mercy, and he would have gone on to the end if the judge hadn't said, 'All this is interesting and some of it even true but, Mr Chittaranjan, you are wasting the court's time.'

Chittaranjan made a great deal of fuss about the wild passion of love. He said Antony had thrown away an empire for the sake of love, just as Hat had thrown away his self-respect. He said that Hat's crime was really a *crime passionel*. In France, he said – and he knew what he was talking about, because he had been to Paris – in France, Hat would have been a hero. Women would have garlanded him.

Eddoes said, 'Is this sort of lawyer who does get man hang, you know.'

Hat was sentenced to four years.

We went to Frederick Street jail to see him. It was a disappointing jail. The walls were light cream, and not very high, and I was surprised to see that most of the visitors were very gay. Only a few women wept, but the whole thing was like a party, with people laughing and chatting.

Eddoes, who had put on his best suit for the occasion, held his hat in his hand and looked around. He said to Hat, 'It don't look too bad here.'

Hat said, 'They taking me to Carrera next week.'

Carrera was the small prison-island a few miles from Port of Spain.

Hat said, 'Don't worry about me. You know me. In two three weeks I go make them give me something easy to do.'

*   *   *

Whenever I went to Carenage or Point Cumana for a bathe, I looked across the green water to the island of Carrera, rising high out of the sea, with its neat pink buildings. I tried to picture what went on inside those buildings, but my imagination refused to work. I used to think, 'Hat there, I here. He know I here, thinking about him?'

But as the months passed I became more and more concerned with myself, and I wouldn't think about Hat for weeks on end. It was useless trying to feel ashamed. I had to face the fact that I was no longer missing Hat. From time to time when my mind was empty, I would stop and think how long it would be before he came out, but I was not really concerned.

I was fifteen when Hat went to jail and eighteen when he came out. A lot happened in those three years. I left school and I began working in the customs. I was no longer a boy. I was a man, earning money.

Hat's homecoming fell a little flat. It wasn't only that we boys had grown older. Hat, too, had changed. Some of the brightness had left him, and conversation was hard to make.

He visited all the houses he knew and he spoke about his experiences with great zest.

My mother gave him tea.

Hat said, 'Is just what I expect. I get friendly with some of the turnkey and them, and you know what happen? I pull two three strings and – bam! – they make me librarian. They have a big library there, you know. All sort of big book. Is the sort of place Titus Hoyt would like. So much book with nobody to read them.'

I offered Hat a cigarette and he took it mechanically.

Then he shouted, 'But, eh-eh, what is this? You come a big man now! When I leave you wasn't smoking. Was a long time now, though.'

I said, 'Yes. Was a long time.'

A long time. But it was just three years, three years in which I had grown up and looked critically at the people around me. I no longer wanted to be like Eddoes. He was so weak and thin, and I hadn't realized that he was so small. Titus Hoyt was stupid and boring, and not funny at all. Everything had changed.

When Hat went to jail, part of me had died.

MY MOTHER SAID, 'You getting too wild in this place. I think is high time you leave.'

'And go where? Venezuela?' I said.

'No, not Venezuela. Somewhere else, because the moment you land in Venezuela they go throw you in jail. I know you and I know Venezuela. No, somewhere else.'

I said, 'All right. You think about it and decide.'

My mother said, 'I go go and talk to Ganesh Pundit about it. He was a friend of your father. But you must go from here. You getting too wild.'

I suppose my mother was right. Without really knowing it, I had become a little wild. I was drinking like a fish, and doing a lot besides. The drinking started in the customs, where we confiscated liquor on the slightest pretext. At first the smell of spirits upset me, but I used to say to myself, 'You must get over this. Drink it like medicine. Hold your nose and close your eyes.' In time I had become a first-class drinker, and I began suffering from drinker's pride.

Then there were the sights of the town Boyee and Errol introduced me to. One night, not long after I began working, they took me to a place near Marine Square. We climbed to the first floor and found ourselves in a small crowded room lit by green bulbs. The green light seemed as thick as jelly. There were many women all about the room, just waiting and looking. A big sign said: OBSCENE LANGUAGE FORBIDDEN.

We had a drink at the bar, a thick sweet drink.

Errol asked me, 'Which one of the women you like?'

I understood immediately, and I felt disgusted. I ran out of the room and went home, a little sick, a little frightened. I said to myself, 'You must get over this.'

Next night I went to the club again. And again.

We made wild parties and took rum and women to Maracas Bay for all-night sessions.

'You getting too wild,' my mother said.

I paid her no attention until the time I drank so much in one evening that I remained drunk for two whole days afterwards. When I sobered up, I made a vow neither to smoke nor drink again.

I said to my mother, 'Is not my fault really. Is just Trinidad. What else anybody can do here except drink?'

About two months later my mother said, 'You must come with me next week. We going to see Ganesh Pundit.'

Ganesh Pundit had given up mysticism for a long time. He had taken to politics and was doing very nicely. He was a minister of something or the other in the Government, and I heard people saying that he was in the running for the M.B.E.

We went to his big house in St Clair and we found the great man, not dressed in *dhoti* and *koortah*, as in the mystic days, but in an expensive-looking lounge suit.

He received my mother with a good deal of warmth.

He said, 'I do what I could do.'

My mother began to cry.

To me Ganesh said, 'What you want to go abroad to study?'

I said, 'I don't want to study anything really. I just want to go away, that's all.'

Ganesh smiled and said, 'The Government not giving away that sort of scholarship yet. Only ministers could do what you say. No, you have to study something.'

I said, 'I never think about it really. Just let me think a little bit.'

Ganesh said, 'All right. You think a little bit.'

My mother was crying her thanks to Ganesh.

I said, 'I know what I want to study. Engineering.' I was thinking about my uncle Bhakcu.

Ganesh laughed and said, 'What *you* know about engineering?'

I said, 'Right now, nothing. But I could put my mind to it.'

My mother said, 'Why don't you want to take up law?'

I thought of Chittaranjan and his brown suit and I said, 'No, not law.'

Ganesh said, 'It have only one scholarship remaining. For drugs.'

I said, 'But I don't want to be a druggist. I don't want to put on a white jacket and sell lipstick to woman.'

Ganesh smiled.

My mother said, 'You mustn't mind the boy, Pundit. He will study drugs.' And to me, 'You could study anything if you put your mind to it.'

Ganesh said, 'Think. It mean going to London. It mean seeing snow and seeing the Thames and seeing the big Parliament.'

I said, 'All right. I go study drugs.'

My mother said, 'I don't know what I could do to thank you, Pundit.'

And, crying, she counted out two hundred dollars and gave it to Ganesh. She said, 'I know it ain't much, Pundit. But it is all I have. Is a long time I did saving it up.'

Ganesh took the money sadly and he said, 'You mustn't let that worry you. You must give only what you can afford.'

My mother kept on crying and in the end even Ganesh broke down.

When my mother saw this, she dried her tears and said, 'If you only know, Pundit, how worried I is. I have to find so much money for so much thing these days, and I don't really know how I going to make out.'

Ganesh now stopped crying. My mother began to cry afresh.

This went on for a bit until Ganesh gave back a hundred dollars to my mother. He was sobbing and shaking and he said, 'Take this and buy some good clothes for the boy.'

I said, 'Pundit, you is a good man.'

This affected him strongly. He said, 'Is when you come back from England, with all sort of certificate and paper, a big man and a big druggist, is then I go come round and ask you for what you owe me.'

I told Hat I was going away.

He said, 'What for? Labouring?'

I said, 'The Government give me a scholarship to study drugs.'

He said, 'Is you who wangle that?'

I said, 'Not me. My mother.'

Eddoes said, 'Is a good thing. A druggist fellow I know – picking up rubbish for him for years now – this fellow rich like anything. Man, the man just rolling in money.'

The news got to Elias and he took it badly. He came to the gate one evening and shouted, 'Bribe, bribe. Is all you could do. Bribe.'

My mother shouted back, 'The only people who does complain about bribe is those who too damn poor to have anything to bribe with.'

In about a month everything was fixed for my departure. The Trinidad Government wrote to the British Consul in New

York about me. The British Consul got to know about me. The Americans gave me a visa after making me swear that I wouldn't overthrow their government by armed force.

The night before I left, my mother gave a little party. It was something like a wake. People came in looking sad and telling me how much they were going to miss me, and then they forgot about me and attended to the serious business of eating and drinking.

Laura kissed me on the cheek and gave me a medallion of St Christopher. She asked me to wear it around my neck. I promised that I would and I put the medallion in my pocket. I don't know what happened to it. Mrs Bhakcu gave me a sixpenny piece which she said she had had specially consecrated. It didn't look different from other sixpenny pieces and I suppose I spent it. Titus Hoyt forgave me everything and brought me Volume Two of the Everyman edition of Tennyson. Eddoes gave me a wallet which he swore was practically new. Boyee and Errol gave me nothing. Hat gave me a carton of cigarettes. He said, 'I know you say you ain't smoking again. But take this, just in case you change your mind.' The result was that I began smoking again.

Uncle Bhakcu spent the night fixing the van which was to take me to the airport next morning. From time to time I ran out and begged him to take it easy. He said he thought the carburettor was playing the fool.

Next morning Bhakcu got up early and was at it again. We had planned to leave at eight, but at ten to, Bhakcu was still tinkering. My mother was in a panic and Mrs Bhakcu was growing impatient.

Bhakcu was underneath the car, whistling a couplet from the *Ramayana*. He came out, laughed, and said, 'You getting frighten, eh?'

Presently we were all ready. Bhakcu had done little damage to the engine and it still worked. My bags were taken to the van and I was ready to leave the house for the last time.

My mother said, 'Wait.'

She placed a brass jar of milk in the middle of the gateway.

I cannot understand, even now, how it happened. The gateway was wide, big enough for a car, and the jar, about four inches wide, was in the middle. I thought I was walking at the edge of the gateway, far away from the jar. And yet I kicked the jar over.

My mother's face fell.

I said, 'Is a bad sign?'

She didn't answer.

Bhakcu was blowing the horn.

We got into the van and Bhakcu drove away, down Miguel Street and up Wrightson Road to South Quay. I didn't look out of the windows.

My mother was crying. She said, 'I know I not going to ever see you in Miguel Street again.'

I said, 'Why? Because I knock the milk down?'

She didn't reply, still crying for the spilt milk.

Only when we had left Port of Spain and the suburbs I looked outside. It was a clear, hot day. Men and women were working in rice-fields. Some children were bathing under a stand-pipe at the side of the road.

We got to Piarco in good time, and at this stage I began wishing I had never got the scholarship. The airport lounge frightened me. Fat Americans were drinking strange drinks at the bar. American women, wearing haughty sun-glasses, raised their voices whenever they spoke. They all looked too rich, too comfortable.

Then the news came, in Spanish and English. Flight 206 had been delayed for six hours.

I said to my mother, 'Let we go back to Port of Spain.'

I had to be with those people in the lounge soon anyway, and I wanted to put off the moment.

And back in Miguel Street the first person I saw was Hat. He was strolling flat-footedly back from the Café, with a paper under his arm. I waved and shouted at him.

All he said was, 'I thought you was in the air by this time.'

I was disappointed. Not only by Hat's cool reception. Disappointed because although I had been away, destined to be gone for good, everything was going on just as before, with nothing to indicate my absence.

I looked at the overturned brass jar in the gateway and I said to my mother, 'So this mean I was never going to come back here, eh?'

She laughed and looked happy.

So I had my last lunch at home, with my mother and Uncle Bhakcu and his wife. Then back along the hot road to Piarco where the plane was waiting. I recognized one of the customs' officers, and he didn't check my baggage.

The announcement came, a cold, casual thing.

I embraced my mother.

I said to Bhakcu, 'Uncle Bhak, I didn't want to tell you before, but I think I hear your tappet knocking.'

His eyes shone.

I left them all and walked briskly towards the aeroplane, not looking back, looking only at my shadow before me, a dancing dwarf on the tarmac.

A FLAG ON THE ISLAND

To Diana Athill

CONTENTS

1 MY AUNT GOLD TEETH

I NEVER KNEW her real name and it is quite likely that she did have one, though I never heard her called anything but Gold Teeth. She did, indeed, have gold teeth. She had sixteen of them. She had married early and she had married well, and shortly after her marriage she exchanged her perfectly sound teeth for gold ones, to announce to the world that her husband was a man of substance.

Even without her gold teeth my aunt would have been noticeable. She was short, scarcely five foot, and she was very fat. If you saw her in silhouette you would have found it difficult to know whether she was facing you or whether she was looking sideways.

She ate little and prayed much. Her family being Hindu, and her husband being a pundit, she, too, was an orthodox Hindu. Of Hinduism she knew little apart from the ceremonies and the taboos, and this was enough for her. Gold Teeth saw God as a Power, and religious ritual as a means of harnessing that Power for great practical good, her good.

I may have given the impression that Gold Teeth prayed because she wanted to be less fat. The fact was that Gold Teeth had no children and she was almost forty. It was her childlessness, not her fat, that oppressed her, and she prayed for the curse to be removed. She was willing to try any means – any ritual, any prayer – in order to trap and channel the supernatural Power.

And so it was that she began to indulge in surreptitious Christian practices.

She was living at the time in a country village called Cunupia, in County Caroni. Here the Canadian Mission had long waged war against the Indian heathen, and saved many. But Gold Teeth stood firm. The Minister of Cunupia expended his Presbyterian piety on her; so did the headmaster of the Mission school. But all in vain. At no time was Gold Teeth persuaded even to think about being converted. The idea horrified her. Her father had been in his day one of the best-known Hindu pundits, and even now her husband's fame as a pundit, as a man who could read and write Sanskrit, had spread far beyond Cunupia. She was in no doubt whatsoever that Hindus were the best people in the world, and that Hinduism was a superior religion. She was willing to select, modify and incorporate alien eccentricities into her worship; but to abjure her own faith – never!

Presbyterianism was not the only danger the good Hindu had to face in Cunupia. Besides, of course, the ever-present threat of open Muslim aggression, the Catholics were to be reckoned with. Their pamphlets were everywhere and it was hard to avoid them. In them Gold Teeth read of novenas and rosaries, of squads of saints and angels. These were things she understood and could even sympathize with, and they encouraged her to seek further. She read of the mysteries and the miracles, of penances and indulgences. Her scepticism sagged, and yielded to a quickening, if reluctant, enthusiasm.

One morning she took the train for the County town of Chaguanas, three miles, two stations and twenty minutes away. The Church of St Philip and St James in Chaguanas stands imposingly at the end of the Caroni Savannah Road, and although Gold Teeth knew Chaguanas well, all she knew of the church was that it had a clock, at which she had glanced on her way to the railway station nearby. She had hitherto been far more interested in the drab ochre-washed edifice opposite, which was the police station.

She carried herself into the churchyard, awed by her own temerity, feeling like an explorer in a land of cannibals. To her relief, the church was empty. It was not as terrifying as she had expected. In the gilt and images and the resplendent cloths she found much that reminded her of her Hindu temple. Her eyes caught a discreet sign: CANDLES TWO CENTS EACH. She undid the knot in the end of her veil, where she kept her money, took out three cents, popped them into the box, picked up a candle and muttered a prayer in Hindustani. A brief moment of elation gave way to a sense of guilt, and she was suddenly anxious to get away from the church as fast as her weight would let her.

She took a bus home, and hid the candle in her chest of drawers. She had half feared that her husband's Brahminical flair for clairvoyance would have uncovered the reason for her trip to Chaguanas. When after four days, which she spent in an ecstasy of prayer, her husband had mentioned nothing, Gold Teeth thought it safe to burn the candle. She burned it secretly at night, before her Hindu images, and sent up, as she thought, prayers of double efficacy.

Every day her religious schizophrenia grew, and presently she began wearing a crucifix. Neither her husband nor her neighbours knew she did so. The chain was lost in the billows of fat around her neck, and the crucifix was itself buried in the valley of her gargantuan breasts. Later she acquired two holy pictures, one of the Virgin Mary, the other of the crucifixion, and took care to conceal them from her husband. The prayers she offered to these Christian things filled her with new hope and buoyancy. She became an addict of Christianity.

Then her husband, Ramprasad, fell ill.

Ramprasad's sudden, unaccountable illness alarmed Gold Teeth. It was, she knew, no ordinary illness, and she knew, too, that her religious transgression was the cause. The District Medical Officer at Chaguanas said it was diabetes, but Gold Teeth knew better. To be on the safe side, though, she used the insulin he prescribed and, to be even safer, she consulted Ganesh Pundit, the masseur with mystic leanings, celebrated as a faith-healer.

Ganesh came all the way from Fuente Grove to Cunupia. He came in great humility, anxious to serve Gold Teeth's husband, for Gold Teeth's husband was a Brahmin among Brahmins, a *Panday*, a man who knew all five Vedas; while he, Ganesh, was a mere *Chaubay* and knew only four.

With spotless white *koortah*, his dhoti cannily tied, and a tasselled green scarf as a concession to elegance, Ganesh exuded the confidence of the professional mystic. He looked at the sick man, observed his pallor, sniffed the air. 'This man,' he said, 'is bewitched. Seven spirits are upon him.'

He was telling Gold Teeth nothing she didn't know. She had known from the first that there were spirits in the affair, but she was glad that Ganesh had ascertained their number.

'But you mustn't worry,' Ganesh added. 'We will "tie" the house – in spiritual bonds – and no spirit will be able to come in.'

Then, without being asked, Gold Teeth brought out a blanket, folded it, placed it on the floor and invited Ganesh to sit on it. Next she brought him a brass jar of fresh water, a mango leaf and a plate full of burning charcoal.

'Bring me some ghee,' Ganesh said, and after Gold Teeth had done so, he set to work. Muttering continuously in Hindustani he sprinkled the water from the brass jar around him with the mango leaf. Then he melted the ghee in the fire and the charcoal hissed so sharply that Gold Teeth could not make out his words. Presently he rose and said, 'You must put some of the ash of this fire on your husband's forehead, but if he doesn't want you to do that, mix it with his food. You must keep the water in this jar and place it every night before your front door.'

Gold Teeth pulled her veil over her forehead.

Ganesh coughed. 'That,' he said, rearranging his scarf, 'is all. There is nothing more I can do. God will do the rest.'

He refused payment for his services. It was enough honour, he said, for a man as humble as he was to serve Pundit Ramprasad, and she, Gold Teeth, had been singled out by fate to be the spouse of such a worthy man. Gold Teeth received the impression that Ganesh spoke from a first-hand knowledge of fate and its designs, and her heart, buried down under inches of mortal, flabby flesh, sank a little.

'Baba,' she said hesitantly, 'revered Father, I have something to say to you.' But she couldn't say anything more and Ganesh, seeing this, filled his eyes with charity and love.

'What is it, my child?'

'I have done a great wrong, Baba.'

'What sort of wrong?' he asked, and his tone indicated that Gold Teeth could do no wrong.

'I have prayed to Christian things.'

And to Gold Teeth's surprise, Ganesh chuckled benevolently. 'And do you think God minds, daughter? There is only one God and different people pray to Him in different ways. It doesn't matter how you pray, but God is pleased if you pray at all.'

'So it is not because of me that my husband has fallen ill?'

'No, to be sure, daughter.'

In his professional capacity Ganesh was consulted by people of many faiths, and with the licence of the mystic he had exploited the commodiousness of Hinduism, and made room for all beliefs. In this way he had many clients, as he called them, many satisfied clients.

Henceforward Gold Teeth not only pasted Ramprasad's pale forehead with the sacred ash Ganesh had prescribed, but mixed substantial amounts with his food. Ramprasad's appetite, enormous even in sickness, diminished; and he shortly entered into a visible and alarming decline that mystified his wife.

She fed him more ash than before, and when it was exhausted

and Ramprasad perilously macerated, she fell back on the Hindu wife's last resort. She took her husband home to her mother. That venerable lady, my grandmother, lived with us in Port-of-Spain.

Ramprasad was tall and skeletal, and his face was grey. The virile voice that had expounded a thousand theological points and recited a hundred *puranas* was now a wavering whisper. We cooped him up in a room called, oddly, 'the pantry'. It had never been used as a pantry and one can only assume that the architect had so designated it some forty years before. It was a tiny room. If you wished to enter the pantry you were compelled, as soon as you opened the door, to climb on to the bed: it fitted the room to a miracle. The lower half of the walls were concrete, the upper close lattice-work; there were no windows.

My grandmother had her doubts about the suitability of the room for a sick man. She was worried about the lattice-work. It let in air and light, and Ramprasad was not going to die from these things if she could help it. With cardboard, oil-cloth and canvas she made the lattice-work air-proof and light-proof.

And, sure enough, within a week Ramprasad's appetite returned, insatiable and insistent as before. My grandmother claimed all the credit for this, though Gold Teeth knew that the ash she had fed him had not been without effect. Then she realized with horror that she had ignored a very important thing. The house in Cunupia had been tied and no spirits could enter, but the house in the city had been given no such protection and any spirit could come and go as it chose. The problem was pressing.

Ganesh was out of the question. By giving his services free he had made it impossible for Gold Teeth to call him in again. But thinking in this way of Ganesh, she remembered his words: 'It doesn't matter how you pray, but God is pleased if you pray at all.'

Why not, then, bring Christianity into play again?

She didn't want to take any chances this time. She decided to tell Ramprasad.

He was propped up in bed, and eating. When Gold Teeth opened the door he stopped eating and blinked at the unwonted light. Gold Teeth, stepping into the doorway and filling it, shadowed the room once more and he went on eating. She placed the palms of her hand on the bed. It creaked.

'Man,' she said.

Ramprasad continued to eat.

'Man,' she said in English, 'I thinking about going to the church to pray. You never know, and it better to be on the safe side. After all, the house ain't tied—'

'I don't want you to pray in no church,' he whispered, in English too.

Gold Teeth did the only thing she could do. She began to cry.

Three days in succession she asked his permission to go to church, and his opposition weakened in the face of her tears. He was now, besides, too weak to oppose anything. Although his appetite had returned, he was still very ill and very weak, and every day his condition became worse.

On the fourth day he said to Gold Teeth, 'Well, pray to Jesus and go to church, if it will put your mind at rest.'

And Gold Teeth straight away set about putting her mind at rest. Every morning she took the trolley-bus to the Holy Rosary Church, to offer worship in her private way. Then she was emboldened to bring a crucifix and pictures of the Virgin and the Messiah into the house. We were all somewhat worried by this, but Gold Teeth's religious nature was well known to us; her husband was a learned pundit and when all was said and done this was an emergency, a matter of life and death. So we could do nothing but look on. Incense and camphor and ghee burned now before the likeness of Krishna and Shiva as well as Mary and Jesus. Gold Teeth revealed an appetite for prayer that equalled her husband's for food, and we marvelled at both, if only because neither prayer nor food seemed to be of any use to Ramprasad.

One evening, shortly after bell and gong and conch-shell had announced that Gold Teeth's official devotions were almost over, a sudden chorus of lamentation burst over the house, and I was summoned to the room reserved for prayer. 'Come quickly, something dreadful has happened to your aunt.'

The prayer-room, still heavy with fumes of incense, presented an extraordinary sight. Before the Hindu shrine, flat on her face, Gold Teeth lay prostrate, rigid as a sack of flour. I had only seen Gold Teeth standing or sitting, and the aspect of Gold Teeth prostrate, so novel and so grotesque, was disturbing.

My grandmother, an alarmist by nature, bent down and put her ear to the upper half of the body on the floor. 'I don't seem to hear her heart,' she said.

We were all somewhat terrified. We tried to lift Gold Teeth

but she seemed as heavy as lead. Then, slowly, the body quivered. The flesh beneath the clothes rippled, then billowed, and the children in the room sharpened their shrieks. Instinctively we all stood back from the body and waited to see what was going to happen. Gold Teeth's hand began to pound the floor and at the same time she began to gurgle.

My grandmother had grasped the situation. 'She's got the spirit,' she said.

At the word 'spirit', the children shrieked louder, and my grandmother slapped them into silence.

The gurgling resolved itself into words pronounced with a lingering ghastly quaver. 'Hail Mary, Hail Ram,' Gold Teeth said, 'the snakes are after me. Everywhere snakes. Seven snakes. Rama! Rama! Full of grace. Seven spirits leaving Cunupia by the four o'clock train for Port-of-Spain.'

My grandmother and my mother listened eagerly, their faces lit up with pride. I was rather ashamed at the exhibition, and annoyed with Gold Teeth for putting me into a fright. I moved towards the door.

'Who is that going away? Who is the young *caffar*, the un-believer?' the voice asked abruptly.

'Come back quickly, boy,' my grandmother whispered. 'Come back and ask her pardon.'

I did as I was told.

'It is all right, son,' Gold Teeth replied, 'you don't know. You are young.'

Then the spirit appeared to leave her. She wrenched herself up to a sitting position and wondered why we were all there. For the rest of that evening she behaved as if nothing had happened, and she pretended she didn't notice that everyone was looking at her and treating her with unusual respect.

'I have always said it, and I will say it again,' my grandmother said, 'that these Christians are very religious people. That is why I encouraged Gold Teeth to pray to Christian things.'

Ramprasad died early next morning and we had the announce-ment on the radio after the local news at one o'clock. Ram-prasad's death was the only one announced and so, although it came between commercials, it made some impression. We buried him that afternoon in Mucurapo Cemetery.

As soon as we got back my grandmother said, 'I have always

said it, and I will say it again: I don't like these Christian things. Ramprasad would have got better if only you, Gold Teeth, had listened to me and not gone running after these Christian things.'

Gold Teeth sobbed her assent; and her body squabbered and shook as she confessed the whole story of her trafficking with Christianity. We listened in astonishment and shame. We didn't know that a good Hindu, and a member of our family, could sink so low. Gold Teeth beat her breast and pulled ineffectually at her long hair and begged to be forgiven. 'It is all my fault,' she cried. 'My own fault, Ma. I fell in a moment of weakness. Then I just couldn't stop.'

My grandmother's shame turned to pity. 'It's all right, Gold Teeth. Perhaps it was this you needed to bring you back to your senses.'

That evening Gold Teeth ritually destroyed every reminder of Christianity in the house.

'You have only yourself to blame,' my grandmother said, 'if you have no children now to look after you.'

1954

2 THE RAFFLE

THEY DON'T PAY primary schoolteachers a lot in Trinidad, but they allow them to beat their pupils as much as they want.

Mr Hinds, my teacher, was a big beater. On the shelf below *The Last of England* he kept four or five tamarind rods. They are good for beating. They are limber, they sting and they last. There was a tamarind tree in the schoolyard. In his locker Mr Hinds also kept a leather strap soaking in the bucket of water every class had in case of fire.

It wouldn't have been so bad if Mr Hinds hadn't been so young and athletic. At the one school sports I went to, I saw him slip off his shining shoes, roll up his trousers neatly to mid-shin and win the Teachers' Hundred Yards, a cigarette between his lips, his tie flapping smartly over his shoulder. It was a wine-coloured tie: Mr Hinds was careful about his dress. That was something else that somehow added to the terror. He wore a brown suit, a cream shirt and the wine-coloured tie.

It was also rumoured that he drank heavily at weekends.

But Mr Hinds had a weak spot. He was poor. We knew he gave those 'private lessons' because he needed the extra money. He gave us private lessons in the ten-minute morning recess. Every boy paid fifty cents for that. If a boy didn't pay, he was kept in all the same and flogged until he paid.

We also knew that Mr Hinds had an allotment in Morvant where he kept some poultry and a few animals.

The other boys sympathized with us – needlessly. Mr Hinds beat us, but I believe we were all a little proud of him.

I say he beat us, but I don't really mean that. For some reason which I could never understand then and can't now, Mr Hinds never beat me. He never made me clean the blackboard. He never made me shine his shoes with the duster. He even called me by my first name, Vidiadhar.

This didn't do me any good with the other boys. At cricket I wasn't allowed to bowl or keep wicket and I always went in at number eleven. My consolation was that I was spending only two terms at the school before going on to Queen's Royal College. I didn't want to go to QRC so much as I wanted to get away from Endeavour (that was the name of the school). Mr Hinds's favour made me feel insecure.

At private lessons one morning Mr Hinds announced that he was going to raffle a goat – a shilling a chance.

He spoke with a straight face and nobody laughed. He made me write out the names of all the boys in the class on two foolscap sheets. Boys who wanted to risk a shilling had to put a tick after their names. Before private lessons ended there was a tick after every name.

I became very unpopular. Some boys didn't believe there was a goat. They all said that if there was a goat, they knew who was going to get it. I hoped they were right. I had long wanted an animal of my own, and the idea of getting milk from my own goat attracted me. I had heard that Mannie Ramjohn, Trinidad's champion miler, trained on goat's milk and nuts.

Next morning I wrote out the names of the boys on slips of paper. Mr Hinds borrowed my cap, put the slips in, took one out, said, 'Vidiadhar, is your goat,' and immediately threw all the slips into the wastepaper basket.

At lunch I told my mother, 'I win a goat today.'

'What sort of goat?'

'I don't know. I ain't see it.'

She laughed. She didn't believe in the goat, either. But when she finished laughing she said: 'It would be nice, though.'

I was getting not to believe in the goat, too. I was afraid to ask Mr Hinds, but a day or two later he said, 'Vidiadhar, you coming or you ain't coming to get your goat?'

He lived in a tumbledown wooden house in Woodbrook and when I got there I saw him in khaki shorts, vest and blue canvas shoes. He was cleaning his bicycle with a yellow flannel. I was overwhelmed. I had never associated him with such dress and such a menial labour. But his manner was more ironic and dismissing than in the classroom.

He led me to the back of the yard. There *was* a goat. A white one with big horns, tied to a plum tree. The ground around the tree was filthy. The goat looked sullen and sleepy-eyed, as if a little stunned by the smell it had made. Mr Hinds invited me to stroke the goat. I stroked it. He closed his eyes and went on chewing. When I stopped stroking him, he opened his eyes.

Every afternoon at about five an old man drove a donkey-cart through Miguel Street where we lived. The cart was piled with fresh grass tied into neat little bundles, so neat you felt grass wasn't a thing that grew but was made in a factory some-where. That donkey-cart became important to my mother and me. We were buying five, sometimes six bundles a day, and every bundle cost six cents. The goat didn't change. He still looked sullen and bored. From time to time Mr Hinds asked me with a smile how the goat was getting on, and I said it was getting on fine. But when I asked my mother when we were going to get milk from the goat she told me to stop aggravating her. Then one day she put up a sign:

RAM FOR SERVICE
Apply Within For Terms

and got very angry when I asked her to explain it.

The sign made no difference. We bought the neat bundles of grass, the goat ate, and I saw no milk.

And when I got home one lunch-time I saw no goat.

'Somebody borrow it,' my mother said. She looked happy.

'When it coming back?'

She shrugged her shoulders.

It came back that afternoon. When I turned the corner into Miguel Street I saw it on the pavement outside our house. A man I didn't know was holding it by a rope and making a big row, gesticulating like anything with his free hand. I knew that sort of man. He wasn't going to let hold of the rope until he had said his piece. A lot of people were looking on through curtains.

'But why all-you want to rob poor people so?' he said, shout-ing. He turned to his audience behind the curtains. 'Look, all-you, just look at this goat!'

The goat, limitlessly impassive, chewed slowly, its eyes half-closed.

'But how all you people so advantageous? My brother stupid and he ain't know this goat but I know this goat. Everybody in Trinidad who know about goat know this goat, from Icacos to Mayaro to Toco to Chaguaramas,' he said, naming the four corners of Trinidad. 'Is the most uselessest goat in the whole world. And you charge my brother for this goat? Look, you better give me back my brother money, you hear.'

My mother looked hurt and upset. She went inside and came

out with some dollar notes. The man took them and handed over the goat.

That evening my mother said, 'Go and tell your Mr Hinds that I don't want this goat here.'

Mr Hinds didn't look surprised. 'Don't want it, eh?' He thought, and passed a well-trimmed thumb-nail over his moustache. 'Look, tell you. Going to buy him back. Five dollars.'

I said, 'He eat more than that in grass alone.'

That didn't surprise him either. 'Say six, then.'

I sold. That, I thought, was the end of that.

One Monday afternoon about a month before the end of my last term I announced to my mother, 'That goat raffling again.'

She became alarmed.

At tea on Friday I said casually, 'I win the goat.'

She was expecting it. Before the sun set a man had brought the goat away from Mr Hinds, given my mother some money and taken the goat away.

I hoped Mr Hinds would never ask about the goat. He did, though. Not the next week, but the week after that, just before school broke up.

I didn't know what to say.

But a boy called Knolly, a fast bowler and a favourite victim of Mr Hinds, answered for me. 'What goat?' he whispered loudly. 'That goat kill and eat long time.'

Mr Hinds was suddenly furious. 'Is true, Vidiadhar?'

I didn't nod or say anything. The bell rang and saved me.

At lunch I told my mother, 'I don't want to go back to that school.'

She said, 'You must be brave.'

I didn't like the argument, but went.

We had Geography the first period.

'Naipaul,' Mr Hinds said right away, forgetting my first name, 'define a peninsula.'

'Peninsula,' I said, 'a piece of land entirely surrounded by water.'

'Good. Come up here.' He went to the locker and took out the soaked leather strap. Then he fell on me. 'You sell my goat?' Cut. 'You kill my goat?' Cut. 'How you so damn ungrateful?' Cut, cut, cut. 'Is the last time you win anything I raffle.'

It was the last day I went to that school.

1957

3 A CHRISTMAS STORY

THOUGH IT IS Christmas Eve my mind is not on Christmas. I look forward instead to the day after Boxing Day, for on that day the inspectors from the Audit Department in Port-of-Spain will be coming down to the village where the new school has been built. I await their coming with calm. There is still time, of course, to do all that is necessary. But I shall not do it, though my family, from whom the spirit of Christmas has, alas, also fled, have been begging me to lay aside my scruples, my new-found faith, and to rescue us all from disgrace and ruin. It is in my power to do so, but there comes a time in every man's life when he has to take a stand. This time, I must confess, has come very late for me.

It seems that everything has come late to me. I continued a Hindu, though of that religion I saw and knew little save meaningless and shameful rites, until I was nearly eighteen. Why I so continued I cannot explain. Perhaps it was the inertia with which that religion deadens its devotees. It did not, after all, require much intelligence to see that Hinduism, with its animistic rites, its idolatry, its emphasis on mango leaf, banana leaf and – the truth is the truth – cowdung, was a religion little fitted for the modern world. I had only to contrast the position of the Hindus with that of the Christians. I had only to consider the differing standards of dress, houses, food. Such differences have today more or less disappeared, and the younger generation will scarcely understand what I mean. I might even be reproached with laying too great a stress on the superficial. What can I say? Will I be believed if I say that to me the superficial has always symbolized the profound? But it is enough, I feel, to state that at eighteen my eyes were opened. I did not have to be 'converted' by the Presbyterians of the Canadian Mission. I had only to look at the work they were doing among the backward Hindus and Moslems of my district. I had only to look at their schools, to look at the houses of the converted.

My Presbyterianism, then, though late in coming, affected me deeply. I was interested in teaching – there was no other thing a man of my limited means and limited education could do – and my Presbyterianism was a distinct advantage. It gave me a grace in the eyes of my superiors. It also enabled me to be a good teacher, for between what I taught and what I felt there was no discordance. How different the position of those who, still unconverted, attempted to teach in Presbyterian schools!

And now that the time for frankness has come I must also remark on the pleasure my new religion gave me. It was a pleasure to hear myself called Randolph, a name of rich historical associations, a name, I feel, thoroughly attuned to the times in which we live and to the society in which I found myself, and to forget that once – I still remember it with shame – I answered, with simple instinct, to the name of – Choonilal. That, however, is so much in the past. I have buried it. Yet I remember it now, not only because the time for frankness has come, but because only two weeks ago my son Winston, going through some family papers – clearly the boy had no right to be going through my private papers, but he shares his mother's curiosity – came upon the name. He teased, indeed reproached me, with it, and in a fit of anger, for which I am now grievously sorry and for which I must make time, while time there still is, to apologize to him, in a fit of anger I gave him a sound thrashing, such as I often gave in my school-teaching days, to those pupils whose persistent shortcomings were matched by the stupidity and backwardness of their parents. Backwardness has always roused me to anger.

As much as by the name Randolph, pleasure was given me by the stately and *clean* – there is no other word for it – rituals sanctioned by my new religion. How agreeable, for instance, to rise early on a Sunday morning, to bathe and breakfast and then, in the most spotless of garments, to walk along the still quiet and cool roads to our place of worship, and there to see the most respectable and respected, all dressed with a similar purity, addressing themselves to the devotions in which I myself could participate, after for long being an outsider, someone to whom the words *Christ* and *Father* meant no more than *winter* or *autumn* or *daffodil*. Such of the unconverted village folk who were energetic enough to be awake and alert at that hour gaped at us as we walked in white procession to our church. And though their admiration was sweet, I must confess that at the same time it filled me with shame to reflect that not long before I too formed part of the gaping crowd. To walk past their gaze was peculiarly painful to me, for I, more perhaps than anyone in that slow and stately procession, *knew* – and by my silence had for nearly eighteen years condoned – the practices those people indulged in in the name of religion. My attitude towards them was therefore somewhat stern, and it gave me some little consolation to know that though we were in some ways alike, we were distinguished from them not only by our names, which after all no man carries pinned to his lapel, but also by our dress. On these Sundays of which I speak the men wore trousers and jackets of white drill, quite unlike the leg-revealing dhoti which it still pleased those others to wear, a garment which I have always felt makes the wearer ridiculous. I even sported a white solar topee. The girls and ladies wore the short frocks which the others held in abhorrence; they wore hats; in every respect, I am pleased to say, they resembled their sisters who had come all the way from Canada and other countries to work among our people. I might be accused of laying too much stress on superficial things. But I ought to say in my own defence that it is my deeply held conviction that progress is not a matter of outward show, but an attitude of mind; and it was this that my religion gave me.

It might seem from what I have so far said that the embracing of Presbyterianism conferred only benefits and pleasure. I wish to make no great fuss of the trials I had to endure, but it is sufficient to state that, while at school and in other associations my fervent adherence to my new faith was viewed with favour, I had elsewhere to put up with the constant ridicule of those of my relations who continued, in spite of my example, in the ways of darkness. They spoke my name, Randolph, with accents of the purest mockery. I bore this with fortitude. It was what I expected, and I was greatly strengthened by my faith, as a miser is by the thought of his gold. In time, when they saw that their ridiculing of my name had not the slightest effect on me – on the contrary, whereas before I had in my signature suppressed my first name behind the blank initial C, now I spelt out Randolph in full – in time they desisted.

But that was not the end of my trials. I had up to that time eaten with my fingers, a manner of eating which is now so repulsive to me, so ugly, so unhygienic, that I wonder how I managed to do it until my eighteenth year. Yet I must now confess that at that time food never tasted as sweet as when eaten with the fingers, and that my first attempts to eat with the proper implements of knife and fork and spoon were almost in the nature of shameful experiments, furtively carried out; and even when I was by myself I could not get rid of the feeling of self-consciousness. It was easier to get used to the name of Randolph than to knife and fork.

Eating, then, in my determined manner one Sunday lunchtime, I heard that I had a visitor. It was a man; he didn't knock, but came straight into my room, and I knew at once that he was a relation. These people have never learned to knock or to close doors behind them.

I must confess I felt somewhat foolish to be caught with those implements in my hand.

'Hello, Randolph,' the boy Hori said, pronouncing the name in a most offensive manner.

'Good afternoon, *Hori*.'

He remained impervious to my irony. This boy, Hori, was the greatest of my tormentors. He was also the grossest. He strained charity. He was a great lump of a man and he gloried in his brutishness. He fancied himself a debater as well, and many were the discussions and arguments we had had, this lout – he strained charity, as I have said – insisting that to squat on the ground and eat off banana leaves was hygienic and proper, that knives and forks were dirty because used again and again by various persons, whereas the fingers were personal and could always be made thoroughly clean by washing. But he never had *his* fingers clean, that I knew.

'Eating, Randolph?'

'I am having my lunch, *Hori*.'

'Beef, Randolph. You are progressing, Randolph.'

'I am glad you note it, *Hori*.'

I cannot understand why these people should persist in this admiration for the cow, which has always seemed to me a filthy animal, far filthier than the pig, which they abhor. Yet it must be stated that this eating of beef was the most strenuous of my tests. If I persevered it was only because I was strengthened by my faith. But to be found at this juncture – I was in my Sunday suit of white drill, my prayer book was on the table, my white solar topee on the wall, and I was eating beef with knife and fork – to be found thus by Hori was a trifle embarrassing. I must have looked the picture of the over-zealous convert.

My instinct was to ask him to leave. But it occurred to me that that would have been too easy, too cowardly a way out. Instead, I plied my knife and fork with as much skill as I could command at that time. He sat, not on a chair, but on the table, just next to my plate, the lout, and gazed at me while I ate. Ignoring his smile, I ate, as one might eat of sacrificial food. He crossed his fat legs, leaned back on his palms and examined me. I paid no attention. Then he took one of the forks that were about and began picking his teeth with it. I was angry and revolted. Tears sprang to my eyes, I rose, pushed away my plate, pushed back my chair, and asked him to leave. The violence of my reaction surprised him, and he did as I asked. As soon as he had gone I took the fork he had handled and bent it and stamped on it and then threw it out of the window.

Progress, as I have said, is an attitude of mind. And if I relate this trifling incident with such feeling, it is because it demonstrates how difficult that attitude of mind is to acquire, for there are hundreds who are ready to despise and ridicule those who they think are getting above themselves. And let people say what they will, the contempt even of the foolish is hard to bear. Let no one think, therefore, that my new religion did not bring its share of trials and tribulations. But I was sufficiently strengthened by my faith to bear them all with fortitude.

My life thereafter was a lonely one. I had cut myself off from my family, and from those large family gatherings which had hitherto given me so much pleasure and comfort, for always, I must own, at the back of my mind there had been the thought that in the event of real trouble there would be people to whom I could turn. Now I was deprived of this solace. I stuck to my vocation with a dedication which surprised even myself. To be a teacher it is necessary to be taught; and after much difficulty I managed to have myself sent to the Training College in Port-of-Spain. The competition for these places was fierce, and for many years I was passed over, because there were many others who were more fitting. Some indeed had been born of Presbyterian parents. But my zeal, which ever mounted as the failures multiplied, eventually was rewarded. I was twenty-eight when I was sent to the Training College, considerably older than most of the trainees.

It was no pleasure to me to note that during those ten years the boy Hori had been prospering. He had gone into the trucking business and he had done remarkably well. He had bought a second truck, then a third, and it seemed that to his success there could be no limit, while my own was always restricted to the predictable contents of the brown-paper pay-packet at the end of the month. The clothes in which I had taken such pride at first became less resplendent, until I felt it as a disgrace to go to church in them. But it became clear to me that this was yet another of the trials I was called upon to undergo, and I endured it, until I almost took pleasure in the darns on my sleeves and elbows.

At this time I was invited to the wedding of Hori's son, Kedar. They marry young, these people! It was an occasion which surmounted religious differences, and it was a distinct pleasure to me to be again with the family, for their attitude had changed. They had become reconciled to my Presbyterianism and indeed treated me with respect for my profession, a respect which, I fear, was sometimes missing in the attitude of my superiors and even my pupils. The marriage rites distressed me. The makeshift though beautiful tent, the coconut-palm arches hung with clusters of fruit, the use of things like mango leaves and grass and saffron, the sacrificial fire, all these things filled me with shame rather than delight. But the rites were only a small part of the celebrations. There was much good food, strictly vegetarian but somehow extremely tempting; and after a period of distaste for Indian food, I had come back to it again. The food, I say, was rich. The music and the dancers were thrilling. The tent and the illuminations had a charm which not even our school hall had on concert nights, though the marriage ceremony did not of course have the grace and dignity of those conducted, as proper marriages should be, in a church.

Kedar received a fabulous dowry, and his bride, of whose face I had just a glimpse when her silk veil was parted, was indeed beautiful. But such beauty has always appeared to me skin deep. Beauty in women is a disturbing thing. But beyond the beauty it is always necessary to look for the greater qualities of manners and – a thing I always remind Winston of – no one is too young or too old to learn – manners and *ways*. She was beautiful. It was sad to think of her joined to Kedar for life, but she was perhaps fitted for nothing else. No need to speak of the resplendent regalia of Kedar himself: his turban, the crown with tassels and pendant glass, his richly embroidered silk jacket, and all those other adornments which for that night concealed so well the truck-driver that he was.

I left the wedding profoundly saddened. I could not help reflecting on my own position and contrasting it with Hori's or even Kedar's. I was now over forty, and marriage, which in the normal way would have come to me at the age of twenty or thereabouts, was still far from me. This was my own fault. Arranged marriages like Kedar's had no part in my scheme of things. I wished to marry, as the person says in *The Vicar of Wakefield*, someone who had qualities that would wear well. My choice was severely restricted. I wished to marry a Presbyterian lady who was intelligent, well brought up and educated, and wished to marry me. This last condition, alas, I could find few willing to fulfil. And indeed I had little to offer. Among Hindus it would have been otherwise. There might have been men of substance who would have been willing to marry their daughters to a teacher, to acquire respectability and the glamour of a learned profession. Such a position has its strains, of course, for it means that the daughter remains, as it were, subject to her family; but the position is not without its charms.

You might imagine – and you would be correct – that at this time my faith was undergoing its severest strain. How often I was on the point of reneging I shudder to tell. I felt myself about to yield; I stiffened in my devotions and prayers. I reflected on the worthlessness of worldly things, but this was a reflection I found few to share. I might add here, in parenthesis and without vanity, that I had had several offers from the fathers of unconverted daughters, whose only condition was the one, about my religion, which I could not accept; for my previous caste had made me acceptable to many.

In this situation of doubt, of nightly wrestling with God, an expression whose meaning I came only then fully to understand, my fortune changed. I was appointed a headmaster. Now I can speak! How many people know of the tribulations, the pettiness, the intrigue which schoolteachers have to undergo to obtain such promotion? Such jockeying, such jealousy, such ill-will comes into play. What can I say of the advances one has to make, the rebuffs one has to suffer in silence, the waiting, the undoing of the unworthy who seek to push themselves forward for positions which they are ill-qualified to fill but which, by glibness and all the outward shows of respectability and efficiency and piety, they manage to persuade our superiors that they alone can fill? I too had my adversaries. My chief rival – but let him rest in peace! I am, I trust, a Christian, and will do no man the injustice of imagining him to persist in error even after we have left this vale of tears.

In my fortune, so opportune, I saw the hand of God. I speak in all earnestness. For without this I would surely have lapsed into the ways of darkness, for who among us can so steel himself as to resist temptation for all time? In my gratitude I applied myself with renewed dedication to my task. And it was this that doubtless evoked the gratification of my superiors which was to lead to my later elevation. For at a time when most men, worn out by the struggle, are content to relax, I showed myself more eager than before. I instituted prayers four times a day. I insisted on attendance at Sunday School. I taught Sunday School myself, and with the weight of my influence persuaded the other teachers to do likewise, so that Sunday became another day for us, a day of rest which we consumed with work for the Lord.

And I did not neglect the educational side. The blackboards all now sparkled with diagrams in chalks of various colours, projects which we had in hand. Oh, the school was such a pretty sight then! I instituted a rigid system of discipline, and forbade indiscriminate flogging by pupil teachers. All flogging I did myself on Friday afternoons, sitting in impartial judgment, as it were, on the school, on pupils as well as teachers. It is surely a better system, and I am glad to say that it has now been adopted throughout the island. The most apt pupils I kept after school, and for some trifling extra fee gave them private lessons. And the school became so involved with work as an ideal that had to be joyously pursued and not as something that had to be endured, that the usefulness of these private lessons was widely appreciated, and soon larger numbers than I could cope with were staying after school for what they affectionately termed their 'private'.

And I married. It was now in my power to marry virtually anyone I pleased and there were among the Sunday School staff not a few who made their attachment to me plain. I am not such a bad-looking fellow! But I wished to marry someone who had qualities that would wear well. I was nearly fifty. I did not wish to marry someone who was much younger than myself. And it was my good fortune at this juncture to receive an offer – I hesitate to use this word, which sounds so much like the Hindu custom and reminds one of the real estate business, but here I must be frank – from no less a person than a schools inspector, who had an unmarried daughter of thirty-five, a woman neglected by the men of the island because of her attainments – yes, you read right – which were considerable, but not of the sort that proclaims itself to the world. In our attitude to women much remains to be changed! I have often, during these past days, reflected on marriage. Such a turning, a point in time whence so many consequences flow. I wonder what Winston, poor boy, will do when his time comes.

My establishment could not rival Hori's or Kedar's for splendour, but within it there was peace and culture such as I had long dreamed of. It was a plain wooden house, but well built, built to last, unlike so many of these modern monstrosities which I see arising these days: and it was well ordered. We had simple bentwood chairs with cane bottoms. No marble-topped tables with ball-fringed lace! No glass cabinets! I hung my treasured framed teaching diploma on the wall, with my religious pictures and some scenes of the English countryside. It was also my good fortune at this time to get an old autographed photograph of one of our first missionaries. In the decoration of our humble home my wife appeared to release all the energy and experience of her thirty-five years which had so far been denied expression.

To her, as to myself, everything came late. It was our fear, confirmed by the views of many friends who behind their expressions of goodwill concealed as we presently saw much uncharitableness, that we would be unable to have children, considering our advanced years. But they, and we, underestimated the power of prayer, for within a year of our marriage Winston was born.

The birth of Winston came to us as a grace and a blessing. Yet it also filled me with anxiety, for I could not refrain from assessing the difference between our ages. It occurred to me, for instance, that he would be thirty when I was eighty. It was a disturbing thought, for the companionship of children is something which, perhaps because of my profession, I hold especially dear. My anxiety had another reason. It was that Winston, in his most formative years, would be without not only my guidance – for what guidance can a man of seventy give to a lusty youngster of twenty? – but also without my financial support.

The problem of money, strange as it might appear, considering my unexpected elevation and all its accruing benefits, was occupying the minds of both my wife and myself. For my retirement was drawing near, and my pension would scarcely be more than what I subsisted on as a simple pupil teacher. It seemed then that like those pilgrims, whose enthusiasm I admire but cannot share, I was advancing towards my goal by taking two steps forward and one step back, though in my case a likelier simile might be that I was taking one step forward and one step back. So success always turns to ashes in the mouth of those who seek it as ardently as I had! And if I had the vision and the depth of faith which I now have, I might have seen even then how completely false are the things of this world, how much they flatter only to deceive.

We were both, as I say, made restless. And now the contemplation of baby Winston was a source of much pain to both of us, for the poor innocent creature could scarcely know what anguish awaited him when we would both be withdrawn from this vale of tears. His helplessness, his dependence tortured me. I was past the age when the taking out of an insurance policy was a practicable proposition; and during my days as a simple teacher I never had the resources to do so. It seemed, then, that I was being destroyed by my own good fortune, by the fruits of all my endeavour. Yet I did not heed this sign.

I continued while I could giving private lessons. I instituted a morning session as well, in addition to the afternoon one. But I did so with a heavy heart, tormented by the thought that in a few years this privilege and its small reward would be denied me, for private lessons, it must be understood, are considered the prerogative of a headmaster: in this way he stamps his character on the school. My results in the exhibition examinations for boys under twelve continued to be heartening; they far surpassed those of many other country schools. My religious zeal continued unabated; and it was this zeal which, burning in those years when most men in my position would have relaxed – they, fortunate souls, having their children fully grown – it was this surprising zeal, I say, which also contributed, I feel, to my later elevation which, as you will see from the plain narration of these events, I did not seek.

My retirement drew nearer. I became fiercer at school. I wished all the boys under me could grow up at once. I was merciless towards the backward. My wife, poor creature, could not control her anxiety with as much success as myself. She had no occupation, no distracting vocation, in which her anxiety might have been consumed. She had only Winston, and this dear infant continually roused her to fears about his future. For his sake she would, I believe, have sacrificed her own life! It was not easy for her. And it required but the exercise of the mildest Christian charity to see that the reproaches she flung with increased acerbity and frequency at my head were but expressions of her anxiety. Sometimes, I must confess, I failed! And then my own unworthiness would torment me, as it torments me now.

We confided our problems to my wife's father, the schools inspector. Though we felt it unfair to let another partake of our troubles, it is none the less a recognized means of lightening any load which the individual finds too heavy to bear. But he, poor man, though as worried on his daughter's behalf as she was on Winston's, could offer only sympathy and little practical help. He reported that the authorities were unwilling to give me an extension of my tenure as headmaster. My despondency found expression in a display of temper, which he charitably forgave; for though he left the house, promising not to do another thing for us, he presently returned, and counselled patience.

So patient we were. I retired. I could hardly bear to remain at home, so used had I been to the daily round, the daily trials. I went out visiting, for no other reason than that I was afraid to be alone at home. My zeal, I believe, was remarked upon, though I took care to avoid the school, the scene of my late labours. I sought to take in for private lessons two or three pupils whose progress had deeply interested me. But my methods were no longer the methods that found favour! The parents of these children reported that the new headmaster had expressed himself strongly, and to my great disfavour, on the subject, to such a degree, in fact, that the progress of their children at school was being hampered. So I desisted; or rather, since the time has come for frankness, they left me.

The schools inspector, a regular visitor now at our humble, sad home, continued to counsel patience. I have so far refrained in this narrative from permitting my wife to speak directly; for

I wish to do nothing that might increase the load she will surely have to bear, for my wife, though of considerable attainments, has not had the advantages of a formal education on which so much stress is nowadays laid. So I will refrain from chronicling the remark with which she greeted this advice of her father's. Suffice it to say that she spoke a children's rhyme without any great care for its metre or rhyme, the last of which indeed she destroyed by accidentally, in her haste, pulling down a vase from the centre-table on to the floor, where the water ran like one of the puddles which our baby Winston so lately made. After this incident relations between my wife and her father underwent a perceptible strain; and I took care to be out of the house as often as possible, and indeed it was pleasant to forget one's domestic troubles and walk abroad and be greeted as 'Headmaster' by the simple village folk.

Then, as it appears has happened so regularly throughout my life, the clouds rolled away and the sky brightened. I was appointed a School Manager. The announcement was made in the most heart-warming way possible, by the schools inspector himself, anticipating the official notification by a week or so. And the occasion became a family reunion. It was truly good to see the harassed schools inspector relaxing at last, and to see father and daughter reasonably happy with one another. My delight in this was almost as great as the delight in my new dignity.

For a school managership is a good thing to come to a man in the evening of his days. It permits an exercise of the most benign power imaginable. It permits a man at a speech day function to ask for a holiday for the pupils; and nothing is as warming as the lusty and sincere cheering that follows such a request. It gives power even over headmasters, for one can make surprise visits and it is in one's power to make reports to the authorities. It is a position of considerable responsibility as well, for a school manager manages a school as much as a managing director manages a company. It is in his power to decide whether the drains, say, need to be remade entirely or need simply be plastered over to look as new; whether one coat of paint or two are needed; whether a ceiling can be partially renovated and painted over or taken out altogether and replaced. He orders the number of desks and blackboards which he considers necessary, and the chalks and the stationery. It is, in short, a dignity ideally suited to one who has led an active life and is dismayed by the prospect of retirement. It brings honour as well as reward. It has the other advantage that school managers are like civil servants; they are seldom dismissed; and their honours tend to increase rather than diminish.

I entered on my new tasks with zeal, and once again all was well at our home. My wife's father visited us regularly, as though, poor man, anxious to share the good fortune for which he was to a large measure responsible. I looked after the school, the staff, the pupils. I visited all the parents of the pupils under my charge and spoke to them of the benefits of education, the dangers of absenteeism, and so on. I know I will be forgiven if I add that from time to time, whenever the ground appeared ripe, I sowed the seed of Presbyterianism or at any rate doubt among those who continued in the ways of darkness. Such zeal was unknown among school managers. I cannot account for it myself. It might be that my early austerity and ambition had given me something of the crusading zeal. But it was inevitable that such zeal should have been too much for some people to stomach.

For all his honour, for all the sweet cheers that greet his request for a holiday for the pupils, the school manager's position is one that sometimes attracts adverse and malicious comment. It is the fate of anyone who finds himself in a position of power and financial responsibility. The rumours persisted; and though they did not diminish the esteem in which I was so clearly held by the community – at the elections, for example, I was approached by all five candidates and asked to lend my voice to their cause, a situation of peculiar difficulty, which I resolved by promising all five to remain neutral, for which they were effusively grateful – it is no good thing for a man to walk among people who every day listen eagerly – for flesh is frail, and nothing attracts our simple villagers as much as scurrilous gossip – to slanders against himself. It was beneath my dignity, or rather, the dignity of my position, to reply to such attacks; and in this situation I turned, as I was turning with growing frequency, to my wife's father for advice. He suggested that I should relinquish one of my managerships, to indicate my disapproval of the gossip and the little esteem in which I held worldly honour. For I had so far succeeded in my new functions that I was now the manager of three schools, which was the maximum number permitted.

I followed his advice. I relinquished the managership of a school which was in a condition so derelict that not even repeated renovations could efface the original gimcrackery of its construction. This school had been the cause of most of the rumours, and my relinquishing of it attracted widespread comment and was even mentioned in the newspapers. It remained dear to me, but I was willing for it to go into other hands. This action of mine had the effect of stilling rumours and gossip. And the action proved to have its own reward, for some months later my wife's father, ever the bearer of good tidings, intimated that there was a possibility of a new school being put up in the area. I was thoroughly suited for its management; and he, the honest broker between the authorities and myself, said that my name was being mentioned in this connection. I was at that time manager of only two schools; I was entitled to a third. He warmly urged me to accept. I hesitated, and my hesitations were later proved to be justified. But the thought of a new school fashioned entirely according to my ideas and principles was too heady. I succumbed to temptation. If now I could only go back and withdraw that acceptance! The good man hurried back with the news; and within a fortnight I received the official notification.

I must confess that during the next few months I lost sight of my doubts in my zeal and enthusiasm for the new project. My two other schools suffered somewhat. For if there is a thing to delight the heart of the school manager, it is the management of a school not yet built. But, alas! We are at every step reminded of the vanity of worldly things. How often does it happen that a person, placed in the position he craves, a position which he is in every way suited to fill, suddenly loses his grip! Given the opportunity for which he longs, he is unable to make use of it. The effort goes all into the striving.

So now it happened with me. Nearly everything I touched failed to go as it should. I, so careful and correct in assessments and estimates, was now found repeatedly in error. None of my calculations were right. There were repeated shortages and stoppages. The school progressed far more slowly than I would have liked. And it was no consolation to me to find that in this moment I was alone, in this long moment of agony! Neither to my wife nor to her father could I turn for comfort. They savoured the joy of my managership of a new school without reference to me. I had my great opportunity; they had no doubt I would make use of it; and I could not bear disillusioning them or breaking into their happiness with my worries.

My errors attracted other errors. My errors multiplied, I tell you! To cover up one error I had to commit twenty acts of concealment, and these twenty had to be concealed. I felt myself caught in a curious inefficiency that seemed entirely beyond my control, something malignant, powered by forces hostile to myself. Until at length it seemed that failure was staring me in the face, and that my entire career would be forgotten in this crowning failure. The building went up, it is true. It had a respectable appearance. It looked a building. But it was far from what I had visualized. I had miscalculated badly, and it was too late to remedy the errors. Its faults, its weaknesses would be at once apparent even to the scantily trained eye. And now night after night I was tormented by this failure of mine. With the exercise of only a little judgement it could so easily have been made right. Yet now the time for that was past! Day after day I was drawn to the building, and every day I hoped that by some miracle it would have been effaced during the night. But there it always stood, a bitter reproach.

Matters were not made easier for me by the reproaches of my wife and her father. They both rounded on me and said with justice that my failure would involve them all. And the days went by! I could not − I have never liked bickering, the answering of insult with insult − I could not reproach them with having burdened me with such an enterprise at the end of my days. I did it for their glory, for I had acquired sufficient to last me until the end of my days. I did it for my wife and her father, and for my son Winston. But who will believe me? Who will believe that a man works for the glory of others, except he work for the glory of God? They reproached me. They stood aside from me. In this moment of need they deserted me.

They were bitter days. I went for long walks through our villages in the cool of the evening. The children ran out to greet me. Mothers looked up from their cooking, fathers from their perches on the roadside culverts, and greeted me, 'Headmaster!' And soon my failure would be apparent even to the humblest among them. I had to act quickly. Failures should be destroyed. The burning down of a school is an unforgiveable thing, but there are surely occasions when it can be condoned, when it is the only way out. Surely this was such an occasion! It is a drastic step. But it is one that has been taken more than once in this island. So I argued with myself. And always the answer was there; my failure had to be destroyed, not only for my own sake, but for the sake of all those, villagers included, whose fates were involved with mine.

Once I had made up my mind, I acted with decision. It was that time of year, mid-November, when people are beginning to think of Christmas to the exclusion of nearly everything else. This served my purpose well. I required – with what shame I now confess it – certain assistants, for it was necessary for me to be seen elsewhere on the day of the accident. Much money, much of what we had set aside for the future of our son Winston, had to go on this. And already it had been necessary to seal the lips of certain officials who had rejoiced in my failure and were willing to proclaim it to the world. But at last it was ready. On Boxing Day we would go to Port-of-Spain, to the races. When we returned the following day, the school would be no more. I say 'we', though my wife had not been apprised of my intentions.

With what fear, self-reproach, and self-disgust I waited for the days to pass! When I heard the Christmas carols, ever associated for me with the indefinable sweetness of Christmas Eve – which I now once more feel, thanks to my decision, though underneath there is a sense of doom and destruction, deserved, but with their own inevitable reward – when I heard carols and Christmas commercials on the radio, my heart sank; for it seemed that I had cut myself off from all about me, that once more I had become a stranger to the faith which I profess. So these days passed in sorrow, in nightly frenzies of prayer and self-castigation. Regret assailed me. Regret for what might have been, regret for what was to come. I was sinking, I felt, into a pit of defilement whence I could never emerge.

Of all this my wife knew nothing. But then she asked one day, 'What have you decided to do?' and, without waiting for my reply, at once drew up such a detailed plan, which corresponded so closely to what I had myself devised, that my heart quailed. For if, in this moment of my need, when the deepest resource was needed, I could devise a plan which might have been devised by anyone else, then discovery was certain. And to my shame,

Winston, who only two or three days before had been teasing me with my previous unbaptized name, Winston took part in this discussion, with no appearance of shame on his face, only thrill and – sad am I to say it – a pride in me greater than I had ever seen the boy display.

How can one tell of the workings of the human heart? How can one speak of the urge to evil – an urge of which Christians more than anyone else are so aware – and of the countervailing urge to good? You must remember that this is the season of good-will. And goodwill it was. For goodwill was what I was feeling towards all. At every carol my heart melted. Whenever a child rushed towards me and cried, 'Headmaster!' I was tormented by grief. For the sight of the unwashed creatures, deprived, so many of them, of schooling, which matters so much in those early years, and the absence of which ever afterwards makes itself felt, condemning a human being to an animal-like existence, the sight of these creatures, grateful towards me who had on so many evenings gone among them propagating the creed with what energy I could, unmanned me. They were proud of their new school. They were even prouder of their association with the man who had built it.

Everywhere I felt rejected. I went to church as often as I could, but even there I found rejection. And as the time drew nearer the enormity of what I proposed grew clearer to me. It was useless to tell myself that what I was proposing had been often done. The carols, the religious services, the talk of birth and life, they all unmanned me.

I walked among the children as one who had it in his power to provide or withhold blessing, and I thought of that other Walker, who said of those among whom I walked that they were blessed, and that theirs was the kingdom of heaven. And as I walked it seemed that at last I had seized the true essence of the religion I had adopted, and whose worldly success I had with such energy promoted. So that it seemed that these trials I was undergoing had been reserved to the end of my days, so that only then I could have a taste of the ecstasy about which I had so far only read. With this ecstasy I walked. It was Christmas Eve. It was Christmas Eve. My head felt drawn out of my body. I had difficulty in assessing the size and distance of objects. I felt myself tall. I felt myself part of the earth and yet removed.

And: 'No!' I said to my wife at teatime. 'No, I will not disgrace

myself by this action of cowardice. Rather, I will proclaim my
failure to the world and ask for my due punishment.'

She behaved as I expected. She had been busy putting up all
sorts of Christmas decorations, expensive ones from the United
States, which are all the rage now, so unlike the simple decorations I used to see in the homes of our early missionaries before
the war. But how changed is the house to which we moved!
How far has simplicity vanished and been replaced by show! And
I gloried in it!

She begged me to change my mind. She summoned Winston
to her help. They both wept and implored me to go through
with our plan. But I was firm. I do believe that if the schools
inspector were alive, he would also have been summoned to
plead with me. But he, fortunate man, passed away some three
weeks ago, entrusting his daughter and grandson to my care; and
this alone is my fear, that by gaining glory for myself I might be
injuring them. But I was firm. And then there started another of
those scenes with which I had become only too familiar, and the
house which that morning was filled with the enthusiasm of
Winston was changed into one of mourning. Winston sobbed,
tears running down his plump cheeks and down his well-shaped
nose to his firm top lip, pleading with me to burn the school
down, and generally behaving as though I had deprived him of
a bonfire. And then a number of things were destroyed by his
mother, and she left the house with Winston, vowing never to
see me again, never to be involved in the disgrace which was
sure to come.

And so here I sit, waiting not for Christmas, but in this
house where the autographed photograph of one of our earliest
missionaries gazes down at me through his rich beard and luxuri-
ant eyebrows, and where the walls carry so many reminders of
my past life of endeavour and hardship and struggle and triumph
and also, alas, final failure, I wait for the day after Boxing Day,
after the races to which we were to have gone, for the visit of the
inspectors of the Audit Department. The house is lonely and
dark. The radios play the Christmas songs. I am very lonely. But
I am strong. And here I lay down my pen. My hand tires; the
beautiful letters we were taught to fashion at the mission school
have begun to weaken and to straggle untidily over the ruled
paper; and someone is knocking.

*   *   *

December 27. How can one speak of the ways of the world, how can one speak of the tribulations that come one's way? Even expiation is denied me. For even as I wrote the last sentence of the above account, there came a knocking at my door, and I went to open unto him who knocked. And lo, there was a boy, bearing tidings. And behold, towards the west the sky had reddened. The boy informed me that the school was ablaze. What could I do? My world fell about my ears. Even final expiation, final triumph, it seemed, was denied me. Certain things are not for me. In this moment of anguish and despair my first thought was for my wife. Where had she gone? I went out to seek her. When I returned, after a fruitless errand, I discovered that she and Winston had come back to seek me. Smiling through our tears, we embraced. So it was Christmas after all for us. And, with lightened heart, made heavy only by my wrestling with the Lord, we went to the races on Boxing Day, yesterday. We did not gamble. It is against our principles. The inspectors from the Audit Department sent word today that they would not, after all, come.

1962

I WALKED UP the back stairs into the veranda, white in the afternoon sun. I could never bring myself to enter that house by the front stairs. We were poor relations; we had been taught to respect the house and the family.

On the right of the veranda was the kitchen, tiled and spruce and with every modern gadget. An ugly Indian girl with a pockmarked face and slack breasts was washing some dishes. She wore a dirty red print frock.

When she saw me she said, 'Hello, Romesh.' She had opened brightly but ended on a subdued tone that was more suitable.

'Hello,' I said softly. 'Is she there?' I jerked my thumb towards the drawing-room that lay straight ahead.

'Yes. Boy, she cries all day. And the baby was so cute too.' The servant girl was adapting herself to the language of the house.

'Can I go in now?'

'Yes,' she whispered. Drying her hands on her frock, she led the way. Her kitchen was clean and pure, but all the impurities seemed to have stuck on her. She tiptoed to the jalousied door, opened it an inch or two, peered in deferentially and said in a louder voice, 'Romesh here, Miss Sheila.'

There was a sigh inside. The girl opened the door and shut it behind me. The curtains had been drawn all around. The room was full of a hot darkness smelling of ammonia and oil. Through the ventilation slits some light came into the room, enough to make Sheila distinct. She was in a loose lemon housecoat; she half sat, half reclined on a pink sofa.

I walked across the polished floor as slowly and silently as I could. I shifted my eyes from Sheila to the table next to the sofa. I didn't know how to begin.

It was Sheila who broke the silence. She looked me up and down in the half-light and said, 'My, Romesh, you are growing up.' She smiled with tears in her eyes. 'How are you? And your mother?'

Sheila didn't like my mother. 'They're all well – all at home are well,' I said. 'And how are you?'

She managed a little laugh. 'Still *living*. Pull up a chair. No, no – not yet. Let me look at you. My, you are getting to be a handsome young man.'

I pulled up a chair and sat down. I sat with my legs wide apart at first. But this struck me as being irreverent and too casual. So I put my knees together and let my hands rest loosely on them. I sat upright. Then I looked at Sheila. She smiled.

Then she began to cry. She reached for the damp handkerchief on the table. I got up and asked whether she would like the smelling salts or the bay rum. Jerking with sobs, she shook her head and told me, in words truncated by tears, to sit down.

I sat still, not knowing what to do.

With the handkerchief she wiped her eyes, pulled out a larger handkerchief from her housecoat and blew her nose. Then she smiled. 'You must forgive me for breaking down like this,' she said.

I was going to say, 'That's all right,' but the words felt too free. So I opened my mouth and made an unintelligible noise.

'You never knew my son, Romesh?'

'I only saw him once,' I lied; and instantly regretted the lie. Suppose she asked me where I had seen him or when I had seen him. In fact, I never knew that Sheila's baby was a boy until he died and the news spread.

But she wasn't going to examine me. 'I have some pictures of him.' She called in a gentle, strained voice: 'Soomintra.'

The servant girl opened the door. 'You want something, Miss Sheila?'

'Yes, Soomin,' Sheila said (and I noticed that she had shortened the girl's name, a thing that was ordinarily not done). 'Yes, I want the snapshots of Ravi.' At the name she almost burst into tears, but flung her head back at the last moment and smiled.

When Soomintra left the room I looked at the walls. In the dim light I could make out an engraving of the Princes in the Tower, a print of a stream lazing bluely beautiful through banks cushioned with flowers. I was looking at the walls to escape looking at Sheila. But her eyes followed mine and rested on the Princes in the Tower.

'You know the story?' she asked.

'Yes.'

'Look at them. They're going to be killed, you know. It's only in the past two days I've really got to understand that picture, you know. The boys. So sad. And look at the dog. Not understanding a thing. Just wanting to get out.'

'It is a sad picture.'

She brushed a tear from her eye and smiled once more. 'But tell me, Romesh, how are you getting on with your studies?'

'As usual.'

'Are you going away?'

'If I do well in the exams.'

'But you're bound to do well. After all, your father is no fool.'

It seemed overbearingly selfish to continue listening. I said, 'You needn't talk, if you don't want to.'

Soomintra brought the snapshot album. It was an expensive album, covered in leather. Ravi had been constantly photographed from the time he had been allowed into the open air to the month before his death. There were pictures of him in bathing costume, digging sand on the east coast, the north coast and the south coast; pictures of Ravi dressed up for Carnival, dressed up for tea parties; Ravi on tricycles, Ravi in motor cars, real ones and toy ones; Ravi in the company of scores of people I didn't know. I turned the pages with due lassitude. From time to time Sheila leaned forward and commented. 'There's Ravi at the home of that American doctor. A wunnerful guy. He looks sweet, doesn't he? And look at this one: that boy always had a smile for the camera. He always knew what we were doing. He was a very smart little kid.'

At last we exhausted the snapshots. Sheila had grown silent towards the end. I felt she had been through the album many times in the past two days.

I tapped my hands on my knees. I looked at the clock on the wall and the Princes in the Tower. Sheila came to the rescue. 'I am sure you are hungry.'

I shook my head faintly.

'Soomin will fix something for you.'

Soomintra did prepare something for me, and I ate in the kitchen – their food was always good. I prepared to face the farewell tears and smiles. But just then the Doctor came. He was Sheila's husband and everyone knew him as 'The Doctor'. He was tall with a pale handsome face that now looked drawn and tired.

'Hello, Romesh.'

'Hello, Doctor.'

'How is she?'

'Not very happy.'

'She'll be all right in a couple of days. The shock, you know. And she's a very delicate girl.'

'I hope she gets over it soon.'

He smiled and patted me on the shoulder. He pulled the blinds to shut out the sun from the veranda, and made me sit down.

'You knew my son?'

'Only slightly.'

'He was a fine child. We wanted – or rather, I wanted – to enter him in the Cow and Gate Baby Contest. But Sheila didn't care for the idea.'

I could find nothing to say.

'When he was four he used to sing, you know. All sorts of songs. In English and Hindi. You know that song – *I'll Be Seeing You?*'

I nodded.

'He used to sing that through and through. He had picked up all the words. Where from I don't know, but he'd picked them up. And even now I don't know half the words myself. He was like that. Quick. And do you know the last words he said to me were "I'll be seeing you in all the old familiar places"? When Sheila heard that he was dead she looked at me and began to cry. "I'll be seeing you," she said.'

I didn't look at him.

'It makes you think, doesn't it? Makes you think about life. Here today. Gone tomorrow. It makes you think about life and death, doesn't it? But here I go, philosophizing again. Why don't you start giving lessons to children?' he asked me abruptly. 'You could make tons of money that way. I know a boy who's making fifty dollars a month by giving lessons one afternoon a week.'

'I am busy with my exams.'

He paid no attention. 'Tell me, have you seen the pictures we took of Ravi last Carnival?'

I hadn't the heart to say yes.

'Soomin,' he called, 'bring the photograph album.'

1950

5 THE NIGHTWATCHMAN'S OCCURRENCE BOOK

November 21. 10.30 p.m. C. A. Cavander takes over duty at C – Hotel all corrected. *Cesar Alwyn Cavander*

7 a.m. C. A. Cavander hand over duty to Mr Vignales at C – Hotel no report. *Cesar Alwyn Cavander*

November 22. 10.30 p.m. C. A. Cavander take over duty at C – Hotel no report. *Cesar Alwyn Cavander*

7 a.m. C. A. Cavander hand over duty to Mr Vignales at C – Hotel all corrected. *Cesar Alwyn Cavander*

> This is the third occasion on which I have found C. A. Cavander, Nightwatchman, asleep on duty. Last night, at 12.45 a.m., I found him sound asleep in a rocking chair in the hotel lounge. Nightwatchman Cavander has therefore been dismissed.
> Nightwatchman Hillyard: This book is to be known in future as 'The Nightwatchman's Occurrence Book'. In it I shall expect to find a detailed account of everything that happens in the hotel tonight. Be warned by the example of ex-Nightwatchman Cavander. *W. A. G. Inskip, Manager*

Mr Manager, remarks noted. You have no worry where I am concern sir. *Charles Ethelbert Hillyard, Nightwatchman*

November 23. 11 p.m. Nightwatchman Hillyard take over duty at C – Hotel with one torch light 2 fridge keys and room keys 1, 3, 6, 10 and 13. Also 25 cartoons Carib Beer and 7 cartoons Heineken and 2 cartoons American cigarettes. Beer cartoons intact Bar intact all corrected no report. *Charles Ethelbert Hillyard*

7 a.m. Nightwatchman Hillyard hand over duty to Mr Vignales at C – Hotel with one torch light 2 fridge keys and room keys, 1, 3, 6, 10 and 13. 32 cartoons beer. Bar intact all corrected no report. *Charles Ethelbert Hillyard*

> Nightwatchman Hillyard: Mr Wills complained bitterly to me this morning that last night he was denied entry to the bar by

you. I wonder if you know exactly what the purpose of this hotel is. In future all hotel guests are to be allowed entry to the bar at whatever time they choose. It is your duty simply to note what they take. This is one reason why the hotel provides a certain number of beer cartons (please note the spelling of this word). *W. A. G. Inskip*

Mr Manager, remarks noted. I sorry I didnt get the chance to take some education sir. *Chas. Ethelbert Hillyard*

November 24. 11 p.m. N. W. Hillyard take over duty with one Torch, 1 Bar Key, 2 Fridge Keys, 32 cartons Beer, all intact. 12 Midnight Bar close and Barman left leaving Mr Wills and others in Bar, and they left at 1 a.m. Mr Wills took 16 Carib Beer, Mr Wilson 8, Mr Percy 8. At 2 a.m. Mr Wills come back in the bar and take Carib and some bread, he cut his hand trying to cut the bread, so please dont worry about the stains on the carpet sir. At 6 a.m. Mr Wills come back for some soda water. It didn't have any so he take a ginger beer instead. Sir you see it is my intention to do this job good sir, I cant see how Nightwatchman Cavander could fall asleep on this job sir. *Chas. Ethelbert Hillyard*

You always seem sure of the time, and guests appear to be in the habit of entering the bar on the hour. You will kindly note the exact time. The clock from the kitchen is left on the window near the switches. You can use this clock but you MUST replace it every morning before you go off duty. *W. A. G. Inskip*

Noted. *Chas. Ethelbert Hillyard*

November 25. Midnight Bar close and 12.23 a.m. Barman left leaving Mr Wills and others in Bar. Mr Owen take bottles Carib, Mr Wilson 6 Bottles Heineken, Mr Wills 18 Carib and they left at 2.52 a.m. Nothing unusual. Mr Wills was helpless, I don't see how anybody could drink so much, eighteen one man alone, this work enough to turn anybody Seventh Day Adventist, and another man come in the bar, I dont know his name, I hear they call him Paul, he assist me because the others couldn't do much, and we take Mr Wills up to his room and take off his boots and slack his other clothes and then we left. Don't know sir if they did take more while I was away, nothing was mark on the Pepsi Cola board, but they was drinking still, it look as if they come back and take some more, but with Mr Wills I want some extra assistance sir.

Mr Manager, the clock break I find it break when I come back from Mr Wills room sir. It stop 3.19 sir. *Chas. E. Hillyard*

> More than 2 lbs of veal were removed from the Fridge last night, and a cake that was left in the press was cut. It is your duty, Nightwatchman Hillyard, to keep an eye on these things. I ought to warn you that I have also asked the Police to check on all employees leaving the hotel, to prevent such occurrences in the future. *W. A. G. Inskip*

Mr Manager, I don't know why people so anxious to blame servants sir. About the cake, the press lock at night and I dont have the key sir, everything safe where I am concern sir. *Chas. Hillyard*

November 26. Midnight Bar close and Barman left. Mr Wills didn't come, I hear he at the American base tonight, all quiet, nothing unusual.

Mr Manager, I request one thing. Please inform the Barman to let me know sir when there is a female guest in the hotel sir. *C. E. Hillyard*

> This morning I received a report from a guest that there were screams in the hotel during the night. You wrote All Quiet. Kindly explain in writing. *W. A. G. Inskip*
> Write Explanation here:

EXPLANATION. Not long after midnight the telephone ring and a woman ask for Mr Jimminez. I try to tell her where he was but she say she cant hear properly. Fifteen minutes later she came in a car, she was looking vex and sleepy, and I went up to call him. The door was not lock, I went in and touch his foot and call him very soft, and he jump up and begin to shout. When he come to himself he said he had Night Mere, and then he come down and went away with the woman, was not necessary to mention.

Mr Manager, I request you again, please inform the Barman to let me know sir when there is a female guest in the hotel. *C. Hillyard*

November 27. 1 a.m. Bar close, Mr Wills and a American 19 Carib and 2.30 a.m. a Police come and ask for Mr Wills, he say the American report that he was robbed of $200.00¢, he was last drinking at C – with Mr Wills and others. Mr Wills and the Police ask to open the Bar to search it, I told them I cannot open the Bar for you like that, the Police must come with the Manager. Then the American say it was only joke he was joking, and they try to get the Police to laugh, but the Police looking the way I feeling. Then laughing Mr Wills left in a garage car as he couldn't drive himself and the American was waiting outside and they both fall down as they was getting in the car, and Mr Wills saying any time you want a overdraft you just come to my bank kiddo. The Police left walking by himself. *C. Hillyard*

> Nightwatchman Hillyard: 'Was not necessary to mention'!! You are not to decide what is necessary to mention in this nightwatchman's occurrence book. Since when have you become sole owner of the hotel as to determine what is necessary to mention? If the guest did not mention it I would never have known that there were screams in the hotel during the night. Also will you kindly tell me who Mr Jimminez is? And what rooms he occupied or occupies? And by what right? You have been told by me personally that the names of all hotel guests are on the slate next to the light switches. If you find Mr Jimminez's name on this slate, or could give me some information about him, I will be most warmly obliged to you. The lady you ask about is Mrs Roscoe, Room 12, as you very well know. It is your duty to see that guests are not pestered by unauthorized callers. You should give no information about guests to such people, and I would be glad if in future you could direct such callers straight to me. *W. A. G. Inskip*

Sir was what I ask you two times, I dont know what sort of work I take up, I always believe that nightwatchman work is a quiet work and I dont like meddling in white people business, but the gentleman occupy Room 12 also, was there that I went up to call him, I didn't think it necessary to mention because was none of my business sir. *C.E.H.*

November 28. 12 Midnight Bar close and Barman left at 12.20 a.m. leaving Mr Wills and others, and they all left at 1.25 a.m. Mr Wills 8 Carib, Mr Wilson 12, Mr Percy 8, and the man they call Paul 12. Mrs Roscoe join the gentlemen at 12.33 a.m., four gins, everybody calling her Minnie from Trinidad, and then they start singing that song, and some others. Nothing unusual. Afterwards there were mild singing and guitar music in Room 12. A man come in and ask to use the phone at 2.17 a.m. and while he was using it about 7 men come in and wanted to beat him up, so he put down the phone and they all ran away. At 3 a.m. I notice the padlock not on the press, I look inside, no cake, but the padlock was not put on in the first place sir. Mr Wills come down again at 6 a.m. to look for his sweet, he look in the Fridge and did not see any. He took a piece of pineapple. A plate was covered in the Fridge, but it didn't have anything in it. Mr Wills put it out, the cat jump on it and it fall down and break. The garage bulb not burning. *C.E.H.*

> You will please sign your name at the bottom of your report. You are in the habit of writing Nothing Unusual. Please take note and think before making such a statement. I want to know what is meant by nothing unusual. I gather, not from you, needless to say, that the police have fallen into the habit of visiting the hotel at night. I would be most grateful to you if you could find the time to note the times of these visits. *W. A. G. Inskip*

Sir, nothing unusual means everything usual. I dont know, nothing I writing you liking. I don't know what sort of work this nightwatchman work getting to be, since when people have to start getting Cambridge certificate to get nightwatchman job, I ain't educated and because of this everybody think they could insult me. *Charles Ethelbert Hillyard*

November 29. Midnight Bar close and 12.15 Barman left leaving Mr Wills and Mrs Roscoe and others in the Bar. Mr Wills and Mrs Roscoe left at 12.30 a.m. leaving Mr Wilson and the man they call Paul, and they all left at 1.00 a.m. Twenty minutes to 2 Mr Wills and party return and left again at 5 to 3. At 3.45 Mr Wills return and take bread and milk and olives and cherries, he ask for nutmeg too, I said we had none, he drink 2 Carib, and left ten minutes later. He also collect Mrs Roscoe bag. All the drinks, except the 2 Carib, was taken by the man they call Paul. I don't know sir I don't like this sort of work, you better hire a night barman. At 5.30 Mrs Roscoe and the man they call Paul come back to the bar, they was having a quarrel, Mr Paul saying you make me sick, Mrs Roscoe saying I feel sick, and then she vomit all over the floor, shouting I didn't want that damned milk.

I was cleaning up when Mr Wills come down to ask for soda water, we got to lay in more soda for Mr Wills but I need extra assistance with Mr Wills Paul and party sir.

The police come at 2, 3.48 and 4.52. They sit down in the bar a long time. Firearms discharge 2 times in the back yard. Detective making inquiries. I don't know sir, I thinking it would be better for me to go back to some other sort of job. At 3 I hear somebody shout Thief, and I see a man running out of the back, and Mr London, Room 9, say he miss 80 cents and a pack of cigarettes which was on his dressing case. I don't know when the people in this place does sleep. *Chas. Ethelbert Hillyard*

Nightwatchman Hillyard: A lot more than 80 cents was stolen. Several rooms were in fact entered during the night, including my own. You are employed to prevent such things occurring. Your interest in the morals of our guests seems to be distracting your attention from your duties. Save your preaching for your roadside prayer meetings. Mr Pick, Room 7, reports that in spite of the most pressing and repeated requests, you did not awaken him at 5. He has missed his plane to British Guiana as a result. No newspapers were delivered to the rooms this morning. I am again notifying you that papers must be handed personally to Doorman Vignales. And the messenger's bicycle, which I must remind you is the property of the hotel, has been damaged. What do you *do* at nights? *W. A. G. Inskip*

Please don't ask me sir.

Relating to the damaged bicycle: I left the bicycle the same place where I meet it, nothing took place so as to damage it. I always take care of all property sir. I dont know how you could think I have time to go out for bicycle rides. About the papers, sir, the police and them read it and leave them in such a state that I didn't think it would be nice to give them to guests. I wake up Mr Pick, room 7, at 4.50 a.m., 5 a.m., 5.15 a.m. and 5.30. He told me to keep off, he would not get up, and one time he pelt a box of matches at me, matches scatter all over the place I always do everything to the best of my ability sir but God is my Witness I never find a nightwatchman work like this, so much writing I dont have time to do anything else, I dont have four hands and six eyes and I want this extra assistance with Mr Wills and party sir. I am a poor man and you could abuse me, but you must not abuse my religion sir because the good Lord sees All and will have

His revenge sir, I don't know what sort of work and trouble I land myself in, all I want is a little quiet night work and all I getting is abuse. *Chas. E. Hillyard*

November 30. 12.25 a.m. Bar close and Barman left 1.00 a.m. leaving Mr Wills and party in Bar. Mr Wills take 12 Carib Mr Wilson 6, Mr Percy 14. Mrs Roscoe five gins. At 1.30 a.m. Mrs Roscoe left and there were a little singing and mild guitar playing in Room 12. Nothing unusual. The police come at 1.35 and sit down in the bar for a time, not drinking, not talking, not doing anything except watching. At 1.45 the man they call Paul come in with Mr McPherson of the S S Naparoni, they was both falling down and laughing whenever anything break and the man they call Paul say Fireworks about to begin tell Minnie Malcolm coming the ship just dock. Mr Wills and party scatter leaving one or two bottles half empty and then the man they call Paul tell me to go up to Room 12 and tell Minnie Roscoe that Malcolm coming. I don't know how people could behave so the thing enough to make anybody turn priest. I notice the padlock on the bar door break off it hanging on only by a little piece of wood. And when I went up to Room 12 and tell Mrs Roscoe that Malcolm coming the ship just dock the woman get sober straight away like she dont want to hear no more guitar music and she asking me where to hide where to go. I dont know, I feel the day of reckoning is at hand, but she not listening to what I saying, she busy straightening up the room one minute packing the next, and then she run out into the corridor and before I could stop she run straight down the back stairs to the annexe. And then 5 past 2, still in the corridor, I see a big man running up to me and he sober as a judge and he mad as a drunkard and he asking me where she is where she is. I ask whether he is a authorized caller, he say you don't give me any of that crap now, where she is, where she is. So remembering about the last time and Mr Jimminez I direct him to the manager office in the annexe. He hear a little scuffling inside Mr Inskip room and I make out Mr Inskip sleepy voice and Mrs Roscoe voice and the red man run inside and all I hearing for the next five minutes is bam bam bodow bodow bow and this woman screaming. I dont know what sort of work this nightwatchman getting I want something quiet like the police. In time things quiet down and the red man drag Mrs Roscoe out of the annexe and they take a taxi, and the Police sitting down quiet in the bar. Then Mr Percy and the others come back one by one to the bar and they talking quiet and they not drinking and they left 3 a.m. 3.15 Mr Wills return and take one whisky and 2 Carib. He asked for pineapple or some sweet fruit but it had nothing.

6 a.m. Mr Wills came in the bar looking for soda but it aint have none. We have to get some soda for Mr Wills sir.

6.30 a.m. the papers come and I deliver them to Doorman Vignales at 7 a.m. *Chas. Hillyard*

Mr Hillyard: In view of the unfortunate illness of Mr Inskip, I am temporarily in charge of the hotel. I trust you will continue to make your nightly reports, but I would be glad if you could keep your entries as brief as possible. *Robt. Magnus, Acting Manager*

December 1. 10.30 p.m. C. E. Hillyard take over duty at C – Hotel all corrected 12 Midnight Bar close 2 a.m. Mr Wills 2 Carib, 1 bread 6 a.m. Mr Wills 1 soda 7 a.m. Nightwatchman Hillyard hand over duty to Mr Vignales with one torch light 2 Fridge keys and Room Keys 1, 3, 6 and 12. Bar intact all corrected no report. *C.E.H.*

1962

6 THE ENEMY

I HAD ALWAYS considered this woman, my mother, as the enemy. She was sure to misunderstand anything I did, and the time came when I thought she not only misunderstood me, but quite definitely disapproved of me. I was an only child, but for her I was one too many.

She hated my father, and even after he died she continued to hate him.

She would say, 'Go ahead and do what you doing. You is your father child, you hear, not mine.'

The real split between my mother and me happened not in Miguel Street, but in the country.

My mother had decided to leave my father, and she wanted to take me to her mother.

I refused to go.

My father was ill, and in bed. Besides, he had promised that if I stayed with him I was to have a whole box of crayons.

I chose the crayons and my father.

We were living at the time in Cunupia, where my father was a driver on the sugar estates. He wasn't a slave-driver, but a driver of free people, but my father used to behave as though the people were slaves. He rode about the estates on a big clumsy brown horse, cracking his whip at the labourers and people said – I really don't believe this – that he used to kick the labourers.

I don't believe it because my father had lived all his life in Cunupia and he knew that you really couldn't push the Cunupia people around. They are not tough people, but they think nothing of killing, and they are prepared to wait years for the chance to kill someone they don't like. In fact, Cunupia and Tableland are the two parts of Trinidad where murders occur often enough to ensure quick promotion for the policemen stationed there.

At first we lived in the barracks, but then my father wanted to move to a little wooden house not far away.

My mother said, 'You playing hero. Go and live in your house by yourself, you hear.'

She was afraid, of course, but my father insisted. So we moved to the house, and then trouble really started.

A man came to the house one day about midday and said to my mother, 'Where your husband?'

My mother said, 'I don't know.'

The man was cleaning his teeth with a twig from a hibiscus plant. He spat and said, 'It don't matter. I have time. I could wait.'

My mother said, 'You ain't doing nothing like that. I know what you thinking, but I have my sister coming here right now.'

The man laughed and said, 'I not doing anything. I just want to know when he coming home.'

I began to cry in terror.

The man laughed.

My mother said, 'Shut up this minute or I give you something really to cry about.'

I went to another room and walked about saying, 'Rama! Rama! Sita Rama!' This was what my father had told me to say when I was in danger of any sort.

I looked out of the window. It was bright daylight, and hot, and there was nobody else in all the wide world of bush and trees.

And then I saw my aunt walking up the road.

She came and she said, 'Anything wrong with you here? I was at home just sitting quite quiet, and I suddenly feel that something was going wrong. I feel I had to come to see.'

The man said, 'Yes, I know the feeling.'

My mother, who was being very brave all the time, began to cry.

But all this was only to frighten us, and we were certainly frightened. My father always afterwards took his gun with him, and my mother kept a sharpened cutlass by her hand.

Then, at night, there used to be voices, sometimes from the road, sometimes from the bushes behind the house. The voices came from people who had lost their way and wanted lights, people who had come to tell my father that his sister had died suddenly in Debe, people who had come just to tell my father that there was a big fire at the sugar-mill. Sometimes there would be two or three of these voices, speaking from different directions, and we would sit awake in the dark house, just waiting, waiting for the voices to fall silent. And when they did fall silent it was even more terrible.

My father used to say, 'They still outside. They want you to go out and look.'

And at four or five o'clock when the morning light was coming up we would hear the tramp of feet in the bush, feet going away.

As soon as darkness fell we would lock ourselves up in the house, and wait. For days there would sometimes be nothing at all, and then we would hear them again.

My father brought home a dog one day. We called it Tarzan. He was more of a playful dog than a watch-dog, a big hairy brown dog, and I would ride on its back.

When evening came I said, 'Tarzan coming in with us?'

He wasn't. He remained whining outside the door, scratching it with his paws.

Tarzan didn't last long.

One morning we found him hacked to pieces and flung on the top step.

We hadn't heard any noise the night before.

My mother began to quarrel with my father, but my father was behaving as though he didn't really care what happened to him or to any of us.

My mother used to say, 'You playing brave. But bravery ain't going to give any of us life, you hear. Let us leave this place.'

My father began hanging up words of hope on the walls of the house, things from the Gita and the Bible, and sometimes things he had just made up.

He also lost his temper more often with my mother, and the time came when as soon as she entered a room he would scream and pelt things at her.

So she went back to her mother and I remained with my father.

During those days my father spent a lot of his time in bed, and so I had to lie down with him. For the first time I really talked to my father. He taught me three things.

The first was this.

'Boy,' my father asked. 'Who is your father?'

I said, 'You is my father.'

'Wrong.'

'How that wrong?'

My father said, 'You want to know who your father really is? God is your father.'

'And what you is, then?'

'Me, what I is? I is – let me see, well, I is just a second sort of father, not your real father.'

This teaching was later to get me into trouble, particularly with my mother.

The second thing my father taught me was the law of gravity.

We were sitting on the edge of the bed, and he dropped the box of matches.

He asked, 'Now, boy, tell me why the matches drop.'

I said, 'But they bound to drop. What you want them to do? Go sideways?'

My father said, 'I will tell why they drop. They drop because of the laws of gravity.'

And he showed me a trick. He half filled a bucket with water and spun the bucket fast over his shoulder.

He said, 'Look, the water wouldn't fall.'

But it did. He got a soaking and the floor was wet.

He said, 'It don't matter. I just put too much water, that's all. Look again.'

The second time it worked.

The third thing my father taught me was the blending of colours. This was just a few days before he died. He was very ill, and he used to spend a lot of time shivering and mumbling; and even when he fell asleep I used to hear him groaning.

I remained with him on the bed most of the time.

He said to me one day, 'You got the coloured pencils?'

I took them from under the pillow.

He said, 'You want to see some magic?'

I said, 'What, you know magic really?'

He took the yellow pencil and filled in a yellow square.

He asked, 'Boy, what colour this is?'

I said, 'Yellow.'

He said, 'Just pass me the blue pencil now, and shut your eyes tight tight.'

When I opened my eyes he said, 'Boy, what colour this square is now?'

I said, 'You sure you ain't cheating?'

He laughed and showed me how blue and yellow make green.

I said, 'You mean if I take a leaf and wash it and wash it and wash it really good, it go be yellow or blue when I finish with it?'

He said, 'No. You see, is God who blend those colours. God, your father.'

I spent a lot of my time trying to make up tricks. The only one I could do was to put two match-heads together, light them, and make them stick. But my father knew that. But at last I found a trick that I was sure my father didn't know. He never got to know about it because he died on the night I was to show it him.

It had been a day of great heat, and in the afternoon the sky had grown low and heavy and black. It felt almost chilly in the house, and my father was sitting wrapped up in the rocking chair. The rain began to fall drop by heavy drop, beating like a hundred fists on the roof. It grew dark and I lit the oil lamp, sticking a pin in the wick, to keep away bad spirits from the house.

My father suddenly stopped rocking and whispered, 'Boy, they here tonight. Listen. Listen.'

We were both silent and I listened carefully, but my ears could catch nothing but the wind and the rain.

A window banged itself open. The wind whooshed in with heavy raindrops.

'God!' my father screamed.

I went to the window. It was a pitch black night, and the world was a wild and lonely place, with only the wind and the rain on the leaves. I had to fight to pull the window in, and before I could close it, I saw the sky light up with a crack of lightning.

I shut the window and waited for the thunder.

It sounded like a steamroller on the roof.

My father said, 'Boy, don't frighten. Say what I tell you to say.'

I went and sat at the foot of the rocking chair and I began to say, 'Rama! Rama! Sita Rama!'

My father joined in. He was shivering with cold and fright.

Suddenly he shouted, 'Boy, they here. They here. I hear them talking under the house. They could do what they like in all this noise and nobody could hear them.'

I said, 'Don't fraid, I have this cutlass here, and you have your gun.'

But my father wasn't listening.

He said, 'But it dark, man. It so dark. It so dark.'

I got up and went to the table for the oil lamp to bring it nearer. But just then there was an explosion of thunder so low it might have been just above the roof. It rolled and rumbled for a long long time. Then another window blew open and the oil lamp was blown out. The wind and the rain tore into the dark room.

My father screamed out once more, 'Oh God, it dark.'

I was lost in the black world. I screamed until the thunder died away and the rain had become a drizzle. I forgot all about the trick I had prepared for my father: the soap I had rubbed into the palms of my hands until it had dried and disappeared.

Everybody agreed on one thing. My mother and I had to leave the country. Port-of-Spain was the safest place. There was too a lot of laughter against my father, and it appeared that for the rest of my life I would have to bear the cross of a father who died from fright. But in a month or so I had forgotten my father, and I had begun to look upon myself as the boy who had no father. It seemed natural.

In fact, when we moved to Port-of-Spain and I saw what the normal relationship between father and son was – it was nothing more than the relationship between the beater and the beaten – when I saw this I was grateful.

My mother made a great thing at first about keeping me in my place and knocking out all the nonsense my father had taught me. I don't know why she didn't try harder, but the fact is that she soon lost interest in me, and she let me run about the street, only rushing down to beat me from time to time.

Occasionally, though, she would take the old firm line.

One day she kept me home. She said, 'No school for you today. I just sick of tying your shoe-laces for you. Today you go have to learn that!'

I didn't think she was being fair. After all, in the country none of us wore shoes and I wasn't used to them.

That day she beat me and beat me and made me tie knot after knot and in the end I still couldn't tie my shoe-laces. For years afterwards it was a great shame to me that I couldn't do a simple thing like that, just as how I couldn't peel an orange. But about the shoes I made up a little trick. I never made my mother buy shoes the correct size. I pretended that those shoes hurt, and I made her get me shoes a size or two bigger. Once the attendant had tied the laces up for me, I never undid them, and merely slipped my feet in and out of the shoes. To keep them on my feet, I stuck paper in the toes.

To hear my mother talk, you would think I was a freak. Nearly every little boy she knew was better and more intelligent. There was one boy she knew who helped his mother paint her house. There was another boy who could mend his own shoes. There was still another boy who at the age of thirteen was earning a good twenty dollars a month, while I was just idling and living off her blood.

Still, there were surprising glimpses of kindness.

There was the time, for instance, when I was cleaning some tumblers for her one Saturday morning. I dropped a tumbler and it broke. Before I could do anything about it my mother saw what had happened.

She said, 'How you break it?'

I said, 'It just slip off. It smooth smooth.'

She said, 'Is a lot of nonsense drinking from glass. They break up so easy.'

And that was all. I got worried about my mother's health.

She was never worried about mine.

She thought that there was no illness in the world a stiff dose of hot Epsom Salts couldn't cure. That was a penance I had to endure once a month. It completely ruined my weekend. And if there was something she couldn't understand, she sent me to the Health Officer in Tragarete Road. That was an awful place. You waited and waited and waited before you went in to see the doctor.

Before you had time to say, 'Doctor, I have a pain—' he would be writing out a prescription for you. And again you had to wait for the medicine. All the Health Office medicines were the same. Water and pink sediment half an inch thick.

Hat used to say of the Health Office, 'The Government taking up faith healing.'

My mother considered the Health Office a good place for me to go to. I would go there at eight in the morning and return any time after two in the afternoon. It kept me out of mischief, and it cost only twenty-four cents a year.

But you mustn't get the impression that I was a saint all the time. I wasn't. I used to have odd fits where I just couldn't take an order from anybody, particularly my mother. I used to feel that I would dishonour myself for life if I took anybody's orders. And life is a funny thing, really. I sometimes got these fits just when my mother was anxious to be nice to me.

The day after Hat rescued me from drowning at Docksite I wrote an essay for my schoolmaster on the subject, 'A Day at the Seaside'. I don't think any schoolmaster ever got an essay like that. I talked about how I was nearly drowned and how calmly

I was facing death, with my mind absolutely calm, thinking, 'Well, boy, this is the end.' The teacher was so pleased he gave me ten marks out of twelve.

He said, 'I think you are a genius.'

When I went home I told my mother, 'That essay I write today, I get ten out of twelve for it.'

My mother said, 'How you so bold-face to lie brave brave so in front of my face? You want me give you a slap to turn your face?'

In the end I convinced her.

She melted at once. She sat down in the hammock and said, 'Come and sit down by me, son.'

Just then the crazy fit came on me.

I got very angry for no reason at all and I said, 'No, I not going to sit by you.'

She laughed and coaxed.

And the angrier she made me.

Slowly the friendliness died away. It had become a struggle between two wills. I was prepared to drown rather than dishonour myself by obeying.

'I ask you to come and sit down here.'

'I not sitting down.'

'Take off your belt.'

I took it off and gave it to her. She belted me soundly, and my nose bled, but still I didn't sit in the hammock.

At times like these I used to cry, without meaning it, 'If my father was alive you wouldn't be behaving like this.'

So she remained the enemy. She was someone from whom I was going to escape as soon as I grew big enough. That was, in fact, the main lure of adulthood.

Progress was sweeping through Port-of-Spain in those days. The Americans were pouring money into Trinidad and there was a lot of talk from the British about colonial development and welfare.

One of the visible signs of this progress was the disappearance of the latrines. I hated the latrines, and I used to wonder about the sort of men who came with their lorries at night and carted away the filth; and there was always the horrible fear of falling into a pit.

One of the first men to have decent lavatories built was Hat, and we made a great thing of knocking down his old latrine.

All the boys and men went to give a hand. I was too small to give a hand, but I went to watch. The walls were knocked down one by one and in the end there was only one remaining.

Hat said, 'Boys, let we try to knock this one down in one big piece.'

And they did.

The wall swayed and began to fall.

I must have gone mad in that split second, for I did a Superman act and tried to prevent the wall falling.

I just remember people shouting, 'O God! Look out!'

I was travelling in a bus, one of the green buses of Sam's Super Service, from Port-of-Spain to Petit Valley. The bus was full of old women in bright bandanas carrying big baskets of eddoes, yams, bananas, with here and there some chickens. Suddenly the old women all began chattering, and the chickens began squawking. My head felt as though it would split, but when I tried to shout at the old women I found I couldn't open my mouth. I tried again, but all I heard, more distinctly now, was the constant chattering.

Water was pouring down my face.

I was flat out under a tap and there were faces above me looking down.

Somebody shouted, 'He recover. Is all right.'

Hat said, 'How you feeling?'

I said, trying to laugh, 'I feeling all right.'

Mrs Bhakcu said, 'You have any pains?'

I shook my head.

But, suddenly, my whole body began to ache. I tried to move my hand and it hurt.

I said, 'I think I break my hand.'

But I could stand, and they made me walk into the house.

My mother came and I could see her eyes glassy and wet with tears.

Somebody, I cannot remember who, said, 'Boy, you had your mother really worried.'

I looked at her tears, and I felt I was going to cry too. I had discovered that she could be worried and anxious for me.

I wished I were a Hindu god at that moment, with two hundred arms, so that all two hundred could be broken, just to enjoy that moment, and to see again my mother's tears.

1955

AND BLUEY IS the hero of this story.

At first Bluey belonged to the Welsh couple in the basement. We heard him throughout the house but we hardly saw him. I used to see him only when I went down to the dustbins just outside the basement window. He was smoky blue; lively, almost querulous, with unclipped wings, he made his cage seem too small.

When the Welsh couple had to go back to Wales – I think Mrs Lewis was going to have a baby – they decided to give Bluey to Mrs Cooksey, the landlady. We were surprised when she accepted. She didn't like the Lewises. In fact, she didn't like any of her tenants. She criticized them all to me and I suppose she criticized me to them. You couldn't blame her: the house was just too full of tenants. Apart from a sitting-room on the ground floor, a kitchen on the landing at the top of the basement steps, and a bedroom somewhere in the basement, the whole of the Cookseys' house had been let. The Cookseys had no children and were saving up for old age. It had come but they didn't know.

Mrs Cooksey was delighted with Bluey. She used to lie in wait behind her half-opened door and spring out at us as we passed through the hall; but now it wasn't to ask who had taken more than his share of the milk or who had left the bath dirty; it was to call us into her room to look at Bluey and listen to him, and to admire the improvements she had made to his cage.

The cage, when I had seen it in the basement window, was an elegant little thing with blue bars to match Bluey's feathers, two toy trapezes, a seed-trough, a water-trough and a spring door. Now every Friday there were additions: Mrs Cooksey shopped on Friday. The first addition was a toy ferris wheel in multi-coloured plastic. The second was a seed-bell; it tinkled when Bluey pecked at it. The third was a small round mirror. Just when it seemed that these additions were going to leave little room for Bluey, Mrs Cooksey added something else. She said it was a friend for Bluey. The friend was a red-beaked chicken emerging from a neatly serrated shell, all in plastic and weighted at the bottom to stay upright.

Bluey loved his toys. He kept the chicken and shell swaying, the trapezes going, the ferris wheel spinning, the seed-bell ringing. He clucked and chattered and whistled and every now and then gave a zestful little shriek.

But he couldn't talk. For that Mrs Cooksey blamed Mrs Lewis. 'They're just like children, d'you see? You've got to train them. But she didn't have the time. Very delicate she was. Just a romp and a giggle all day long.'

Mrs Cooksey bought a booklet, *Your Budgie*, and kept it under the heavy glass ashtray on the table. She said it was full of good hints; and when she had read them, she began to train Bluey. She talked and talked to him, to get him used to her voice. Then she gave him a name: Joey. Bluey never recognized it. When I went down to pay for the milk one Saturday Mrs Cooksey told me that she was also finger-training him, getting him to come out of his cage and remain on her finger. Two or three days later she called me in to get Bluey down from the top of the curtains where he was squawking and shrieking and flapping his wings with energy. He wouldn't come down to calls of 'Joey!' or to Mrs Cooksey's cluckings or at her outstretched finger. I had a lot of trouble before I got him back into his cage.

The finger-training was dropped and the name Joey was dropped. Mrs Cooksey just called him Bluey.

Spring came. The plane tree two back-gardens away, the only tree between the backs of the houses and the back of what we were told was the largest cinema in England, became touched with green. The sun shone on some days and for an hour or two lit up our back-garden, or rather the Cookseys' garden: tenants weren't allowed. Mrs Cooksey put Bluey and his cage outside and sat beside him, knitting a bed-jacket. Sparrows flew about the cage; but they came to dig up Mr Cooksey's cindery, empty flowerbeds, not to attack Bluey. And Bluey was aware of no danger. He hopped from trapeze to trapeze, spun his ferris wheel, rubbed his beak against his little mirror and cooed at his reflection. His seed-bell tinkled, the red-beaked chicken bobbed up and down. Bluey was never to be so happy again.

Coming into the hall late one Friday afternoon I saw that Mrs Cooksey's door was ajar. I let her take me by surprise. Behind her pink-rimmed glasses her watery blue eyes were full of mischief. I followed her into the room.

Bluey was not alone. He had a companion. A live one. It was a green budgerigar.

'He just flew into the garden this morning,' Mrs Cooksey said. 'Really. Oh, he must have been a smart fellow to get away from all those naughty little sparrows. Smart, aren't you, Greenie?'

Greenie was plumper than Bluey and I thought he had an arrogant breast. He wasted no time showing us what he could do. He fanned out one wing with a series of small snapping sounds, folded it back in, and fanned out the other. He could lean over sideways on one leg too, and when he pecked at a bar it didn't look so strong. He was noisier than Bluey and, for all his size, more nimble. He looked the sort of budgerigar who could elude sparrows. But his experience of freedom and his triumph over danger had made him something of a bully. Even while we stood over the cage he baited Bluey. By shrieks and flutterings he attracted Bluey to the ferris wheel. Bluey went, gave the wheel a spin with his beak and stood by to give another. Before he could do so, Greenie flew at him, flapping his wings so powerfully that the sand on the floor of the cage flew up. Bluey retreated, complaining. Greenie outsquawked his complaints. The ferris wheel meant nothing to Greenie; in his wanderings he hadn't picked up the art of making a wheel spin. After some moments he flew away from the wheel and rested on a trapeze. He invited Bluey to the wheel again. Bluey went, and the whole shameful squabble began all over.

Mrs Cooksey was giving little oohs and ahs. 'You have a real friend now, haven't you, Bluey?'

Bluey wasn't listening. He was hurrying away from the wheel to the red-beaked chicken. He pecked at it frenziedly.

'Just like children,' Mrs Cooksey said. 'They'll quarrel and fight, but they are good friends.'

Life became hard for Bluey. Greenie never stopped showing off and Bluey, continually baited and squawked at, retaliated less and less. At the end of the week he seemed to have lost the will even to protest. It was Greenie now who kept the little trapeze going, Greenie who punched the seed-bell and made it ring, Greenie who filled the room with noise. Mrs Cooksey didn't try to teach Greenie to talk and I don't imagine the thought of finger-training him ever entered her head. 'Greenie's a big boy,' she said.

It gave me some pleasure to see how the big boy fretted at the ferris wheel. He shook it and made it rattle; but he couldn't make it spin.

'Why don't you show him, Bluey?' Mrs Cooksey said.

But Bluey had lost interest in all Mrs Cooksey's embellishments, even in the plastic chicken. He remained on the floor of the cage and hardly moved. Finally he stood quite still, his feathers permanently ruffled, shivering from time to time. His eyes were half-shut and the white lined lids looked tender and vulnerable. His feet began to swell until they became white and scaly.

'He's just hopeless,' Mrs Cooksey said, with surprising vehemence. 'Don't blame Greenie. I did my best to train Bluey. He didn't care. And who's paying for it now?'

She was contrite a few days later. 'It isn't his fault, poor little Bluey. He's got ingrowing toe-nails. And his feet are so dirty too. He hasn't had a bath for a long time.'

I stayed to watch. Mrs Cooksey emptied the glass ashtray of pins and paper-clips and elastic bands and filled it with warm water. She turned on the electric fire and warmed a towel in front of it. She put a hand into the cage, had it pecked and squawked at by Greenie, pulled Bluey out and dropped him into the water in the ashtray. Instantly Bluey dwindled to half his size. His feathers stuck to him like a second skin. He was rubbed with carbolic soap, rinsed in the ashtray and dried in the warm towel. At the end he looked damp and dishevelled. 'There you are, Bluey. Dry. And now let's have a look at your nails.' She put Bluey on the palm of her left hand and held a pair of nail scissors to his swollen feet. A month before, given such freedom, Bluey would have flown to the top of the curtains. Now he lay still. Suddenly he shrieked and gave a little wriggle.

'Poor little Bluey,' Mrs Cooksey said. 'We've cut his little foot.'

Bluey didn't recover. His feet became scalier, more swollen and gnarled. A paper-thin growth, shaped like a fingernail, appeared on his lower beak and grew upwards, making it hard for him to eat, impossible for him to peck. The top of his beak broke out into a sponge-like sore.

And now even Greenie no longer baited him.

In summer Mr Cooksey did something he had been talking about for a long time. He painted the hall and the stairs. The paint he used was a dull ordinary blue which quickly revealed extraordinary qualities. It didn't dry. The inside of the door became smudged and dirty and all up the banisters there were streaks of sticky blue from the fingers of tenants. Mr Cooksey painted the door again, adding a notice: WET PAINT PLEASE, with the PLEASE underlined three times. He also chalked warnings on the steps outside. But after a fortnight the paint hadn't dried and it looked as though the door would have to be painted again. Mr Cooksey left notices on the glass-topped table in the hall, each note curter than the last. He had a good command of curt language. This wasn't surprising, because Mr Cooksey was a commissionaire or caretaker or something like that at the head office of an important public corporation. Anyway, it was a big position: he told me he had thirty-four cleaners under him.

I never got used to the wet paint and one day, as I came into the hall, wondering in my exasperation whether I shouldn't wipe the paint off on to the wallpaper, the Cookseys' door opened and I saw Mr Cooksey.

''Ave a drink,' he said. 'Cocktail.'

I feared Mr Cooksey's cocktails: they were too obviously one of the perquisites of his calling. But I went in, wiping my fingers on my evening paper. The room smelled of paint and linseed oil.

Mrs Cooksey sat in her armchair and beamed at me. Her hands were resting a little too demurely on her lap. She clearly had something to show.

The cage on the sewing machine was covered with a blue cloth, part of one of Mrs Cooksey's old dresses. It was late evening, still light outside, but dark inside: the Cookseys didn't like to use more electricity than was strictly necessary. Mr Cooksey passed around his cocktails. Mrs Cooksey refused with a shake of the head. I accepted but delayed sipping, Mr Cooksey sipped.

Muted rustlings and tumblings and cheeps came from behind the blue cloth. Mr and Mrs Cooksey sat silent and listened. I listened.

'Got a new one,' Mr Cooksey said, sipping his cocktail and smacking his lips with a little *pop-pop* sound.

'He came into the garden too?' I asked.

'It's a *she*!' Mrs Cooksey cried.

'*Pop-pop.* Ten bob,' said Mr Cooksey. 'Man wanted twelve and six.'

'And we've got a nesting-box for her too.'

'But we didn't pay for that, Bess.'

Mrs Cooksey went and stood by the cage. She rested her hands on the blue cloth, delaying the unveiling. 'She's the daintiest little thing.'

'Yellow,' said Mr Cooksey.

'Just the sort of mate for Greenie.' And, with a flourish, Mrs Cooksey lifted the blue cloth from the cage.

It wasn't the cage I had known. It was a bigger, cruder thing, made from wire netting, with rudimentary embellishments – just two bars supported on the wire netting. And I saw Greenie alone. He had composed himself to sleep. Yellow I didn't see.

Mrs Cooksey giggled, enjoying my disappointment. 'She's there all right. But *in her nesting-box*!' I saw a small wooden box hanging at the back of the cage. Mrs Cooksey tapped it. 'Come out, Yellow. Let Uncle have a look at you. Come out, come out. We know where you are.' Through the round hole of the box a little yellow head popped out, restlessly turning this way and that. Mrs Cooksey tapped the box again, and Yellow slipped out of the box into the cage.

Yellow was smaller than Greenie or Bluey. She wandered about the cage fussily, inquisitively. She certainly had no intention of going to sleep just yet, and she wasn't going to let Greenie sleep either. She hopped up to where he stood on his bar, his head hunched into his breast, and pecked at him. Greenie shook himself but didn't open his eyes. Yellow gave him a push. Perhaps it was chivalry – though I had never credited Greenie with that – or perhaps he was just too sleepy. But Greenie didn't fight back. He yielded and yielded until he could move no further. Then he went down to the other bar. Yellow followed. When she had dislodged him a second time she lost interest in him and went back into her nesting-box.

'D'you see?' Mrs Cooksey said. 'She's interested. The man at the shop says that when they're interested you can expect eggs in ten days.'

'Twelve, Bess.'

'He told *me* ten.'

I tried to get them off the subject. I said, 'They've got a new cage.'

'Mr Cooksey made it.'

Mr Cooksey pop-popped.

He had painted it too. With the blue paint.

Yellow pushed her head through the hole of her box.

'Oh, she *is* interested.' Mrs Cooksey replaced the blue cloth on the cage. 'We mustn't be naughty. Leave them alone.'

'One of my cleaners,' Mr Cooksey said, pausing and throwing the possessive adjective into relief, 'one of my cleaners keeps chickens and turkeys. Makes a packet at Christmas. Nabsolute packet.'

Mrs Cooksey said, 'I wouldn't like to sell any of my little Greenies and Yellows.'

Abruptly I remembered. 'Where's Bluey?'

I don't think Mrs Cooksey liked being reminded. She showed me where Bluey's cage was, on the floor, overshadowed by an armchair and the bookcase that had few books and many china animals. Alone among the luxurious furnishings of his cage, Bluey stood still, on one foot, his feathers ruffled, his head sunk low.

'I can't throw him out, can I?' Mrs Cooksey shrugged her shoulders. 'I've done my best for him.'

The love life didn't agree with Greenie.

'She's taming him,' Mrs Cooksey said.

He had certainly quietened down.

'P'raps he's missing Bluey,' Mr Cooksey said.

'Hark at him,' said Mrs Cooksey.

Yellow was still eager, restless, inquisitive, going in and out of her box. Mrs Cooksey showed me how cleverly the box had been made: you could slide out the back to see if there were eggs. She counted the days.

'Seven days now.'

'Nine, Bess.'

'Seven.'

Then: 'Greenie's playing the fool,' Mr Cooksey said.

'Look who's talking,' Mrs Cooksey said.

Two days later she met me in the hall and said, 'Something's happened to Greenie.'

I went to look. Greenie had the same unhealthy stillness as Bluey now: his feathers were ruffled, his eyes half-closed, his head sunk into his breast. Yellow fussed about him, not belligerently or playfully, but in puzzlement.

'She *loves* him, d'you see? I've tried to feed him. Milk from an eye-dropper. But he isn't taking a thing. Tell me where it hurts, Greenie. Tell Mummy where.'

It was Friday. When Mrs Cooksey rang up the RSPCA they told her to bring Greenie in on Monday. All during the weekend Greenie deteriorated. Mrs Cooksey did her best. Although it was warm she kept the electric fire going all the time, a luxury the Cookseys denied themselves even in winter. A towel was always warming in front of the fire. Greenie was wrapped in another towel.

On Monday Mrs Cooksey wrapped Greenie in a clean towel and took him to the doctor. He prescribed a fluid of some sort and warned Mrs Cooksey against giving Greenie milk.

'He said something about poison,' Mrs Cooksey said. 'As though I would want to do anything to my Greenie. But you should have seen the doctor. Doctor! He was just a boy. He told me to bring Greenie again on Friday. That's four days.'

When I came in next evening, my fingers stained with blue paint from the door, Mrs Cooksey met me in the hall. I followed her into the room.

'Greenie's dead,' she said. She was very calm.

The door opened authoritatively and Mr Cooksey came in, mackintoshed and bowler-hatted.

'Greenie's dead,' Mrs Cooksey said.

'*Pop-pop.*' Mr Cooksey took off his hat and mackintosh and rested them carefully on the chair next to the sideboard.

In the silence that followed I didn't look at the Cookseys or the cage on the sewing machine. It was dark in the corner where Bluey's cage was and it was some moments before I could see things clearly. Bluey's cage was empty. I looked up at the sewing machine. He was in the cage with Yellow; he drooped on the floor, eyes closed, one swollen foot raised. Yellow paid him no attention. She fussed about from bar to bar, with a faint continuous rustle. Then she slipped through the hole into the nesting-box and was silent.

'She's still *interested*,' Mr Cooksey said. He looked at Bluey. 'You never know.'

'It's no good,' Mrs Cooksey said. 'She loved Greenie.' Her old woman's face had broken up and she was crying.

Mr Cooksey opened doors on the sideboard, noisily looking for cocktails.

Mrs Cooksey blew her nose. 'Oh, they're like children. You get so fond of them.'

It was hard to think of something to say. I said, 'We were all

fond of Greenie, Mrs Cooksey. I was fond of him and I am sure
Mr Cooksey was too.'

'*Pop-pop.*'

'Him? He doesn't care. He's *tough*. D'you know, he had a look
at Greenie this morning. Told me he looked better. But he's
always like that. Look at him. Nothing worries him.'

'Not true, Bess. Was a trific shock. Trific.'

Yellow never came out of her nesting-box. She died two days
later and Mrs Cooksey buried her in the garden, next to Greenie.
I saw the cage and the nesting-box, smashed, on the heap of old
wood Mr Cooksey kept in the garden shed.

In the Cookseys' sitting-room Bluey and his cage took their
place again on the sewing machine. Slowly, week by week, Bluey
improved. The time came when he could stand on both feet,
when he could shuffle an inch or two on the floor of his cage.
But his feet were never completely well again, and the growths
on his beak didn't disappear. The trapezes never swung and the
ferris wheel was still.

It must have been three months later. I went down one Saturday
morning to pay Mrs Cooksey for the milk. I had to get some
change and she had to hunt about for her glasses, then for the vase
in which she kept small change. She poured out buttons from one
vase, pins from another, fasteners from a third.

'Poor old lady,' she kept on muttering – that was how she had
taken to speaking of herself. She fumbled about with more vases,
then stopped, twisted her face into a smile and held out her open
palm towards me. On it I saw two latch keys and a small white
skull, finished, fragile.

'Greenie or Yellow,' she said. 'I couldn't really tell you which.
The sparrows dug it up.'

We both looked at Bluey in his cage.

1957

WE HEARD ABOUT the Dakins before they arrived. 'They're the perfect tenants,' Mrs Cooksey, the landlady, said. 'Their landlady brought them to me personally. She says she's sorry to lose them, but she's leaving London and taking over a hotel in Benson.'

The Dakins moved in so quietly it was some days before I realized they were in the house. On Saturday and Sunday I heard sounds of washing and scrubbing and carpet-sweeping from the flat above. On Monday there was silence again.

Once or twice that week I saw them on the steps. Mrs Dakin was about forty, tall and thin, with a sweet smile. 'She used to be a policewoman,' Mrs Cooksey said. 'Sergeant, I think.' Mr Dakin was as old as his wife and looked as athletic. But his rough, handsome face was humourless. His greetings were brief and firm and didn't encourage conversation.

Their behaviour was exemplary. They never had visitors. They never had telephone calls. Their cooking never smelled. They never allowed their milk bottles to accumulate and at the same time they never left an empty milk bottle on the doorstep in daylight. And they were silent. They had no radio. The only sounds were of scrubbing brush, broom and carpet-sweeper. Sometimes at night, when the street fell silent, I heard them in their bedroom: a low whine punctuated infrequently with brief bass rumbles.

'There's respectable people in every class,' Mrs Cooksey said. 'The trouble these days is that you never know where you are. Look at the Seymours. Creeping up late at night to the bathroom and splashing about together. You can't even trust the BBC people. Remember that Arab.'

The Dakins quickly became the favourite tenants. Mr Cooksey invited Mr Dakin down to 'cocktails'. Mrs Dakin had Mrs Cooksey up to tea and Mrs Cooksey told us that she was satisfied with the appearance of the flat. 'They're very fussy,' Mrs Cooksey said. She knew no higher praise, and we all felt reproached.

*   *   *

It was from Mrs Cooksey that I learned with disappointment that the Dakins had their troubles. 'He fell off a ladder and broke his arm, but they won't pay any compensation. The arm's bent and he can't even go to the seaside. What's more, he can't do his job properly. He's an electrician, and you know how they're always climbing. But there you are, d'you see. *They* don't care. What's three hundred pounds to *them*? But will they give it? Do you know the foreman actually burned the ladder?'

I hadn't noticed any disfigurement about Mr Dakin. He had struck me as a man of forbidding vigour, but now I looked on him with greater interest and respect for putting up so silently with his misfortune. We often passed on the stairs but never did more than exchange greetings, and so it might have gone on had it not been for the Cookseys' New Year's Eve party.

At that time I was out of favour with the Cookseys. I had left a hoard of about fifteen milk bottles on the doorstep and the milkman had refused to take them all at once. For a whole day six partly washed milk bottles had remained on the doorstep, lowering Mrs Cooksey's house. Some unpleasantness between Mrs Cooksey and the milkman had followed and quickly been passed on to me.

When I came in that evening the door of the Cookseys' sitting-room was open and through it came laughter, stamping and television music. Mr Cooksey, coming from the kitchen with a tray, looked at me in embarrassment. He brought his lips rapidly over his false teeth and made a popping sound.

'*Pop-pop.* Come in,' he said. 'Drink. Cocktail.'

I went in. Mrs Cooksey was sober but gay. The laughter and the stamping came from the Dakins alone. They were dancing. Mrs Dakin shrieked whenever Mr Dakin spun her around, and for a man whose left arm was permanently damaged he was doing it quite well. When she saw me Mrs Dakin shrieked, and Mrs Cooksey giggled, as though it was her duty to cheer the Dakins up. The couple from the flat below mine were there too, she on the seat of an armchair, he on the arm. They were dressed in their usual sub-county manner and looked constrained and unhappy. I thought of this couple as the Knitmaster and the Knitmistress. They had innumerable minor possessions: contemporary coffee tables and lampstands, a Cona coffee machine, a record-player, a portable television-and-VHF set, a 1946 Anglia which at the appropriate season carried a sticker: FREE LIFT

TO GLYNDEBOURNE AT YOUR OWN RISK, and a Knitmaster machine which was never idle for long.

The music stopped, Mrs Dakin pretended to swoon into her husband's injured arms, and Mrs Cooksey clapped.

''Elp yourself, 'elp yourself,' Mr Cooksey shouted.

'Another drink, darling?' the Knitmaster whispered to his wife.

'Yes, yes,' Mrs Dakin cried.

The Knitmistress smiled malevolently at Mrs Dakin.

'Whisky?' said Mr Cooksey. 'Beer? Sherry? Guinness?'

'Give her the cocktail,' Mrs Cooksey said.

Mr Cooksey's cocktails were well known to his older tenants. He had a responsible position in an important public corporation – he said he had thirty-four cleaners under him – and the origin and blend of his cocktails were suspect.

The Knitmistress took the cocktail and sipped without enthusiasm.

'And you?' Mr Cooksey asked.

'Guinness,' I said.

'Guinness!' Mr Dakin exclaimed, looking at me for the first time with interest and kindliness. 'Where did you learn to drink Guinness?'

We drew closer and talked about Guinness.

'Of course it's best in Ireland,' he said. 'Thick and creamy. What's it like where you come from?'

'I can't drink it there. It's too warm.'

Mr Dakin shook his head. 'It isn't the climate. It's the Guinness. It can't travel. It gets sick.'

Soon it was time to sing Auld Lang Syne.

The next day the Dakins reverted to their exemplary behaviour, but now when we met we stopped to have a word about the weather.

One evening, about four weeks later, I heard something like a commotion in the flat above. Footsteps pounded down the stairs, there was a banging on my door, and Mrs Dakin rushed in and cried, 'It's my 'usband! 'E's rollin' in agony.'

Before I could say anything she ran out and raced down to the Knitmasters.

'My husband's rollin' in agony.'

The whirring of the Knitmaster machine stopped and I heard the Knitmistress making sympathetic sounds.

The Knitmaster said, 'Telephone for the doctor.'

I went and stood on the landing as a sympathetic gesture. Mrs Dakin roused the Cookseys, there were more exclamations, then I heard the telephone being dialled. I went back to my room. After some thought I left my door wide open: another gesture of sympathy.

Mrs Dakin, Mrs Cooksey and Mr Cooksey hurried up the stairs.

The Knitmaster machine was whirring again.

Presently there was a knock on my door and Mr Cooksey came in. '*Pop-pop*. It's as hot as a bloomin' oven up there.' He puffed out his cheeks. 'No wonder he's ill.'

I asked after Mr Dakin.

'A touch of indigestion, if you ask me.' Then, like a man used to more momentous events, he added, 'One of my cleaners took ill sudden last week. Brain tumour.'

The doctor came and the Dakins' flat was full of footsteps and conversation. Mr Cooksey ran up and down the steps, panting and pop-popping. Mrs Dakin was sobbing and Mrs Cooksey was comforting her. An ambulance bell rang in the street and soon Mr Dakin, Mrs Dakin and the doctor left.

'Appendix,' Mr Cooksey told me.

The Knitmaster opened his door.

'Appendix,' Mr Cooksey shouted down. 'It was like an oven up there.'

'He was cold,' Mrs Cooksey said.

'Pah!'

Mrs Cooksey looked anxious.

'Nothing to it, Bess,' Mr Cooksey said. ''Itler had the appendix took out of all his soldiers.'

The Knitmaster said, 'I had mine out two years ago. Small scar.' He measured off the top of his forefinger. 'About that long. It's a nervous thing really. You get it when you are depressed or worried. My wife had to have hers out just before we went to France.'

The Knitmistress came out and smiled her terrible smile, baring short square teeth and tall gums, and screwing up her small eyes. She said, 'Hallo,' and pulled on woollen gloves, which perhaps she had just knitted on her machine. She wore a tweed skirt, a red sweater, a brown velveteen jacket and a red-and-white beret.

'Appendix,' Mr Cooksey said.

The Knitmistress only smiled again, and followed her husband downstairs to the 1946 Anglia.

'A terrible thing,' I said to Mrs Cooksey tentatively.

'*Pop-pop.*' Mr Cooksey looked at his wife.

'Terrible thing,' Mrs Cooksey said.

Our quarrel over the milk bottles was over.

Mr Cooksey became animated. 'Nothing to it, Bess. Just a lot of fuss for nothing at all. Gosh, they kept that room like an oven.'

Mrs Dakin came back at about eleven. Her eyes were red but she was composed. She spoke about the kindness of the nurses. And then, to round off an unusual evening, I heard – at midnight on a weekday – the sound of the carpet-sweeper upstairs. The Knitmistress complained in her usual way. She opened her door and talked loudly to her husband about the nuisance.

Next morning Mrs Dakin went again to the hospital. She returned just before midday and as soon as she got into the hall she began to sob so loudly that I heard her on the second floor.

I found her in Mrs Cooksey's arms when I went down. Mrs Cooksey was pale and her eyes were moist.

'What's happened?' I whispered.

Mrs Cooksey shook her head.

Mrs Dakin leaned against Mrs Cooksey, who was much smaller.

'And my brother is getting married tomorrow!' Mrs Dakin burst out.

'Come now, Eva,' Mrs Cooksey said firmly. 'Tell me what happened at the hospital.'

'They're feeding him through a glass tube. They've put him on the danger list. And – his bed is near the door!'

'That doesn't mean anything, Eva.'

'It does! It does!'

'Nonsense, Eva.'

'They've got him screened round.'

'You must be brave, Eva.'

We led Mrs Dakin to Mrs Cooksey's sitting-room, made her sit down and watched her cry.

'It burst inside 'im.' Mrs Dakin made a wild gesture across her body. 'They had to cut him clean open, and – *scrape* it out.' Having uttered this terrible word, she abandoned herself to her despair.

'Come now, Eva,' Mrs Cooksey said. 'He wouldn't like you to behave like this.'

We all took turns to look after Mrs Dakin between her trips to the hospital. The news didn't get better. Mrs Dakin had tea with the Cookseys. She had tea with the Knitmistress. She had tea with me. We talked gaily about everything except the sick man, and Mrs Dakin was very brave. She even related some of her adventures in the police force. She also complained.

'The first thing Mr Cooksey said when he came up that evening was that the room was like an oven. But I couldn't help that. My husband was cold. Fancy coming up and saying a thing like that!'

I gave Mrs Dakin many of the magazines which had been piling up on the enormous Victorian dresser in my kitchen. The Knitmistress, I noticed, was doing the same thing.

Mr Cooksey allowed himself to grow a little grave. He discussed the operation in a sad but clinical way. 'When it bursts inside 'em, you see, it poisons the whole system. That's why they had to cut 'im open. Clean it out. They hardly ever live afterwards.'

Mrs Cooksey said, 'He was such a nice man. I am so glad now we enjoyed ourselves on New Year's Eve. It's her I'm really sorry for. He was her second, you know.'

'Aah,' Mr Cooksey said. 'There are women like that.'

I told the Knitmistress, 'And he was such a nice man.'

'Wasn't he?'

I heard Mrs Dakin sobbing in everybody's rooms. I heard her sobbing on the staircase.

Mrs Cooksey said, 'It's all so terrible. Her brother got married yesterday, but she couldn't go to the wedding. She had to send a telegram. They are coming up to see Mr Dakin. What a thing to happen on anybody's honeymoon!'

Mrs Dakin's brother and his bride came up from Wales on a motorbike. Mrs Dakin was at the hospital when they came and Mrs Cooksey gave them tea.

I didn't see Mrs Dakin that evening, but late that night I saw the honeymoon couple running upstairs with bottles wrapped in tissue paper. He was a huge man – a footballer, Mrs Cooksey said – and when he ran up the steps you heard it all over the house. His bride was small, countrified and gay. They stayed awake for some time.

Next morning, when I went down to get the paper, I saw the footballer's motorbike on the doorstep. It had leaked a lot of oil.

Again that day Mrs Dakin didn't come to our rooms. And that evening there was another party in the flat above. We heard the footballer's heavy footsteps, his shouts, his wife's giggles, Mrs Dakin's whine.

Mrs Dakin had ceased to need our solace. It was left to us to ask how Mr Dakin was getting on, whether he had liked the magazines we had sent, whether he wanted any more. Then, as though reminded of some sadness bravely forgotten, Mrs Dakin would say yes, Mr Dakin thanked us.

Mrs Cooksey didn't like the new reticence. Nor did the rest of us. For some time, though, the Knitmaster persevered and he had his reward when two days later Mrs Dakin said, 'I told 'im what you said about the nervousness, and he wondered how you ever knew.' And she repeated the story about the fall from the defective ladder, the bent arm, the foreman burning the ladder.

We were astonished. It was our first indication that the Dakins were taking an interest in the world outside the hospital.

'Well, really!' Mrs Cooksey said.

The Knitmistress began to complain about the noise in the evenings.

'Pah!' Mr Cooksey said. 'It *couldn't* 'ave burst inside him. Feeding through a glass tube!'

We heard the honeymoon couple bounding down the stairs. The front door slammed, then we heard the thunderous stutter of the motorbike.

'He could be had up,' Mr Cooksey said. 'No silencer.'

'Well!' Mrs Cooksey said. 'I am glad *somebody's* having a nice time. So cheap too. Where do you think they're off to?'

'Not the hospital,' Mr Cooksey said. 'Football, more likely.'

This reminded him. The curtains were drawn, the tiny television set turned on. We watched horse-racing, then part of the football match. Mrs Cooksey gave me tea. Mr Cooksey offered me a cigarette. I was back in favour.

The next day, eight days after Mr Dakin had gone to the hospital, I met Mrs Dakin outside the tobacconist's. She was shopping and her bulging bag reflected the gaiety on her face.

'He's coming back tomorrow,' she said.

I hadn't expected such a rapid recovery.

'Everybody at the hospital was surprised,' Mrs Dakin said. 'But it's because he's so strong, you see.' She opened her shopping bag. 'I've got some sherry and whisky and' – she laughed – 'some Guinness of course. And I'm buying a duck, to have with apple sauce. He loves apple sauce. He says the apple sauce helps the duck to go down.'

I smiled at the little family joke. Then Mrs Dakin asked me, 'Guess who went to the hospital yesterday.'

'Your brother and his wife.'

She shook her head. 'The foreman!'

'The one who burned the ladder?'

'Oh, and he was ever so nice. He brought grapes and magazines and told my husband he wasn't to worry about anything. They're frightened now all right. As soon as my husband went to hospital my solicitor wrote them a letter. And my solicitor says we stand a good chance of getting more than three hundred pounds now.'

I saw the Knitmaster on the landing that evening and told him about Mr Dakin's recovery.

'Complications couldn't have been serious,' he said. 'But it's a nervous thing. A nervous thing.'

The Knitmistress opened the kitchen door.

'He's coming back tomorrow,' the Knitmaster said.

The Knitmistress gave me one of her terrible smiles.

'Five hundred pounds for falling off a ladder,' Mr Cooksey said. 'Ha! It's as easy as falling off a log, ain't it, Bess?'

Mrs Cooksey sighed. 'That's what the Labour has done to this country. They didn't do a thing for the middle class.'

'Bent arm! Can't go to the seaside! Pamperin', that's what it is. You wouldn't've found 'Itler pampering that lot.'

A motorbike lacerated the silence.

'Our happy honeymooners,' Mr Cooksey said.

'They'll soon be leaving,' Mrs Cooksey said, and went out to meet them in the hall.

'Whose key are you using?'

'Eva's,' the footballer said, running up the stairs.

'We'll see about that,' Mrs Cooksey called.

* * *

Mrs Dakin said: 'I went down to Mrs Cooksey and I said, "Mrs Cooksey, what do you mean by insulting my guests? It's bad enough for them having their honeymoon spoilt without being insulted." And she said she'd let the flat to me and my 'usband and not to my brother and his wife and they'd have to go. And I told her that they were leaving tomorrow anyway because my husband's coming back tomorrow. And I told her I hoped she was satisfied that she'd spoiled their honeymoon, which comes only once in a lifetime. And she said some people managed to have two, which I took as a reference to myself because, as you know, my first husband died during the war. And then I told her that if that was the way she was going to behave then I could have nothing more to say to her. And she said she hoped I would have the oil from my brother's bike cleaned up. And I said that if it wasn't for my husband being so ill I would've given notice then and there. And she said it was *because* my husband was ill that she didn't give me notice, which any other landlady would've done.'

Three things happened the next day. The footballer and his wife left. Mrs Dakin told me that the firm had given her husband four hundred pounds. And Mr Dakin returned from hospital, no more noticed by the rest of the house than if he had returned from a day's work. No sounds came from the Dakins' flat that evening except for the whine and rumble of conversation.

Two days later I heard Mrs Dakin racing down to my flat. She knocked and entered at the same time. 'The telly's coming today,' she said.

Mr Dakin was going to put up the aerial himself. I wondered whether he was as yet strong enough to go climbing about the roof.

'They wanted ten pounds to do it. But my husband's an electrician and he can do it himself. You must come up tonight. We're going to celebrate.'

I went up. A chromium-plated aeroplane and a white doily had been placed on the television set. It looked startlingly new.

Mrs Dakin emptied a bottle of Tio Pepe into three tumblers.

'To good 'ealth,' she said, and we drank to that.

Mr Dakin looked thin and fatigued. But his fatigue was tinged with a certain quiet contentment. We watched a play about a 400-year-old man who took certain drugs and looked no more than twenty. From time to time Mrs Dakin gave little cries of pleasure, at the play, the television set, and the quality of the sherry.

Mr Dakin languidly took up the empty bottle and studied the label. '*Spanish* sherry,' he said.

Mr Cooksey waylaid me the following day. 'Big telly they've got.'

'Eighteen inch.'

'Those big ones hurt the eyes, don't you find?'

'They do.'

'Come in and have a drink. BBC and Commercial?'

I nodded.

'Never did hold with those commercials. Ruining the country. We're not going to have ours adapted.'

'We're waiting for the colour,' Mrs Cooksey said.

Mrs Cooksey loved a battle. She lived for her house alone. She had no relations or friends, and little happened to her or her husband. Once, shortly after Hess had landed in Scotland, Mr Cooksey had been mistaken by a hostile crowd at Victoria Station for Mussolini, but for the most part Mrs Cooksey's conversation was about her victories over tenants. In her battles with them she stuck to the rules. *The Law of Landlord and Tenant* was one of the few books among the many china animals in the large bookcase in her sitting-room. And Mrs Cooksey had her own idea of victory. She never gave anyone notice. That was almost an admission of defeat. Mrs Cooksey asked me, 'You didn't throw a loaf of stale bread into the garden, did you?'

I said I hadn't.

'I didn't think you had. That's what the other people in this street do, you know. It's a fight to keep this house the way it is, I can tell you. There's the mice, d'you see. You haven't any mice up here, have you?'

'As a matter of fact I had one yesterday.'

'I knew it. The moment you let up these things start happening. All the other houses in this street have mice. That's what the sanitary inspector told me. He said this was the cleanest house in the whole street. But the moment you start throwing food about you're bound to get mice.'

That evening I heard Mrs Dakin complaining loudly. She was doing it the way the Knitmistress did: talking loudly to her husband through an open door.

'Coming up here and asking if I had thrown a loaf of bread into 'er 'orrible little garden. And talking about people having too much to eat these days. Well, if it's one thing I like, it is a warm room. I don't wrap myself up in a blanket and '*uddle* in front of cinders and then come and say that somebody else's room is like an oven.'

Mrs Dakin left her kitchen door open and did the washing up with many bangs, jangles, and clatters. The television sound was turned up and in my room I could hear every commercial, every song, every scrap of dialogue. The carpet-sweeper was brought into action; I heard it banging against walls and furniture.

The next day Mrs Cooksey continued her mice hunt. She went into all the flats and took up the linoleum and put wads of newspaper in the gaps between the floorboards. She also emptied Mrs Dakin's dustbin. 'To keep away the mice,' she told us.

I heard the Dakins' television again that night.

The next morning there was a large notice in the hall. I recognized Mr Cooksey's handwriting and style: WILL THE PERSON OR PERSONS RESPONSIBLE SEE ABOUT THE IMMEDI-ATE REMOVAL OF THE OIL STAINS ON THE FRONT STEPS. In the bathroom there was a notice tied to the pipe that led to the geyser: WILL THE PERSON OR PERSONS WHO HAVE BEEN TAMPERING WITH THIS TAP PLEASE STOP IT. And in the lava-tory: WE NEVER THOUGHT WE WOULD HAVE TO MAKE THIS REQUEST BUT WILL THE PERSON OR PERSONS RESPONSIBLE PLEASE LEAVE THESE OFFICES AS THEY WOULD LIKE TO FIND THEM.

The Dakins retaliated at once. Four unwashed milk bottles were placed on the stains on the steps. An empty whisky bottle was placed, label outwards, next to the dustbin.

I felt the Dakins had won that round.

'Liquor and football pools,' Mr Cooksey said. 'That's all that class spends its money on. Pamperin'! You mustn't upset your-self, Bess. We're giving them enough rope to hang themselves.'

The television boomed through the house that evening. The washing-up was done noisily, the carpet-sweeper banged against walls and furniture, and Mrs Dakin sang loudly. Presently I heard scuffling sounds and shrieks. The Dakins were dancing. This went on for a short time. Then I heard a bath being run.

There was a soft knock on my door and Mrs Cooksey came in. 'I just wanted to find out who was having the bath,' she said.

For some moments after she left the bath continued to run. Then there was a sharper sound of running water, hissing and metallic. And soon the bath was silent.

There was no cistern to feed the geyser ('Unhygienic things, cisterns,' Mr Cooksey said) and the flow of water to it depended on the taps in the house. By turning on a tap in your kitchen you could lessen the flow and the heat of the water from the geyser. The hissing sound indicated that a tap had been turned full on downstairs, rendering the geyser futile.

From the silent bathroom I heard occasional splashes. The hissing sound continued. Then Mr Dakin sneezed.

The bathroom door opened and was closed with a bang. Mr Dakin sneezed again and Mrs Dakin said, 'If you catch pneumonia, I know who your solicitor will have to be writing to next.'

And all they could do was to smash the gas mantle in the bathroom.

It seemed that they had accepted defeat, for they did nothing further the next day. I was with the Cookseys when the Dakins came in from work that afternoon. In a few minutes they had left the house again. The light in the Cookseys' sitting-room had not been turned on and we stared at them through the lace curtains. They walked arm in arm.

'Going to look for a new place, I suppose,' Mrs Cooksey said.

There was a knock and the Knitmistress came in, her smile brilliant and terrible even in the gloom. She said, 'Hullo.' Then she addressed Mrs Cooksey: 'Our lights have gone.'

'Power failure,' Mr Cooksey said. But the street lights were on. The light in the Cookseys' room was turned on but nothing happened.

Mrs Cooksey's face fell.

'Fuse,' Mr Cooksey said briskly. He regarded himself as an electrical expert. With the help of a candle he selected fuse wire, went down to the fuse box, urged us to turn off all lights and fires and stoves, and set to work. The wire fused again. And again.

'He's been *up* to something,' Mr Cooksey said.

But we couldn't find out what that was. The Dakins had secured their rooms with new Yale locks.

The Knitmistress complained.

'It's no use, Bess,' Mr Cooksey said. 'You'll just have to give them notice. Never *did* hold with that class of people anyway.'

*   *   *

And defeat was made even more bitter because it turned out that victory had been very close. After Mrs Cooksey asked them to leave, the Dakins announced that they had used part of the compensation money to pay down on a house and were just about to give notice themselves. They packed and left without saying goodbye.

Three weeks later the Dakins' flat was taken over by a middle-aged lady with a fat shining dachshund called Nicky. Her letters were posted on from a ladies' club whose terrifying interiors I had often glimpsed from the top of a number sixteen bus.

1957

9 THE HEART

WHEN THEY DECIDED that the only way to teach Hari to swim would be to throw him into the sea, Hari dropped out of the sea scouts. Every Monday afternoon for a term he had put on the uniform, practised rowing on the school grounds, and learned to run up signals and make knots. The term before he had dropped out of the boy scouts, to avoid going to camp. At the school sports the term before that he had entered for all the races for the under-elevens, but when the time came he was too shy to strip (the emblem of his house had been fancifully embroidered on his vest by his mother), and he didn't run.

Hari was an only child. He was ten and had a weak heart. The doctors had advised against over-exertion and excitement, and Hari was unexercised and fat. He would have liked to play cricket, fancying himself as a fast bowler, but he was never picked for any of the form teams. He couldn't run quickly, he couldn't bowl, he couldn't bat, and he threw like a girl. He would also have liked to whistle, but he could only make hissing noises through his small plump lips. He had an almost Chinese passion for neatness. He wrote with a blotter below his hand and blotted each line as he wrote; he crossed out with the help of a ruler. His books were clean and unmarked, except on the fly-leaf, where his name had been written by his father. He would have passed unnoticed at school if he hadn't been so well provided with money. This made him unpopular and attracted bullies. His expensive fountain pens were always stolen; and he had learned to stay away from the tuck shop.

Most of the boys from Hari's district who went to the school used Jameson Street. Hari wished to avoid this street. The only way he could do this was to go down Rupert Street. And at the bottom of that street, just where he turned right, there was the house with the Alsatians.

The house stood on the right-hand corner and walking on the other side would have made his cowardice plain, to dogs and passers-by. The Alsatians bounded down from the veranda, barking, leapt against the wire fence and made it shake. Their paws touched the top of the fence and it always seemed to Hari that with a little effort they could jump right over. Sometimes a thin old lady with glasses and grey hair and an irritable expression limped out to the veranda and called in a squeaky voice to the Alsatians. At once they stopped barking, forgot Hari, ran up to the veranda and wagged their heavy tails, as though apologizing for the noise and at the same time asking to be congratulated. The old lady tapped them on the head and they continued to wag their tails; if she slapped them hard they moved away with their heads bowed, their tails between their legs, and lay down on the veranda, gazing out, blinking, their muzzles beneath their forelegs.

Hari envied the old lady her power over the dogs. He was glad when she came out; but he also felt ashamed of his own fear and weakness.

The city was full of unlicensed mongrels who barked in relay all through the day and night. Of these dogs Hari was not afraid. They were thin and starved and cowardly. To drive them away one had only to bend down as though reaching for a stone; it was a gesture the street dogs all understood. But it didn't work with the Alsatians; it merely aggravated their fury.

Four times a day – he went home for lunch – Hari had to pass the Alsatians, hear their bark and breath, see their long white teeth, black lips and red tongues, see their eager, powerful bodies, taller than he when they leapt against the fence. He took his revenge on the street dogs. He picked up imaginary stones; and the street dogs always bolted.

When Hari asked for a bicycle he didn't mention the boys in Jameson Street or the Alsatians in Rupert Street. He spoke about the sun and his fatigue. His parents had misgivings about the bicycle, but Hari learned to ride without accident. And then, with the power of his bicycle, he was no longer afraid of the dogs in Rupert Street. The Alsatians seldom barked at passing cyclists. So Hari stopped in front of the house at the corner, and when the Alsatians ran down from the veranda he pretended to throw things at them until they were thoroughly enraged and their breath grew loud. Then he cycled slowly away, the Alsatians following along the fence to the end of the lot, growling with anger and frustration. Once, when the old lady came out, Hari pretended he had stopped only to tie his laces.

Hari's school was in a quiet, open part of the city. The streets were wide and there were no pavements, only broad, well-kept grass verges. The verges were not level; every few yards there were shallow trenches which drained off the water from the road. Hari liked cycling on the verges, gently rising and falling.

Late one Friday afternoon Hari was cycling back from school after a meeting of the Stamp Club (he had joined that after leaving the sea scouts and with the large collections and expensive albums given him by his father he enjoyed a continuing esteem). It was growing dark as Hari cycled along the verge, falling and rising, looking down at the grass.

In a trench he saw the body of an Alsatian.

The bicycle rolled down into the trench and over the thick tail of the dog. The dog rose and, without looking at Hari, shook himself. Then Hari saw another Alsatian. And another. Steering to avoid them he ran into more. They lay in the trenches and all over the verge. They were of varying colours; one was brown-black. Hari had not pedalled since he had seen the first dog and was now going so slowly he felt he was losing his balance. From behind came a low, brief bark, like a sneeze. At this, energy returned to him. He rode on to the asphalt and it was only then, as though they too had just recovered from their surprise, that the Alsatians all rose and came after him. He pedalled, staring ahead, not looking at what was behind him or beside him. Three Alsatians, the brown-black one among them, were running abreast of his bicycle. Calmly, as he pedalled, Hari waited for their attack. But they only ran beside him, not barking. The bicycle hummed; the dogs' paws on the asphalt sounded like pigeons' feet on a tin roof. And then Hari felt that the savagery of the Alsatians was casual, without anger or malice: an evening gathering, an evening's pleasure. He fixed his eyes on the main road at the end, with the street lamps just going on, the lighted trolley-buses, the motor-cars, the people.

Then he was there. The Alsatians had dropped behind. He didn't look for them. It was only when he was in the main road, with the trolley-poles sparking blue in the night already fallen, that he realized how frightened he had been, how close to painful death from the teeth of those happy dogs. His heart beat fast, from the exertion. Then he felt a sharp pain he had never known before. He gave a choked, deep groan and fell off the bicycle.

* * *

He spent a month in a nursing home and didn't go to school for the rest of that term. But he was well enough again when the new term began. It was decided that he should give up the bicycle; and his father changed his hours of work so that he could drive Hari to and from the school.

His birthday fell early that term, and when he was driven home from school in the afternoon his mother handed him a basket and said, 'Happy birthday!'

It was a puppy.

'He won't bite you,' his mother said. 'Touch him and see.'

'Let me see you touch him,' Hari said.

'You must touch him,' his mother said. 'He is yours. You must get him used to you. They are one-man dogs.'

He thought of the old lady with the squeaky voice and he held out his hand to the puppy. The puppy licked it and pressed a damp nose against it. Hari was tickled. He burst out laughing, felt the puppy's hair and the puppy rubbed against his hand; he passed his hand over the puppy's muzzle, then he lifted the puppy and the puppy licked his face and Hari was tickled into fresh laughter.

The puppy had small sharp teeth and liked to pretend that he was biting. Hari liked the feel of his teeth; there was friendliness in them, and soon there would be power. His power. 'They are one-man dogs,' his mother said.

He got his father to drive to school down Rupert Street. Sometimes he saw the Alsatians. Then he thought of his own dog, and felt protected and revenged. They drove up and down the street with grass verges along which he had been chased by the Alsatians. But he never again saw any Alsatian there.

The puppy was always waiting when they got back home. His father drove right up to the gate and blew his horn. His mother came out to open the gate, and the puppy came out too, wagging his tail, leaping up against the car even as it moved.

'Hold him! Hold him!' Hari cried.

More than anything now he feared losing his dog.

He liked hearing his mother tell visitors about his love for the puppy. And he was given many books about dogs. He learned with sadness that they lived for only twelve years; so that when he was twenty-three, a man, he would have no dog. In the circumstances training seemed pointless, but the books all recommended training, and Hari tried it. The puppy responded

with a languor Hari thought enchanting. At school he was
moved almost to tears when they read the poem beginning
'A barking sound the shepherd hears'. He went to see the film
Lassie Come Home and wept. From the film he realized that he
had forgotten an important part of the puppy's training. And, to
prevent his puppy eating food given by strangers, he dipped
pieces of meat in pepper-sauce and left them about the yard.

The next day the puppy disappeared. Hari was distressed and
felt guilty, but he got some consolation from the film; and when,
less than a week later, the puppy returned, dirty, scratched and
thinner, Hari embraced him and whispered the words of the film:
'You're my Lassie – my Lassie come home.'

He abandoned all training and was concerned only to see the
puppy become healthy again. In the American comic books he
read, dogs lived in dog-houses and ate from bowls marked DOG.
Hari didn't approve of the dog-houses because they looked small
and lonely; but he insisted that his mother should buy a bowl
marked DOG.

When he came home for lunch one day she showed him a
bowl on which DOG had been painted. Hari's father said he was
too hot to eat and went upstairs; his mother followed. Before
Hari ate he washed the bowl and filled it with dog-food. He
called for the puppy and displayed the bowl. The puppy jumped
up, trying to get at the bowl.

Hari put the bowl down and the puppy, instantly ignoring
Hari, ran to it. Disappointed, Hari squatted beside the puppy and
waited for some sign of recognition. None came. The puppy ate
noisily, seeming to catch his food for every chew. Hari passed his
hand over the puppy's head.

The puppy, catching a mouthful of food, growled and shook
his head.

Hari tried again.

With a sharper growl the puppy dropped the food he had in
his mouth and snapped at Hari's hand. Hari felt teeth sinking into
his flesh; he could sense the anger driving the teeth, the thought
that finally held them back. When he looked at his hand he saw
torn skin and swelling blobs of blood. The puppy was bent over
the bowl again, catching and chewing, his eyes hard.

Hari seized the bowl marked DOG and threw it with his girl's
throw out of the kitchen door. The puppy's growl abruptly
ended. When the bowl disappeared he looked up at Hari,

puzzled, friendly, his tail swinging slowly. Hari kicked hard at the puppy's muzzle and felt the tip of his shoe striking the bone. The puppy backed away to the door and looked at Hari with bewilderment.

'Come,' Hari said, his voice thick with saliva.

Swinging his tail briskly, the puppy came, passing his neat pink tongue over his black lips, still oily from the food. Hari held out his bitten hand. The puppy licked it clean of blood. Then Hari drove his shoe up against the puppy's belly. He kicked again, but the puppy had run whining out of the kitchen door, and Hari lost his balance and fell. Tears came to his eyes. His hands burned at those points where the puppy's teeth had sunk, and he could still feel the puppy's saliva on his hand, binding the skin.

He got up and went out of the kitchen. The puppy stood by the gate, watching him. Hari bent down, as though to pick up a stone. The puppy made no move. Hari picked up a pebble and flung it at the puppy. It was a clumsy throw and the pebble rose high. The puppy ran to catch it, missed, stopped and stared, his tail swinging, his ears erect, his mouth open. Had threw another pebble. This one kept low and struck the puppy hard. The puppy whined and ran into the front garden. Hari followed. The puppy ran around the side of the house and hid among the anthurium lilies. Hari aimed one stone after another, and suddenly he had a sense of direction. Again and again he hit the puppy, who whined and ran until he was cornered below the narrow trellis with the Bleeding Heart vine. There he stood still, his eyes restless, his tail between his legs. From time to time he licked his lips. This action infuriated Hari. Blindly he threw stone after stone and the puppy ran from tangle to tangle of Bleeding Heart. Once he tried to rush past Hari, but the way was too narrow and Hari too quick. Hari caught him a drumming kick and he ran back to the corner, watching, faintly whining.

In a choked voice Hari said, 'Come.'

The puppy raised its ears.

Hari smiled and tried to whistle.

Hesitantly, his legs bent, his back curved, the puppy came. Hari stroked his head until the puppy stood erect. Then he held the muzzle with both his hands and squeezed it hard. The puppy yelped and pulled away.

'Hari!' He heard his mother's voice. 'Your father is nearly ready.'

He had had no lunch.

'I have no appetite,' Hari said. They were words his father often used.

She asked about the broken bowl and the food scattered about the yard.

'We were playing,' Hari said.

She saw his hand. 'Those animals don't know their own strength,' she said.

It was his resolve to get the puppy to allow himself to be stroked while eating. Every refusal had to be punished, by beating and stoning, imprisonment in the cupboard below the stairs or imprisonment behind the closed windows of the car, when that was available. Sometimes Hari took the puppy's plate, led the puppy to the lavatory, emptied the plate into the toilet bowl and pulled the flush. Sometimes he threw the food into the yard; then he punished the puppy for eating off the ground. Soon he extended his judgment to all the puppy's actions, punishing those he thought unfriendly, disobedient or ungrateful. If the puppy didn't come to the gate when the car horn sounded, he was to be punished; if he didn't come when called, he was to be punished. Hari kept a careful check of the punishments he had to inflict because he could punish only when his parents were away or occupied, and he was therefore always behindhand. He feared that the puppy might run away again; so he tied him at nights. And when his parents were about, Hari was enraged, as enraged as he had been by that licking of the oily lips, to see the puppy behaving as though unaware of the punishments to come: lying at his father's feet, yawning, curling himself into comfortable positions, or wagging his tail to greet Hari's mother. Sometimes, then, Hari stooped to pick up an imaginary stone, and the puppy ran out of the room. But there were also days when punishments were forgotten, for Hari knew that he controlled the puppy's power and made it an extension of his own, not only by his punishments but also by the complementary hold of affection.

Then came the triumph. The puppy, now almost a dog, attacked Hari one day and had to be pulled back by Hari's parents. 'You can never trust those dogs,' Hari's mother said, and the dog was permanently chained. For days, whenever he could get the chance, Hari beat the dog. One evening, when his parents were out, he beat the dog until it ceased to whine. Then, knowing he was alone, and wishing to test his strength and fear, he unchained the dog. The dog didn't attack, didn't growl. It ran to hide among the anthurium lilies. And after that it allowed itself to be stroked while it ate.

Hari's birthday came again. He was given a Brownie 6-20 camera and wasted film on absurd subjects until his father suggested that a photograph should be taken of Hari and the dog. The dog didn't stand still; eventually they put its collar on and Hari held on to that and smiled for the camera.

Hari's father was busy that Friday and couldn't drive Hari home. Hari stayed at school for the meeting of the Stamp Club and took a taxi home. His father's car was in the drive. He called for the dog. It didn't come. Another punishment. His parents were in the small dining-room next to the kitchen; they sat down to tea. On the dining table Hari saw the yellow folder with the negatives and the prints. They had not come out well. The dog looked strained and awkward, not facing the camera; and Hari thought he himself looked very fat. He felt his parents' eyes on him as he went through the photographs. He turned over one photograph. On the back of it he saw, in his father's handwriting: *In memory of Rex*. Below that was the date.

'It was an accident,' his mother said, putting her arms around him. 'He ran out just as your father was driving in. It was an accident.'

Tears filled Hari's eyes. Sobbing, he stamped up the stairs.

'Mind, son,' his mother called, and Hari heard her say to his father, 'Go after him. His heart. His heart.'

1960

LOOK AT ME. Black as the Ace of Spades, and ugly to match. Nobody looking at me would believe they looking at one of the richest men in this city of Port-of-Spain. Sometimes I find it hard to believe it myself, you know, especially when I go out on some of the holidays that I start taking the wife and children to these days, and I catch sight of the obzocky black face in one of those fancy mirrors that expensive hotels have all over the place, as if to spite people like me.

Now everybody – particularly black people – forever asking me how this thing start, and I does always tell them I make my dough from dough. Ha! You like that one? But how it start? Well, you hearing me talk, and I don't have to tell you I didn't have no education. In Grenada, where I come from – and that is one thing these Trinidad black people don't forgive a man for being: a black Grenadian – in Grenada I was one of ten children, I believe – everything kind of mix up out there – and I don't even know who was the feller who hit my mother. I believe he hit a lot of women in all the other parishes of that island, too, because whenever I go back to Grenada for one of those holidays I tell you about, people always telling me that I remind them of this one and that one, and they always mistaking me for a shop assistant whenever I in a shop. (If this thing go on, one day I going to sell somebody something, just for spite.) And even in Trinidad, whenever I run into another Grenadian, the same thing does happen.

Well, I don't know what happen in Grenada, but mammy bring me alone over to Trinidad when she was still young. I don't know what she do with the others, but perhaps they wasn't even she own. Anyway, she get a work with some white people in St Ann's. They give she a uniform; they give she three meals a day; and they give she a few dollars a month besides. Somehow she get another man, a real Trinidad 'rangoutang, and somehow, I don't know how, she get somebody else to look after me while she was living with this man, for the money and the food she was getting was scarcely enough to support this low-minded Trinidad rango she take up with.

It used to have a Chinee shop not far from this new aunty I was living with, and one day, when the old girl couldn't find the cash no how to buy a bread – is a hell of a thing, come to think of it now, that it have people in this island who can't lay their hands on enough of the ready to buy a bread – well, when she couldn't buy this bread she send me over to this Chinee shop to ask for trust. The Chinee woman – eh, but how these Chinee people does make children! – was big like anything, and I believe I catch she at a good moment, because she say nothing doing, no trust, but if I want a little work that was different, because she want somebody to take some bread she bake for some Indian people. But how she could trust me with the bread? This was a question. And then I pull out my crucifix from under my dirty merino that was more holes than cloth and I tell she to keep it until I come back with the money for the bake bread. I don't know what sort of religion these Chinee people have, but that woman look impressed like anything. But she was smart, though. She keep the crucifix and she send me off with the bread, which was wrap up in a big old *châle-au-pain*, just two or three floursack sew together. I collect the money, bring it back, and she give me back the crucifix with a few cents and a bread.

And that was how this thing really begin. I always tell black people that was God give me my start in life, and don't mind these Trinidadians who does always tell you that Grenadians always praying. Is a true thing, though, because whenever I in any little business difficulty even these days I get down bam! straight on my two knees and I start praying like hell, boy.

Well, so this thing went on, until it was a regular afternoon work for me to deliver people bread. The bakery uses to bake ordinary bread – hops and pan and machine – which they uses to sell to the poorer classes. And how those Chinee people uses to work! This woman, with she big-big belly, clothes all dirty, sweating in front of the oven, making all this bread and making all this money, and I don't know what they doing with it, because all the time they living poor-poor in the back room, with only a bed, some hammocks for the young ones, and a few boxes. I couldn't talk to the husband at all. He didn't know a word of English and all the writing he uses to write uses to be in Chinee. He was a thin nashy feller, with those funny flapping khaki short

pants and white merino that Chinee people always wear. He uses
to work like a bitch, too. We Grenadians understand hard work,
so that is why I suppose I uses to get on so well with these Chinee
people, and that is why these lazy black Trinidadians so jealous
of we. But was a funny thing. They uses to live so dirty. But the
children, man, uses to leave that ramshackle old back room as
clean as new bread, and they always had this neatness, always with
their little pencil-case and their little rubbers and rulers and
blotters, and they never losing anything. They leaving in the
morning in one nice little line and in the afternoon they coming
back in this same little line, still cool and clean, as though nothing
at all touch them all day. Is something they could teach black
people children.

But as I was saying this bakery uses to bake ordinary bread for
the poorer classes. For the richer classes they uses to bake, too.
But what they would do would be to collect the dough from
those people house, bake it, and send it back as bread, hot and
sweet. I uses to fetch and deliver for this class of customer. They
never let me serve in the shop; it was as though they couldn't
trust me selling across the counter and collecting money in that
rush. Always it had this rush. You know black people: even if it
only have one man in the shop he always getting on as if it have
one hell of a crowd.

Well, one day when I deliver some bread in this *châle-au-pain*
to a family, there was a woman, a neighbour, who start saying
how nice it is to get bread which you knead with your own hands
and not mix up with all sort of people sweat. And this give me
the idea. A oven is a oven. It have to go on, whether it baking
one bread or two. So I tell this woman, was a Potogee woman,
that I would take she dough and bring it back bake for she,
and that it would cost she next to nothing. I say this in a sort of
way that she wouldn't know whether I was going to give the
money to the Chinee people, or whether it was going to cost
she next to nothing because it would be I who was going to take
the money. But she give me a look which tell me right away that
she wanted me to take the money. So matter fix. So. Back in the
châle-au-pain the next few days I take some dough, hanging it in
the carrier of the bakery bicycle. I take it inside, as though I just
didn't bother to wrap up the *châle-au-pain*, and the next thing is
that this dough mix up with the other dough, and see me knead-
ing and baking, as though all is one. The thing is, when you go

in for a thing like that, to go in brave-brave. It have some people who make so much fuss when they doing one little thing that they bound to get catch. So, and I was surprise like hell, mind you. I get this stuff push in the oven, and is this said Chinee man, always with this sad and sorrowful Chinee face, who pulling it out of the oven with the long-handle shovel, looking at it, and pushing it back in.

And when I take the bread back, with some other bread, I collect the money cool-cool. The thing with a thing like this is that once you start is damn hard to stop. You start calculating this way and that way. And I have a calculating mind. I forever sitting down and working out how much say .50 a day every day for seven days, and every week for a year, coming to. And so this thing get to be a big thing with me. I wouldn't recommend this to any and everybody who want to go into business. But is what I mean when I tell people that I make my dough by dough.

The Chinee woman wasn't too well now. And the old man was getting on a little funny in a Chinee way. You know how those Chinee fellers does gamble. You drive past Marine Square in the early hours of the Sabbath and is two to one if you don't see some of those Chinee fellers sitting down outside the Treasury, as though they want to be near money, and gambling like hell. Well, the old man was gambling and the old girl was sick, and I was pretty well the only person looking after the bakery. I work damn hard for them, I could tell you. I even pick up two or three words of Chinee, and some of those rude black people start calling me Black Chinee, because at this time I was beginning to dress in short khaki pants and merino like a Chinee and I was drinking that tea Chinee people drinking all day long and I was walking and not saying much like a Chinee. And, now, don't believe what these black people say about Chinee and prejudice, eh. They have nothing at all against black people, provided they is hard-working and grateful.

But life is a funny thing. Now when it look that I all set, that everything going fine and dandy, a whole set of things happen that start me bawling. First, the Chinee lady catch a pleurisy and dead. Was a hell of a thing, but what else you expect when she was always bending down in front of that fire and then getting wet and going out in the dew and everything, and then always making these children too besides. I was sorry like hell, and a little frighten. Because I wasn't too sure how I was going to manage alone with the old man. All the time I work with him he never speak one word straight to me, but he always talking to me through his wife.

And now, look at my crosses. As soon as the woman dead, the Chinee man like he get mad. He didn't cry or anything like that, but he start gambling like a bitch, and the upshot was that one day, perhaps about a month after the old lady dead, the man tell his children to pack up and start leaving, because he gamble and lose the shop to another Chinee feller. I didn't know where I was standing, and nobody telling me nothing. They only packing. I don't know, I suppose they begin to feel that I was just part of the shop, and the old man not even saying that he sorry he lose me. And, you know, as soon as I drop to my knees and start praying, I see it was really God who right from the start put that idea of the dough in my head, because without that I would have been nowhere at all. Because the new feller who take over the shop say he don't want me. He was going to close the bakery and set up a regular grocery, and he didn't want me serving there because the grocery customers wouldn't like black people serving them. So look at me. Twenty-three years old and no work. No nothing. Only I have this Chinee-ness and I know how to bake bread and I have this extra bit of cash I save up over the years.

I slip out of the old khaki short pants and merino and I cruise around the town a little, looking for work. But nobody want bakers. I had about $700.00, and I see that this cruising around would do but it wouldn't pay, because the money was going fast. Now look at this. You know, it never cross my mind in those days that I could open a shop of my own. Is how it is with black people. They get so use to working for other people that they get to believe that because they black they can't do nothing else but work for other people. And I must tell you that when I start praying and God tell me to go out and open a shop for myself I feel that perhaps God did mistake or that I hadn't hear Him good. Because God only saying to me, 'Youngman, take your money and open a bakery. You could bake good bread.' He didn't say to open a parlour, which a few black fellers do, selling rock cakes and mauby and other soft drinks. No, He say open a bakery. Look at my crosses.

I had a lot of trouble borrowing the extra few hundred dollars, but I eventually get a Indian feller to lend me. And this is what I always tell young fellers. That getting credit ain't no trouble at all if you know exactly what you want to do. I didn't go round telling people to lend me money because I want to build house or buy lorry. I just did want to bake bread. Well, to cut a long story short, I buy a break-down old place near Arouca, and I spend most of what I had trying to fix the place up. Nothing extravagant, you understand, because Arouca is Arouca and you don't want to frighten off the country-bookies with anything too sharp. Too besides, I didn't have the cash. I just put in a few second-hand glass cases and things like that. I write up my name on a board, and look, I in business.

Now the funny thing happen. In Laventille the people couldn't have enough of the bread I was baking – and in the last few months was me was doing the baking. But now trouble. I baking better bread than the people of Arouca ever see, and I can't get one single feller to come in like man through my rickety old front door and buy a penny hops bread. You hear all this talk about quality being its own advertisement? Don't believe it, boy. Is quality plus something else. And I didn't have this something else. I begin to wonder what the hell it could be. I say is because I new in Arouca that this thing happening. But no. I new, I get stale, and the people not flocking in their hundreds to the old shop. Day after day I baking two or three quarts good and all this just remaining and going dry and stale, and the only bread I selling is to the man from the government farm, buying stale cakes and bread for the cows or pigs or whatever they have up there. And was good bread. So I get down on the old knees and I pray as though I want to wear them out. And still I getting the same answer: 'Youngman' – was always the way I uses to get call in these prayers – 'Youngman, you just bake bread.'

Pappa! This was a thing. Interest on the loan piling up every month. Some months I borrow from aunty and anybody else who kind enough to listen just to pay off the interest. And things get so low that I uses to have to go out and pretend to people that I was working for another man bakery and that I was going to bake their dough cheap-cheap. And in Arouca cheap mean cheap. And the little cash I picking up in this disgraceful way was just about enough to keep the wolf from the door, I tell you.

Jeezan. Look at confusion. The old place in Arouca so damn out of the way – was why I did buy it, too, thinking that they didn't have no bakery there and that they would be glad of the good Grenadian-baked – the place so out of the way nobody would want to buy it. It ain't even insure or anything, so it can't get in a little fire accident or anything – not that I went in for that sort of thing. And every time I go down on my knees, the answer coming straight back at me: 'Youngman, you just bake bread.'

Well, for the sake of the Lord I baking one or two quarts regular every day, though I begin to feel that the Lord want to break me, and I begin to feel too that this was His punishment for what I uses to do to the Chinee people in their bakery. I was beginning to feel bad and real ignorant. I uses to stay away from the bakery after baking those quarts for the Lord – nothing to lock up, nothing to thief – and, when any of the Laventille boys drop in on the way to Manzanilla and Balandra and those other beaches on the Sabbath, I uses to tell them, making a joke out of it, that I was 'loafing'. They uses to laugh like hell, too. It have nothing in the whole world so funny as to see a man you know flat out on his arse and catching good hell.

The Indian feller was getting anxious about his cash, and you couldn't blame him, either, because some months now he not even seeing his interest. And this begin to get me down, too. I remember how all the man did ask me when I went to him for money was: 'You sure you want to bake bread? You feel you have a hand for baking bread?' And yes-yes, I tell him, and just like that he shell out the cash. And now he was getting anxious. So one day, after baking those loaves for the Lord, I take a Arima Bus Service bus to Port-of-Spain to see this feller. I was feeling brave enough on the way. But as soon as I see the old sea and get a whiff of South Quay and the bus touch the Railway Station terminus my belly start going pweh-pweh. I decide to roam about the city for a little.

Was a hot morning, *petit-carême* weather, and in those days a coconut uses still to cost .04. Well, it had this coconut cart in the old square and I stop by it. It was a damn funny thing to see. The seller was a black feller. And you wouldn't know how funny this was, unless you know that every coconut seller in the island is Indian. They have this way of handling a cutlass that black people don't have. Coconut in left hand; with right hand bam, bam, bam with cutlass, and coconut cut open, ready to drink. I ain't never see a coconut seller chop his hand. And here was this black feller doing this bam-bam business on a coconut with a cutlass. It was as funny as seeing a black man wearing dhoti and turban.

The sweetest part of the whole business was that this black feller was, forgetting looks, just like an Indian. He was talking Hindustani to a lot of Indian fellers, who was giving him jokes like hell, but he wasn't minding. It does happen like that sometimes with black fellers who live a lot with Indians in the country. They putting away curry, talking Indian, and behaving just like Indians. Well, I take a coconut from this black man and then went on to see the feller about the money.

He was more sad than vex when I tell him, and if I was in his shoes I woulda be sad, too. Is a hell of a thing when you see your money gone and you ain't getting the sweet little kisses from the interest every month. Anyway, he say he would give me three more months' grace, but that if I didn't start shelling out at the agreed rate he would have to foreclose. 'You put me in a hell of a position,' he say. 'Look at me. You think I want a shop in Arouca?'

I was feeling a little better when I leave the feller, and who I should see when I leave but Percy. Percy was an old rango who uses to go to the Laventille elementary school with me. I never know a boy get so much cut-arse as Percy. But he grow up real hard and ignorant with it, and now he wearing fancy clothes like a saga boy, and talking about various business offers. I believe he was selling insurance – is a thing that nearly every idler doing in Trinidad, and, mark my words, the day coming when you going to see those fellers trying to sell insurance to one another. Anyway, Percy getting on real flash, and he say he want to stand me a lunch for old times' sake. He makes a few of the usual ignorant Trinidadian jokes about Grenadians, and we went up to the Angostura Bar. I did never go there before, and wasn't the sort of place you would expect a rango like Percy to be welcome. But we went up there and Percy start throwing his weight around with the waiters, and, mind you, they wasn't even a quarter as black as Percy. Is a wonder they didn't abuse him, especially with all those fair people around. After the drinks Percy say, 'Where you want to have this lunch?'

Me, I don't know a thing about the city restaurants, and when Percy talk about food all I was expecting was rice and peas or a roti off a Indian stall or a mauby and rock cake in some parlour. And is a damn hard thing to have people, even people as ignorant as Percy, showing off on you, especially when you carrying two nails in your pocket to make the jingling noise. So I tell Percy we could go to a parlour or a bar. But he say, 'No, no. When I treat my friends, I don't like black people meddling with my food.'

And was only then that the thing hit me. I suppose that what Trinidadians say about the stupidness of Grenadians have a little truth, though you have to live in a place for a long time before you get to know it really well. Then the thing hit me, man.

When black people in Trinidad go to a restaurant they don't like to see black people meddling with their food. And then I see that though Trinidad have every race and every colour, every race have to do special things. But look, man. If you want to buy a snowball, who you buying it from? You wouldn't buy it from a Indian or a Chinee or a Potogee. You would buy it from a black man. And I myself, when I was getting my place in Arouca fix up, I didn't employ Indian carpenters or masons. If a Indian in Trinidad decide to go into the carpentering business the man would starve. Who ever see a Indian carpenter? I suppose the only place in the world where they have Indian carpenters and Indian masons is India. Is a damn funny thing. One of these days I must make a trip to that country, to just see this thing. And as we walking I see the names of bakers; Coelho, Pantin, Stauble. Potogee or Swiss, or something, and then all those other Chinee places. And, look at the laundries. If a black man open a laundry, you would take your clothes to it? *I* wouldn't take my clothes there. Well, I walking to this restaurant, but I jumping for joy. And then all sorts of things fit into place. You remember that the Chinee people didn't let me serve bread across the counter? I uses to think it was because they didn't trust me with the rush. But it wasn't that. It was that, if they did let me serve, they would have had no rush at all. You ever see anybody buying their bread off a black man?

I ask Percy why he didn't like black people meddling with his food in public places. The question throw him a little. He stop and think and say, 'It don't *look* nice.'

Well, you could guess the rest of the story. Before I went back to Arouca that day I made contact with a yellow boy call Macnab. This boy was half black and half Chinee, and, though he had a little brown colour and the hair a little curly, he could pass for one of those Cantonese. They a little darker than the other Chinee people, I believe. Macnab I find beating a steel pan in somebody yard – they was practising for Carnival – and I suppose the only reason that Macnab was willing to come all the way to Arouca was because he was short of the cash to buy his costume for the Carnival band.

But he went up with me. I put him in front of the shop, give him a merino and a pair of khaki short pants, and tell him to talk as Chinee as he could, if he wanted to get that Carnival bonus. I stay in the back room, and I start baking bread. I even give Macnab a old Chinee paper, not to read, because Macnab could scarcely read English, but just to leave lying around, to make it look good. And I get hold of one of those big Chinee calendars with Chinee women and flowers and waterfalls and hang it up on the wall. And when this was all ready, I went down on my knees and thank God. And still the old message coming, but friendly and happy now: 'Youngman, you just bake bread.'

And, you know, that solve another problem. I was worrying to hell about the name I should give the place. New Shanghai, Canton, Hongkong, Nanking, Yang-tse-Kiang. But when the old message came over I know right away what the name should be. I scrub off the old name – no need to tell you what that was – and I get a proper sign painter to copy a few letters from the Chinee newspaper. Below that, in big letters, I make him write:

YUNG MAN
BAKER

I never show my face in the front of the shop again. And I tell you, without boasting, that I bake damn good bread. And the people of Arouca ain't that foolish. They know a good thing. And soon I was making so much money that I was able to open a branch in Arima and then another in Port-of-Spain self. Was hard in the beginning to get real Chinee people to work for a black man. But money have it own way of talking, and when today you pass any of the Yung Man establishments all you seeing behind the counter is Chinee. Some of them ain't even know they working for a black man. My wife handling that side of the business, and the wife is Chinee. She come from down Cedros way. So look at me now, in Port-of-Spain, giving Stauble and Pantin and Coelho a run for their money. As I say, I only going in the shops from the back. But every Monday morning I walking brave brave to Marine Square and going in the bank, from the front.

1962

11 A FLAG ON THE ISLAND
A Fantasy for a Small Screen

I

IT WAS AN ISLAND around which I had been circling for some years. My duties often took me that way and I could have called there any time. But in my imagination the island had ceased to be accessible; and I wanted it to remain so. A lassitude always fell upon me whenever – working from the name made concrete and ordinary on say an airport board – I sought to re-create a visit. So easy then to get into a car, to qualify a name with trees, houses, people, their quaint advertisements and puzzling journeys. So easy to destroy more than a name. All landscapes are in the end only in the imagination; to be faced with the reality is to start again.

And now the island was upon me. It was not on our itinerary. But out there, among the tourist isles to the north, there was the big annual event of the hurricanes; and it was news of one of these hurricanes, called Irene, that was making us put in. The island, we were told in the ship's bulletin, was reasonably safe. There had been a hurricane here, and a mild one, only once, in the 1920s; and scientists at that time had said, in the way scientists have, that the island was safe for another hundred years. You wouldn't have thought so, though, from the excitement in the announcements from the local radio station, which our transistors had begun to pick up as we came slowly into the harbour through the narrow channel, still and clear and dangerous, between tall green-thatched rocky islets.

Channel and islets which I had never hoped or wished to see again. Still there. And I had been so calm throughout the journey northwards. Abstemiousness, even self-mortification, had settled on me almost as soon as I had gone aboard; and had given me a deep content. I had been eating little and drinking not at all. I fancied that I was shrinking from day to day, and this daily assessment had been pleasing. When I sat I tried to make myself as small as possible; and it had been a pleasure to me then to put on my spectacles and to attempt to read, to be the ascetic who yet knew the greater pleasure of his own shrinking flesh. To be the ascetic, to be mild and gentle and soft-spoken, withdrawn and ineffectual; to have created for oneself that little clearing in the jungle of the mind; and constantly to reassure oneself that the clearing still existed.

Now as we moved into the harbour I could feel the jungle press in again. I was jumpy, irritated, unsatisfied, suddenly incomplete. Still, I made an effort. I decided not to go ashore with the others. We were to stay on the island until the hurricane had blown itself out. The shipping company had arranged trips and excursions.

'What's the name of this place? They always give you the name of the place in airports. Harbours try to keep you guessing. I wonder why?'

'Philosopher!'

Husband and wife, playing as a team.

Already we were news. On the transistors there came a new announcement, breathless like the others: 'Here is an appeal from the Ministry of Public Order and Education. Five hundred tourists will be on our island for the next few days. The Ministry urges that these tourists be treated with our customary courtesy and kindness.'

'The natives are excited,' a tourist said to me.

'Yes,' I said, 'I think there is a good chance they will eat us. We look pretty appetizing.'

Red dust hung in a cloud above the bauxite loading station, disfiguring the city and the hills. The tourists gazed, lining the rails in bermuda shorts, bright cotton shirts and straw hats. They looked vulnerable.

'Here is an appeal from the Ministry of Public Order and Education....'

I imagined the appeal going to the barbershops, rumshops, cafés and back-yards of the ramshackle town I had known.

The radio played a commercial for a type of shirt; an organ moaned and some deaths were announced; there was a commercial for a washing powder; then the time was tremendously announced and there were details of weather and temperature.

A woman said, 'They get worked up about the time and the weather here too.'

Her husband, his bitterness scarcely disguised by the gaiety of his tourist costume, said, 'Why the hell shouldn't they?'

They were not playing as a team.

I went down to my cabin. On the way I ran into the happier team, already dressed as for a carnival.

'You're not going ashore?' asked the male.

'No. I think I will just stay here and read.'

And in my self-imposed isolation, I did try to read. I put on my spectacles and tried to savour my shrinking, mortified flesh. But it was no use; the jungle pressed; confusion and threat were already being converted into that internal excitement which is in itself fulfilment, and exhaustion.

Here on this Moore-McCormack liner everything was Moore-McCormack. In my white cabin the name called to me from every corner, from every article, from towels, from toilet paper, from writing paper, from table cloth, from pillow-cases, from bed sheets, from blankets, from cups and menus. So that the name appeared to have gone deep, to have penetrated, like the radiation we have been told to fear, the skin of all those exposed to it, to have shaped itself in living red corpuscles within bodies.

Moore-McCormack, Moore-McCormack. Man had become God. Impossible in this cabin to escape; yet I knew that once we were out of the ship the name would lose its power. So that my decision was almost made for me. I would go ashore; I would spend the night ashore. My mood was on me; I let it settle; I let it take possession of me. Then I saw that I too, putting away briefcase, papers, letters, passport, was capable of my own feeble assertions. I too had tried to give myself labels, and none of my labels could convince me that I belonged to myself.

This is part of my mood; it heightens my anxiety; I feel the whole world is being washed away and that I am being washed away with it. I feel my time is short. The child, testing his courage, steps into the swiftly moving stream, and though the water does not go above his ankles, in an instant the safe solid earth vanishes, and he is aware only of the terror of sky and trees and the force at his feet. Split seconds of lucidity add to his terror. So, we can use the same toothpaste for years and end by not seeing the colour of the tube; but set us among strange labels, set us in disturbance, in an unfamiliar landscape; and every un-regarded article we possess becomes isolated and speaks of our peculiar dependence.

'You are going to spend the night ashore?'

The question came from a small intelligent-looking man with a round, kind face. He had been as withdrawn from the life of the ship as myself, and I had always seen him in the company of a big grey-suited man whose face I had never been able to commit to memory. I had heard rumours that he was very rich, but I had paid no attention; as I had paid no attention to the other rumour that we had a Russian spy on board as a prisoner.

'Yes, I am going to be brave.'

'Oh, I am glad,' he said, 'we are going to have lots of fun together.'

'Thanks for asking me.'

'When I say fun, I don't mean what you mean.'

'I don't know what you mean either.'

He did not stop smiling. 'I imagine that you are going ashore for pleasure.'

'Well, I suppose that you could call it that.'

'I am glad we put in here.' His expression became that of a man burdened by duty. 'You see I have a little business to do here.' He spoke gravely, but his excitement was clear. 'Do you know the island?'

'I used to know it very well.'

'Well, I am so glad we have met. You are just the sort of person I want to meet. You could be of great help to me.'

'I can simplify matters for you by giving you a list of places you must on no account go to.'

He looked pained. 'I am really here on business.'

'You can do good business here. I used to.'

Pleasure? I was already exhausted. My stomach felt tight; and all the unexpended energy of days, of weeks, seemed to have turned sour. Already the craving for shellfish and seafood was on me. I could almost feel its sick stale taste in my mouth, and I knew that for all that had happened in the past, I would eat no complete meal for some time ahead, and that while my mood lasted the pleasures I looked for would quickly turn to a distressing-satisfying endurance test, would end by being pain.

I had been the coldest of tourists, unexcited by the unexpected holiday. Now, as we landed, I was among the most eager.

'Hey, that was a pretty quick read.'

'I read the last page – the butler did it.'

In the smart reception building, well-groomed girls, full of self-conscious charm, chosen for race and colour, with one or two totally, diplomatically black, pressed island souvenirs on us: toy steel-drums, market-women dolls in cotton, musicians in wire, totem-like faces carved from coconuts. Beyond the wire-netting fence, the taxi drivers of the city seethed. It seemed a frail barrier.

'It's like the zoo,' the woman said.

'Yes,' said her embittered husband. 'They might even throw you some nuts.'

I looked for a telephone. I asked for a directory. It was a small directory.

'A toy directory,' the happy tourist said.

'It's full of the numbers of dolls,' I said.

I dialled, I waited. A voice I knew said, 'Hullo.' I closed my eyes to listen. The voice said, 'Hullo, hullo.' I put the receiver down.

'Naughty.'

It was my friend from the ship. His companion stood at the other end of the room, his back to us; he was looking at books on a revolving bookstand.

'What do you think Sinclair is interested in? Shall we go and see?'

We moved over. Sinclair shuffled off.

Most of the books displayed were by a man called H. J. B. White. The back of each book had a picture of the author. A tormented writer's-photograph face. But I imagined it winking at me. I winked back.

'Do you know him?' my friend asked.

'I don't know whether any of us really knew Mr Blackwhite,' I said. 'He was a man who moved with the times.'

'Local writer?'

'Very local.'

He counted the titles with an awed finger. 'He looks tremendous. Oh, I hope I can see him. Oh, this looks very good.'

The book he picked up was called *I Hate You*, with the sub-title *One Man's Search for Identity*. He opened the book greedily and began moving his lips, ' "I am a man without identity. Hate has consumed my identity. My personality has been distorted by hate. My hymns have not been hymns of praise, but of hate. How terrible to be Caliban, you say. But I say, how tremendous. Tremendousness is therefore my unlikely subject." '

He stopped reading, held the book out to the assistant and said, 'Miss, Miss, I would like to buy this.' Then, indicating one title after the other: 'And this, and this, and this, and this.'

He was not the only one. Many of the tourists had been deftly guided to the bookstall.

'Native author.'

'Don't use that word.'

'Lots of local colour, you think?'

'Mind your language.'

'But look, he's attacking us.'

'No, he's only attacking tourists.'

The group moved on, leaving a depleted shelf.

I bought all H. J. B. White's books.

The girl who sold them to me said, 'Tourists usually go for *I Hate You*, but I prefer the novels myself. They're heart-warming stories.'

'Good clean sex?'

'Oh no, inter-racial.'

'Sorry, I need another language.'

I put on my spectacles and read on the dedication page of one book: 'Thanks are due to the Haaker Foundation whose generous support facilitated the composition of this work.' Another book offered thanks to the Stockwell Foundation. My companion – he was becoming my companion – held all his own books under his arm and read with me from mine.

'You see,' he said, 'they're all after him. I don't imagine he'll want to look at me.'

We were given miniature rum bottles with the compliments of various firms. Little leaflets and folders full of photographs and maps with arrows and X's told us of the beauties of the island, now fully charted. The girl was especially friendly when she explained about the sights.

'You have mud volcanoes here,' I said, 'and that's pretty good. But the leaflet doesn't say. Which is the best whorehouse in town nowadays?'

Tourists stared. The girl called: 'Mr Phillips.' And my companion held my arm, smiled as to a child and said soothingly: 'Hey, I believe I am going to have to look after you. I know how it is when things get on top of you.'

'You know, I believe you do.'

'My name's Leonard.'

'I am Frank,' I said.

'Short for Frankenstein. Forget it, that's my little joke. And you see my friend over there, but you can't see his face? His name's Sinclair.'

Sinclair stood, with his back to us, studying some tormented paintings of black beaches below stormy skies.

'But Sinclair won't talk to you, especially now that he's seen me talking to you.'

In the turmoil of the reception building we were three fixed points.

'Why won't Sinclair talk to me?'

'He's jealous.'

'Hooray for you.'

I broke away to get a taxi.

'Hey, you can't leave me. I'm worried about you, remember?'

Below a wooden arch that said WELCOME TO THE COLOUR-FUL ISLAND the taxi drivers, sober in charcoal-grey trousers, white shirts, some even with ties, behaved like people maddened by the broadcast pleas for courtesy. They rushed the tourists, easy targets in their extravagantly Caribbean cottons stamped with palm-fringed beaches, thatched huts and grass skirts. The tropics appeared to be on their backs alone; when they got into their taxis the tropics went with them.

We came out into an avenue of glass buildings, air-conditioned bars, filling stations and snappily worded advertisements. The slogan PRIDE, TOIL, CULTURE, was everywhere. There was a flag over the customs building. It was new to me: rays from a yellow sun lighting up a wavy blue sea.

'What did you do with the Union Jack?'

The taxi driver said, 'They take it away, and they send this. To tell the truth I prefer the old Union Jack. Now don't misunderstand me, I talking about the flag as a flag. They send us this thing and they try to sweeten us up with some old talk about *or, a pile gules, argenta bordure, barry-wavy.* They try to sweeten us up with that, but I prefer the old Union Jack. It look like a real flag. This look like something they make up. You know, like foreign money?'

Once the island had seemed to me flagless. There was the Union Jack of course, but it was a remote affirmation. The island was a floating suspended place to which you brought your own flag if you wanted to. Every evening on the base we used to pull down the Stars and Stripes at sunset; the bugle would sound and through the city of narrow streets, big trees and old wooden houses, every American serviceman would stand to attention. It was a ridiculous affirmation – the local children mocked us – but only one in a city of ridiculous affirmations. For a long time Mr Blackwhite had a coloured portrait of Haile Selassie in his front room; and in his corner grocery Ma-Ho had a photograph of Chiang Kai-shek between his Chinese calendars. On the flagless island we, saluting the flag, were going back to America; Ma-Ho was going back to Canton as soon as the war was over; and the picture of Haile Selassie was there to remind Mr Black-white, and to remind us, that he too had a place to go back to. 'This place doesn't exist,' he used to say, and he was wiser than any of us.

Now, driving through the city whose features had been so altered, so that alteration seemed to have spread to the land itself, the nature of the soil, I felt again that the reality of landscape and perhaps of all relationships lay only in the imagination. The place existed now: that was the message of the flag.

The road began to climb. On a culvert two calypsonians, dressed for the part, sat disconsolately waiting for custom. A little later we saw two who had been successful. They were serenading the happy wife. The taxi driver, hands in pockets, toothpick in mouth, stood idle. The embittered husband stood equally idle, but he was like a man fighting an inward rage.

The hotel was new. There were murals in the lobby which sought to exalt the landscape and the people which the hotel's very existence seemed to deny. The noticeboard in the lobby gave the name of our ship and added: 'Sailing Indefinite'. A poster advertised The Coconut Grove. Another announced a Barbecue Night at the Hilton, Gary Priestland, popular TV personality, Master of Ceremonies. A photograph showed him with his models. But I saw only Priest, white-robed Priest, handler of the language, handler of his six little hymn-singing girls. He didn't wink at me. He scowled; he threatened. I covered his face with my hand.

In my moods I tell myself that the world is not being washed away; that there is time; that the blurring of fantasy with reality which gives me the feeling of helplessness exists only in my mind. But then I know that the mind is alien and unfriendly, and I am never able to regulate things. Hilton, Hilton. Even here,

even in the book on the bedside table. And The Coconut Grove
again in a leaflet on the table, next to the bowl of fruit in green
cellophane tied with a red ribbon.

I telephoned for a drink; then I telephoned again to hear the
voice and to say nothing. Even before lunch I had drunk too
much.

'Frank, your eye is still longer than your tongue.'

It was an island saying; I thought I could hear the words on
the telephone.

Lunch, lunch. Let it be ordered in every sense. Melon or
avocado to start, something else to follow – but what? But what?
And as soon as I entered the dining-room the craving for oysters
and shellfish became overpowering. The liveried page strolled
through the dining-room beating a toy steel pan and calling out
a name. I fancied it was mine: 'Frankie, Frankie.' But of course
I knew better.

I saw Sinclair's back as he walked to a table. He sat at the far
end like a man controlling the panorama.

'Are you feeling better?'

'Leonard?'

'Frank.'

'Do you like seafood, Leonard?'

'In moderation.'

'I am going to have some oysters.'

'A good starter. Let's have some, I'll have half a dozen.'

The waiter carried the emblem of yellow sun and wavy sea on
his lapel; my eyes travelled down those waves.

'Half a dozen for him. Fifty for me.'

'Fifty,' Leonard said.

'Well, let's make it a hundred.'

Leonard smiled. 'Boy, I'm glad I met you. You believe me,
don't you, Frank?'

'I believe you.'

'You know, people don't believe I have come here to work.
They think I am making it up.'

The waiter brought Leonard his six oysters and brought me
my hundred. The oysters were of the tiny island variety; six
scarcely filled one indentation of Leonard's oyster plate.

'Are these six oysters?' Leonard asked the waiter.

'They are six oysters.'

'Okay, okay,' Leonard said soothingly, 'I just wanted to find

out. Of course,' he said to me, 'it doesn't sound like work. You
see—'

And here the liveried page walked back through the dining-
room beating a bright tune on his toy pan and calling out a name.

'—you see, I have got to give away a million dollars.'

My oysters had come in a tumbler. I scooped up about a dozen
and swallowed them.

'Exactly,' Leonard said. 'It doesn't sound like work. But it is.
One wants to be sure that one is using the money sensibly. It's
easy enough to make a million dollars, I always say. Much harder
to spend it.'

'That's what I have always felt. Excuse me.'

I went up to my room. The oysters had been too many for me.
The sick tightness was in my stomach. Even at this early stage it
was necessary for me to drive myself on.

I was careful, as I always am on these occasions, to prepare
sensibly. I lined the waist-band of my trousers with the new
funny island money; I distributed notes all over my pockets;
I even lay some flat in my shoes.

A letter from home among my papers. Nothing important; no
news; just a little bit about the drains, the wonderful workmen
who had helped. Brave girl. Brave.

I remembered again. I lifted the telephone, asked for a line,
dialled. The same voice answered and again my courage left me
and I listened to the squawks until the phone went dead.

I had stripped myself of all my labels, of all my assertions. Soon
I would be free. Hilton, Hilton: man as God. Goodbye to that
now. My excitement was high.

I went to the desk, transferred a fixed sum to the hotel vault.
The final fraudulence that we cannot avoid: we might look for
escape, but we are always careful to provide for escape from that
escape.

While the clerk was busy I took the pen from the desk, blacked
out the whites of Gary Priestland's eyes and sent an arrow
through his neck. The clerk was well trained. It was only after
I had turned that he removed the disfigured poster and replaced
it by a new one.

The liveried doorman whistled up a taxi. I gave him a local
dollar; too much, but I enjoyed his attempt to look unsurprised.
He opened the taxi door, closed it, saluted. It was the final
moment of responsibility. I did not give the taxi driver the name

of any bar; I gave him the name of a department store in the centre of the city. And when I got off I actually went into the store, as though the taxi driver was watching me and it was important that I should not step out of the character which he must have built up for me.

The store was air-conditioned. The world was cool and muffled. My irritation was sharpened.

'Can I help you, sir?'

'No thank you, I am just passing through.'

I spoke with unnecessary aggressiveness; one or two customers stared and I instinctively waited for Leonard's interjection.

'Leonard,' I whispered, turning.

But he wasn't there.

The shop girl took a step backwards and I hurried out through the other door into the shock of damp heat, white light, and gutter smells. Hooray for air-conditioning. My mood had taken possession of me. I was drunk on more, and on less, than alcohol.

The money began to leak out of my fingers. This is part of the excitement; money became paper over which other people fought. Two dollars entrance here; one dollar for a beer there; cigarettes at twice the price: I paid in paper. Bright rooms, killing bright, and noisy as the sea. The colours yellow, green, red, on drinks, labels, calendars on the walls. On the television intermittently through a series of such bars, Gary Priestland, chairing a discussion on love and marriage. And from a totally black face, a woman's, black enough to be featureless, issued: 'Well, I married for love.' 'No, she married for hate.' Laughter was like the sea. Someone played with the knob on the set; and the thought, perhaps expressed, came to me. 'It is an unkind medium.'

In bright rooms, bright seas, I floated. And I explored dark caves, so dark you groped and sat still and in the end you found that you were alone.

'Where is everybody?'

'They are coming just now.'

In an almost empty room – dim lights, dark walls, dark chairs – the man sitting at the edge of the table invited us to come close up to him. We all six in the room moved up to him, as to a floor show. He crossed his legs and swung them. 'Is he going to strip?'

Confusion again. The door; the tiled entrance; the discreet board:

BRITISH COUNCIL
The Elizabethan Lyric
A Course of Six Lectures

I always feel it would be so much better if I could wait to pick and choose. Time after time I promise myself to do so. But when the girl came and said – so sad it seemed to me – 'I am going to screw you,' I knew that this was how it would begin; that I wouldn't have the will to resist.

PRIDE, flashed the neon light across the square.

She ordered a stout.

'You are an honest girl.'

'Stout does build me up.'

TOIL

The stout came.

'Ah,' she said, 'my old bulldog.'

And from the neck label the bulldog growled at me. With the stout there also came two men dressed like calypsonians in the travel brochures, dressed like calypsonians on the climbing road to the hotel.

'Allow me to welcome the gentleman to our colourful island.'

CULTURE

'Get away,' I shouted.

She looked a little nervous; she nodded uncertainly to some-one behind me and said, 'Is all right, Percy.' Then to me: 'Why you driving them away?'

'They embarrass me.'

'How you mean, they embarrass you?'

'They're not real. Look, I could put my hand through them.'

The man with the guitar lifted his arm; my hand went through.

The song went on: 'In two-twos, this gentleman got the alcoholic blues.'

'God!'

When I uncovered my face I saw a ringed hand before it. It was an expectant hand. I paid; I drank.

A fat white woman began to do a simple little dance on the raised floor. I couldn't look.

'What wrong with you?'

And when the woman made as if to discard the final garment, I stood up and shouted. 'No!'

'But how a big man like you could shame me so?'

The man who had been sitting with a stick at the top of the steps came to our table. He waved around the room, past paintings of steel-bands and women dancing on golden sand, and pointed to a sign:

> Patrons are requested to abstain from
> lewd and offensive gestures
> By order, Ministry of Order and Public Education

'Is all right, Percy,' the girl said.

Percy could only point. Speech was out of the question because of the steel orchestra. I sat down.

Percy went away and the girl said gently: 'Sit down and tell me why you finding everything embarrassing. What else you tourists come here for?' She beckoned to the waitress. 'I want a fry chicken.'

'No,' I said. 'No damn fry chicken for you.'

At that moment the band stopped, and my words filled the room. The Japanese sailors – we had seen their trawlers in the harbour – looked up. The American airmen looked up. Percy looked up.

And in the silence the girl shouted to the room, 'He finding everything embarrassing, and he damn mean with it.' She stood up and pointed at me. 'He travelling all over the world. And all I want is a fry chicken.'

'Frank,' I heard a voice whisper.

'Leonard,' I whispered back.

'O boy, I am glad I've found you. I've had such a time looking for you. I have been in so many different bars, so many. I've got all these nice names, all these interesting people I've got to assist and give money to. Sometimes I had trouble getting the names. You know how people misunderstand. I was worried about you. Sinclair was worried about you too.'

Sinclair was sitting at a table in the distance with his back to us, drinking.

Caught between Leonard and a demand for fried chicken, I bought the fried chicken.

'You know,' Leonard said confidentially, 'it seems that the place to go to is The Coconut Grove. It sounds terrific, just what I am looking for. You know it?'

'I know it.'

'Well look, why don't we all three of us just go there now.'

'Not me at The Coconut Grove,' the girl said.

Leonard said to me, 'I meant you and me and Sinclair.'

'What the hell you mean?' She stood up and held the bottle of stout at an angle over Leonard's head, as though ready to pour. She called, 'Percy!'

Leonard closed his eyes, passive and expectant.

'I'll be with you in a minute, Leonard,' I said, and I ran down the steps with the girl who was still holding the bottle of stout.

'How you get so impatient so sudden?'

'I don't know, but this is your big chance.'

The open car door at the foot of the steps was like an invitation. We got in, the door slammed behind us.

'I've got to get away from those people upstairs. They're mad, they're quite mad. You don't know what I rescued you from.'

She looked at me.

So it began: the walking out past tables; the casual stares; the refusal to walk the hundred yards to the hotel; the two-dollar taxi; the unswept concrete steps; the dimly lit rooms; the cheap wooden furniture; the gaudy calendars on the wall, mocking desire, mocking flesh; the blue shimmer of television screens; Gary Priestland, now with the news of the hurricane; the startling gentility of glass cabinets; the much-used bed.

And in lucid intermissions, the telephone: the squawks, the slams.

So it began. The bars, the hotels, pointless conversations with girls. 'What's your name? Where do you come from? What do you want?' The drinks; the bloated feeling in the stomach; the sick taste of island oysters and red pepper sauce; the airless rooms; the wastepaper baskets, wetly and whitely littered; and white washbasins which, supine on stale beds, one associated with hospitals, medicines, operations, feverishness, delirium.

'No!'

'But I ain't even touched you yet.'

Above me a foolish face, the poor body offering its charms that were no charms. Poor body, poor flesh; poor man.

And again confusion. I must have spoken the words. A woman wailed, claiming insult and calling for brave men, and the bare wooden staircase resounded. Then among trellis and roses, dozens of luminous white roses, a dog barked, and growled. The offended black body turned white with insult. The same screams, the same call for vengeance. Down an aisle, between hundreds and hundreds of fully clothed men with spectacles and pads and pencils, the body chased me. To another entrance; another tiled floor; another discreet board:

ALLIANCE FRANÇAISE
Art Course
Paris Model
(Admission free)

And the glimpses of Leonard: like scenes imagined, the man with the million dollars to give away, the Pied Piper whom as in a dream I saw walking down the street followed by processions of steel-bandsmen, singers, and women calling for his money. At the head he walked, benign, stunned, smiling.

The day had faded, the night moved in jerks, in great swallows of hours. Lighted docks had wise and patient faces.

The bar smelled of rum and latrines. The beer and some notes and some silver were pushed at me through the gap in the wire-netting. My right hand was gripped and the black face, smiling, menacing, humorous, frightening, which I seemed to study pore by pore, hair by hair, was saying, 'Leave the change for me, nuh.'

Confusion. Glimpses of faces expressing interest rather than hostility. A tumbling and rumbling; a wet floor; my own shouts of 'No', and the repeated answering sentence: 'Next time you walk with money.'

And in the silent street off the deserted square, midnight approaching, the Cinderella hour, I was sitting on the pavement, totally lucid, with my feet in the gutter, sucking an orange. Sitting below the old straw-hatted lady, lit by the yellow smoking flame of a bottle flambeau. On the television in the shop window, Gary Priestland and the Ma-Ho Four, frantic and mute behind plate-glass.

'Better?' she said.

'Better.'

'These people nowadays, they never have, they only want.'

'What do they want?'

'What you have. Look.'

The voice was mock American: 'Man, I can get anything for you?'

'What do you have?'

'I have white,' the taxi driver said. 'I have Chinese, I have Portuguese, I have Indian, I have Spanish. Don't ask me for black. I don't do black.'

'That's right, boy,' the old lady said. 'Keep them out of mischief.'

'I couldn't do black or white now.'

'Was what I was thinking,' the orange lady said.

'Then you want The Coconut Grove,' the taxi driver said. 'Very cultural. All the older shots go there.'

'You make it sound very gay.'

'I know what you mean. This culture would do, but it wouldn't pay. Is just a lot of provocation if you ask me. A lot of wicked scanty clothing and all you doing with your two hands at the end is clapping. The spirit of the older shots being willing, but the flesh being weak.'

'That sounds like me. After mature consideration I think we will go to The Coconut Grove.'

'And too besides, I was going to say, they wouldn't take you in like this, old man. Look at you.'

'I don't know, I believe I have lost you somewhere. Do you want me to go to this place?'

'I don't want nothing. I was just remarking that they wouldn't take you in.'

'Let's try.'

'In these cultural joints they have big bouncers, you know.'

We drove through silent streets in which occasionally neon lights flashed PRIDE, TOIL, CULTURE. On the car radio came the news of midnight. Terrific news, from the way it was presented. Then came news of wind velocity and temperature, and of the hurricane, still out there.

'You see what I mean,' the taxi driver said when we stopped.

'It has changed,' I said. 'It used to be an ordinary house, you know. You know those wooden houses with gables and fretwork along the eaves?'

'Oh, the old-fashioned ones. We are pulling them down all the time now. You mustn't think a lot of them still remain.'

Henry's was new and square, with much glass. Behind the glass, potted greenery; and behind that, blinds. Rough stone walls, recessed mortar, a heavy glass door, heavy, too, with recommendations from clubs and travel associations, like the suitcase of an old-fashioned traveller. And behind the door, the bouncer.

'Big, eh?' the taxi driver said.

'He's a big man.'

'You want to try your luck?'

'Perhaps a little later. Just now I just want you to drive slowly down the street.'

The bouncer watched us move off. I looked back at him; he continued to look at me. And how could I have forgotten? Opposite The Coconut Grove, what? I looked. I saw.

> Ministry of Order and Public Education
> University College
> Creative Writing Department
> Principal: H. J. B. White
> Grams: Olympus

'You don't mind going so slowly?' I asked the driver.

'No, I do a lot of funeral work when I'm not hustling.'

No overturned dustbins on the street now; no pariah dogs timidly pillaging. The street we moved down was like a street in an architect's drawing. Above the neat new buildings trees tossed. The wind was high; the racing clouds were black and silver. We came to an intersection.

'Supermarket,' the driver said, pointing.

'Supermarket.'

A little further on my anxiety dissolved. Where I had expected and feared to find a house, there was an empty lot. I got out of the car and went to look.

'What are you looking for?' the taxi driver asked.

'My house.'

'You sure you left it here? That was a damn careless thing to do.'

'They've pulled down my house.' I walked among the weeds, looking.

'The house not here,' the taxi driver said. 'What you looking for?'

'An explanation. Here, go leave me alone.' I paid him off.

He didn't go. He remained where he was and watched me. I began to walk briskly back towards The Coconut Grove, the wind blowing my hair, making my shirt flap, and it seemed that it was just in this way, though not at night and under a wild sky, but in broad daylight, below a high light sky, that I had first come to this street. The terror of sky and trees, the force at my feet.

II

I used to feel in those days that it was we who brought the tropics to the island. When I knew the town, it didn't end in sandy beaches and coconut trees, but in a tainted swamp, in mangrove and mud. Then the land was reclaimed from the sea, and the people who got oysters from the mangrove disappeared. On the reclaimed land we built the tropics. We put up our army huts, raised our flag, planted our coconut trees and our hedges. Among the great wooden buildings with wire-netting windows we scattered pretty little thatched huts.

We brought the tropics to the island. Yet to the islanders it must have seemed that we had brought America to them. Everyone worked for us. You asked a man what he did; he didn't say that he drove a truck or was a carpenter; he simply said he worked for the Americans. Every morning trucks drove through the city, picking up workers; and every afternoon the trucks left the base to take them back.

The islanders came to our bit of the tropics. We explored theirs. Nothing was organized in those days. There were no leaflets telling you where to shop or where to go. You had to find out yourself. You found out quickly about the bars; it wasn't pleasant to be beaten up or robbed.

I heard about Henry's place from a man on the base. He said Henry kept a few goats in his back-yard and sometimes slaughtered them on a Sunday. He said Henry was a character. It didn't seem a particularly enticing thing. But I got into a taxi outside the base one Thursday afternoon and decided to look. Taxi drivers know everything; so they say.

'Do you know a man called Henry?' I asked the taxi driver. 'He keeps a few goats.'

'The island small, boss, but not that small.'

'You must know him. He keeps these goats.'

'No, boss, you be frank with me, I be frank with you. If goats you after . . .'

I allowed him to take me where he wished. We drove through the old ramshackle city, wooden houses on separate lots, all decay, it seemed, in the middle of the brightest vegetation. It scarcely seemed a city where you would, by choice, seek pleasure; it made you think only of empty afternoons. All these streets look so quiet and alike. All the houses looked so tame and dull and alike: very little people attending to their very little affairs.

The taxi driver took me to various rooms, curtained, hot, stuffed with furniture, and squalid enough to kill all thoughts of pleasure. In one room there was even a baby. 'Not mine, not mine,' the girl said. I was a little strained, and the driver was strained, by the time we came to the street where he said I would find Henry's place.

The brave young man looking for fun. The spark had gone; and to tell the truth, I was a little embarrassed. I wished to arrive at Henry's alone. I paid the taxi driver off.

I imagine I was hoping to find something which at least looked like a commercial establishment. I looked for boards and signs. I saw nothing. I walked past shuttered houses to a shuttered grocery, the only clue even there being a small black noticeboard saying, in amateurish letters, that Ma–Ho was licensed to deal in spirituous liquors. I walked down the other side of the street. And here was something I had missed. Outside a house much hung with ferns a board said:

> Premier Commercial College
> Shorthand and Bookkeeping
> H. J. Blackwhite, Principal

Here and there a curtain flapped. My walks up and down the short street had begun to attract attention. Too late to give up, though. I walked back past the Premier Commercial College. This time a boy was hanging out of a window. He was wearing a tie and he was giggling.

I asked him, 'Hey, does your sister screw?'

The boy opened his mouth and wailed and pulled back his head. There were giggles from behind the ferns. A tall man pushed open a door with coloured glass panes and came out to the veranda. He looked sombre. He wore black trousers, a white shirt, and a black tie. He had a rod in his hand!

He said in an English accent, 'Will you take your filth elsewhere. This is a school. We devote ourselves to things of the mind.' He pointed sternly to the board.

'Sorry, Mr—'

He pointed to the board again. 'Blackwhite. Mr H. J. Black-white. My patience is at an end. I shall sit down and type out a letter of protest to the newspapers.'

'I feel like writing some sort of protest myself. Do you know a place called Henry's?'

'This is not Henry's.'

'Sorry, sorry. But before you go away, tell me, what do you people do?'

'What do you mean, do?'

'What do you people do when you are doing nothing? Why do you keep on?'

There were more giggles behind the ferns. Mr Blackwhite turned and ran through the coloured glass doors into the drawing-room. I heard him beating on a desk with a rod and shouting: 'Silence, silence.' In the silence which he instantly obtained he beat a boy. Then he reappeared on the veranda, his sleeves rolled up, his face shining with sweat. He seemed willing enough to keep on exchanging words with me, but just then some army jeeps turned the corner and we heard men and women shouting. Overdoing the gaiety, I thought. Blackwhite's look of exaltation was replaced by one of distaste and alarm.

'Your colleagues and companions,' he said.

He disappeared, with a sort of controlled speed, behind the glass panes. His class began to sing, 'Flow gently, sweet Afton.'

The jeeps stopped at the unfenced lot opposite Mr Black-white's. This lot contained two verandaless wooden houses. Small houses on low concrete pillars; possibly there were more houses at the back. I stood on the pavement, the jeep-loads tumbled out. I half hoped that the gay tide would sweep me in. But men and girls just passed on either side of me, and when the tide had washed into the houses and the yard I remained where I was, stranded on the pavement.

Henry's, it was clear, was like a club. Everybody seemed to know everybody else and was making a big thing of it. I stood around. No one took any notice of me. I tried to give the impression that I was waiting for someone. I felt very foolish. Pleasure was soon the last thing in my mind. Dignity became much more important.

Henry's was especially difficult because it appeared to have no commercial organization. There was no bar, there were no waiters. The gay crowd simply sat around on the flights of concrete steps that led from the rocky ground to the doors. No tables outside, and no chairs. I could see things like this inside some of the rooms, but I wasn't sure whether I had the right to go into any of them. It was clearly a place to which you couldn't come alone.

It was Henry in the end who spoke to me. He said that I was making him nervous and that I was making the girls nervous. The girls were like racehorses, he said, very nervous and sensitive. Then, as though explaining everything, he said, 'The place is what you see it is.'

'It's very nice,' I said.

'You don't have to flatter me; if you want to stay here, fine; if you don't want to stay here, that's fine too.'

Henry wasn't yet a character. He was still only working up to it. I don't like characters. They worry me, and perhaps it was because Henry wasn't yet a character – a public performer, jolly but excluding – that I fell in so easily with him. Later, when he became a character, I was one of the characters with him; it was we that did the excluding.

I clung to him that first afternoon for the sake of dignity, as I say. Also, I felt a little resentful of the others, so very gay and integrated, and did not wish to be alone.

'We went out,' Henry said. 'A little excursion, you know. That bay over the hills, the only one you people leave us. I don't know, you people say you come here to fight a war, and the first thing you do you take away our beaches. You take all the white sand beaches; you leave us only black sand.'

'You know these bureaucrats. They like things tidy.'

'I know,' he said. 'They like it tidy here too. I can't tell you the number of people who would like to run me out of town.'

'Like that man across the road?'

'Oh, you meet old Blackwhite?'

'He is going to type out a letter about me to the newspapers. And about you, too, I imagine. And your colleagues and companions.'

'They don't print all Blackwhite's letters. Good relations and all that, you know. He believe he stand a better chance with the typewriter. Tell me what you do to provoke him. I never see a man look as quiet as you.'

'I asked one of his boys whether he had a sister who screwed.'

Amusement went strangely on Henry's sour face. He looked the ascetic sort. His hair was combed straight back and his narrow-waisted trousers were belted with a tie. This was the one raffish, startling thing about his dress.

Henry went on: 'The trouble with the natives—'

I started at the word.

'Yes, natives. The trouble with the natives is that they don't like me. I don't belong here, you know. I am like you. I come from another place. A pretty island, if I tell you. I build up all this from scratch.' He waved at his yard. 'These people here lazy and they damn jealous with it too. They always trying to get me deported. Illegal immigrant and so on. But they can't touch me. I have all the shots in the palm of my hand. You hear people talk about Gordon? Black man; but the best lawyer we have. Gordon was always coming here until that divorce business. Big thing. You probably hear about that on the base.'

'Sure, we heard about it.'

'And whenever I have any little trouble about this illegal immigrant business, I just go straight, like man, to Gordon office. The clerks – you know, those fellows with ties – try to be rude, and I just telling them, "You tell Alfred" – his name is Alfred Gordon – "you tell Alfred that Henry here." And everybody falling back in amazement when Mr Gordon come out heself and shaking me by the hand and muching me up in front of everybody. "All you wait," he say, "I got to see my old friend Henry." And teeth.'

'Teeth?'

'Teeth. Whenever I want to have any teeth pull out, I just run up to old Ling-Wing – Chinee, but the best dentist we have in the place – and he pulling out the teeth straight way. You got to have a philosophy of life. Look, I go tell you,' he said, 'my father was a good-for-nothing. Always gambling, a game called wappee and all-fours. And whenever my mother complain and start bawling out, "Hezekiah, what you going to leave for your children?" my father he only saying, "I ain't got land. I ain't got money. But I going to leave my children a wonderful set of friends."'

'That's a fine philosophy,' I said.

'We all have to corporate in some way. Some people corporate in one way, some corporate another way. I think that you and me going to get on good. Mavis, pour this man a drink. He is a wonderful talker.'

Henry, sipping at rum-and-cokes all the time, was maudlin. I was a little high myself.

One of the Americans who had been on the excursion to the bay came up to us. He tottered a little. He said he had to leave.

'I know,' Henry said. 'The war etcetera.'

'How much do I owe you, Henry?'

'You know what you owe me. I don't keep no check.'

'Let me see. I think I had a chicken pilau. Three or four rum-and-cokes.'

'Good,' Henry said. 'You just pay for that.'

The man paid. Henry took his money without any comment. When the man left he said, 'Drink is never any excuse. I don't believe people ever not knowing what they do. He not coming back in here. He had two chicken pilaus, six rum-and-coke, five bottles soda water and two whiskies. That's what I call vice.'

'It is vice, and I am ashamed of him.'

'I will tell you, you know.' Henry said. 'When the old queen pass on—'

'The old queen?'

'My mother. I was in a sort of daze. Then I had this little dream. The old man, he appear to me.'

'Your father Hezekiah?'

'No. God. He say, "Henry, surround yourself with love, but avoid vice." On this island I was telling you about, pretty if I tell you, they had this woman, pretty but malevolent. She make two-three children for me, and bam, you know what, she want to rush me into marriage.'

The sun was going down. From the base, the bit of the tropics we had created, the bugle sounded Retreat. Henry snapped his fingers, urging us all to stand. We stood up and saluted to the end.

'I like these little customs,' he said. 'Is a nice little custom you boys bring with you.'

'About this woman on the pretty island with two or three children?'

Henry said, 'I avoided vice. I ran like hell. I get the rumour spread that I dead. I suppose I am dead in a way. Can't go back to my pretty little island. Oh, prettier than this. Pretty, pretty. But she waiting for me.'

We heard hymns from the street.

'Money,' Henry said, 'all you girls got your money ready?'

They all got out little coins and we went out to the pavement.

A tall bearded man, white-robed and sandalled, was leading a little group of hymn-singers, six small black girls in white gowns. They were sweet hymns; we listened in silence.

Then the bearded man said, 'Brothers and sisters, it is customary on such occasions to say that there is still time to repent.' He was like a man in love with his own fluency. His accent was very English. 'It is, however, my belief that this, at this time, is one of the optimistic assertions of fraudulent evangelists more concerned with the counting of money than what I might call the count-down of our imminent destruction.' Suddenly his manner changed. He paused, closed his eyes, swayed a little, lifted up his arms and shouted, in an entirely different voice: 'The word of the Bible is coming to pass.'

Some of Henry's girls chanted back: 'What word?' And others: 'What part?'

The white-robed man said, 'The part where it say young people going to behave bad, and evil and violence going to stalk the land. That part.'

His little chorus began to sing; and he went round collecting from us, saying, 'It is nothing personal, you understand, nothing personal. I know you boys have to be here defending us and so on, but the truth is the truth.'

He collected his money, slipped it into a pocket of his robe, patted the pocket; then he seemed to go on patting. He patted each of his singers, either out of a great love, or to make sure that they had not hidden any of the coins they had received. Then: 'Right-wheel!' he called above their singing; and, patting them on the shoulder as they passed him, followed them to the grocery at the corner. His hymn meeting continued there, under the rusty corrugated-iron eaves.

It was now dark. A picnic atmosphere came to Henry's yard. Meals were being prepared in various rooms; gramophones were playing. From distant yards came the sound of steel-bands. Night provided shelter, and in the yard it was very cosy, very like a family gathering. Only, I was not yet of the family.

A girl with a sling bag came in. She greeted Henry, and he greeted her with a largeness of gesture which yet concealed a little reserve, a little awe. He called her Selma. I noted her. I became the third in the party; I became nervous.

I am always nervous in the presence of beauty; and in such a setting, faced with a person I couldn't assess, I was a little frightened.

I didn't know the rules of Henry's place and it was clear that the place had its own rules. I was inexperienced. Inexperienced, I say. Yet what good has experience brought me since? I still, in such a situation and in such a place, move between the extremes of courtesy and loudness.

Selma was unattached and cool. I thought she had the coolness that comes either from ownership or from being owned. It was this as much as dress and manner and balance which marked her out from the others in the yard. She might have been Henry's girl, the replacement for that other, abandoned on the pretty little island; or she might have belonged to someone who had not yet appeared.

The very private greetings over, Henry introduced us.

'He's quite a talker,' he said.

'He's a good listener,' I said.

She asked Henry, 'Did he hear Priest talk?'

I answered, 'I did. That was some sermon.'

'I always like hearing a man use language well,' she said.

'He certainly does,' I said.

'You can see,' she said, 'that he's an educated man.'

'You could see that.'

There was a pause. 'He sells insurance,' she said, 'when he's not preaching.'

'It sounds a wonderful combination. He frightens us about death, and then sells us insurance.'

She wasn't amused. 'I would like to be insured.'

'You are far too young.'

'But that is just the time. The terms are better. I don't know, I would just like it. I feel it's nice. I have an aunt in the country. She is always making old style because she's insured. Whenever she buys a little more she always lets you know.'

'Well, why don't you buy some insurance yourself?'

She said, 'I am very poor.'

And she said the words in such a way that it seemed to put a fullstop to our conversation. I hate the poor and the humble. I think poverty is something we should all conceal. Selma spoke of it as something she was neither proud nor ashamed of; it was a condition which was soon to be changed. Little things like this occur in all relationships, little warning abrasions in the smoothness of early intercourse which we choose to ignore. We always deceive ourselves; we cannot say we have not been warned.

'What would you do if you had a lot of money?'

'I would buy lots of things,' she said after some thought. 'Lots of nice modern things.'

'What sort of things?'

'A three-piece suite. One of those deep ones. You sink into them. I'd buy a nice counterpane, satiny and thick and criss-crossed with deep lines. I saw Norma Shearer using one in *Escape.*'

'A strange thing. That's all I remember of that picture. What do you think she was doing in that bed then? But that was an eiderdown she had, you know. You don't need an eiderdown in this part of the world. It's too warm.'

'Well, whatever you call it, I'd like that. And shoes, I'd buy lots of shoes. Do you have nightmares?'

'Always.'

'You know mine?'

'Tell me.'

'I am in town, you know. Walking down Regent Street. People staring at me, and I feel: this is new. I don't feel embarrassed. I feel like a beauty queen. Then I see myself in a shop window. I am barefoot. I always wake up then. My feet are hanging over the bed.'

I was still nervous. The conversation always seemed to turn away from the point to which I felt I ought to bring it, though to tell the truth I had lost the wish to do so. Still, we owe a duty to ourselves.

I said, 'Do you come from the city?'

'I come from the country.'

Question, answer, fullstop. I tried again. Henry was near us, a bottle in his hand.

I said, 'What makes a girl like you come to a place like this?' And, really, I was ashamed of the words almost before I said them.

'That's what I call a vicious question,' Henry said.

At the same time Selma slapped me.

'You think that's a nice question?' Henry said. 'I think that's a vicious question. I think that's obscene.' He pointed through the open doorway to a little sign in one of the inner rooms: Be obscene but not heard. 'It's not something we talk about.'

'I am sorry.'

'It's not for me that I am worried,' he said. 'It's for Selma. I don't know, but that girl always bringing out the vice in people. She bring out the vice in Blackwhite across the road. Don't say anything, but I see it in his eye: he want to reform her. And you know what reform is? Reform mean: keep off, for me alone. She bring out the vice in Priest. He don't want to reform. He just want. Look, Frankie, one set of people come here and then too another set come here. Selma is a educated girl, you know. Cambridge Junior Certificate. Latin and French and geometry and all that sort of thing. She does work in one of the big stores. Not one of those little Syrian shops, you know. She come here every now and then, you come here. That is life. Let us leave the vice outside, let us leave the vice outside. A lot of these girls work in stores. Any time I want a shirt, I just pass around these stores, and these girls give me shirts. We have to help one another.'

I said, 'You must have a lot of shirts.'

'Yes, I have a lot of shirts. Look, I will tell you. Selma and one or two of the other people you see here, we call *wabeen*.'

'Wabeen?'

'One of our freshwater fish. A lil loose. A *lil*. Not for any and everybody. You understand? Wabeen is not *spote*.'

'Spote?'

'Spote is – don't make me use obscene language, man, Frank. Spote is what you see.' He waved his hands about the yard.

The steel-bands sounded nearer, and then through a gate in the corrugated-iron fence at the back of the lot the musicians came in. Their instruments were made out of old dustbins, and on these instruments they played a coarse music I had never heard before.

'They have to hide, you know,' Henry told me. 'It's illegal. The war and so on. Helping the war effort.'

There was a little open shed at the back. It had a blackboard. I had noticed that blackboard and wondered about it. In this shed two or three people now began to dance. They drew watchers to them; they converted watchers into participants. From rooms in the houses on Henry's lot, from rooms in other back-yards, and from the sewerage trace at the back, people drifted in steadily to watch. Each dancer was on his own. Each dancer lived with a private frenzy. Women among the watchers tore twigs from the hibiscus hedges and from time to time, as though offering bene-diction and reward, beat the dancer's dusty feet with green leaves.

Henry put his arm over my shoulder and led me to where

Selma was standing. He kept one hand on my shoulder; he put the other on her shoulder. We stood silently together, watching. His hands healed us, bound us.

A whistle blew. There were cries of 'Police!' and in an instant the yard was transformed. Dustbins appeared upright here and there; liquor bottles disappeared inside some; the dancers and the audience sat in neat rows under the shed and one man stood at the blackboard, writing. Many of Henry's girls put on spectacles. One or two carried pieces of embroidery.

It seemed to me that the police were a long time in entering. When they did, the Inspector shook Henry by the hand and said, 'The old Adult Education class, eh?'

'As you see,' Henry said. 'Each one teach one.'

The Inspector closed his fingers when he took away his hand from Henry's. He became chatty. 'I don't know, boy,' he said. 'We just have to do this. Old Blackwhite really on your tail. And that Mrs Lambert, she too lodge a complaint.'

I wonder, though, whether I would have become involved with Selma and the others, if, during that first evening after I had undressed and was lying with Selma, I hadn't seen my clothes dancing out of the window. They danced; it was as though they had taken on a life of their own.

I called out to Selma.

She didn't seem surprised. She said, 'I think they are fishing tonight.'

'Fishing?' I ran to the window after my disappearing clothes.

'Yes, you know, fishing through the windows. Lifting a shirt here, a pair of trousers there. It is no good chasing them. Carnival coming, you know, and everybody wants a pretty costume.'

She was right. In the morning I woke up and remembered that I had no clothes except for my pants and vest. I threw open the back window and saw naked Americans hanging out of windows. We looked at one another. We exchanged no words. The evening was past; this was the morning.

Boys and girls were going to Mr Blackwhite's college. Some stopped to examine contraceptives thrown into the gutters. Selma herself was fully dressed when I saw her. She said she was going to work. So it seemed after all that Henry's story about some of his girls working in stores was right. Henry himself brought me a cup of coffee.

'You can have one of my shirts. I just pass around and ask them for one, you know.'

The morning life of Henry's yard was different from the evening life. There was a subdued workaday bustle everywhere. A tall thin man was doing limbering-up exercises. He wore a vest and a pair of shorts, and from time to time he rubbed himself with oil from a little phial.

'Canadian Healing Oil,' Henry said. 'I like to give him a little encouragement. Mano is a walker, you know. But a little too impatient; he does always end up by running and getting disqualified.'

'This is terrible,' I said. 'But what about my clothes?'

'You've got to learn tolerance. This is the one thing you have got to learn on the island.'

Mano was squatting and springing up. All about him coalpots were being fanned on back steps and women were preparing morning meals. A lot of green everywhere, more than I had remembered. Beyond the sewerage trace I could see the equally forested back-yards of the houses of the other street, and it was in some of these yards that I saw khaki uniforms and white sailor uniforms hanging limp from lines.

Henry followed my eyes. 'Carnival coming, Frank. And you people got the whole world. Some people corporate in one way, some in another.'

I didn't want Henry's philosophy just then. I ran out as I was on to the pavement. By the standards of the street I wasn't too badly dressed in my vest and pants. Next door an old negro sat sunning himself in the doorway of a room which looked like a declining secondhand bookshop. He was dressed in a tight-fitting khaki suit. The open door carried on its inside a flowery sign – MR W. LAMBERT, BOOKBINDER – so that I understood how, with the front door closed, the house was the respectable shuttered residence I had seen the day before, and how now, with the front door open, it was a shop. Beside Mr Lambert – I thought it safe to assume that he was Mr Lambert – was a small glass of rum. As I passed him he lifted the glass against the light, squinted at it, nodded to me and said, 'Good morning, my Yankee friend, may God all blessings to you send.' Then he drank the rum at a gulp and the look of delight on his face was replaced by one of total torment, as though the rum and the morning greeting formed part of an obnoxious daily penance.

'Good morning.'

'If it is not being rude, tell me, my good sir, why you are nude.'

'I don't have any clothes.'

'Touché, I say. Naked we come, and naked go away.'

This was interesting and worth exploring but just then at the end of the road I saw the jeep. I didn't know what the punishment was for losing your uniform and appearing naked in public. I ran back past Mr Lambert. He looked a little startled, like a man seeing visions. I ran into the side of Henry's yard and went up to the front house by the back steps. At the same time Mano, the walker, began walking briskly out from the other side of the house into the road.

I heard someone say from the jeep, 'Doesn't it look to you that he went in white and came out black?'

A window opened in the next room and an American voice called out, 'Did you see a naked white man running down here this morning, a few minutes ago?'

A woman's voice said, 'Look, mister, the morning is my period of rest, and the last thing I want to see in the morning is a prick.'

A pause, and the SPs drove off.

For me there remained the problem of clothing. Henry offered to lend me some of his. They didn't exactly fit. 'But,' he said, 'you could pass around by Selma's store and get a shirt. Look, I'll give you the address.'

A bicycle bell rang from the road. It was the postman in his uniform.

'Henry, Henry,' he said. 'Look what I bringing today.'

He came inside and showed a parcel. It was for Mr Blackwhite and had been sent to him from a publisher in the United States.

'Another one come back, another one.'

'O my God!' Henry said. 'I'm going to have Blackwhite crying on my hands again. What was this one about?'

'Usual thing,' the postman said. 'Love. I had a good little read. In fact, it was funny in parts.' He pulled out the manuscript. 'You want to hear?'

Henry looked at me.

'I am a captive audience,' I said.

'Make yourself comfortable,' the postman said. He began to read: ' "Lady Theresa Phillips was the most sought-after girl in all the county of Shropshire. Beautiful, an heiress to boot, intelligent, well-versed in the classics, skilful in repartee and with the embroidery needle, superbly endowed in short, she had but one failing, that of pride. She spurned all who wooed her. She had sent frustrated lovers to Italy, to the distant colonies, there to pine away in energetic solitude. Yet Nemesis was at hand. At a ball given by Lord Severn, the noblest lord in the land, Lady Theresa met Lord Alistair Grant. He was tall, square-shouldered and handsome, with melancholy eyes that spoke of deep suffering; he had in fact been left an orphan." '

'Christ! Is this what he always writes about?'

'All the time,' Henry said. 'Only lords and ladies. Typing like a madman all day. And Sundays especially you hear that machine going.'

The front door was open and through it now came the voice of Mr Blackwhite. 'Henry, I have seen everything this morning, and Mrs Lambert has just been to see me. I shall be typing out a letter to the newspapers. I just can't have naked men running about my street.' He caught sight of the postman and caught sight of the manuscript in the postman's hand. His face fell. He raced up the concrete steps into the room and snatched the manuscript away. 'Albert, I've told you before. You must stop this tampering with His Majesty's mail. It is the sort of thing they chop off your head for.'

'They send it back, old man,' Henry said. 'If you ask me, Blackwhite, I think it's just a case of prejudice. Open-and-shut case. I sit down quiet-quiet and listen to what Albert read out, and it was really nice. It was really nice.'

Blackwhite softened. 'You really think so, Henry?'

'Yes, man, it was really nice. I can't wait to hear what happen to Lady Theresa Phillips.'

'No. You are lying, you are lying.'

'What happened in the end, Mr Blackwhite?' I slapped at an ant on my leg.

'You just scratch yourself and keep quiet,' he said to me. 'I hate you. I don't believe you can even read. You think that black people don't write, eh?'

Albert the postman said, 'It was a real nice story, Blackwhite. And I prophesy, boy, that one day all those white people who now sending back your books going to be coming here and begging you to write for them.'

'Let them beg, let them beg. I won't write for them when they beg. Oh, my God. All that worrying, all that typing. Not going to write a single line more. Not a blasted line.' He grew wild again. 'I hate you, Henry, too. I am going to have this place closed, if it's the last thing I do.'

Henry threw up his hands.

'To hell with you,' Blackwhite said. 'To hell with Lady Theresa Phillips.' To me he said pointing, 'You don't like me.' And then to Henry: 'And you don't like me either. Henry, I don't know how a man could change like you. At one time it was always Niya Binghi and death to the whites. Now you could just wrap yourself in the Stars and Stripes and parade the streets.'

'Niya Binghi?' I asked.

'Was during the Abyssinian War,' Henry said, 'and the old queen did just die. Death to the whites. Twenty million on the march. You know our black people. The great revenge. Twenty million on the march. And always when you look back, is you alone. Nobody behind you. But the Stars and Stripes,' he added. 'You know, Blackwhite, I believe you have an idea there. Good idea for Carnival. Me as sort of Uncle Sam. Gentleman, it have such a thing as Stars and Stripes at the base?'

'Oh, he's one of those, is he?' Blackwhite said. 'One of our American merchantmen?'

'I believe I can get you a Stars and Stripes,' I said.

Blackwhite went silent. I could see he was intrigued. His aggressiveness when he spoke wasn't very convincing. 'I suppose that you people have the biggest typewriters in the world, as you have the biggest everything else?'

'It's too early in the morning for obscene language,' Henry said.

'I am not boasting,' I said. 'But I am always interested in writing and writers. Tell me, Mr Blackwhite, do you work regularly, or do you wait for inspiration?'

The question pleased him. He said, 'It is a mixture of both, a mixture of both.'

'Do you write it out all in longhand, or do you use a typewriter?'

'On the typewriter. But I am not being bribed, remember. I am not being bribed. But if the naked gentleman is interested in our native customs and local festivals, I am prepared to listen.' His manner changed. 'Tell me, man, you have a little pattern book of uniforms? I don't want to appear in any and every sort of costume at Carnival, you know.'

'Some of those costumes can be expensive,' I said.

'Money, money,' Blackwhite said. 'It had to come up. But of course I will pay.'

This was how it started; this was how I began to be a purveyor of naval supplies. First to Mr Henry and to Mr Blackwhite and then to the street. I brought uniforms; money changed hands. I brought steel drums; money changed hands. I brought cartons of cigarettes and chewing gum; money changed hands. I brought a couple of Underwood standard typewriters. Money didn't change hands.

Blackwhite said, 'Frankie, I think art ought to be its own reward.'

It wasn't though. A new line went up on Blackwhite's board:

ALSO TYPING LESSONS

'Also typing lessons, Blackwhite?'

'Also typing lessons. Black people don't type?'

This had become his joke. We were in his room. His walls were hung with coloured drawings of the English countryside in spring. There were many of these, but they were not as numerous as the photographs of himself, in black and white, in sepia, in coarse colour. He had an especially large photograph of himself between smaller ones of Churchill and Roosevelt.

'The trouble, you know, Blackwhite,' I said, 'is that you are not black at all.'

'What do you mean?'

'You are terribly white.'

'God, I am not going to be insulted by a beachcomber.'

'Beachcomber. That's very good. But you are not only white. You are English. All those lords and ladies, Blackwhite. All that Jane Austen.'

'What's wrong with that? Why should I deny myself any aspect of the world?'

'Rubbish. I was wondering, though, whether you couldn't start writing about the island. Writing about Selma and Mano and Henry and the others.'

'But you think they will want to read about these people?

These people don't exist, you know. This is just an interlude for you, Frankie. This is your little Greenwich Village. I know, I can read. Bam bam, bram, bram. Fun. Afterwards you leave us and go back. This place, I tell you, is nowhere. It doesn't exist. People are just born here. They all want to go away, and for you it is only a holiday. I don't want to be any part of your Greenwich Village. You beachcomb, you buy sympathy. The big rich man always behind the love, the I-am-just-like-you. I have been listening to you talking to people in Henry's yard about the States; about the big cinemas with wide screens and refrigerators as big as houses and everybody becoming film stars and presidents. And you are damn frightened of the whole thing. Always ready for the injection of rum, always looking for the nice and simple natives to pick you up.'

It was so. We turn experience continually into stories to lend drama to dullness, to maintain our self-respect. But we never see ourselves; only occasionally do we get an undistorted reflection. He was right. I was buying sympathy, I was buying fellowship. And I knew, better than he had said, the fraudulence of my position in the street.

He pointed to Churchill on the wall. 'What do you think would have happened to him if he was born here?'

'Hold your head that way, Blackwhite. Yes, definitely Churchillian.'

'Funny. You think we would have been hearing about him today? He would have been working in a bank. He would have been in the civil service. He would have been importing sewing machines and exporting cocoa.'

I studied the photograph.

'You like this street. You like those boys in the back-yard beating the pans. You like Selma who has nowhere to go, poor little wabeen. Big thing, big love. But she is only a wabeen and you are going back, and neither of you is fooling the other. You like Mr Lambert sitting on the steps drinking his one glass of rum in the morning and tacking up a few ledgers. Because Mr Lambert can only drink one glass of rum in the morning and tack up a few ledgers. You like seeing Mano practising for the walking race that is never going to come off. You look at these things and you say, "How nice, how quaint, this is what life should be." You don't see that we here are all mad and we are getting madder all the time, turning life into a Carnival.'

And Carnival came.

It had been permitted that year under stringent police super-vision. The men from the yards near Henry's made up their bands in the uniforms I had provided; and paraded through the streets. Henry was Uncle Sam; Selma was the Empress Theodora; the other girls were slave girls and concubines. There were marines and infantrymen and airforce pilots on the Pacific atolls; and in a jeep with which I had provided him stood Mr Blackwhite. He stood still, dressed in a fantastically braided uniform. He wore dark glasses, smoked a corncob pipe and his left hand was held aloft in a salute which was like a benediction. He did not dance, he did not sway to the music. He was MacArthur, promising to return.

On the Tuesday evening, when the streets were full of great figures – Napoleon, Julius Caesar, Richard the Lionheart: men parading with concentration – Blackwhite was also abroad, dressed like Shakespeare.

Selma and I settled down into a relationship which was only occasionally stormy. I had taken Mr Henry's advice that first morning and had gone around to the store where she worked. She did not acknowledge me. My rough clothes, which were really Henry's, attracted a good deal of critical attention and much critical comment on the behaviour of Americans. She acknowledged me later: she was pleased that I had gone to see her in a period as cool and disenchanted as the morning after.

Henry's, as I said, seemed to have its own especial rules. It was a club, a meeting-place, a haven, a place of assignation. It attracted all sorts. Selma belonged to the type of island girl who moved from relationship to relationship, from man to man. She feared marriage because marriage, for a girl of the people, was full of perils and quick degradation. She felt that once she surren-dered completely to any one man, she lost her hold on him, and her beauty was useless, a wasted gift.

She said, 'Sometimes when I am walking I look at these *warra-hoons*, and I think that for some little girl somewhere this animal is lord and master. *He. He* doesn't like cornflakes. *He* doesn't like rum. *He* this, *he* that.'

Her job in the store and Henry's protection gave her independence. She did not wish to lose this; she never fell for glamour. She was full of tales of girls she had known who had broken the code of their group and actually married visitors; and then had led dreadful lives, denied both the freedom they had had and the respectability, the freedom from struggle, which marriage ought to have brought.

So we settled down, after making a little pact.

'Remember,' she said, 'you are free and I am free. I am free to do exactly what I want, and you are free too.'

The pressing had always been mine. It wasn't an easy pact. I knew that this freedom might at any time embrace either Black-white, shy reformer in the background, or the white-robed preacher whom we called Priest. They both continued to make their interest in her plain.

But in the beginning it was not from these men that we found opposition after we had settled down in one of the smaller jalou-sied houses in the street – and in those days it was possible to buy a house for fifteen hundred dollars. No, it was not from these men that there was opposition, but from Mrs Lambert, Henry's neighbour, the wife of the man in the khaki suit who sipped the glass of rum in the mornings and spoke in rhyme to express either delight or pain.

Now Mrs Lambert was a surprise. I had seen her in the street for some time without connecting her with Mr Lambert. Mr Lambert was black and Mrs Lambert was white. She was about fifty and she had the manners of the street. It was my own fault, in a way, that I had attracted her hostility. I had put money in the Lamberts' way and had given them, too late in life, a position to keep up or to lose.

Mr Lambert had been excited by the boom conditions that had begun to prevail in the street. The words were Ma-Ho's, he who ran the grocery at the corner. Ma-Ho had begun to alter and extend his establishment to include a café where many men from the base and many locals sat on high stools and ate hot dogs and drank Coca-Colas, and where the children from several streets around congregated, waiting to be treated.

'Offhand,' Ma-Ho said, for he was fond of talking, 'I would say, boom.' And the words 'offhand' and 'boom' were the only really distinct ones. He began every sentence with 'offhand'; what followed was very hard to understand. Yet he was always engaged in conversation with some captive customer.

The walls of his grocery carried pictures of Chiang Kai-shek and Madame Chiang. They also had pictorial calendars, several years out of date, with delicately tinted Chinese beauties languid or coy against a background of ordered rocks and cultivated weeds, picturesque birds and waterfalls which poured like oil: incongruous in the shop with its chipped grimy counter, its open sacks of flour, its khaki-coloured sacks of sugar, its open tins of red, liquid butter. These pictures were like a longing for another world; and indeed, Ma-Ho did not plan to stay on the island. When you asked him, making conversation, especially on those occasions when you were short of change and wanted a little trust from him, 'You still going back?' the answer was: 'Offhand, I say two-four years.'

His children remained distinctive, and separate from the life of the street: a small neat crocodile, each child armed with neat bags and neat pencil boxes, going coolly off to school in the morning and returning just as coolly in the afternoon, as though nothing had touched them during the whole day, or caused them to be sullied. In the morning the back door of his shop opened to let out these children; in the afternoon the back door opened to swallow them in again; and nothing more was heard from them, and nothing more was seen of them.

The boom touched Ma-Ho. It touched Mrs Lambert. Mr Lambert called very formally one evening in his khaki suit and put a proposal to me.

'I don't want to see you get into trouble,' he said. 'Mrs Lambert and I have been talking things over, and we feel you are running an unnecessary risk in bringing these – what should I say? – these supplies to the needy of our poor island.'

I said, 'It's worked quite all right so far. You should see all the stuff we throw away.'

'Now don't misunderstand,' he said. 'I am not blaming you for what you are doing. But Mrs Lambert is particularly concerned about the trucks. She feels that by having them come out with these supplies and then having them go back, there is a chance of them being checked twice.'

'I see what you mean. Thanks, Mr Lambert. You mean that Mrs Lambert thinks that perhaps a truck might just slip out of the base and stay out?'

'Mrs Lambert thought it might be safer. Mrs Lambert has a relation who knows all there is to be known about trucks and motor vehicles generally.'

I said nothing just then, thinking of the possibilities.

Mr Lambert's manner broke up. It became familiar. All the people in the street had two sets of manners, one extremely formal, one rallying and casual.

'Look,' Mr Lambert said. 'The truck go back to the base, they start one set of questioning. It stay out here, ten to one they forget all about it. You people own the whole world.'

So into Mr Lambert's yard a truck one day rolled; and when, a fortnight or so later, it rolled out again, it was scarcely recognizable.

'Lend-lease, lease-lend,' Mr Lambert said with pure delight. 'The trend, my friend.'

And it was this truck that the Lamberts hired out to the contractors on the base. The contractors provided a driver and were willing – in fact, anxious – for the truck to work two shifts a day.

'We are getting twenty dollars a day,' Mr Lambert said. 'My friend, what luck! What luck you've given with a simple truck!'

Part of this luck, needless to say, I shared.

Yet all this while Mrs Lambert remained in the background. She was a figure in a curtained window; she was someone walking briskly down the street. She was never someone you exchanged words with. She never became part of the life of the street.

'That is one person whose old age you spoil,' Henry said. 'You see? She behaving as though they *buy* that truck. I don't think this is going to end good.'

Twenty dollars a day, minus commission and gasoline. The money was piling up; and then one day we saw a whole group of workmen around the Lamberts' house, like ants around a dead cockroach. The street came out to watch. The house, small and wooden, was lifted off its pillars by the workmen. The front door with the sign 'Mr W. Lambert, Bookbinder' swung open and kept on flapping while the house was taken to the back of the lot, to rest not on pillars but flat on the ground. The workmen drank glasses of rum to celebrate. The street cheered. But then we saw Mr Lambert pushing his way through the crowd. He looked like a man expecting news of death. He saw the pillars; he saw his house on the ground; and he said: 'My house! My house brought low! But I did not want a bungalow. Here the old pillars stand, in the middle of naked land.' He left and went to Ma-Ho's. He became drunk; he addressed verse to everyone.

The habit grew on him. It seemed to us that he remained drunk until he died.

Henry said, 'Once upon a time – and really now it sounded like a fairy tale – once upon a time Mrs Lambert was a very poor girl. Family from Corsica. Living up there in the cocoa valleys with the tall *immortelle* trees. Times was hard. You couldn't even give away cocoa. And Lambert had this job in the Civil Service. Messenger. Uniform, regular pay, the old pension at the end, and nobody sacking you. Marriage up there in the hills with the bush and red *immortelle* flowers. Oh, happy! Once-upon-a-time fairy tale. Wurthering Heights. Hansel and Gretel in the witch-broom cocoa woods. Then the world sort of catch up with them.'

The pillars were knocked down, and where the old wooden house stood there presently began to rise a house of patterned concrete blocks. The house, I could see, was going to be like hundreds of others in the city: three bedrooms down one side, a veranda, drawing-room and dining-room down the other side, and a back veranda.

No longer a doorstep at which Mr Lambert could sit, greeting us in the morning with his glass of rum. The old wooden house was sold, for the materials; frame by frame, jalousie by jalousie, the house was dismantled and re-erected far away by the man who had bought it, somewhere in the country. And then there was no longer a Mr Lambert in the morning. He left the yard early. In his khaki suit he was like a workman hurrying off to a full day. We often saw him walking with Mano. Mano, the walker in Henry's yard, who after his morning's exercise put on his khaki messenger's uniform and walked to the government office where he worked. Their dress was alike, but they were an ill-assorted pair, Mano lean and athletic, Mr Lambert even at that early hour shambling drunk.

Mr Lambert had a sideline. At sports meetings, on race days, at cricket and football matches, he ran a stall. He sold a vile sweet liquid of his own manufacture. On these occasions he appeared, not with his cork hat, but with a handkerchief knotted around his head. He rang a bell and sang his sales rhymes, which were often pure gibberish. 'Neighbour! Neighbour! Where are you? Here I am! Rat-tat-too.' Sometimes he would point to the poisonous tub in which hunks of ice floated in red liquid, and sing: 'Walk in! Jump in! Run in! Hop in! Flop in! Leap in! Creep in!'

This was the Mr Lambert of happier days. Now, after the degradation of his house, it seemed that he had given up his stall. But he had grown friendly with Mano and this friendship led him to announce that he was going to the sports meeting in which Mano was to take part.

Henry said, 'Mrs Lambert doesn't like it. She feel that this old black man hopping around with a handkerchief on his head and ringing his bell is a sort of low-rating, especially now that she building this new house. And she say that if he go and ring that bell any more she finish with him. She not going to let him set foot in the new house.'

So we were concerned about both Mr Lambert and Mano. We often went in the afternoons to the great park to cycle around with Mano as he walked, to help him to fight the impatience that made him run in walking races and get disqualified.

Henry said, 'Frankie, I think you trying too hard with Mano. You should watch it. You see what happen to Mrs Lambert. You know, I don't think people want to do what they say they want to do. I think we always make a lot of trouble for people by helping them to get what they say they want to get. Some people look at black people and only see black. You look at poor people and you only see poor. You think the only thing they want is money. All-you wrong, you know.'

One day while we were coming back in procession from the park, Mano pumping away beside us past the crocodile of Ma-Ho's children, we were horrified to see Mr Lambert stretched out on the pavement like a dead man. He was not dead; that was a relief. He was simply drunk, very complicatedly drunk. Selma ran to Mrs Lambert and brought back a cool message: 'Mrs Lambert says we are not to worry our heads with that good-for-nothing idler.'

Henry said, 'We are not doing Lambert any good by being so friendly with him. Mrs Lambert, I would say, is hostile to us all, definitely hostile.'

Mr Lambert at this stage revived a little and said, 'They say I am black. But black I am not. I tell you, good sirs, I am a Scot.'

Henry said, 'Is not so funny, you know. His grandfather was a big landowner, a big man. We even hear a rumour some years before the war that according to some funny law of succession Mr Lambert was the legal head of some Scottish clan.'

The house went up. The day of the sports meeting came.

Mano was extremely nervous. As the time drew nearer he even began to look frightened. This was puzzling, because I had always thought him quite withdrawn, indifferent to success, failure or encouragement.

Henry said, 'You know, Mano never read the papers. On the road yesterday some crazy thing make him take up the evening paper and he look at the horoscope and he read: "You will be exalted today." '

'But that's nice,' I said.

'It get him frightened. Was a damn funny word for the paper to use. It make Mano think of God and the old keys of the kingdom.'

Mano was very frightened when we started for the sports ground. There was no sign in the street of Mr Lambert and we felt that he had in the end been scared off by Mrs Lambert and that to save face he had gone away for a little. But at the sports ground, after the meeting had begun and Mano was started on his walk – it was a long walk, and you must picture it going on and on, with lots of other sporting activities taking place at the same time, each activity unrelated to any other, creating a total effect of a futile multifarious frenzy – it was when Mano was well on his walk that we heard the bell begin to ring. To us it rang like doom.

'Mano will not run today, Mano will walk to heaven today.'

Exaltation was not in Mr Lambert's face alone or in his bell or in his words. It was also in his dress.

'On me some alien blood has spilt. I make a final statement, I wear a kilt.' And then came all his old rhymes.

And Mano didn't run. He walked and won. And Mr Lambert rang his bell and chanted: 'Mano will not run today. He will walk into the arms of his Lord today.'

We had worked for Mano's victory. Now that it had come it seemed unnatural. He himself was like a stunned man. He rejected congratulations. We offered him none. When we looked for Mr Lambert we couldn't find him. And with a sense of a double and deep unsettling of what was fixed and right, we walked home. We had a party. It turned into more than a party. We did not notice when Mano left us.

Later that night we found Mr Lambert drunk and sprawling on the pavement.

He said, 'I led her up from the gutter. I gave her bread. I gave her butter. And this is how she pays me back. White is white and black is black.'

We took him to his house. Henry went to see Mrs Lambert. It was no use. She refused to take him in. She refused to come out to him.

'To my own house I have no entrance. Come, friends, all on my grave dance.'

We had a double funeral the next day. Mano had done what so many others on the island had done. He had gone out swimming, far into the blue waters, beyond the possibility of return.

'You know,' Henry said, as we walked to the cemetery, 'the trouble with Mano was that he never had courage. He didn't want to be a walker. He really wanted to be a runner. But he didn't have the courage. So when he won the walking race, he went and drowned himself.'

Albert the postman was in our funeral procession. He said, 'News, Frankie. They send back another one of Blackwhite's books.'

Blackwhite heard. He said to me, 'Was your fault. You made me start writing about all *this*. Oh, I feel degraded. Who wants to read about this place?'

I said, 'Once you were all white, and that wasn't true. Now you are trying to be all black and that isn't true either. You are really a shade of grey, Blackwhite.'

'Hooray for me, to use one of your expressions. This place is nowhere. It is a place where everyone comes to die. But I am not like Mano. You are not going to kill me.'

'Blackwhite, you old virgin, I love you.'

'Virgin? How do you know?'

'We are birds of a feather.'

'Frankie, why do you drink? It's only a craving for sugar.'

And I said to him: 'Dickie-bird, why do you weep? Sugar, sugar. A lovely word, sugar. I love its sweetness on my breath. I love its sweetness seeping through my skin.'

And in the funeral procession, which dislocated traffic and drew doffed hats and grave faces from passers-by, I wept for Mano and Lambert and myself, wept for my love of sugar; and Blackwhite wept for the same things and for his virginity. We walked side by side.

*   *   *

Selma said Henry was right. 'I don't think you should go around interfering any more in other people's lives. People don't really want what you think they want.'

'Right,' I said. 'From now on we will just live quietly.'

Quietly. It was a word with so many meanings. The quietness of the morning after, for instance, the spectacles on my nose, quiet in an abstemious corner. I was a character now. I had licence. Sugar sweetened me. In Henry's yard, in Selma's house, and on the sands of the desolate bay over the hills, the healing bay where the people of the island sought privacy from joy and grief.

Priest's denunciations of us, of me, grew fiercer. And Black-white, seen through the flapping curtain of his front room, pounded away at his typewriter in sympathetic rage.

Then one blurred aching morning I found on the front step a small coffin, and in the coffin a mutilated sailor doll and a toy wreath of rice fern.

They came around to look.

'Primitive,' Blackwhite said. 'Disgusting. A disgrace to us.'

'This is Priest work,' Henry said.

'I have been telling you to insure me,' Selma said.

'What, is that his game?'

Henry said, 'Priest does take his work seriously. The only thing is, I wish I know what his work is. I don't know whether it is preaching, or whether it is selling insurance. I don't think he know either. For him the two seem to come together.'

To tell the truth, the coffins on Selma's doorstep worried me. They kept on appearing and I didn't know what to do. Selma became more and more nervous. At one moment she suggested I should take her away; at another moment she said that I myself should go away. She also suggested that I should try to appease Priest by buying some insurance.

'Appease Priest? The words don't sound right. Henry, you hear?'

Henry said, 'I will tell you about this insurance. I don't know how it happen on the island, but it becoming a social thing, you know. Like having a shower, like taking schooling, like getting married. If you not insured these days you can't hold up your head at all. Everybody feel you poor as a church rat. But look. The man coming himself.'

It was Priest, wearing a suit and looking very gay and not at all malevolent.

'Dropping in for a little celebration,' he said.

Selma was awed, and it was hard to say whether it was because of Priest's suit, the coffins, or his grand manner.

'What are you celebrating?' I said. 'A funeral?'

He wasn't put out. 'New job, Frankie, new job. More money, you know. Higher commission, bigger salary. Frankie, where you say you living in the States? Well, look out for me. I might be going up there any day. So the bosses say.'

I said, 'I'd love to have you.'

'You know,' he said, 'how in this insurance business I have this marvellous record. But these local people' – and here he threw up his beard, scratched under his chin, screwed up his eyes – 'but these local people, you know how mean they is with the money. Then this new company come down, you know, and they get to know about me. I didn't go to see them. They send for me. And when I went to see them they treat me as a God, you know. And a damn lot of them was white to boot. You know, man, I was like – what I can say? – I was like a *playboy* in that crowd, a playboy. And look how the luck still with me, look how the luck still in my hand. You know what I come in here to celebrate especially? You know how for years I begging Ma-Ho to take out insurance. And you know how he, Ma-Ho, don't want to take out no insurance. He just saying he want to go back to China, back to the old wan-ton soup and Chiang Kai-shek. Well, he insured as from today.'

Henry said, 'He pass his medical?'

I said, 'Offhand, that man looks damn sick to me, you know.'

'He pass his medical,' Priest said.

'He went to the doctor?' Henry asked. 'Or the doctor went to him?'

'What you worrying with these *details*? You know these Chinese people. Put them in their little shop and they stay there until kingdom come. Is a healthy life, you know.'

Henry said, 'Ma-Ho tell me one day that when he come to the island in 1920 and the ship stop in the bay and he look out and he see only mangrove, he started to cry.'

Selma said, 'I can't imagine Ma-Ho crying.'

Henry said, 'To me it look as though he never stop crying.'

'Offhand,' I said, 'no more coffins, eh?'

'Let me not hear of death,' Priest said in his preaching manner. He burst out laughing and slapped me on the back.

And, indeed, no more coffins and dead sailors and toy wreaths appeared on Selma's steps.

I knocked on Selma's door one day two weeks later. 'Any coffins today, Ma'am?'

'Not today, thank you.'

Selma had become houseproud. The little house glittered and smelt of all sorts of polishes. There were pictures in passe-partout frames on the walls and potted ferns in brass vases on the marble-topped three-legged tables for which she had a passion. That day she had something new to show me: a marble-topped dresser with a clay basin and ewer.

'Do you like it?'

'It's lovely. But do you really need it?'

'I always wanted one. My aunt always had one. I don't want to use it. I just want to look at it.'

'Fine.' And after a while I said, 'What are you going to do?'

'What do you mean?'

'Well, the war's not going to go on for ever. I can't stay here for ever.'

'Well, it's as Blackwhite says. You are going to go back, we are going to stay here. Don't weep for me, and' – she waved around at all the little possessions in her room – 'and I won't weep for you. No. That's not right. Let's weep a little.'

'I feel,' I said, 'that you are falling for old Blackwhite. He's talked you round, Selma. Let me warn you. He's no good. He's a virgin. Such men are dangerous.'

'Not Blackwhite. To tell you the truth, he frightens me a little.'

'More than Priest?'

'I am not frightened of Priest at all,' she said. 'You know, I always feel Priest handles the language like a scholar and gentleman.'

I was at the window. 'I wonder what you will say now.'

Priest was running down the street in his suit and howling: 'All-you listen, all-you listen. Ma-Ho dead, Ma-Ho dead.'

And from houses came the answering chant. 'Who dead?'

'Ma-Ho dead.'

'The man was good. Good, good.'

'Who?'

'Ma-Ho.'

'I don't mean he was not bad. I mean,' Priest said, subsiding into personal grief, 'I mean he was well. He was strong. He was healthy. And now, and now, he dead.'

'Who dead?'

'Ma-Ho. I not crying because I blot my book in my new job. I not crying because this is the first time I sell insurance to someone who dead on my hands. I not crying because those white people did much me up when I get this new job.'

'But, Priest, it look so.'

'It look so, but it wrong. O my brothers, do not misunderstand. I cry for the man.'

'What man?'

'Ma-Ho.'

'He did want to go back.'

'Where?'

'China.'

'China?'

'China.'

'Poor Ma-Ho.'

'You know he have those Chinese pictures in the back-room behind the shop.'

'And plenty children.'

'And you know how nice the man was.'

'The man was nice.'

'You go to Ma-Ho and ask for a cent red butter. And he give you a big lump.'

'And a chunk of lard with it.'

'And he was always ready to give a little trust.'

'A little trust.'

'Now he dead.'

'Dead.'

'He not going to give any lard again.'

'No lard.'

'He not going to China again.'

'Dead.'

Through the roused street Priest went, howling from man to man, from woman to woman. And that evening under the eaves of Ma-Ho's shop, before the closed doors, he delivered a tremendous funeral oration. And his six little girls sang hymns. Afterwards he came in, sad and sobered, to Henry's and began to drink beer.

Henry said, 'To tell you the truth, Priest, I was shocked when

I hear you sell Ma-Ho insurance. Is a wonder you didn't know the man had diabetes. But with all these coffins all over the place, I didn't think it was any of my business. So I just keep my mouth shut. I ain't say nothing. I always say everybody know their own business.'

'Diabetes?' Priest said, almost dipping his beard into his beer. 'But the doctor pass him in everything.' He made circular gestures with his right hand. 'The doctor give him a test and everything was correct. Everything get test. The man was good, good, good, I tell you. He was small, but all of all–you used to see him lifting those heavy sugar bags and flour bags over the counter.'

Henry asked, 'You did test his pee?'

'It was good. It was damned good pee.' Priest wept a little. 'You know how those Chinese people neat. He went into the little back-room with all those children, and he bring out a little bottle – a little Canadian Healing Oil bottle.' Still weeping, he indicated with his thumb and finger the size of the bottle.

'Was not his pee,' Henry said. 'That was why he didn't want to *go* to the doctor. That was why he wanted the doctor to come to *him*.'

'O God!' Priest said. 'O God! The Chinese bitch. He make me lose my bonus. And you, Henry. You black like me and you didn't tell me nothing. You see,' he said to the room, 'why black people don't progress in this place. No corporation.'

'Some people corporate in one way,' Henry said. 'Some people corporate in another way.'

'Priest,' I said, 'I want you to insure Selma for me.'

'No,' Selma said nervously. 'I don't want Priest to insure me. I feel the man blight.'

'Do not mock the fallen,' Priest said. 'Do not mock the fallen. I will leave. I will move to another part of the city. I will fade away. But not for long.'

And he did move to another area of the city. He became a nervous man, frightened of selling insurance, instilling terror, moreover, into those to whom he tried to sell insurance: the story of Ma-Ho's sudden death got around pretty quickly.

Ma-Ho went, and with him there also went the Chinese emblems in his shop. No longer the neat crocodile left and entered the back door of the shop; and from being people who kept themselves to themselves, who gave the impression of being

only temporary residents on the island, always packed for departure, Ma-Ho's family came out. The girls began to ride bicycles.
The insurance money was good. The boys began to play cricket
on the pavement. And Mrs Ma-Ho, who had never spoken a
word of English, revealed that she could speak the language.

'I begin to feel,' Blackwhite said, 'that I am wrong. I begin to
feel that the island is just about beginning to have an existence
in its own right.'

Our own flag was also about to go down. The war ended. And,
after all these years, it seemed to end so suddenly. When the news
came there was a Carnival. No need to hide now. Bands sprang
out of everywhere. A song was created out of nothing: *Mary Ann*.
And the local men, who had for so long seen the island taken
over by others, sang, but without malice, 'Spote, spote, Yankee
sufferer,' warning everyone of the local and lean times to come.

The atmosphere at Henry's subtly changed. Gradually through
the boom war years there had been improvements. But now, too,
the people who came changed. Officers came from the base with
their wives, to look at the dancing. So did some of the island's
middle class. Men with tape recorders sometimes appeared in the
audience. And in the midst of this growing esteem, Henry
became more and more miserable. He was a character at last,
mentioned in the newspapers. The looser girls faded away; and
more *wabeens* appeared, so expensive as to be indistinguishable
from women doomed to marriage. Henry reported one day that
one of his drummers, a man called Snake, had been seized by
somebody's wife, put into a jacket and tie, and sent off to the
United States to study music.

Henry, now himself increasingly clean and increasingly better
shaven, was despondent. Success had come to him, and it made
him frightened. And Blackwhite, who had for years said that
people like Snake were letting down the island, adding to the
happy-go-lucky-native idea, Blackwhite was infuriated. He used
to say, 'Snake is doing a difficult thing, beating out music on
dustbins. That is like cutting down a tree with a penknife and
asking for applause.' Now, talking of the kidnapping of Snake,
he spoke of the corruption of the island's culture.

'But you should be happy,' I said. 'Because this proves that the
island exists.'

'No sooner exists,' he said, 'than we start to be destroyed. You know, I have been doing a lot of thinking. You know, Frankie, I begin to feel that what is wrong with my books is not me, but the language I use. You know, in English, black is a damn bad word. You talk of a black deed. How then can I write in this language?'

'I have told you already. You are getting too black for me.'

'What we want is our own language. I intend to write in our own language. You know this patois we have. Not English, not French, but something we have made up. This is our own. You were right. Damn those lords and ladies. Damn Jane Austen. This is ours, this is what we have to work with. And Henry, I am sure, whatever his reasons, is with me in this.'

'Yes,' Henry said. 'We must defend our culture.' And sadly regarding his new customers, he added: 'We must go back to the old days.'

On the board outside Blackwhite's house there appeared this additional line: PATOIS TAUGHT HERE.

Selma began going to the Imperial Institute to take sewing lessons. The first lessons were in hemstitching, I believe, and she was not very good. A pillowcase on which she was working progressed very slowly and grew dirtier and dirtier, so that I doubted whether in the end any washing could make it clean again. She was happy in her house, though, and was unwilling to talk about what was uppermost in my own mind: the fact that we at the base had to leave soon.

We did talk about it late one night when perhaps I was in no position to talk about anything. I had gone out alone, as I had often done. We all have our causes for irritation, and mine lay in this: that Selma refused to exercise any rights of possession over me. I was free to come and go as I wished. This had been a bad night. I could not get the key into the door; I collapsed on the steps. She let me in in the end. She was concerned and sympathetic, but not as concerned as she might have been. And yet that tiny moment of rescue stayed with me: that moment of helplessness and self-disgust and total despair at the door, which soon, to my scratchings, had miraculously opened.

We began by talking, not about my condition, but about her sewing lessons. She said, 'I will be able to earn a little money with my sewing after these lessons.'

I said, 'I can't see you earning a penny with your sewing.'

She said, 'Every evening in the country my aunt would sit

down by the oil lamp and embroider. She looked very happy when she did this, very contented. And I promised myself that when I grew up I too would sit down every evening and embroider. But really I wonder, Frank, who is afraid for who.'

Again the undistorted reflection. I said, 'Selma, I don't think you have ever been nicer than you were tonight when you let me in.'

'I did nothing.'

'You were very nice.' Emotion is foolish and dangerous; the sweetness of it carried me away. 'If anyone ever hurts you, I'll kill him.'

She looked at me with amusement.

'I really will, I'll kill him.'

She began to laugh.

'Don't laugh.'

'I am not really laughing. But for this, for what you've just said, let us make a bargain. You will leave soon. But after you leave, whenever we meet again, and whatever has happened, let us make a bargain that we will spend the first night together.'

We left it at that.

So now there gathered at Henry's, more for the company than for the pleasure, and to celebrate what was changing, the four of us whose interests seemed to coincide: Henry, Blackwhite, Selma and myself. What changes, changes. We were not together for long. Strangers were appearing every day now on the street, and one day there appeared two who split us up, it seemed, for ever.

We were at Henry's one day when a finely-suited middle-aged man came up hesitantly to our table and introduced himself as Mr de Ruyter of the Council for Colonial Cultures. He and Blackwhite got on well from the start. Blackwhite spoke of the need to develop the new island language. He said he had already done much work on it. He had begun to carry around with him a few duplicated sheets: a glossary of words he had made up.

'I make up new words all the time. What do you think of *squinge*? I think that's a good word.'

'A lovely word,' Mr de Ruyter said. 'What does it mean?'

'It means screwing up your eyes. Like this.'

'An excellent word,' Mr de Ruyter said.

'I visualize,' Blackwhite said, 'an institute which would dedicate itself to translating all the great books of the world into this language.'

'Tremendous job.'

'The *need* is tremendous.'

I said to Henry and Selma: 'You know, I feel that all three of us are losing Blackwhite.'

'I think you are wrong,' Mr de Ruyter said. 'This is just the sort of thing that we must encourage. We have got to move with the times.'

'One of my favourite expressions,' Blackwhite said.

Mr de Ruyter said, 'I have a proposal which I would like to put to you, though I do so with great diffidence. How would you like to go to Cambridge to do some more work on your language? Oxford of course has a greater reputation for philology but—' Mr de Ruyter laughed.

And Blackwhite laughed with him, already playing the Oxford and Cambridge game. Almost before the question had been completed I could see that he had succumbed. Still he went down fighting. 'Cambridge, Oxford? But my work is here, among my people.'

'Indeed, indeed,' Mr de Ruyter said. 'But you will see the Cam.'

'A hell of a long way to go to see a Cam,' Henry said.

'It's a river,' Mr de Ruyter said.

'Big river?' Henry said.

'In England we think big things are rather vulgar.'

'It sounds a damn small river,' Henry said.

Mr de Ruyter went on, 'You will see King's College Chapel. You will see the white cliffs of Dover.'

With every inducement Blackwhite's eyes lit up with increased wattage.

Mr de Ruyter threw some more switches. 'You will cross the Atlantic. You will sail down the Thames. You will see the Tower of London. You will see snow and ice. You will wear an overcoat. You will look good in an overcoat.'

At the same time Henry, rising slowly and furtively, began to excuse himself. He said, 'I never thought I would see this.'

At the end of the room we saw a fat and ferocious woman who was looking closely at the darkened room as though searching for someone. She was the woman whose picture Henry often showed and around whom he had been in the habit of weaving stories of romance and betrayal. Even now, in this moment of distress, he found time to say, 'She wasn't fat when I did know she.'

Success, the columns in the newspapers, had betrayed him. He got away that evening, but within a fortnight he had been recaptured, cleaned up and brought back. And now it was Mrs Henry, if she was a Mrs Henry, who ruled. She worked like a new broom in the establishment, introducing order, cleanliness, cash registers, bill-pads, advertisements in the newspapers, and a signboard: THE COCONUT GROVE – *Overseas Visitors Welcome*.

No place for us now. Change, change. It was fast and furious. Through mine-free, dangerless channels ships came from Europe and the United States to the island: some grey, some still with their wartime camouflage, but one or two already white: the first of the tourist boats.

And on the base, where before there had been stern notices about a 5 mph speed limit and about the dangers to unauthorized persons, there now appeared a sign: TO BE SOLD BY PUBLIC AUCTION.

The base was sold and a time was fixed for local possession. Until that time my authority still mattered. From house to house in the street I went. And in that no man's time – between the last Retreat and the arrival of the local buyer who had put up a new board:

To Be Erected Here Shortly
THE FLORIDA SHIRT FACTORY

– in that no man's time, at dawn, through the open unguarded gates of the base the people of the street came in and took away whatever they could carry. They took away typewriters, they took away stoves, they took away bathtubs, wash-basins, refrigerators, cabinets. They took away doors and windows and panels of wire-netting.

I saw the buildings bulldozed. I saw the quick tropical grass spreading into the cracks on the asphalted roads. I saw the flowers, the bougainvillaea, poinsettia, the hibiscus, grow straggly in the tropics we had created.

In a house stuffed with refrigerators and wash-basins and stoves and typewriters I took my leave.

'It is our way,' Selma said. 'Better this than that.' She pointed to Henry's, where Henry stood, miserable in his own doorway, Mrs Henry, you could feel, oppressive in the background. 'That is how love and the big thing always ends.'

Blackwhite was typing when I left.

III

In the doorway now stood the bouncer.

'I've been keeping my eye on you.'

'Me too. You are very pretty.'

He made a gesture.

'As pretty as a picture in a magazine. What are you advertising today? Bourbon?'

'You can't come in here.'

'No, I don't think bourbon. I think rice.'

'Even with a tie I don't think you could come in here.'

'Bourbon, rice: I'm not interested. I'm turning the page over to the funnies.'

'You can't come in here.'

'You've a nice place to break up.'

It was lush inside, like the film set of an old musical. There were waiters dressed in fancy clothes which I took to be a type of folk costume. There were tourists at candlelit tables; there was a stage with a thatched roof. And sitting at a long table in the company of some expensively-dressed elderly men was Mr Blackwhite.

'You can't come in here without a tie.'

I pulled hard at his.

A voice said, 'You better lend him yours before you hang yourself on it.'

The voice was Henry's. Poor Henry, in a suit and with a tie; his eyes red and impotent with drink; thinner than I had remembered, his face more sour.

'Henry, what have they done to you?'

'I think,' another voice said, 'I think that is a question he might more properly put to you.'

It was Blackwhite. H. J. B. White, of the tormented winking writer's-photograph face. Very ordinary now.

'I have bought *all* your books.'

'Hooray for you, as the saying was. Frank, it is awfully nice seeing you here again. But you frighten us a little.'

'You frighten me too.' I lifted my arms in mock terror. 'Oh, I am frightened of you.'

Henry said, 'Do that more often and they will get you up on the stage.' He nodded towards the back of the room.

Blackwhite gave a swift, anxious look at the room. Some

tourists, among them the happy team and the embittered team of the morning, were looking at me with alarm and shame. Letting down the side.

Blackwhite said, 'I don't think you only frighten us, you know.'

I was struggling with the tie the doorman had given me. Greasy.

'Look,' I said to Henry, pointing to the doorman. 'This man hasn't got a tie. Throw him out.'

'You are in one of your moods,' Blackwhite said. 'I don't think you can see that we have moved with the times.'

'Oh, I am frightened of you.'

'Drunkard,' Blackwhite said.

'It's only sugar, remember?'

'I believe, Frank, speaking as a friend, that you want another island. Another bunch of happy-go-lucky natives.'

'So you went to Cambridge?'

'A tedious place.'

'Still, it shows.'

The band began to tune up. Blackwhite became restless, anxious to get back to his guests. 'Come, Frankie, why don't you go down to the kitchen with Henry and have a drink and talk over old times? You can see we have some very distinguished guests from various foundations tonight. Very important negotiations on hand, boy. And we mustn't give them a wrong idea of the place, must we? Don't waste your time. Take a tip. Start looking for another island.' He looked at me; he softened. 'Though I don't think there is any place for you now except home. Take him down, Henry. And Henry, look, when Pablo and those other idlers come, clean them up a little bit in the kitchen first before you send them up, eh?'

Men and women in fancy costumes which were like the waiters' costumes came out on to the stage and began doing a fancy folk dance. They symbolically picked cotton, symbolically cut cane, symbolically carried water. They squatted and swayed on the floor and moaned a dirge. From time to time a figure with a white mask over his face ran among them, cracking a whip; and they lifted their hands in pretty fear.

'You see how us niggers suffered,' Henry said, leading me to a door marked STAFF ONLY. 'Is all Blackwhite doing, you know. He say it was you who give him the idea. You make him stop writing all those books about lords and ladies in England. You ask him to write about black people. You know, Frankie, come to think of it, you did interfere a damn lot, you know. Is a wonder you didn't try to marry me off: Is a *wonder*? Is a pity. Remember what you did use to say about what you would do if you had a million dollars? What you would do for the island, for the street?'

'A million dollars.'

Footsteps behind me. I turned.

'Frankie.'

'Leonard.'

'Frankie, I am glad I found you. I was really worried about you. But goodness, isn't this a terrific place? Did you see that last dance?'

From where we were we could hear the cracking of whips, orchestrated wails, the stamp and scuttling of feet. Then it came: muted, measured applause.

'Leonard, you'd better get back,' I said. 'There are some people from various foundations upstairs who have seized Mr White. If you aren't careful you will lose him.'

'Oh, is that who they were? Thanks for telling me. I will run up straight away. I don't know how I will make myself known to him. People just don't believe me . . .'

'You will think of something. Henry, where is the telephone?'

'You still play this telephone game. One day the police are going to catch up with you.'

I dialled. The telephone rang. I waited. A booming male voice shouted, 'Frankie. Stay away.' So loud that even Henry could hear.

'Priest,' I said. 'Gary Priestland. How do you think he knew?'

Henry said, 'From the way you've been getting on, I don't imagine there is a single person in town who doesn't know. You know you broke up the British Council lecture on Shakespeare or something?'

'My God.' I remembered the room. Six people, a man in khaki trousers swinging jolly, friendly legs over a table.

'You thought it was a bar.'

'But, Henry, what's happened to the place? You mean they've actually begun to give you culture now? Shakespeare and all the rest of it?'

'They give we, we give them. A two-way process, as old Black-white always saying. And they always saying how much they have to learn from us. I don't know how the thing catch on so sudden. You see the place is like a little New York now. I imagine that's why they like it. Everybody feel at home. Ice-cubes in the fridge, and at the same time they getting the exotic old culture. The old Coconut Grove even have a board of governors. I think, you know, the next thing is they going to ask me to run for the City Council. They already make me a MBE, you know.'

'MBE?'

'Member of the Order of the British Empire. Something they give singers and people in culture. Frankie, you don't even care about the MBE. Forget the telephone. Forget Selma. Sometimes you want the world to end. You can't go back and do things again. They begin just like that, they get good. The only thing is you never know they good until they finish. I wish the hurricane would come and blow away all this. I feel the world need this sort of thing every now and then. A clean break, a fresh start. But the damn world don't end. And we don't dead at the right time.'

'What about Selma?'

'You really want to know?'

'Tell me.'

'I hear she buy a mixmaster the other day.'

'Now this is what I really call news.'

'I don't know what else to tell you. I went the other day to the Hilton. Barbecue night. I see Selma there, picking and choosing with the rest. Everybody moving with the times, Frankie. Only you and me moving backwards.'

Mrs Henry came into the room. She didn't have to say that she didn't like me. Henry cringed.

She said, 'I don't know, Henry. Leave you in charge in front for five minutes, and the place start going to pieces. I just had to sack the doorman. He didn't have no tie or anything. And Mr White did ask you to take special care this evening.'

I fingered the doorman's tie. When Mrs Henry left Henry sprayed the door with an imaginary tommy gun. I was aware of the room. We were among flowers. Hundreds of plastic blooms.

'You looking,' Henry said. 'Is not my doing. I like a flowers, but I don't like a flowers so bad.'

The back door was pushed open again. Henry cringed, lowered his voice. But it wasn't Mrs Henry.

'I is Pablo,' an angry man said. 'What that fat woman mean, telling we to come round by the back?'

'That was no woman,' Henry said. 'That was my wife.'

Pablo was one of three angry men. Three men of the people: freshly washed hair, freshly oiled, freshly suited. They looked like triplets.

Pablo said, 'Mr White sent for us specially. He send for me. He send for he.' He pointed to one of his friends.

The friend said, 'I is Sandro.'

'He send for he.'

'I is Pedro.'

'Pablo, Sandro, Pedro,' Henry said, 'cool down.'

'Mr White won't like it,' Pablo said.

'Making guests and artisses come through the back,' said Sandro.

'When they get invite to a little supper,' said Pedro.

Henry sized them up. 'Guests and artisses. A lil supper. Well, all-you look all right, I suppose. Making, as they say, the best of a bad job. Go up. Mr White waiting for you.'

They left, mollified. Determination to deter further insult was in their walk. Henry, following them, seemed to sag.

I noticed an angry face behind the window. It was the sacked doorman. I could scarcely recognize him without his tie. He made threatening gestures; he seemed about to climb in. I straightened his tie around my collar and hurried after Henry into the main hall.

At the long table the little supper seemed about to begin. Blackwhite rose to meet Pablo, Sandro and Pedro. The three expensively-suited men with Blackwhite rose to be introduced. Leonard and Sinclair were hanging around uncertainly.

Blackwhite eyed Leonard. Leonard flinched. He saw me and ran over.

'I don't have the courage,' he whispered.

'I'll introduce you.'

I led him to the table.

'I'll introduce you,' I said again. 'Blackwhite is an old friend.'

I pulled up two chairs from another table. I put one chair on Blackwhite's right. For Leonard. One chair on Blackwhite's left. For me. Astonishment on the faces of the foundation men; anxiety on Blackwhite's; a mixture of assessment and sympathy on the faces of Pablo, Sandro and Pedro, uncomfortable among the crystal and linen, the flowers and the candles.

A waiter passed around menus. I tried to take one. He pulled it back. He looked at Blackwhite, questioning. Blackwhite looked at me. He looked down at Leonard. Leonard gave a little smile and a little wave and looked down at the table at a space between settings. He drew forks from his right and knives from his left.

'Yes,' Blackwhite said. 'I suppose. Feed them.'

They hurried up with knives and forks and spoons.

Pablo and Sandro and Pedro were lip-reading the menus.

Pablo said, 'Steak Chatto Brian for me.'

'But, sir,' the waiter said. 'That's for two.'

Pablo said, 'You didn't hear me? Chatto Brian.'

'Chatto Brian,' Sandro said.

'Chatto Brian,' Pedro said.

'Oysters,' I said. 'Fifty. No, a hundred.'

'As a starter?'

'And ender.'

'Prawns for me,' Leonard said. 'You know. Boiled. And with the shells. I like peeling them.'

'He is a great admirer of yours, Blackwhite,' I said. 'His name is Leonard. He is a patron of the arts.'

'Yes, indeed,' Leonard said. 'Mr White, this is a great pleasure. I think *Hate* is wonderful. It is – it is – a most *endearing* work.'

'It was not meant to be an endearing work,' Blackwhite said.

'Goodness, I hope I haven't said the wrong thing.'

'You can't, Leonard,' I said. 'Leonard has got some money to give away.'

Blackwhite adjusted the nature of his gaze. Pablo, Sandro and Pedro looked up. The men from the foundations stared.

'Do you know him, Chippy?'

'Can't say I do. I'll ask Bippy.'

'I don't know him, Tippy.'

'Leonard,' Chippy said. 'I've never heard of that name in Foundationland.'

'This is possible,' Blackwhite said. 'But Leonard has the right idea.'

'Mr White,' Bippy said, affronted.

'We have never let you down,' said Tippy.

'You won't want to run out on us now, will you, Mr White?' Chippy asked.

'What about you, Mr White?' asked the waiter.

Blackwhite considered the menu. 'I think I'll start with the Avocado Lucullus.'

'Avocado Lucullus.' The waiter made an approving note.

'What do you mean by the right idea, Mr White?'

'Then I think I'll try a sole. What's the bonne femme like tonight? The right idea?'

The waiter brought his thumb and index finger together to make a circle.

'Well, let's say the sole bonne femme. With a little spinach. Gentlemen, I'll tell you straight. The artist in the post-colonial era is in a position of peculiar difficulty.'

'How would you like the spinach, Mr White?'

'En branches. And the way you or anyone else can help him is with – money. There it is, gentlemen. The way you can help Pablo here—'

'The wine list, Mr White.'

'Go on. We are listening.'

'The way to help Pablo – ah, sommelier. But let's ask our hosts.'

'No, no. We leave that to you, Mr White.'

'Is with – money. Shall we break some rules? Pablo, would you and your boys mind a hock? Or would you absolutely insist on a burgundy to go with your Chateaubriand?'

'Anything you say, Mr White.'

'I think the hock. Tell me, do you have any of that nice Rudesheimer left?'

'Indeed, Mr White. Chilled.'

'All right, gentlemen? A trifle sweet. But still.'

'Sure. Waiter, bring a couple of bottles of what Mr White just said. How do we help Pablo?'

'Pablo? You give Pablo ten thousand dollars. And let him get on with the job.'

'What does he do?' asked Bippy.

'That's a *detail*,' Blackwhite said. 'So far as my present argument goes.'

'I entirely agree,' Chippy said.

'Waiter,' Blackwhite called. 'I believe you have forgotten our hosts.'

'Sorry, gentlemen. For you?'

'But if you are interested, Pablo and his boys are a painting group. They work together at the same time on one canvas.'

'Steak tartare. Like the Italians. Or the Dutch.'

'Steak tartare. One man painting the face.'

'Steak tartare. The other painting the scenery. Steak tartare. What am I saying? Just a salad.'

'Not quite,' Blackwhite said. 'This is more an experiment in recovering the tribal subconscious.'

'Shall we say, en vinaigrette?'

'What do you mean?'

'You know about Jung and the racial memory.'

'With vinegar.'

'That's just about how I feel.'

'They have produced some very interesting results. A sort of artistic stream-of-consciousness relay. But in paint. A sort of continuous mutual interference.'

'This sounds very interesting, Mr White,' Bippy said.

'We don't want to offend Pablo,' Tippy said.

'Or Sandro or Pedro,' Chippy added.

'But we have to be sure, Mr White.'

'Foundationland has its own rules, Mr White.'

'Mr White, we have to write reports.'

'Mr White, help us.'

'Mr White, we have made this journey to see *you*.'

'I don't know, gentlemen. We can't just *brush* off Pablo and his boys just like that. An appropriate word, don't you think? Let us see how they feel.'

Bippy, Tippy and Chippy looked at Pablo, Sandro and Pedro.

'Ask them,' Blackwhite said. 'Go on, ask them.'

'What do you feel about this, Mr Pablo?' Bippy asked.

'If any money going, give it to Blackwhite,' Pablo said.

'Give it to Mr White,' Sandro said.

'Is what I say too,' said Pedro.

'You see, Mr White,' Chippy said. 'You must shoulder your responsibilities. We appreciate your desire to nurse struggling talent. But—'

'Exactly,' said Tippy.

Blackwhite didn't look disappointed.

The food came. Pablo and his friends began sawing. Blackwhite scooped avocado, poured wine.

Blackwhite said, 'I didn't want it to appear that I was pushing myself forward. I wanted you to meet Pablo and his boys because

I thought you might want to encourage something new. I feel that you chaps have got quite enough out of me as it is.'

There was a little dismissing laughter. I swallowed oysters. Leonard peeled prawns.

'And also,' Blackwhite went on, 'because I felt that you might not be altogether happy with the experimental work I have on hand.'

'Experimental?' Tippy said.

'Oh, this sounds good,' Leonard said.

'Gentlemen, no artist should repeat himself. My interracial romances, though I say it myself, have met with a fair amount of esteem, indeed acclaim.'

'Indeed,' said Bippy, Tippy and Chippy.

'Gentlemen, before you say anything, listen. I have decided to abandon the problem.'

'This is good,' Leonard said. 'This is very good.'

'How do we abandon the problem?' Blackwhite said.

Pablo reached forward and lifted up a wine bottle. It was empty. He held it against the light and shook it. Chippy took the bottle from him and set it on the table. 'There is nothing more there,' he said.

'I have thought about this for a long time. I think I should move with the times.'

'Good old Blackwhite,' I said.

'I want,' Blackwhite said, 'to write a novel about a black man.'

'Oh, good,' Leonard said.

'A novel about a black man falling in love.'

'Capital,' said Bippy, Tippy and Chippy.

'With a black woman.'

'Mr White!'

'Mr White!'

'Mr White!'

'I thought you would be taken aback,' Blackwhite said. 'But I would regard such a novel as the statement of a final emancipation.'

'It's a terrific idea,' Leonard said.

'Tremendous problems, of course,' Blackwhite said.

'Mr White!' Bippy said.

'We have to write too,' said Chippy.

'Our reports,' said Tippy.

'Calm down boys,' Bippy said. 'Mr White, you couldn't tell us how you are going to treat this story?'

'That's my difficulty,' Blackwhite said.

'*Your* difficulty,' Chippy said. 'What about ours?'

'Black boy meets black girl,' Tippy said.

'They fall in love,' said Bippy.

'And have some black children,' said Chippy.

'Mr White, that's not a story.'

'It's more like the old-fashioned coon show. The thing we've been fighting against.'

'You'll have the liberals down your throat.'

'You will get us the sack. Mr White, look at it from our point of view.'

'Calm down, boys. Let me talk to him. This is a strange case of regression, Mr White.'

'I'll say. You've regressed right back to Uncle Remus, right back to Brer Rabbit and Brer Fox.'

'Do us another *Hate* and we'll support you to the hilt.'

'Give us more of the struggler, Mr White.'

'Calm *down* boys. Much depends on the treatment, of course. The treatment is everything in a work of art.'

'Of course,' Blackwhite said, scooping up the bonne femme sauce from the dish in the waiter's reverential hand.

'I don't know. You might just work something. You might have the black man rescued from a bad white woman.'

'Or the black woman rescued from a bad white man.'

'Or *something*.'

'We've got to be careful,' Blackwhite said. 'I have gone into this thing pretty thoroughly. I don't want to offend any ethnic group.'

'What do you mean, Mr White?'

'He is right,' Leonard said. 'Mr White, I think you are terrific.'

'Thank you, Leonard. And also, I was toying with the idea of having a bad black man as my hero. Just toying.'

'Mr White!'

'Mr White!'

'Mr White!'

'I am sorry. I have used a foolish word. One gets into such a way of talking. Reducing the irreducible to simple terms. I don't mean bad. I just mean ordinary.'

'Mr White!'

'Calm down, Tippy.'

'What do you mean, Mr White? Someone bad at ball games?'

'And tone deaf?'

'You just want a cripple,' Leonard said.

'The thought occurred to me too, Leonard,' Blackwhite said. 'They just want a cripple.'

'Who the hell said anything about a cripple?'

'Calm down, Bippy.'

'Kid,' Chippy said. 'Forgive me for talking to you like this. But you are committing suicide. You've built up a nice little reputation. Why go and throw it away now for the sake of a few crazy ideas?'

'Why don't you go home and write us another *Shadowed Livery*?'

'Do us another *Hate*.'

Leonard said, 'I intend to support you, Mr White.'

Blackwhite said, 'I am rather glad this has turned out as it has. I believe I understand you gentlemen and what you stand for. It mightn't be a bad idea, after all, for you to extend your patronage to Pablo and his boys.'

'Anything to follow, Mr White?' the waiter said. 'A zabaglione? Crème de marrons?'

'I require nothing but the bill,' Blackwhite said. 'Though those boys look as though they require feeding.' He nodded towards Pablo and his friends.

The waiter produced the bill. Blackwhite waved towards Bippy, Tippy and Chippy, each of whom extended a trained hand to receive it.

'Mr White, we didn't mean to offend you.'

'But you have,' Leonard said.

'I hate you,' Blackwhite said to Bippy. He pointed to Chippy. 'I hate you.' He pointed to Tippy. 'And I hate you.'

They began to smile.

'This is the old H. J. B. White.'

'We might have lost a friend.'

'But we feel we have saved an artist.'

'Feed Pablo and his boys from now on,' Blackwhite said.

'Yes,' Leonard said, rising. 'Feed Pablo. Mr White, I am with you. I think your black idea is terrific. I will support you. You will want for nothing.'

'Who is this guy?' Bippy asked.

'Thanks for the oysters,' I said. 'He's got a million to play with. He's going to make you look pretty silly.'

'Who knows?' Chippy said. 'The mad idea might come off.'

'New York won't like it if it does,' Bippy said.

'Calm down,' said Tippy.

They walked towards the bar.

'No more winter trips.'

'Or extended journeys.'

'No more congresses.'

'By day or night.'

'No more chewing over literate-chewer.'

'Or seminars on cinema.'

'But wait,' said Bippy. 'Perhaps Blackwhite was right. Perhaps Pablo and his boys do have something. The tribal subconscious.'

They were still eating.

'Mr Pablo?'

'Mr Sandro?'

'Mr Pedro?'

I left Blackwhite and Leonard together. I left Sinclair too. He had been in the dining-room throughout. I went down to the kitchen.

On the TV screen Gary Priestland was announcing: 'Here is some important news. Hurricane Irene has altered course fractionally. This means the island now lies in her path. Irene, as you know' – he spoke almost affectionately – 'has flattened the islands of Cariba and Morocoy.' On the screen there appeared stills. Flattened houses; bodies; motor-cars in unlikely places; a coconut grove in which uprooted coconut trees lay almost parallel to one another as though laid there by design, to await erection. Gary Priestland gave details of death and injuries and financial loss. He was like a sports commentator, excited by a rising score. 'To keep you in touch the Island Television Service will not be closing down tonight. ITS will remain on the air, to keep you in constant touch with developments. I have a message from the Red Cross. But first—'

The Ma-Ho girls came on in their frilly short skirts and sang a brisk little whinnying song for a local rum.

While they were singing the telephone rang.

Henry had been gazing at the television set, held, it seemed, by more than news. He roused himself and answered the telephone.

'For you.'

'Frankie.'

The voice was not that of Gary Priestland, TV compere, master of ceremonies. It was the voice of Priest.

'Frankie, I am telling you. Stay away. Do not interfere. My thoughts are of nothing but death tonight. Leave Selma alone. Do not provoke her.'

On the TV I saw him put the telephone down, saw the manner change instantly from that of Priest to that of Priestland. Like a deity, then, he supervised more stills of disaster on the islands of Cariba and Morocoy.

The kitchen had a low ceiling. The light was fluorescent. No wind, no noise save that from the air extractor. The world was outside. Protection was inside.

Henry, gazing at the pictures of death and disorder, was becoming animated.

'Hurricane, Frankie. Hurricane, boy. Do you think it will really come?'

'Do you want it to come?'

He looked dazed.

I left him and made for the lavatories. The oyster sickness. One door carried a metal engraving of a man, the other of a woman. Their coyness irritated me. One at a time, they raced unsteadily up to me. I cuffed the woman. Squeals. I hurried through the door with the man.

The mirror was steamed over. I cleared part of it with my hand. For the first time that day, that night, that morning, I saw my face. My face, my eyes. My shirt, the doorman's tie. I was overwhelmed. The tribal subconscious. Portrait of the artist. I signed it in one corner.

'Yes. When all is said and done, I think you are pretty tremendous. Very brave. Moving among men like a man. You take taxis. You buy shirts. You run houses. You travel. You hear other people's voices and are not afraid. You are pretty terrific. Where do you get the courage?'

A hand on my elbow.

'Leonard,' I whispered, turning.

But it was Henry, a little firmer than he had been so far that evening, a little more rallying, a little less dejected.

'Hurricane coming, man. The first time. And you want to meet it here?'

I went out. And saw Selma.

'You,' I said.

'The mystery man on the telephone,' she said. 'No mystery to me, though, after the first few times. I knew it was you. Henry sent a message to me. I left the Hilton as soon as I could.'

'Barbecue night. Gary Priestland, master of ceremonies. I know. Selma, I have to talk to you. Selma, you have pulled down our house. I went and looked. You pulled it down.'

'I've got a nicer one.'

'Poor Selma.'

'Rich Selma,' Henry said. 'Poor Henry.'

We were in the kitchen. The television was blue. The air extractor roared.

'I sold the house to a foundation. They are going to put up a national island theatre.' She nodded towards the television set. 'It was Gary's idea. It was a good deal.'

'You've all done good deals. Who is going to write the plays? Gary?'

'It's only for happenings. No scenery or anything. Audiences walking across the stage whenever they want. Taking part even. Like Henry's in the old days.'

'Hurricane coming,' Henry said.

'It was all Gary's idea.'

'Not the hurricane,' I said.

'Even that.' She gazed at the screen as if to say, look.

Priestland, Priest, was lifting back his head. From details of death and destruction on other islands, details delivered with the messenger's thrill, he was rising to a type of religious exaltation. And now there followed not the Ma-Ho girls with their commercials but six little black girls with hymns.

She looked away. 'Come, shall I take you home?'

'You want me to see your home?'

'It is up to you.'

'Hurricane coming,' Henry said. He began to sway. 'All this is over. We all become new men.'

'Repent!' Priest cried from the television screen.

'Repent?' Henry shouted back. 'All this is over.'

'Rejoice!' Priest said. 'All this is over.'

'Why run away now?' Henry said.

'Why run away?' Priest said. 'There is nothing to run to. Soon there will be nothing to run from. There is a way which seemeth right unto a man but at the end thereof are the ways of death. Repent! Rejoice! How shall we escape, if we neglect so great a salvation.'

'Emelda!' Henry called. 'Emelda!' To Selma and to me he said, 'Not yet. Don't go. A last drink. A last drink. Emelda!' He wandered about the kitchen and the adjoining room. 'All these plastic flowers! All these furnitures! All these decorations! Consume them, O Lord!'

Mrs Henry appeared in the doorway.

'Emelda, my dear,' Henry said.

'What get into you now?'

He unhooked a flying bird from the wall and aimed it at her head. She ducked. The bird broke against the door.

'That cost forty dollars,' she said.

He aimed another at her. 'Eighty now.'

'Henry, the wind get in your head!'

'Let us make it a hundred.' He lifted a vase.

Selma said, 'Let us go.'

I said, 'I think the time has come.'

'No. You're my friends. You must have a farewell drink. Emelda, will you serve my friends?'

'Yes, Henry.'

'Call me mister, Emelda. Let us maintain the old ways.'

'Yes, Mr Henry.'

'Vodka and coconut water, Emelda.' He put down the vase.

The black girls sang hymns.

'You let me in that night, Selma,' I said. 'I've remembered that.'

'I remember. That was why I came.'

Emelda, Mrs Henry brought back a bottle, a pitcher and some tumblers.

Henry said, 'Emelda, after all this time you spend teaching me manners, you mean you want to give my friends glasses with hairs in it?'

'Then look after them yourself, you drunken old trout.'

'Old trout, old tout,' Henry said. And then, with shouts of pure joy, the hymns pouring out in the background, he smashed bottle, pitcher and tumblers. He went round breaking things. Emelda followed him, saying, 'That cost twenty dollars. That cost thirty-two dollars. That cost fifteen dollars. In a sale.'

'Sit down, Emelda.'

She sat down.

'Show them your mouth.'

She opened her mouth.

'Nice and wide. Is a big mouth you have, you know, Emelda. The dentist could just climb in inside with his lunch parcel and scrape away all day.'

Emelda had no teeth.

'Frankie, look at what you leave me with. Sit down, Emelda. She and she sister setting competition. Sister take out all her teeth. So naturally Miss Emelda don't want to keep a single one of she own. Look. I got to watch this morning, noon and night. I mad to hit you, mouth. Mouth, I mad to hit you.'

'No, Henry. That mouth cost almost a thousand dollars, you know.'

'All that, and the world ending!'

'Rejoice!' Priest called from the television screen. He lifted the telephone on his desk and dialled.

The telephone in Henry's kitchen rang.

'Don't answer,' Selma said. 'Come, our bargain. Our first evening. Let me take you home.'

Hymns from the blue screen; screams from Emelda; the crash of glasses and crockery. The main room of The Coconut Grove, all its lights still on, was deserted. The thatched stage was empty.

'The perfection of drama. No scenery. No play. No audience. Let us watch.'

She led me outside. People here. Some from The Coconut Grove, some from neighbouring buildings. They stood still and silent.

'Like an aquarium,' Selma said.

Low, dark clouds raced. The light ever changed.

'Your car, Selma?'

'I always wanted a sports model.'

'The car is the man, is the woman. Where are you taking me to?'

'Home.'

'You haven't told me. Where is that?'

'Manhattan Park. A new area. It used to be a citrus plantation. The lots are big, half an acre.'

'Lovely lawns and gardens?'

'People are going in a lot for shrubs these days. It's something you must have noticed. You'll like the area. It's very nice.'

It was a nice area, and Selma's house was in the modernistic style of the island. Lawn, garden, a swimming pool shaped like a teardrop. The roof of the veranda was supported on sloping lengths of tubular metal. The ceiling was in varnished pitchpine. The furnishings were equally contemporary. Little bits of driftwood; electric lights pretending to be oil lamps; irregularly shaped tables whose tops were sections of tree trunks complete with bark. She certainly hated straight lines and circles and rectangles and ovals.

'Where do you get the courage, Selma?'

'This is just your mood. We all have the courage.'

Local paintings on the wall, contemporary like anything.

'I always think women have a lot of courage. Imagine putting on the latest outrageous thing and walking out in that. That takes courage.'

'But you have managed. What do you sell? I am sure that you sell things.'

'Encyclopaedias. Textbooks. Inoffensive culture. *Huckleberry Finn* without nigger Jim, for ten cents.'

'You see. That's something I could never do. The world isn't a frightening place, really. People are playing a lot of the time. Once you realize that, you begin to see that people are just like yourself. Not stronger or weaker.'

'Oh, they are stronger than me. Blackwhite, Priest, you, even Henry – you are all stronger than me.'

'You are looking at the driftwood? Lovely things can be found in Nature.'

'But we don't leave it there. Lovely house, Selma. Lovely, ghastly, sickening, terrible home.'

'My home is not terrible.'

'No, of course not to you.'

'You can't insult me. You are too damn frightened. You don't like homes. You prefer houses. To fit into other people's lives.'

'Yes. I prefer houses. My God. I am on a treadmill. I can't get off. I am surrounded by other people's very big names.'

'You are getting worse, Frank. Come. Be a good boy. Bargain, remember. Let me show you my bedroom.'

'Adultery has its own rules. Never on the matrimonial bed.'

'Not matrimonial yet. That is to come.'

'I have no exalted idea of my prowess.'

'You were always lousy as a lover. But still.'

'What language, Selma. So snappy, man. Let me put on the old TV. I don't want to miss anything.'

The man on the screen had changed his clothes. He was wearing a white gown. He had abandoned news; he was only preaching.

He said, 'All we like sheep have gone astray; we have turned everyone to his own way.'

As if in sympathy with his undress, I began unbuttoning my shirt.

In the bedroom it was possible to hear him squawking on. On the bed lay a quilted satin eiderdown.

'You are like Norma Shearer in *Escape*.'

'Shut up. Come. Be good.'

'I will be good if I come.'

Our love-making was not a success.

'It was bad.'

'Drink is good for a woman,' Selma said. 'Bad for a man. You prepared yourself too well today, Frank. You waste your courage in fear.'

'I waste my courage in fear. "Now *look* what you have done." '

'Explain.'

'It was what a woman said to me many years ago. I was fifteen. She called me in one afternoon when I was coming back from school and asked me to get on top of her. And that was what she said at the end. "Now *look* what you have done." As though *I* had done the asking. Talking to me as though she was talking to a baby. Terrible. Sex is a hideous thing. I've decided. I'm anti-sex.'

'That makes two of us.'

'All I can say is that we've been behaving strangely for a very long time.'

'You started it. Tell me, did you expect me to keep our bargain?'

'I don't know. It is like one of those stories you hear. That a woman always sleeps with the man who took her maidenhead. Is it true? I don't know. Is it true?'

'It is,' Selma said, rising from the bed, 'an old wives' tale.'

In the drawing-room the television still groaned on. The black girls sang hymns. I went to the bathroom. The mat said RESERVED FOR DRIPS. On the lavatory seat there was a notice, flowers painted among the words: GENTLEMEN LIFT THE SEAT IT IS SHORTER THAN YOU THINK LADIES REMAIN SEATED

THROUGHOUT THE PERFORMANCE. An ashtray; a little book of
lavatory and bedroom jokes. The two so often going together.
Poor Selma. I pulled the lavatory chain twice.

The wind was high.

'Selma, be weak like me. Henry is right. Priest is right. It is all
going to be laid flat. Let us rejoice. Let us go to the bay. Let us
take Henry with us. And afterwards, if there is an afterwards,
Henry will take us to his pretty little island.'

'There are no more islands. It's not you talking. It's the wind.'

The oil lamp which was really an electric lamp was overturned. Darkness, except for the blue of the television screen.
And the wind drowned Priest's voice.

Selma became hysterical.

'Let us get out of here. Let us go back to town. In the street
with the others.'

'No, let us go to the bay.'

Henry sat among disarrayed plastic flowers, in a deserted
Coconut Grove.

'The bay!'

'The bay.'

We drove up and over the hills, the three of us. We heard the
wind. We ran down on to the beach, and heard the sea. At least
that couldn't be changed. Once the beach was dangerous with
coconut trees, dropping nuts. Now most had been cut down to
make a parking lot. Standing foursquare on the beach was a great
concrete pavilion, derelict: a bit of modernity that had failed: a
tourist convenience that had served no purpose. The village had
grown. It had spread down almost to the beach, a rural marine
slum. Lights were on in many of the shacks.

'I never thought you could destroy the bay.'

'We might have a chance to start afresh.'

We walked in the wind. Pariah dogs came up to wait, to follow
fearfully. The smell of rotting fish came fitfully with the wind.
We decided to spend the night in the tourist pavilion.

Morning, dark and turbulent, revealed the full dereliction of
the beach. Fishing boats reclined or were propped up on the
sand that was still golden, but there were also yellow oil drums
on the beach for the refuse of the fishermen, whose houses, of
unplastered hollow-clay bricks and unpainted timber, jostled
right up to the limit of dry sand. The sand was scuffed and
marked and bloody like an arena; it was littered with the heads

and entrails of fish. Mangy pariah dogs, all rib and bone, all bleached to a nondescript fawn colour, moved listlessly, their tails between their legs, from drum to yellow drum. Black vultures weighed down the branches of coconut trees; some hopped awkwardly on the sand; many more circled overhead.

Henry was peeing into the sea.

I called out to him, 'Let us go back. It is more than I can stand.'

'I always wanted to do this,' he said. 'In public.'

'You mustn't blame yourself,' Selma said. 'It is never very good in the morning.'

It hadn't been good.

We drove back to the city. We drove, always, under a low dark sky. It was early, yet the island was alive. The streets were full of people. Their first hurricane, their first drama, and they had come out into the streets so as to miss nothing. All normal activity had been suspended. It was like a continuation of the night before; the streets were even more like aquaria, thick with life, but silent. Only the absence of the blackness of night seemed to have marked the passage of time; only that and the screens, now blank, of television sets seen through the open doors of houses – some still with useless lights on – and in cafés doing no business.

Then it was night again. The useless lights had meaning. Against the black sky blacker points moved endlessly: all the birds of the island, flying south. It was like the final abandonment. We were in the midst of noise, in which it was at times possible to distinguish the individual groans of houses, trees, and the metallic flapping of loose corrugated-iron sheets. No fear on any face, though. Only wonder and expectation.

The television screens shimmered. Priest reappeared, tired, shining with fatigue, telling us what we already knew, that the end of our world was at hand.

'Behold,' he said, 'now is the day of salvation.'

The city responded. Faintly at first, like distant temple bells, the sound of steel orchestras came above the roar of the wind. The pariah dogs, and those dogs that lived in houses, began to bark in relay, back and forth and crossways. Feet began to shuffle. Priest railed like a seer, exhausted by the effort of concentration. He railed; the city was convulsed with music and dance.

The world was ending and the cries that greeted this end were cries of joy. We all began to dance. We saw dances such as we had seen in the old days in Henry's yard. No picking of cotton, no cutting of cane; no carrying of water, no orchestrated wails. We danced with earnestness. We did contortions of which we had never thought ourselves capable.

We saw Blackwhite dancing with Leonard. Blackwhite not white, not black, but Blackwhite as we all would have liked to see him, a man released from endeavour, released from the strain of seeing himself (portrait of the artist: the tribal subconscious), at peace with the world, accepting, like Leonard. We saw Bippy, Tippy and Chippy arm in arm with Pablo, Sandro and Pedro, as though the wooing that had begun at The Coconut Grove had gone on all night: a gesture now without meaning, a fixed attitude of ritual in which news of the hurricane had caught them all. Occasionally the men from Foundationland pleaded with Blackwhite. Still, without malice or triumph, he spurned them, and did stylized stamps of simple negation: a private man, at last. As on a flat stage, stretching to infinity before our eyes, infinity the point where the painted floorboards met, companionship and wooing and pursuit and evasion played back and forth before us. But Leonard, obstinately dancing, dancing with earnestness, like the man anxious to catch the right mood and do the right thing: Leonard remained, in spite of his exertions, what he had always been, bemused, kind, blank. Arm in arm he danced with Blackwhite whenever they met; and Sinclair, big, heavy Sinclair, swung between them. And the tourist teams of the day before: the happy now like people who had forgotten the meaning of the word, which implied an opposite, the embittered, oh, infinitely less so. And for me, no terror of sky and trees: the courage of futility, the futility of courage, the empty, total response.

Through the streets, flattened to stage-boards, we danced, waiting for the final benediction. The sky hung low, grew high, hung low. The wind sweetly filled our ears, slackened, filled our ears again. We danced and waited. We waited and danced.

Benediction never came. Our dancing grew listless. Fatigue consumed anguish. But hope was not entirely consumed, even when on the television sets we saw Priest being transformed into Priestland, the seer into the newscaster, the man whose thoughts had only been of death, into the man who diminished life. But how could we deny?

We gave up the hurricane. We sat in the streets. Light was grey, then silver. The stage was becoming a street again; house took on volume. I heard Bippy, Tippy and Chippy wailing. Pablo and the boys comforted them.

Sinclair straightened his jacket and tie. In the light of a day that had now truly broken he went to Leonard, detached him from Blackwhite, and said, 'Come, Leonard. Come, boy. We have had our fun. It is time to go home!'

'Goodbye, Mr White,' Leonard said. 'Very well, Sinclair. You have been very good. Let us go.'

Blackwhite saw and understood. 'Leonard!' he said, stupefied. 'Leonard, what about my black novel? You promised help. You drove away the men from Foundationland. You said I was to want for nothing.'

'Goodbye, Mr White. How are you feeling, Sinclair?'

'Leonard! You promised support! Bippy, Tippy, Chippy. Wait, wait. Pablo, call off your idlers! Pablo! Bippy! Mr Tippy! Mr Chippy!'

He, once the pursued, now became the pursuer. Pablo, Sandro and Pedro fled before him, as did Bippy, Tippy and Chippy. He pursued them; they evaded him and often the six came together. On the stage stretching to infinity the chase took place, pursuer and the six pursued dwindling to nothing before us. The sun was bright; there were shadows.

I went with Selma to The Coconut Grove. Henry was cleaning up the kitchen. Emelda stood over him. He rearranged plastic flowers; he put broken vases together.

On the television set Gary Priestland was announcing that the hurricane had not come. But he had news for us, news of the destruction of some other island. He had news. He had facts and the figures of death. He had stills.

In the harbour the ships blew the all-clear.

The Ma-Ho girls came on and did a commercial for a local cigarette.

The programmes for the day were announced.

'Home,' Selma said.

'The old driftwood calls. Lovely things can be found in Nature.'

'Gary will be tired.'

'I'll say.'

And in the city where each exhausted person had once more

to accommodate himself to his fate, to the life that had not been arrested, I went back to the hotel.

> Hilton, Hilton.
> *Sailing 1 p.m.*, the board said in the lobby.
> Moore-McCormack, Moore-McCormack.

August 1965

From IN A FREE STATE

CONTENTS

IT WAS ONLY a two-day crossing from Piraeus to Alexandria, but as soon as I saw the dingy little Greek steamer I felt I ought to have made other arrangements. Even from the quay it looked overcrowded, like a refugee ship; and when I went aboard I found there wasn't enough room for everybody.

There was no deck to speak of. The bar, open on two sides to the January wind, was the size of a cupboard. Three made a crowd there, and behind his little counter the little Greek barman, serving bad coffee, was in a bad mood. Many of the chairs in the small smoking-room, and a good deal of the floor space, had been seized by overnight passengers from Italy, among them a party of overgrown American schoolchildren in their mid-teens, white and subdued but watchful. The only other public room was the dining-room, and that was being got ready for the first of the lunch sittings by stewards who were as tired and bad-tempered as the barman. Greek civility was something we had left on shore; it belonged perhaps to idleness, unemployment and pastoral despair.

But we on the upper part of the ship were lucky. We had cabins and bunks. The people on the lower deck didn't. They were deck passengers; night and day they required only sleeping room. Below us now they sat or lay in the sun, sheltering from the wind, humped figures in Mediterranean black among the winches and orange-coloured bulkheads.

They were Egyptian Greeks. They were travelling to Egypt, but Egypt was no longer their home. They had been expelled; they were refugees. The invaders had left Egypt; after many humiliations Egypt was free; and these Greeks, the poor ones, who by simple skills had made themselves only just less poor than Egyptians, were the casualties of that freedom. Dingy Greek ships like ours had taken them out of Egypt. Now, briefly, they were going back, with tourists like ourselves, who were neutral, travelling only for the sights; with Lebanese businessmen; a troupe of Spanish night-club dancers; fat Egyptian students returning from Germany.

The tramp, when he appeared on the quay, looked very English; but that might only have been because we had no English people on board. From a distance he didn't look like a tramp. The hat and the rucksack, the lovat tweed jacket, the grey flannels and the boots might have belonged to a romantic wanderer of an earlier generation; in that rucksack there might have been a book of verse, a journal, the beginnings of a novel.

He was slender, of medium height, and he moved from the knees down, with short springy steps, each foot lifted high off the ground. It was a stylish walk, as stylish as his polka-dotted saffron neck-scarf. But when he came nearer we saw that all his clothes were in ruin, that the knot on his scarf was tight and grimy; that he was a tramp. When he came to the foot of the gangway he took off his hat, and we saw that he was an old man, with a tremulous worn face and wet blue eyes.

He looked up and saw us, his audience. He raced up the gangway, not using the hand-ropes. Vanity! He showed his ticket to the surly Greek; and then, not looking about him, asking no questions, he continued to move briskly, as though he knew his way around the ship. He turned into a passageway that led nowhere. With comical abruptness he swung right round on one heel and brought his foot down hard.

'Purser,' he said to the deck-boards, as though he had just remembered something. 'I'll go and see the purser.'

And so he picked his way to his cabin and bunk.

Our sailing was delayed. While their places in the smoking-room were being watched over, some of the American school-children had gone ashore to buy food; we were waiting for them to come back. As soon as they did – no giggles: the girls were plain, pale and abashed – the Greeks became especially furious and rushed. The Greek language grated like the anchor chain. Water began to separate us from the quay and we could see, not far from where we had been, the great black hulk of the liner *Leonardo da Vinci*, just docked.

The tramp reappeared. He was without his hat and rucksack and looked less nervous. Hands in trouser pockets already stuffed and bulging, legs apart, he stood on the narrow deck like an experienced sea-traveller exposing himself to the first sea breeze of a real cruise. He was also assessing the passengers; he was looking for company. He ignored people who stared at him; when others, responding to his own stare, turned to look at him he swivelled his head away.

In the end he went and stood beside a tall blond young man. His instinct had guided him well. The man he had chosen was a Yugoslav who, until the day before, had never been out of Yugoslavia. The Yugoslav was willing to listen. He was baffled by the tramp's accent but he smiled encouragingly; and the tramp spoke on.

'I've been to Egypt six or seven times. Gone around the world about a dozen times. Australia, Canada, all those countries. Geologist, or used to be. First went to Canada in 1923. Been there about eight times now. I've been travelling for thirty-eight years. Youth-hostelling, that's how I do it. Not a thing to be despised. New Zealand, have you been there? I went there in 1934. Between you and me, they're a cut above the Australians. But what's nationality these days? I myself, I think of myself as a citizen of the world.'

His speech was like this, full of dates, places and numbers, with sometimes a simple opinion drawn from another life. But it was mechanical, without conviction; even the vanity made no impression; those quivering wet eyes remained distant.

The Yugoslav smiled and made interjections. The tramp neither saw nor heard. He couldn't manage a conversation; he wasn't looking for conversation; he didn't even require an audience. It was as though, over the years, he had developed this way of swiftly explaining himself to himself, reducing his life to names and numbers. When the names and numbers had been recited he had no more to say. Then he just stood beside the Yugoslav. Even before we had lost sight of Piraeus and the *Leonardo da Vinci* the tramp had exhausted that relationship. He hadn't wanted company; he wanted only the camouflage and protection of company. The tramp knew he was odd.

At lunch I sat with two Lebanese. They were both overnight passengers from Italy and were quick to explain that it was luggage, not money, that had prevented them travelling by air. They looked a good deal less unhappy with the ship than they said they were. They spoke in a mixture of French, English and

Arabic and were exciting and impressing each other with talk of
the money other people, mainly Lebanese, were making in this
or that unlikely thing.

They were both under forty. One was pink, plump and casually dressed, with a canary pullover; his business in Beirut was,
literally, money. The other Lebanese was dark, well-built, with
moustached Mediterranean good looks, and wore a three-piece
check suit. He made reproduction furniture in Cairo and he said
that business was bad since the Europeans had left. Commerce
and culture had vanished from Egypt; there was no great demand
among the natives for reproduction furniture; and there was
growing prejudice against Lebanese like himself. But I couldn't
believe in his gloom. While he was talking to us he was winking
at one of the Spanish dancers.

At the other end of the room a fat Egyptian student with thick-
lensed glasses was being raucous in German and Arabic. The
German couple at his table were laughing. Now the Egyptian
began to sing an Arabic song.

The man from Beirut said in his American accent, 'You should
go modern.'

'Never,' the furniture-maker said. 'I will leave Egypt first.
I will close my factory. It is a horror, the modern style. It is
grotesque, totally grotesque. *Mais le style Louis Seize, ah, voilà
l'âme*—' He broke off to applaud the Egyptian and to shout his
congratulations in Arabic. Wearily then, but without malice, he
said under his breath, 'Ah, these natives.' He pushed his plate
from him, sank in his chair, beat his fingers on the dirty tablecloth. He winked at the dancer and the tips of his moustache
flicked upwards.

The steward came to clear away. I was eating, but my plate
went as well.

'You were dining, monsieur?' the furniture-maker said. 'You
must be *calme*. We must all be *calme*.'

Then he raised his eyebrows and rolled his eyes. There was
something he wanted us to look at.

It was the tramp, standing in the doorway, surveying the room.
Such was the way he held himself that even now, at the first glance,
his clothes seemed whole. He came to the cleared table next to
ours, sat on a chair and shifted about in it until he was settled.
Then he leaned right back, his arms on the rests, like the head of a
household at the head of his table, like a cruise-passenger waiting

to be served. He sighed and moved his jaws, testing his teeth. His jacket was in an appalling state. The pockets bulged; the flaps were fastened with safety pins.

The furniture-maker said something in Arabic and the man from Beirut laughed. The steward shooed us away and we followed the Spanish girls to the windy little bar for coffee.

Later that afternoon, looking for privacy, I climbed some steep steps to the open railed area above the cabins. The tramp was standing there alone, stained trouser-legs swollen, turn-ups shredded, exposed to the cold wind and the smuts from the smokestack. He held what looked like a little prayer-book. He was moving his lips and closing and opening his eyes, like a man praying hard. How fragile that face was, worked over by distress; how frail that neck, below the tight knot of the polka-dotted scarf. The flesh around his eyes seemed especially soft; he looked close to tears. It was strange. He looked for company but needed solitude; he looked for attention, and at the same time wanted not to be noticed.

I didn't disturb him. I feared to be involved with him. Far below, the Greek refugees sat or lay in the sun.

In the smoking-room after dinner the fat young Egyptian shouted himself hoarse, doing his cabaret act. People who understood what he was saying laughed all the time. Even the furniture-maker, forgetting his gloom about the natives, shouted and clapped with the rest. The American schoolchildren lay in their own promiscuous seasick heap and looked on, like people helplessly besieged; when they spoke among themselves it was in whispers.

The non-American part of the room was predominantly Arab and German and had its own cohesion. The Egyptian was our entertainer, and there was a tall German girl we could think of as our hostess. She offered us chocolate and had a word for each of us. To me she said: 'You are reading a very good English book. These Penguin books are very good English books.' She might have been travelling out to join an Arab husband; I wasn't sure.

I was sitting with my back to the door and didn't see when the tramp came in. But suddenly he was there before me, sitting on a chair that someone had just left. The chair was not far from the German girl's, but it stood in no intimate relationship to that chair or any other group of chairs. The tramp sat squarely on it, straight up against the back. He faced no one directly, so that in that small room he didn't become part of the crowd but appeared instead to occupy the centre of a small stage within it.

He sat with his old man's legs wide apart, his weighted jacket sagging over his bulging trouser-pockets. He had come with things to read, a magazine, the little book which I had thought was a prayer-book. I saw now that it was an old pocket diary with many loose leaves. He folded the magazine in four, hid it under his thigh, and began to read the pocket diary. He laughed, and looked up to see whether he was being noticed. He turned a page, read and laughed again, more loudly. He leaned towards the German girl and said to her over his shoulder, 'I say, do you read Spanish?'

She said, carefully, 'No.'

'These Spanish jokes are awfully funny.'

But though he read a few more, he didn't laugh again.

The Egyptian continued to clown; that racket went on. Soon the German girl was offering chocolate once more. '*Bitte?*' Her voice was soft.

The tramp was unfolding his magazine. He stopped and looked at the chocolate. But there was none for him. He unfolded his magazine. Then, unexpectedly, he began to destroy it. With nervous jigging hands he tore at a page, once, twice. He turned some pages, began to tear again; turned back, tore. Even with the raucousness around the Egyptian the sound of tearing paper couldn't be ignored. Was he tearing out pictures – sport, women, advertisements – that offended him? Was he hoarding toilet paper for Egypt?

The Egyptian fell silent and looked. The American school-children looked. Now, too late after the frenzy, and in what was almost silence, the tramp made a show of reason. He opened the tattered magazine wide out, turned it around angrily, as though the right side up hadn't been easy to find, and at last pretended to read. He moved his lips; he frowned; he tore and tore. Strips and shreds of paper littered the floor around his chair. He folded the loose remains of the magazine, stuffed it into his jacket pocket, pinned the flaps down, and went out of the room, looking like a man who had been made very angry.

'I will kill him,' the furniture-maker said at breakfast the next morning.

He was in his three-piece suit but he was unshaven and the dark rings below his eyes were like bruises. The man from Beirut, too, looked tired and crumpled. They hadn't had a good night. The third bunk in their cabin was occupied by an Austrian boy, a passenger from Italy, with whom they were on good terms. They had seen the rucksack and the hat on the fourth bunk; but it wasn't until it was quite late, all three in their bunks, that they had discovered that the tramp was to be the fourth among them.

'It was pretty bad,' the man from Beirut said. He felt for delicate words and added, 'The old guy's like a child.'

'Child! If the English pig comes in now' – the furniture-maker raised his arm and pointed at the door – 'I will *kill* him. *Now.*'

He was pleased with the gesture and the words; he repeated them, for the room. The Egyptian student, hoarse and hungover after the evening's performance, said something in Arabic. It was obviously witty, but the furniture-maker didn't smile. He beat his fingers on the table, stared at the door and breathed loudly through his nose.

No one was in a good mood. The drumming and the throbbing and bucking of the ship had played havoc with stomachs and nerves; the cold wind outside irritated as much as it refreshed; and in the dining-room the air was stale, with a smell as of hot rubber. There was no crowd, but the stewards, looking unslept and unwashed, even their hair not well combed, were as rushed as before.

The Egyptian shrieked.

The tramp had come in, benign and rested and ready for his coffee and rolls. He had no doubts about his welcome now. He came without hesitation or great speed to the table next to ours, settled himself in his chair and began to test his teeth. He was quickly served. He chewed and drank with complete relish.

The Egyptian shrieked again.

The furniture-maker said to him, 'I will send him to your room tonight.'

The tramp didn't see or hear. He was only eating and drinking. Below the tight knot of his scarf his Adam's apple was very busy. He drank noisily, sighing afterwards; he chewed with rabbit-like swiftness, anxious to be free for the next mouthful; and between mouthfuls he hugged himself, rubbing his arms and elbows against his sides, in pure pleasure at food.

The fascination of the furniture-maker turned to rage. Rising, but still looking at the tramp, he called, 'Hans!'

The Austrian boy, who was at the table with the Egyptian, got up. He was about sixteen or seventeen, square and chunky, enormously well-developed, with a broad smiling face. The man from Beirut also got up, and all three went outside.

The tramp, oblivious of this, and of what was being prepared for him, continued to eat and drink until, with a sigh which was like a sigh of fatigue, he was finished.

It was to be like a tiger-hunt, where bait is laid out and the hunter and spectators watch from the security of a platform. The bait here was the tramp's own rucksack. They placed that on the deck outside the cabin door, and watched it. The furniture-maker still pretended to be too angry to talk. But Hans smiled and explained the rules of the game as often as he was asked.

The tramp, though, didn't immediately play. After breakfast he disappeared. It was cold on the deck, even in the sunshine, and sometimes the spray came right up. People who had come out to watch didn't stay, and even the furniture-maker and the man from Beirut went from time to time to rest in the smoking-room among the Germans and Arabs and the Spanish girls. They were given chairs; there was sympathy for their anger and exhaustion. Hans remained at his post. When the cold wind made him go inside the cabin he watched through the open door, sitting on one of the lower bunks and smiling up at people who passed.

Then the news came that the tramp had reappeared and had been caught according to the rules of the game. Some of the American schoolchildren were already on deck, studying the sea. So were the Spanish girls and the German girl. Hans blocked the cabin door. I could see the tramp holding the strap of his rucksack; I could hear him complaining in English through the French and Arabic shouts of the furniture-maker, who was raising his arms and pointing with his right hand, the skirts of his jacket dancing.

In the dining-room the furniture-maker's anger had seemed only theatrical, an aspect of his Mediterranean appearance, the moustache, the wavy hair. But now, in the open, with an expectant audience and a victim so nearly passive, he was working himself into a frenzy.

'Pig! Pig!'

'It's not true,' the tramp said, appealing to people who had only come to watch.

'Pig!'

The grotesque moment came. The furniture-maker, so strongly built, so elegant in his square-shouldered jacket, lunged with his left hand at the old man's head. The tramp swivelled his head, the way he did when he refused to acknowledge a stare. And he began to cry. The furniture-maker's hand went wide and he stumbled forward against the rails into a spatter of spray. Putting his hands to his breast, feeling for pen and wallet and other things, he cried out, like a man aggrieved and desperate, 'Hans! Hans!'

The tramp stooped; he stopped crying; his blue eyes popped. Hans had seized him by the polka-dotted scarf, twisting it, jerking it down. Kicking the rucksack hard, Hans at the same time flung the tramp forward by the knotted scarf. The tramp stumbled over Hans's kicking foot. The strain went out of Hans's smiling face and all that was left was the smile. The tramp could have recovered from his throw and stumble. But he preferred to fall and then to sit up. He was still holding the strap of his rucksack. He was crying again.

'It's not true. These remarks they've been making, it's not true.'

The young Americans were looking over the rails.

'Hans!' the furniture-maker called.

The tramp stopped crying.

'Ha-ans!'

The tramp didn't look round. He got up with his rucksack and ran.

The story was that he had locked himself in one of the lavatories. But he reappeared among us, twice.

About an hour later he came into the smoking-room, without his rucksack, with no sign of distress on his face. He was already restored. He came in, in his abrupt way, not looking to right or left. Just a few steps brought him right into the small room and almost up against the legs of the furniture-maker, who was stretched out in an upholstered chair, exhausted, one hand over his half-closed eyes. After surprise, anger and contempt filled the tramp's eyes. He started to swivel his head away.

'Hans!' the furniture-maker called, recovering from his astonishment, drawing back his legs, leaning forward. 'Ha-ans!'

Swivelling his head, the tramp saw Hans rising with some playing cards in his hands. Terror came to the tramp's eyes. The swivelling motion of his head spread to the rest of his body. He swung round on one heel, brought the other foot down hard, and bolted. Entry, advance, bandy-legged swivel and retreat had formed one unbroken movement.

'Hans!'

It wasn't a call to action. The furniture-maker was only under-lining the joke. Hans, understanding, laughed and went back to his cards.

The tramp missed his lunch. He should have gone down immediately, to the first sitting, which had begun. Instead, he went into hiding, no doubt in one of the lavatories, and came out again only in time for the last sitting. It was the sitting the Lebanese and Hans had chosen. The tramp saw from the doorway.

'Ha-ans!'

But the tramp was already swivelling.

Later he was to be seen with his rucksack, but without his hat, on the lower deck, among the refugees. Without him, and then without reference to him, the joke continued, in the bar, on the narrow deck, in the smoking-room. 'Hans! Ha-ans!' Towards the end Hans didn't laugh or look up; when he heard his name he completed the joke by giving a whistle. The joke lived; but by night-fall the tramp was forgotten.

At dinner the Lebanese spoke again in their disinterested way about money. The man from Beirut said that, because of certain special circumstances in the Middle East that year, there was a fortune to be made from the well-judged exporting of Egyptian shoes; but not many people knew. The furniture-maker said the fact had been known to him for months. They postulated an investment, vied with each other in displaying knowledge of hidden, local costs, and calmly considered the staggering profits. But they weren't really exciting one another any longer. The game was a game; each had taken the measure of the other. And they were both tired.

Something of the lassitude of the American schoolchildren had come over the other passengers on this last evening. The Americans themselves were beginning to thaw out. In the smoking-room, where the lights seemed dimmer, their voices were raised in friendly boy–girl squabbles; they did a lot more coming and going; especially active was a tall girl in a type of ballet-dancer's costume, all black from neck to wrist to ankle. The German girl, our hostess of the previous evening, looked quite ill. The Spanish girls were flirting with nobody. The Egyptian, whose hangover had been compounded by seasickness, was playing bridge. Gamely from time to time he croaked out a witticism or a line of a song, but he got smiles rather than laughs. The furniture-maker and Hans were also playing cards. When a good card or a disappointing one was played the furniture-maker said in soft exclamation, expecting no response, 'Hans, Hans.' It was all that remained of the day's joke.

The man from Beirut came in and watched. He stood beside Hans. Then he stood beside the furniture-maker and whispered to him in English, their secret language. 'The guy's locked himself in the cabin.'

Hans understood. He looked at the furniture-maker. But the furniture-maker was weary. He played his hand, then went out with the man from Beirut.

When he came back he said to Hans, 'He says that he will set fire to the cabin if we try to enter. He says that he has a quantity of paper and a quantity of matches. I believe that he will do it.'

'What do we do?' the man from Beirut asked.

'We will sleep here. Or in the dining-room.'

'But those Greek stewards sleep in the dining-room. I saw them this morning.'

'That proves that it is possible,' the furniture-maker said.

Later, the evening over, I stopped outside the tramp's cabin. At first I heard nothing. Then I heard paper being crumpled: the tramp's warning. I wonder how long he stayed awake that night, listening for footsteps, waiting for the assault on the door and the entry of Hans.

In the morning he was back on the lower deck, among the refugees. He had his hat again; he had recovered it from the cabin.

Alexandria was a long shining line on the horizon: sand and the silver of oil-storage tanks. The sky clouded over; the green sea grew choppier. We entered the breakwater in cold rain and stormlight.

Long before the immigration officials came on board we queued to meet them. Germans detached themselves from Arabs,

Hans from the Lebanese, the Lebanese from the Spanish girls. Now, as throughout the journey since his meeting with the tramp, the tall blond Yugoslav was a solitary. From the lower deck the refugees came up with their boxes and bundles, so that at last they were more than their emblematic black wrappings. They had the slack bodies and bad skins of people who ate too many carbohydrates. Their blotched faces were immobile, distant, but full of a fierce, foolish cunning. They were watching. As soon as the officials came aboard the refugees began to push and fight their way towards them. It was a factitious frenzy, the deference of the persecuted to authority.

The tramp came up with his hat and rucksack. There was no nervousness in his movements but his eyes were quick with fear. He took his place in the queue and pretended to frown at its length. He moved his feet up and down, now like a man made impatient by officials, now like someone only keeping out the cold. But he was of less interest than he thought. Hans, mountainous with his own rucksack, saw him and then didn't see him. The Lebanese, shaved and rested after their night in the dining-room, didn't see him. That passion was over.

1 ONE OUT OF MANY

I AM NOW AN American citizen and I live in Washington, capital of the world. Many people, both here and in India, will feel that I have done well. But.

I was so happy in Bombay. I was respected, I had a certain position. I worked for an important man. The highest in the land came to our bachelor chambers and enjoyed my food and showered compliments on me. I also had my friends. We met in the evenings on the pavement below the gallery of our chambers. Some of us, like the tailor's bearer and myself, were domestics who lived in the street. The others were people who came to that bit of pavement to sleep. Respectable people; we didn't encourage riff-raff.

In the evenings it was cool. There were few passers-by and, apart from an occasional double-decker bus or taxi, little traffic. The pavement was swept and sprinkled, bedding brought out from daytime hiding-places, little oil-lamps lit. While the folk upstairs chattered and laughed, on the pavement we read newspapers, played cards, told stories and smoked. The clay pipe passed from friend to friend; we became drowsy. Except of course during the monsoon, I preferred to sleep on the pavement with my friends, although in our chambers a whole cupboard below the staircase was reserved for my personal use.

It was good after a healthy night in the open to rise before the sun and before the sweepers came. Sometimes I saw the street lights go off. Bedding was rolled up; no one spoke much; and soon my friends were hurrying in silent competition to secluded lanes and alleys and open lots to relieve themselves. I was spared this competition; in our chambers I had facilities.

Afterwards for half an hour or so I was free simply to stroll. I liked walking beside the Arabian Sea, waiting for the sun to come up. Then the city and the ocean gleamed like gold. Alas for those morning walks, that sudden ocean dazzle, the moist salt breeze on my face, the flap of my shirt, that first cup of hot sweet tea from a stall, the taste of the first leaf-cigarette.

Observe the workings of fate. The respect and security I enjoyed were due to the importance of my employer. It was this very importance which now all at once destroyed the pattern of my life.

My employer was seconded by his firm to Government service and was posted to Washington. I was happy for his sake but frightened for mine. He was to be away for some years and there was nobody in Bombay he could second me to. Soon, therefore, I was to be out of a job and out of the chambers. For many years I had considered my life as settled. I had served my apprenticeship, known my hard times. I didn't feel I could start again. I despaired. Was there a job for me in Bombay? I saw myself having to return to my village in the hills, to my wife and children there, not just for a holiday but for good. I saw myself again becoming a porter during the tourist season, racing after the buses as they arrived at the station and shouting with forty or fifty others for luggage. Indian luggage, not this lightweight American stuff! Heavy metal trunks!

I could have cried. It was no longer the sort of life for which I was fitted. I had grown soft in Bombay and I was no longer young. I had acquired possessions, I was used to the privacy of my cupboard. I had become a city man, used to certain comforts.

My employer said, 'Washington is not Bombay! Santosh. Washington is expensive. Even if I was able to raise your fare, you wouldn't be able to live over there in anything like your present style.'

But to be barefoot in the hills, after Bombay! The shock, the disgrace! I couldn't face my friends. I stopped sleeping on the pavement and spent as much of my free time as possible in my cupboard among my possessions, as among things which were soon to be taken from me.

My employer said, 'Santosh, my heart bleeds for you.'

I said, 'Sahib, if I look a little concerned it is only because I worry about you. You have always been fussy, and I don't see how you will manage in Washington.'

'It won't be easy. But it's the principle. Does the representative of a poor country like ours travel about with his cook? Will that create a good impression?'

'You will always do what is right, sahib.'

He went silent.

After some days he said, 'There's not only the expense,

Santosh. There's the question of foreign exchange. Our rupee isn't what it was.'

'I understand, sahib. Duty is duty.'

A fortnight later, when I had almost given up hope, he said, 'Santosh, I have consulted Government. You will accompany me. Government has sanctioned, will arrange accommodation. But not expenses. You will get your passport and your P form. But I want you to think, Santosh. Washington is not Bombay.'

I went down to the pavement that night with my bedding.

I said, blowing down my shirt, 'Bombay gets hotter and hotter.'

'Do you know what you are doing?' the tailor's bearer said. 'Will the Americans smoke with you? Will they sit and talk with you in the evenings? Will they hold you by the hand and walk with you beside the ocean?'

It pleased me that he was jealous. My last days in Bombay were very happy.

I packed my employer's two suitcases and bundled up my own belongings in lengths of old cotton. At the airport they made a fuss about my bundles. They said they couldn't accept them as luggage for the hold because they didn't like the responsibility. So when the time came I had to climb up to the aircraft with all my bundles. The girl at the top, who was smiling at everybody else, stopped smiling when she saw me. She made me go right to the back of the plane, far from my employer. Most of the seats there were empty, though, and I was able to spread my bundles around and, well, it was comfortable.

It was bright and hot outside, cool inside. The plane started, rose up in the air, and Bombay and the ocean tilted this way and that. It was very nice. When we settled down I looked around for people like myself, but I could see no one among the Indians or the foreigners who looked like a domestic. Worse, they were all dressed as though they were going to a wedding and, brother, I soon saw it wasn't they who were conspicuous. I was in my ordinary Bombay clothes, the loose long-tailed shirt, the wide-waisted pants held up with a piece of string. Perfectly respectable domestic's wear, neither dirty nor clean, and in Bombay no one would have looked. But now on the plane I felt heads turning whenever I stood up.

I was anxious. I slipped off my shoes, tight even without the laces, and drew my feet up. That made me feel better. I made myself a little betel-nut mixture and that made me feel better still. Half the pleasure of betel, though, is the spitting; and it was only when I had worked up a good mouthful that I saw I had a problem. The airline girl saw too. That girl didn't like me at all. She spoke roughly to me. My mouth was full, my cheeks were bursting, and I couldn't say anything. I could only look at her. She went and called a man in uniform and he came and stood over me. I put my shoes back on and swallowed the betel juice. It made me feel quite ill.

The girl and the man, the two of them, pushed a little trolley of drinks down the aisle. The girl didn't look at me but the man said, 'You want a drink, chum?' He wasn't a bad fellow. I pointed at random to a bottle. It was a kind of soda drink, nice and sharp at first but then not so nice. I was worrying about it when the girl said, 'Five shillings sterling or sixty cents US.' That took me by surprise. I had no money, only a few rupees. The girl stamped, and I thought she was going to hit me with her pad when I stood up to show her who my employer was.

Presently my employer came down the aisle. He didn't look very well. He said, without stopping, 'Champagne, Santosh? Already we are overdoing?' He went on to the lavatory. When he passed back he said, 'Foreign exchange, Santosh! Foreign exchange!' That was all. Poor fellow, he was suffering too.

The journey became miserable for me. Soon, with the wine I had drunk, the betel juice, the movement and the noise of the aeroplane, I was vomiting all over my bundles, and I didn't care what the girl said or did. Later there were more urgent and terrible needs. I felt I would choke in the tiny, hissing room at the back. I had a shock when I saw my face in the mirror. In the fluorescent light it was the colour of a corpse. My eyes were strained, the sharp air hurt my nose and seemed to get into my brain. I climbed up on the lavatory seat and squatted. I lost control of myself. As quickly as I could I ran back out into the comparative openness of the cabin and hoped no one had noticed. The lights were dim now; some people had taken off their jackets and were sleeping. I hoped the plane would crash.

The girl woke me up. She was almost screaming, 'It's you, isn't it? Isn't it?'

I thought she was going to tear the shirt off me. I pulled back and leaned hard on the window. She burst into tears and nearly tripped on her sari as she ran up the aisle to get the man in uniform.

Nightmare. And all I knew was that somewhere at the end, after the airports and the crowded lounges where everybody was dressed up, after all those take-offs and touchdowns, was the city of Washington. I wanted the journey to end but I couldn't say I wanted to arrive at Washington. I was already a little scared of that city, to tell the truth. I wanted only to be off the plane and to be in the open again, to stand on the ground and breathe and to try to understand what time of day it was.

At last we arrived. I was in a daze. The burden of those bundles! There were more closed rooms and electric lights. There were questions from officials.

'Is he diplomatic?'

'He's only a domestic,' my employer said.

'Is that his luggage? What's in that pocket?'

I was ashamed.

'Santosh,' my employer said.

I pulled out the little packets of pepper and salt, the sweets, the envelopes with scented napkins, the toy tubes of mustard. Airline trinkets. I had been collecting them throughout the journey, seizing a handful, whatever my condition, every time I passed the galley.

'He's a cook,' my employer said.

'Does he always travel with his condiments?'

'Santosh, Santosh,' my employer said in the car afterwards, 'in Bombay it didn't matter what you did. Over here you represent your country. I must say I cannot understand why your behaviour has already gone so much out of character.'

'I am sorry, sahib.'

'Look at it like this, Santosh. Over here you don't only represent your country, you represent me.'

For the people of Washington it was late afternoon or early evening, I couldn't say which. The time and the light didn't match, as they did in Bombay. Of that drive I remember green fields, wide roads, many motor-cars travelling fast, making a steady hiss, hiss, which wasn't at all like our Bombay traffic noise. I remember big buildings and wide parks; many bazaar areas; then smaller houses without fences and with gardens like bush, with the *hubshi* standing about or sitting down, more usually sitting down, everywhere. Especially I remember the *hubshi*.

I had heard about them in stories and had seen one or two in Bombay. But I had never dreamt that this wild race existed in such numbers in Washington and were permitted to roam the streets so freely. O father, what was this place I had come to?

I wanted, I say, to be in the open, to breathe, to come to myself, to reflect. But there was to be no openness for me that evening. From the aeroplane to the airport building to the motor-car to the apartment block to the elevator to the corridor to the apartment itself, I was forever enclosed, forever in the hissing, hissing sound of air-conditioners.

I was too dazed to take stock of the apartment. I saw it as only another halting place. My employer went to bed at once, completely exhausted, poor fellow. I looked around for my room. I couldn't find it and gave up. Aching for the Bombay ways, I spread my bedding in the carpeted corridor just outside our apartment door. The corridor was long: doors, doors. The illuminated ceiling was decorated with stars of different sizes; the colours were grey and blue and gold. Below that imitation sky I felt like a prisoner.

Waking, looking up at the ceiling, I thought just for a second that I had fallen asleep on the pavement below the gallery of our Bombay chambers. Then I realized my loss. I couldn't tell how much time had passed or whether it was night or day. The only clue was that newspapers now lay outside some doors. It disturbed me to think that while I had been sleeping, alone and defenceless, I had been observed by a stranger and perhaps by more than one stranger.

I tried the apartment door and found I had locked myself out. I didn't want to disturb my employer. I thought I would get out into the open, go for a walk. I remembered where the elevator was. I got in and pressed the button. The elevator dropped fast and silently and it was like being in the aeroplane again. When the elevator stopped and the blue metal door slid open I saw plain concrete corridors and blank walls. The noise of machinery was very loud. I knew I was in the basement and the main floor was not far above me. But I no longer wanted to try; I gave up ideas of the open air. I thought I would just go back up to the apartment. But I hadn't noted the number and didn't even know what floor we were on. My courage flowed out of me. I sat on the floor of the elevator and felt the tears come to my eyes. Almost without noise the elevator door closed, and I found I was being taken up silently at great speed.

The elevator stopped and the door opened. It was my employer, his hair uncombed, yesterday's dirty shirt partly unbuttoned. He looked frightened.

'Santosh, where have you been at this hour of morning? Without your shoes.'

I could have embraced him. He hurried me back past the newspapers to our apartment and I took the bedding inside. The wide window showed the early morning sky, the big city; we were high up, way above the trees.

I said, 'I couldn't find my room.'

'Government sanctioned,' my employer said. 'Are you sure you've looked?'

We looked together. One little corridor led past the bathroom to his bedroom; another, shorter, corridor led to the big room and the kitchen. There was nothing else.

'Government sanctioned,' my employer said, moving about the kitchen and opening cupboard doors. 'Separate entrance, shelving. I have the correspondence.' He opened another door and looked inside. 'Santosh, do you think it is possible that this is what Government meant?'

The cupboard he had opened was as high as the rest of the apartment and as wide as the kitchen, about six feet. It was about three feet deep. It had two doors. One door opened into the kitchen; another door, directly opposite, opened into the corridor.

'Separate entrance,' my employer said. 'Shelving, electric light, power point, fitted carpet.'

'This must be my room, sahib.'

'Santosh, some enemy in Government has done this to me.'

'Oh no, sahib. You mustn't say that. Besides, it is very big. I will be able to make myself very comfortable. It is much bigger than my little cubby-hole in the chambers. And it has a nice flat ceiling. I wouldn't hit my head.'

'You don't understand, Santosh. Bombay is Bombay. Here if we start living in cupboards we give the wrong impression. They will think we all live in cupboards in Bombay.'

'O sahib, but they can just look at me and see I am dirt.'

'You are very good, Santosh. But these people are malicious. Still, if you are happy, then I am happy.'

'I am very happy, sahib.'

And after all the upset, I was. It was nice to crawl in that evening, spread my bedding and feel protected and hidden. I slept very well.

In the morning my employer said, 'We must talk about money, Santosh. Your salary is one hundred rupees a month. But Washington isn't Bombay. Everything is a little bit more expensive here, and I am going to give you a Dearness Allowance. As from today you are getting one hundred and fifty rupees.'

'Sahib.'

'And I'm giving you a fortnight's pay in advance. In foreign exchange. Seventy-five rupees. Ten cents to the rupee, seven hundred and fifty cents. Seven fifty US. Here, Santosh. This afternoon you go out and have a little walk and enjoy. But be careful. We are not among friends, remember.'

So at last, rested, with money in my pocket, I went out in the open. And of course the city wasn't a quarter as frightening as I had thought. The buildings weren't particularly big, not all the streets were busy, and there were many lovely trees. A lot of the *hubshi* were about, very wild-looking some of them, with dark glasses and their hair frizzed out, but it seemed that if you didn't trouble them they didn't attack you.

I was looking for a café or a tea-stall where perhaps domestics congregated. But I saw no domestics, and I was chased away from the place I did eventually go into. The girl said, after I had been waiting some time, 'Can't you read? We don't serve hippies or bare feet here.'

O father! I had come out without my shoes. But what a country, I thought, walking briskly away, where people are never allowed to dress normally but must forever wear their very best! Why must they wear out shoes and fine clothes for no purpose? What occasion are they honouring? What waste, what presumption! Who do they think is noticing them all the time?

And even while these thoughts were in my head I found I had come to a roundabout with trees and a fountain where – and it was like a fulfilment in a dream, not easy to believe – there were many people who looked like my own people. I tightened the string around my loose pants, held down my flapping shirt and ran through the traffic to the green circle.

Some of the *hubshi* were there, playing musical instruments and looking quite happy in their way. There were some Americans sitting about on the grass and the fountain and the kerb. Many of them were in rough, friendly-looking clothes; some were without shoes; and I felt I had been over-hasty in condemning the entire race. But it wasn't these people who had attracted me to the circle. It was the dancers. The men were bearded, bare-footed and in saffron robes, and the girls were in saris and canvas shoes that looked like our own Bata shoes. They were shaking little cymbals and chanting and lifting their heads up and down and going round in a circle, making a lot of dust. It was a little bit like a Red Indian dance in a cowboy movie, but they were chanting Sanskrit words in praise of Lord Krishna.

I was very pleased. But then a disturbing thought came to me. It might have been because of the half-caste appearance of the dancers; it might have been their bad Sanskrit pronunciation and their accent. I thought that these people were now strangers, but that perhaps once upon a time they had been like me. Perhaps, as in some story, they had been brought here among the *hubshi* as captives a long time ago and had become a lost people, like our own wandering gipsy folk, and had forgotten who they were. When I thought that, I lost my pleasure in the dancing; and I felt for the dancers the sort of distaste we feel when we are faced with something that should be kin but turns out not to be, turns out to be degraded, like a deformed man, or like a leper, who from a distance looks whole.

I didn't stay. Not far from the circle I saw a café which appeared to be serving bare feet. I went in, had a coffee and a nice piece of cake and bought a pack of cigarettes; matches they gave me free with the cigarettes. It was all right, but then the bare feet began looking at me, and one bearded fellow came and sniffed loudly at me and smiled and spoke some sort of gibberish, and then some others of the bare feet came and sniffed at me. They weren't unfriendly, but I didn't appreciate the behaviour; and it was a little frightening to find, when I left the place, that two or three of them appeared to be following me. They weren't unfriendly, but I didn't want to take any chances. I passed a cinema; I went in. It was something I wanted to do anyway. In Bombay I used to go once a week.

And that was all right. The movie had already started. It was in English, not too easy for me to follow, and it gave me time to think. It was only there, in the darkness, that I thought about the money I had been spending. The prices had seemed to me very reasonable, like Bombay prices. Three for the movie ticket, one fifty in the café, with tip. But I had been thinking in rupees and paying in dollars. In less than an hour I had spent nine days' pay.

I couldn't watch the movie after that. I went out and began to make my way back to the apartment block. Many more of the *hubshi* were about now and I saw that where they congregated the pavement was wet, and dangerous with broken glass and bottles. I couldn't think of cooking when I got back to the apartment. I couldn't bear to look at the view. I spread my bedding in the cupboard, lay down in the darkness and waited for my employer to return.

When he did I said, 'Sahib, I want to go home.'

'Santosh, I've paid five thousand rupees to bring you here. If I send you back now, you will have to work for six or seven years without salary to pay me back.'

I burst into tears.

'My poor Santosh, something has happened. Tell me what has happened?'

'Sahib, I've spent more than half the advance you gave me this morning. I went out and had a coffee and cake and then I went to a movie.'

His eyes went small and twinkly behind his glasses. He bit the inside of his top lip, scraped at his moustache with his lower teeth, and he said, 'You see, you see. I told you it was expensive.'

I understood I was a prisoner. I accepted this and adjusted. I learned to live within the apartment, and I was even calm.

My employer was a man of taste and he soon had the apartment looking like something in a magazine, with books and Indian paintings and Indian fabrics and pieces of sculpture and bronze statues of our gods. I was careful to take no delight in it. It was of course very pretty, especially with the view. But the view remained foreign and I never felt that the apartment was real, like the shabby old Bombay chambers with the cane chairs, or that it had anything to do with me.

When people came to dinner I did my duty. At the appropriate time I would bid the company goodnight, close off the kitchen behind its folding screen and pretend I was leaving the apartment. Then I would lie down quietly in my cupboard and smoke. I was free to go out; I had my separate entrance. But I didn't like being out of the apartment. I didn't even like going down to the laundry room in the basement.

Once or twice a week I went to the supermarket on our street. I always had to walk past groups of *hubshi* men and children. I tried not to look, but it was hard. They sat on the pavement, on steps and in the bush around their redbrick houses, some of which had boarded-up windows. They appeared to be very much a people of the open air, with little to do; even in the mornings some of the men were drunk.

Scattered among the *hubshi* houses were others just as old but with gas-lamps that burned night and day in the entrance. These were the houses of the Americans. I seldom saw these people; they didn't spend much time on the street. The lighted gas-lamp was the American way of saying that though a house looked old outside it was nice and new inside. I also felt that it was like a warning to the *hubshi* to keep off.

Outside the supermarket there was always a policeman with a gun. Inside, there were always a couple of *hubshi* guards with truncheons, and, behind the cashiers, some old *hubshi* beggar men in rags. There were also many young *hubshi* boys, small but muscular, waiting to carry parcels, as once in the hills I had waited to carry Indian tourists' luggage.

These trips to the supermarket were my only outings, and I was always glad to get back to the apartment. The work there was light. I watched a lot of television and my English improved. I grew to like certain commercials very much. It was in these commercials I saw the Americans whom in real life I so seldom saw and knew only by their gas-lamps. Up there in the apartment, with a view of the white domes and towers and greenery of the famous city, I entered the homes of the Americans and saw them cleaning those homes. I saw them cleaning floors and dishes. I saw them buying clothes and cleaning clothes, buying motor-cars and cleaning motor-cars. I saw them cleaning, cleaning.

The effect of all this television on me was curious. If by some chance I saw an American on the street I tried to fit him or her into the commercials; and I felt I had caught the person in an interval between his television duties. So to some extent Americans have remained to me, as people not quite real, as people temporarily absent from television.

Sometimes a *hubshi* came on the screen, not to talk of *hubshi* things, but to do a little cleaning of his own. That wasn't the same. He was too different from the *hubshi* I saw on the street and I knew he was an actor. I knew that his television duties were only make-believe and that he would soon have to return to the street.

One day at the supermarket, when the *hubshi* girl took my money, she sniffed and said, 'You always smell sweet, baby.'

She was friendly, and I was at last able to clear up that mystery, of my smell. It was the poor country weed I smoked. It was a peasant taste of which I was slightly ashamed, to tell the truth; but the cashier was encouraging. As it happened, I had brought a quantity of the weed with me from Bombay in one of my bundles, together with a hundred razor blades, believing both weed and blades to be purely Indian things. I made an offering to the girl. In return she taught me a few words of English. 'Me black and beautiful' was the first thing she taught me. Then she pointed to the policeman with the gun outside and taught me: 'He pig.'

My English lessons were taken a stage further by the *hubshi* maid who worked for someone on our floor in the apartment block. She too was attracted by my smell, but I soon began to feel that she was also attracted by my smallness and strangeness. She herself was a big woman, broad in the face, with high cheeks and bold eyes and lips that were full but not pendulous. Her largeness disturbed me; I found it better to concentrate on her face. She misunderstood; there were times when she frolicked with me in a violent way. I didn't like it, because I couldn't fight her off as well as I would have liked and because in spite of myself I was fascinated by her appearance. Her smell mixed with the perfumes she used could have made me forget myself.

She was always coming into the apartment. She disturbed me while I was watching the Americans on television. I feared the smell she left behind. Sweat, perfume, my own weed: the smells lay thick in the room, and I prayed to the bronze gods my employer had installed as living-room ornaments that I would not be dishonoured. Dishonoured, I say; and I know that this might seem strange to people over here, who have permitted the *hubshi* to settle among them in such large numbers and must therefore esteem them in certain ways. But in our country we frankly do not care for the *hubshi*. It is written in our books, both holy and not so holy, that it is indecent and wrong for a man of our blood to embrace the *hubshi* woman. To be dishonoured in this life, to be born a cat or a monkey or a *hubshi* in the next!

But I was falling. Was it idleness and solitude? I was found attractive: I wanted to know why. I began to go to the bathroom of the apartment simply to study my face in the mirror. I cannot easily believe it myself now, but in Bombay a week or a month could pass without my looking in the mirror; and then it wasn't to consider my looks but to check whether the barber had cut off too much hair or whether a pimple was about to burst. Slowly I made a discovery. My face was handsome. I had never thought of myself in this way. I had thought of myself as unnoticeable, with features that served as identification alone.

The discovery of my good looks brought its strains. I became obsessed with my appearance, with a wish to see myself. It was like an illness. I would be watching television, for instance, and I would be surprised by the thought: are you as handsome as that man? I would have to get up and go to the bathroom and look in the mirror.

I thought back to the time when these matters hadn't interested me, and I saw how ragged I must have looked, on the aeroplane, in the airport, in that café for bare feet, with the rough and dirty clothes I wore, without doubt or question, as clothes befitting a servant. I was choked with shame. I saw, too, how good people in Washington had been, to have seen me in rags and yet to have taken me for a man.

I was glad I had a place to hide. I had thought of myself as a prisoner. Now I was glad I had so little of Washington to cope with: the apartment, my cupboard, the television set, my employer, the walk to the supermarket, the *hubshi* woman. And one day I found I no longer knew whether I wanted to go back to Bombay. Up there, in the apartment, I no longer knew what I wanted to do.

I became more careful of my appearance. There wasn't much I could do. I bought laces for my old black shoes, socks, a belt. Then some money came my way. I had understood that the weed I smoked was of value to the *hubshi* and the bare feet; I disposed of what I had, disadvantageously as I now know, through the *hubshi* girl at the supermarket. I got just under two hundred dollars. Then, as anxiously as I had got rid of my weed, I went out and bought some clothes.

I still have the things I bought that morning. A green hat, a green suit. The suit was always too big for me. Ignorance, inexperience; but I also remember the feeling of presumption. The salesman wanted to talk, to do his job. I didn't want to listen. I took the first suit he showed me and went into the cubicle and changed. I couldn't think about size and fit. When I considered all that cloth and all that tailoring I was proposing to adorn my simple body with, that body that needed so little, I felt I was asking to be destroyed. I changed back quickly, went out of the cubicle and said I would take the green suit. The salesman began to talk; I cut him short; I asked for a hat. When I got back to the apartment I felt quite weak and had to lie down for a while in my cupboard.

I never hung the suit up. Even in the shop, even while counting out the precious dollars, I had known it was a mistake. I kept the suit folded in the box with all its pieces of tissue paper. Three or four times I put it on and walked about the apartment and sat down on chairs and lit cigarettes and crossed my legs, practising. But I couldn't bring myself to wear the suit out of doors. Later I wore the pants, but never the jacket. I never bought another suit; I soon began wearing the sort of clothes I wear today, pants with some sort of zippered jacket.

Once I had had no secrets from my employer; it was so much simpler not to have secrets. But some instinct told me now it would be better not to let him know about the green suit or the few dollars I had, just as instinct had already told me I should keep my own growing knowledge of English to myself.

Once my employer had been to me only a presence. I used to tell him then that beside him I was as dirt. It was only a way of talking, one of the courtesies of our language, but it had something of truth. I meant that he was the man who adventured in the world for me, that I experienced the world through him, that I was content to be a small part of his presence. I was content, sleeping on the Bombay pavement with my friends, to hear the talk of my employer and his guests upstairs. I was more than content, late at night, to be identified among the sleepers and greeted by some of those guests before they drove away.

Now I found that, without wishing it, I was ceasing to see myself as part of my employer's presence, and beginning at the same time to see him as an outsider might see him, as perhaps the people who came to dinner in the apartment saw him. I saw that he was a man of my own age, around thirty-five; it astonished me that I hadn't noticed this before. I saw that he was plump, in need of exercise, that he moved with short, fussy steps; a man with glasses, thinning hair, and that habit, during conversation, of scraping at his moustache with his teeth and nibbling at the inside of his top lip; a man who was frequently anxious, took pains over his work, was subjected at his own table to unkind remarks by his office colleagues; a man who looked as uneasy in Washington as I felt, who acted as cautiously as I had learned to act.

I remember an American who came to dinner. He looked at the pieces of sculpture in the apartment and said he had himself brought back a whole head from one of our ancient temples; he had got the guide to hack it off.

I could see that my employer was offended. He said, 'But that's illegal.'

'That's why I had to give the guide two dollars. If I had a bottle of whisky he would have pulled down the whole temple for me.'

My employer's face went blank. He continued to do his duties as host but he was unhappy throughout the dinner. I grieved for him.

Afterwards he knocked on my cupboard. I knew he wanted to talk. I was in my underclothes but I didn't feel underdressed, with the American gone. I stood in the door of my cupboard; my employer paced up and down the small kitchen; the apartment felt sad.

'Did you hear that person, Santosh?'

I pretended I hadn't understood, and when he explained I tried to console him. I said, 'Sahib, but we know these people are Franks and barbarians.'

'They are malicious people, Santosh. They think that because we are a poor country we are all the same. They think an official in Government is just the same as some poor guide scraping together a few rupees to keep body and soul together, poor fellow.'

I saw that he had taken the insult only in a personal way, and I was disappointed. I thought he had been thinking of the temple.

A few days later I had my adventure. The *hubshi* woman came in, moving among my employer's ornaments like a bull. I was greatly provoked. The smell was too much; so was the sight of her armpits. I fell. She dragged me down on the couch, on the saffron spread which was one of my employer's nicest pieces of Punjabi folk-weaving. I saw the moment, helplessly, as one of dishonour. I saw her as Kali, goddess of death and destruction, coal-black, with a red tongue and white eyeballs and many powerful arms. I expected her to be wild and fierce; but she added insult to injury by being very playful, as though, because I was small and strange, the act was not real. She laughed all the time. I would have liked to withdraw, but the act took over and completed itself. And then I felt dreadful.

I wanted to be forgiven, I wanted to be cleansed, I wanted her to go. Nothing frightened me more than the way she had ceased to be a visitor in the apartment and behaved as though she possessed it. I looked at the sculpture and the fabrics and thought of my poor employer, suffering in his office somewhere.

I bathed and bathed afterwards. The smell would not leave me. I fancied that the woman's oil was still on that poor part of my poor body. It occurred to me to rub it down with half a lemon. Penance and cleansing; but it didn't hurt as much as I expected, and I extended the penance by rolling about naked on the floor of the bathroom and the sitting-room and howling. At last the tears came, real tears, and I was comforted.

It was cool in the apartment; the air-conditioning always hummed; but I could see that it was hot outside, like one of our own summer days in the hills. The urge came upon me to dress as I might have done in my village on a religious occasion. In one of my bundles I had a dhoti-length of new cotton, a gift from the tailor's bearer that I had never used. I draped this around my waist and between my legs, lit incense sticks, sat down cross-legged on the floor and tried to meditate and become still. Soon I began to feel hungry. That made me happy; I decided to fast.

Unexpectedly my employer came in. I didn't mind being caught in the attitude and garb of prayer; it could have been so much worse. But I wasn't expecting him till late afternoon.

'Santosh, what has happened?'

Pride got the better of me. I said, 'Sahib, it is what I do from time to time.'

But I didn't find merit in his eyes. He was far too agitated to notice me properly. He took off his lightweight fawn jacket, dropped it on the saffron spread, went to the refrigerator and drank two tumblers of orange juice, one after the other. Then he looked out at the view, scraping at his moustache.

'Oh, my poor Santosh, what are we doing in this place? Why do we have to come here?'

I looked with him. I saw nothing unusual. The wide window showed the colours of the hot day: the pale-blue sky, the white, almost colourless, domes of famous buildings rising out of dead-green foliage; the untidy roofs of apartment blocks where on Saturday and Sunday mornings people sunbathed; and, below, the fronts and backs of houses on the tree-lined street down which I walked to the supermarket.

My employer turned off the air-conditioning and all noise was absent from the room. An instant later I began to hear the noises outside: sirens far and near. When my employer slid the window open the roar of the disturbed city rushed into the room. He closed the window and there was near-silence again. Not far from the supermarket I saw black smoke, uncurling, rising, swiftly turning colourless. This was not the smoke which some of the apartment blocks gave off all day. This was the smoke of a real fire.

'The *hubshi* have gone wild, Santosh. They are burning down Washington.'

I didn't mind at all. Indeed, in my mood of prayer and repentance, the news was even welcome. And it was with a feeling of release that I watched and heard the city burn that afternoon and watched it burn that night. I watched it burn again and again on television; and I watched it burn in the morning. It burned like a famous city and I didn't want it to stop burning. I wanted the fire to spread and spread and I wanted everything in the city, even the apartment block, even the apartment, even myself, to be destroyed and consumed. I wanted escape to be impossible; I wanted the very idea of escape to become absurd. At every sign that the burning was going to stop I felt disappointed and let down.

For four days my employer and I stayed in the apartment and watched the city burn. The television continued to show us what we could see and what, whenever we slid the window back, we could hear. Then it was over. The view from our window hadn't changed. The famous buildings stood; the trees remained. But for the first time since I had understood that I was a prisoner I found that I wanted to be out of the apartment and in the streets.

The destruction lay beyond the supermarket. I had never gone into this part of the city before, and it was strange to walk in those long wide streets for the first time, to see trees and houses and shops and advertisements, everything like a real city, and then to see that every signboard on every shop was burnt or stained with smoke, that the shops themselves were black and broken, that flames had burst through some of the upper windows and scorched the red bricks. For mile after mile it was like that. There were *hubshi* groups about, and at first when I passed them I pretended to be busy, minding my own business, not at all interested in the ruins. But they smiled at me and I found I was smiling back. Happiness was on the faces of the *hubshi*. They were like people amazed they could do so much, that so much lay in their power. They were like people on holiday. I shared their exhilaration.

The idea of escape was a simple one, but it hadn't occurred to me before. When I adjusted to my imprisonment I had wanted only to get away from Washington and to return to Bombay. But then I had become confused. I had looked in the mirror and seen myself, and I knew it wasn't possible for me to return to Bombay to the sort of job I had had and the life I had lived. I couldn't easily become part of someone else's presence again. Those evening chats on the pavement, those morning walks: happy times, but they were like the happy times of childhood: I didn't want them to return.

I had taken, after the fire, to going for long walks in the city. And one day, when I wasn't even thinking of escape, when I was just enjoying the sights and my new freedom of movement, I found myself in one of those leafy streets where private houses had been turned into business premises. I saw a fellow countryman superintending the raising of a signboard on his gallery. The signboard told me that the building was a restaurant, and I assumed that the man in charge was the owner. He looked worried and slightly ashamed, and he smiled at me. This was unusual, because the Indians I had seen on the streets of Washington pretended they hadn't seen me; they made me feel that they didn't like the competition of my presence or didn't want me to start asking them difficult questions.

I complimented the worried man on his signboard and wished him good luck in his business. He was a small man of about fifty and he was wearing a double-breasted suit with old-fashioned wide lapels. He had dark hollows below his eyes and he looked as though he had recently lost a little weight. I could see that in our country he had been a man of some standing, not quite the sort of person who would go into the restaurant business. I felt at one with him. He invited me in to look around, asked my name and gave his. It was Priya.

Just past the gallery was the loveliest and richest room I had ever seen. The wallpaper was like velvet; I wanted to pass my hand over it. The brass lamps that hung from the ceiling were in a lovely cut-out pattern and the bulbs were of many colours. Priya looked with me, and the hollows under his eyes grew darker, as though my admiration was increasing his worry at his extravagance. The restaurant hadn't yet opened for customers and on a shelf in one corner I saw Priya's collection of good-luck objects: a brass plate with a heap of uncooked rice, for prosperity; a little copybook and a little diary pencil, for good luck with the accounts; a little clay lamp, for general good luck.

'What do you think, Santosh? You think it will be all right?'

'It is bound to be all right, Priya.'

'But I have enemies, you know, Santosh. The Indian restaurant people are not going to appreciate me. All mine, you know, Santosh. Cash paid. No mortgage or anything like that. I don't believe in mortgages. Cash or nothing.'

I understood him to mean that he had tried to get a mortgage and failed, and was anxious about money.

'But what are you doing here, Santosh? You used to be in Government or something?'

'You could say that, Priya.'

'Like me. They have a saying here. If you can't beat them, join them. I joined them. They are still beating me.' He sighed and spread his arms on the top of the red wall-seat. 'Ah, Santosh, why do we do it? Why don't we renounce and go and meditate on the riverbank?' He waved about the room. 'The yemblems of the world, Santosh. Just yemblems.'

I didn't know the English word he used, but I understood its meaning; and for a moment it was like being back in Bombay, exchanging stories and philosophies with the tailor's bearer and others in the evening.

'But I am forgetting, Santosh. You will have some tea or coffee or something?'

I shook my head from side to side to indicate that I was agreeable, and he called out in a strange harsh language to someone behind the kitchen door.

'Yes, Santosh. Yem-*blems*!' And he sighed and slapped the red seat hard.

A man came out from the kitchen with a tray. At first he looked like a fellow countryman, but in a second I could tell he was a stranger.

'You are right,' Priya said, when the stranger went back to the kitchen. 'He is not of Bharat. He is a Mexican. But what can I do? You get fellow countrymen, you fix up their papers and everything, green card and everything. And then? Then they run away. Run-run-runaway. Crooks this side, crooks that side, I can't tell you. Listen, Santosh. I was in cloth business before. Buy for fifty rupees that side, sell for fifty dollars this side. Easy. But then. Caftan, everybody wants caftan. Caftan-aftan, I say, I will settle your caftan. I buy one thousand, Santosh. Delays India-side, of course. They come one year later. Nobody wants caftan then. We're not organized, Santosh. We don't do enough consumer research. That's what the fellows at the embassy tell me. But if I do consumer research, when will I do my business? The trouble, you know, Santosh, is that this shopkeeping is not in my blood. The damn thing goes *against* my blood. When I was in cloth business I used to hide sometimes for shame when a customer came in. Sometimes I used to pretend I was a shopper myself. Consumer research! These people make us dance, Santosh. You and I, we will renounce. We will go together and walk beside Potomac and meditate.'

I loved his talk. I hadn't heard anything so sweet and philosophical since the Bombay days. I said, 'Priya, I will cook for you, if you want a cook.'

'I feel I've known you a long time, Santosh. I feel you are like a member of my own family. I will give you a place to sleep, a little food to eat and a little pocket money, as much as I can afford.'

I said, 'Show me the place to sleep.'

He led me out of the pretty room and up a carpeted staircase. I was expecting the carpet and the new paint to stop somewhere, but it was nice and new all the way. We entered a room that was like a smaller version of my employer's apartment.

'Built-in cupboards and everything, you see, Santosh.'

I went to the cupboard. It had a folding door that opened outward. I said, 'Priya, it is too small. There is room on the shelf for my belongings. But I don't see how I can spread my bedding inside here. It is far too narrow.'

He giggled nervously. 'Santosh, you are a joker. I feel that we are of the same family already.'

Then it came to me that I was being offered the whole room. I was stunned.

Priya looked stunned too. He sat down on the edge of the soft bed. The dark hollows under his eyes were almost black and he looked very small in his double-breasted jacket. 'This is how they make us dance over here, Santosh. You say staff quarters and they say staff quarters. This is what they mean.'

For some seconds we sat silently, I fearful, he gloomy, meditating on the ways of this new world.

Someone called from downstairs, 'Priya!'

His gloom gone, smiling in advance, winking at me, Priya called back in an accent of the country, 'Hi, Bab!'

I followed him down.

'Priya,' the American said, 'I've brought over the menus.'

He was a tall man in a leather jacket, with jeans that rode up above thick white socks and big rubber-soled shoes. He looked like someone about to run in a race. The menus were enormous; on the cover there was a drawing of a fat man with a moustache and a plumed turban, something like the man in the airline advertisements.

'They look great, Bab.'

'I like them myself. But what's that, Priya? What's that shelf doing there?'

Moving like the front part of a horse, Bab walked to the shelf with the rice and the brass plate and the little clay lamp. It was only then that I saw that the shelf was very roughly made.

Priya looked penitent and it was clear he had put the shelf up himself. It was also clear he didn't intend to take it down.

'Well, it's yours,' Bab said. 'I suppose we had to have a touch of the East somewhere. Now, Priya—'

'Money-money-money, is it?' Priya said, racing the words together as though he was making a joke to amuse a child. 'But, Bab, how can *you* ask *me* for money? Anybody hearing you would believe that this restaurant is mine. But this restaurant isn't mine, Bab. This restaurant is yours.'

It was only one of our courtesies, but it puzzled Bab and he allowed himself to be led to other matters.

I saw that, for all his talk of renunciation and business failure, and for all his jumpiness, Priya was able to cope with Washington.

I admired this strength in him as much as I admired the richness of his talk. I didn't know how much to believe of his stories, but I liked having to guess about him. I liked having to play with his words in my mind. I liked the mystery of the man. The mystery came from his solidity. I knew where I was with him. After the apartment and the green suit and the *hubshi* woman and the city burning for four days, to be with Priya was to feel safe. For the first time since I had come to Washington I felt safe.

I can't say that I moved in. I simply stayed. I didn't want to go back to the apartment even to collect my belongings. I was afraid that something might happen to keep me a prisoner there. My employer might turn up and demand his five thousand rupees. The *hubshi* woman might claim me for her own; I might be condemned to a life among the *hubshi*. And it wasn't as if I was leaving behind anything of value in the apartment. The green suit I was even happy to forget. But.

Priya paid me forty dollars a week. After what I was getting, three dollars and seventy-five cents, it seemed a lot; and it was more than enough for my needs. I didn't have much temptation to spend, to tell the truth. I knew that my old employer and the *hubshi* woman would be wondering about me in their respective ways and I thought I should keep off the streets for a while. That was no hardship; it was what I was used to in Washington. Besides, my days at the restaurant were pretty full; for the first time in my life I had little leisure.

The restaurant was a success from the start, and Priya was fussy. He was always bursting into the kitchen with one of those big menus in his hand, saying in English, 'Prestige job, Santosh, prestige.' I didn't mind. I liked to feel I had to do things perfectly; I felt I was earning my freedom. Though I was in hiding, and though I worked every day until midnight, I felt I was much more in charge of myself than I had ever been.

Many of our waiters were Mexicans, but when we put turbans on them they could pass. They came and went, like the Indian staff. I didn't get on with these people. They were frightened and jealous of one another and very treacherous. Their talk amid the biryanis and the pillaus was all of papers and green cards. They were always about to get green cards or they had been cheated out of green cards or they had just got green cards. At first I didn't know what they were talking about. When I understood I was more than depressed.

I understood that because I had escaped from my employer I had made myself illegal in America. At any moment I could be denounced, seized, jailed, deported, disgraced. It was a complication. I had no green card; I didn't know how to set about getting one; and there was no one I could talk to.

I felt burdened by my secrets. Once I had none; now I had so many. I couldn't tell Priya I had no green card. I couldn't tell him I had broken faith with my old employer and dishonoured myself with a *hubshi* woman and lived in fear of retribution. I couldn't tell him that I was afraid to leave the restaurant and that nowadays when I saw an Indian I hid from him as anxiously as the Indian hid from me. I would have felt foolish to confess. With Priya, right from the start, I had pretended to be strong; and I wanted it to remain like that. Instead, when we talked now, and he grew philosophical, I tried to find bigger causes for being sad. My mind fastened on to these causes, and the effect of this was that my sadness became like a sickness of the soul.

It was worse than being in the apartment, because now the responsibility was mine and mine alone. I had decided to be free, to act for myself. It pained me to think of the exhilaration I had felt during the days of the fire; and I felt mocked when I remembered that in the early days of my escape I had thought I was in charge of myself.

The year turned. The snow came and melted. I was more afraid than ever of going out. The sickness was bigger than all the causes. I saw the future as a hole into which I was dropping. Sometimes at night when I awakened my body would burn and I would feel the hot perspiration break all over.

I leaned on Priya. He was my only hope, my only link with what was real. He went out; he brought back stories. He went out especially to eat in the restaurants of our competitors.

He said, 'Santosh, I never believed that running a restaurant was a way to God. But it is true. I eat like a scientist. Every day I eat like a scientist. I feel I have already renounced.'

This was Priya. This was how his talk ensnared me and gave me the bigger causes that steadily weakened me. I became more and more detached from the men in the kitchen. When they spoke of their green cards and the jobs they were about to get I felt like asking them: Why? Why?

And every day the mirror told its own tale. Without exercise, with the sickening of my heart and my mind, I was losing my looks. My face had become pudgy and sallow and full of spots; it was becoming ugly. I could have cried for that, discovering my good looks only to lose them. It was like a punishment for my presumption, the punishment I had feared when I bought the green suit.

Priya said, 'Santosh, you must get some exercise. You are not looking well. Your eyes are getting like mine. What are you pining for? Are you pining for Bombay or your family in the hills?'

But now, even in my mind, I was a stranger in those places.

Priya said one Sunday morning, 'Santosh, I am going to take you to see a Hindi movie today. All the Indians of Washington will be there, domestics and everybody else.'

I was very frightened. I didn't want to go and I couldn't tell him why. He insisted. My heart began to beat fast as soon as I got into the car. Soon there were no more houses with gas-lamps in the entrance, just those long wide burnt-out *hubshi* streets, now with fresh leaves on the trees, heaps of rubble on bulldozed, fenced-in lots, boarded-up shop windows, and old smoke-stained signboards announcing what was no longer true. Cars raced along the wide roads; there was life only on the roads. I thought I would vomit with fear.

I said, 'Take me back, *sahib*.'

I had used the wrong word. Once I had used the word a hundred times a day. But then I had considered myself a small part of my employer's presence, and the word was not servile; it was more like a name, like a reassuring sound, part of my employer's dignity and therefore part of mine. But Priya's dignity could never be mine; that was not our relationship. Priya I had always called Priya; it was his wish, the American way, man to man. With Priya the word was servile. And he responded to the word. He did as I asked; he drove me back to the restaurant. I never called him by his name again.

I was good-looking; I had lost my looks. I was a free man; I had lost my freedom.

One of the Mexican waiters came into the kitchen late one evening and said, 'There is a man outside who wants to see the chef.'

No one had made this request before, and Priya was at once agitated. 'Is he an American? Some enemy has sent him here. Sanitary-anitary, health-ealth, they can inspect my kitchens at any time.'

'He is an Indian,' the Mexican said.

I was alarmed. I thought it was my old employer; that quiet approach was like him. Priya thought it was a rival. Though Priya regularly ate in the restaurants of his rivals he thought it unfair when they came to eat in his. We both went to the door and peeked through the glass window into the dimly lit dining-room.

'Do you know that person, Santosh?'

'Yes, sahib.'

It wasn't my old employer. It was one of his Bombay friends, a big man in Government, whom I had often served in the chambers. He was by himself and seemed to have just arrived in Washington. He had a new Bombay haircut, very close, and a stiff dark suit, Bombay tailoring. His shirt looked blue, but in the dim multi-coloured light of the dining-room everything white looked blue. He didn't look unhappy with what he had eaten. Both his elbows were on the curry-spotted tablecloth and he was picking his teeth, half closing his eyes and hiding his mouth with his cupped left hand.

'I don't like him,' Priya said. 'Still, big man in Government and so on. You must go to him, Santosh.'

But I couldn't go.

'Put on your apron, Santosh. And that chef's cap. Prestige. You must go, Santosh.'

Priya went out to the dining-room and I heard him say in English that I was coming.

I ran up to my room, put some oil on my hair, combed my hair, put on my best pants and shirt and my shining shoes. It was so, as a man about town rather than as a cook, I went to the dining-room.

The man from Bombay was as astonished as Priya. We exchanged the old courtesies, and I waited. But, to my relief, there seemed little more to say. No difficult questions were put to me; I was grateful to the man from Bombay for his tact. I avoided talk as much as possible. I smiled. The man from Bombay smiled back. Priya smiled uneasily at both of us. So for a while we were, smiling in the dim blue-red light and waiting.

The man from Bombay said to Priya, 'Brother, I just have a few words to say to my old friend Santosh.'

Priya didn't like it, but he left us.

I waited for those words. But they were not the words I feared. The man from Bombay didn't speak of my old employer. We continued to exchange courtesies. Yes, I was well and he was well and everybody else we knew was well; and I was doing well and he was doing well. That was all. Then, secretively, the man from Bombay gave me a dollar. A dollar, ten rupees, an enormous tip for Bombay. But, from him, much more than a tip: an act of graciousness, part of the sweetness of the old days. Once it would have meant so much to me. Now it meant so little. I was saddened and embarrassed. And I had been anticipating hostility!

Priya was waiting behind the kitchen door. His little face was tight and serious, and I knew he had seen the money pass. Now, quickly, he read my own face, and without saying anything to me he hurried out into the dining-room.

I heard him say in English to the man from Bombay, 'Santosh is a good fellow. He's got his own room with bath and everything. I am giving him a hundred dollars a week from next week. A thousand rupees a week. This is a first-class establishment.'

A thousand chips a week! I was staggered. It was much more than any man in Government got, and I was sure the man from Bombay was also staggered, and perhaps regretting his good gesture and that precious dollar of foreign exchange.

'Santosh,' Priya said, when the restaurant closed that evening, 'that man was an enemy. I knew it from the moment I saw him. And because he was an enemy I did something very bad, Santosh.'

'Sahib.'

'I lied, Santosh. To protect you. I told him, Santosh, that I was going to give you seventy-five dollars a week after Christmas.'

'Sahib.'

'And now I have to make that lie true. But, Santosh, you know that is money we can't afford. I don't have to tell you about overheads and things like that. Santosh, I will give you sixty.'

I said, 'Sahib, I couldn't stay on for less than a hundred and twenty-five.'

Priya's eyes went shiny and the hollows below his eyes darkened. He giggled and pressed out his lips. At the end of that week I got a hundred dollars. And Priya, good man that he was, bore me no grudge.

Now here was a victory. It was only after it happened that I realized how badly I had needed such a victory, how far, gaining my freedom, I had begun to accept death not as the end but as the goal. I revived. Or rather, my senses revived. But in this city what was there to feed my senses? There were no walks to be taken, no idle conversations with understanding friends. I could buy new clothes. But then? Would I just look at myself in the mirror? Would I go walking, inviting passers-by to look at me and my clothes? No, the whole business of clothes and dressing up only threw me back into myself.

There was a Swiss or German woman in the cake-shop some doors away, and there was a Filipino woman in the kitchen. They were neither of them attractive, to tell the truth. The Swiss or German could have broken my back with a slap, and the Filipino, though young, was remarkably like one of our older hill women. Still, I felt I owed something to the senses, and I thought I might frolic with these women. But then I was frightened of the responsibility. Goodness, I had learned that a woman is not just a roll and a frolic but a big creature weighing a hundred-and-so-many pounds who is going to be around afterwards.

So the moment of victory passed, without celebration. And it was strange, I thought, that sorrow lasts and can make a man look forward to death, but the mood of victory fills a moment and then is over. When my moment of victory was over I discovered below it, as if waiting for me, all my old sickness and fears: fear of my illegality, my former employer, my presumption, the *hubshi* woman. I saw then that the victory I had had was not something I had worked for, but luck; and that luck was only fate's cheating, giving an illusion of power.

But that illusion lingered, and I became restless. I decided to act, to challenge fate. I decided I would no longer stay in my room and hide. I began to go out walking in the afternoons. I gained courage; every afternoon I walked a little farther. It became my ambition to walk to that green circle with the fountain where, on my first day out in Washington, I had come upon those people in Hindu costumes, like domestics abandoned a long time ago, singing their Sanskrit gibberish and doing their strange Red Indian dance. And one day I got there.

One day I crossed the road to the circle and sat down on a bench. The *hubshi* were there, and the bare feet, and the dancers in saris and the saffron robes. It was mid-afternoon, very hot, and no one was active. I remembered how magical and inexplicable that circle had seemed to me the first time I saw it. Now it seemed so ordinary and tired: the roads, the motor-cars, the shops, the trees, the careful policemen: so much part of the waste and futility that was our world. There was no longer a mystery. I felt I knew where everybody had come from and where those cars were going. But I also felt that everybody there felt like me, and that was soothing. I took to going to the circle every day after the lunch rush and sitting until it was time to go back to Priya's for the dinners.

Late one afternoon, among the dancers and the musicians, the *hubshi* and the bare feet, the singers and the police, I saw her. The *hubshi* woman. And again I wondered at her size; my memory had not exaggerated. I decided to stay where I was. She saw me and smiled. Then, as if remembering anger, she gave me a look of great hatred; and again I saw her as Kali, many-armed, goddess of death and destruction. She looked hard at my face; she considered my clothes. I thought: is it for this I bought these clothes? She got up. She was very big and her tight pants made her much more appalling. She moved towards me. I got up and ran. I ran across the road and then, not looking back, hurried by devious ways to the restaurant.

Priya was doing his accounts. He always looked older when he was doing his accounts, not worried, just older, like a man to whom life could bring no further surprises. I envied him.

'Santosh, some friend brought a parcel for you.'

It was a big parcel wrapped in brown paper. He handed it to me, and I thought how calm he was, with his bills and pieces of paper, and the pen with which he made his neat figures, and the book in which he would write every day until that book was exhausted and he would begin a new one.

I took the parcel up to my room and opened it. Inside there was a cardboard box; and inside that, still in its tissue paper, was the green suit.

I felt a hole in my stomach. I couldn't think. I was glad I had to go down almost immediately to the kitchen, glad to be busy until midnight. But then I had to go up to my room again, and I was alone. I hadn't escaped; I had never been free. I had been abandoned. I was like nothing; I had made myself nothing. And I couldn't turn back.

In the morning Priya said, 'You don't look very well, Santosh.'

His concern weakened me further. He was the only man I could talk to and I didn't know what I could say to him. I felt tears coming to my eyes. At that moment I would have liked the whole world to be reduced to tears. I said, 'Sahib, I cannot stay with you any longer.'

They were just words, part of my mood, part of my wish for tears and relief. But Priya didn't soften. He didn't even look surprised. 'Where will you go, Santosh?'

How could I answer his serious question?

'Will it be different where you go?'

He had freed himself of me. I could no longer think of tears. I said, 'Sahib, I have enemies.'

He giggled. 'You are a joker, Santosh. How can a man like yourself have enemies? There would be no profit in it. *I* have enemies. It is part of your happiness and part of the equity of the world that you cannot have enemies. That's why you can run-run-runaway.' He smiled and made the running gesture with his extended palm.

So, at last, I told him my story. I told him about my old employer and my escape and the green suit. He made me feel I was telling him nothing he hadn't already known. I told him about the *hubshi* woman. I was hoping for some rebuke. A rebuke would have meant that he was concerned for my honour, that I could lean on him, that rescue was possible.

But he said, 'Santosh, you have no problems. Marry the *hubshi*. That will automatically make you a citizen. Then you will be a free man.'

It wasn't what I was expecting. He was asking me to be alone for ever. I said, 'Sahib, I have a wife and children in the hills at home.'

'But this is your home, Santosh. Wife and children in the hills, that is very nice and that is always there. But that is over. You have to do what is best for you here. You are alone here. *Hubshi-ubshi*, nobody worries about that here, if that is your choice. This isn't Bombay. Nobody looks at you when you walk down the street. Nobody cares what you do.'

He was right. I was a free man; I could do anything I wanted.

I could, if it were possible for me to turn back, go to the apartment and beg my old employer for forgiveness. I could, if it were possible for me to become again what I once was, go to the police and say, 'I am an illegal immigrant here. Please deport me to Bombay.' I could run away, hang myself, surrender, confess, hide. It didn't matter what I did, because I was alone. And I didn't know what I wanted to do. It was like the time when I felt my senses revive and I wanted to go out and enjoy and I found there was nothing to enjoy.

To be empty is not to be sad. To be empty is to be calm. It is to renounce. Priya said no more to me; he was always busy in the mornings. I left him and went up to my room. It was still a bare room, still like a room that in half an hour could be someone else's. I had never thought of it as mine. I was frightened of its spotless painted walls and had been careful to keep them spotless. For just such a moment.

I tried to think of the particular moment in my life, the particular action, that had brought me to that room. Was it the moment with the *hubshi* woman, or was it when the American came to dinner and insulted my employer? Was it the moment of my escape, my sight of Priya in the gallery, or was it when I looked in the mirror and bought the green suit? Or was it much earlier, in that other life, in Bombay, in the hills? I could find no one moment; every moment seemed important. An endless chain of action had brought me to that room. It was frightening; it was burdensome. It was not a time for new decisions. It was time to call a halt.

I lay on the bed watching the ceiling, watching the sky. The door was pushed open. It was Priya.

'My goodness, Santosh! How long have you been here? You have been so quiet I forgot about you.'

He looked about the room. He went into the bathroom and came out again.

'Are you all right, Santosh?'

He sat on the edge of the bed and the longer he stayed the more I realized how glad I was to see him. There was this: when I tried to think of him rushing into the room I couldn't place it in time; it seemed to have occurred only in my mind. He sat with me. Time became real again. I felt a great love for him. Soon I could have laughed at his agitation. And later, indeed, we laughed together.

I said, 'Sahib, you must excuse me this morning. I want to go for a walk. I will come back about tea time.'

He looked hard at me, and we both knew I had spoken truly.

'Yes, yes, Santosh. You go for a good long walk. Make yourself hungry with walking. You will feel much better.'

Walking, through streets that were now so simple to me, I thought how nice it would be if the people in Hindu costumes in the circle were real. Then I might have joined them. We would have taken to the road; at midday we would have halted in the shade of big trees; in the late afternoon the sinking sun would have turned the dust clouds to gold; and every evening at some village there would have been welcome, water, food, a fire in the night. But that was a dream of another life. I had watched the people in the circle long enough to know that they were of their city; that their television life awaited them; that their renunciation was not like mine. No television life awaited me. It didn't matter. In this city I was alone and it didn't matter what I did.

As magical as the circle with the fountain the apartment block had once been to me. Now I saw that it was plain, not very tall, and faced with small white tiles. A glass door; four tiled steps down; the desk to the right, letters and keys in the pigeonholes; a carpet to the left, upholstered chairs, a low table with paper flowers in the vase; the blue door of the swift, silent elevator. I saw the simplicity of all these things. I knew the floor I wanted. In the corridor, with its illuminated star-decorated ceiling, an imitation sky, the colours were blue, grey and gold. I knew the door I wanted. I knocked.

The *hubshi* woman opened. I saw the apartment where she worked. I had never seen it before and was expecting something like my old employer's apartment, which was on the same floor. Instead, for the first time, I saw something arranged for a television life.

I thought she might have been angry. She looked only puzzled. I was grateful for that.

I said to her in English, 'Will you marry me?'

And there, it was done.

'It is for the best, Santosh,' Priya said, giving me tea when I got back to the restaurant. 'You will be a free man. A citizen. You will have the whole world before you.'

I was pleased that he was pleased.

* * *

So I am now a citizen, my presence is legal, and I live in Washington. I am still with Priya. We do not talk together as much as we did. The restaurant is one world, the parks and green streets of Washington are another, and every evening some of these streets take me to a third. Burnt-out brick houses, broken fences, overgrown gardens; in a levelled lot between the high brick walls of two houses, a sort of artistic children's playground which the *hubshi* children never use; and then the dark house in which I now live.

Its smells are strange, everything in it is strange. But my strength in this house is that I am a stranger. I have closed my mind and heart to the English language, to newspapers and radio and television, to the pictures of *hubshi* runners and boxers and musicians on the wall. I do not want to understand or learn any more.

I am a simple man who decided to act and see for himself, and it is as though I have had several lives. I do not wish to add to these. Some afternoons I walk to the circle with the fountain. I see the dancers but they are separated from me as by glass. Once, when there were rumours of new burnings, someone scrawled in white paint on the pavement outside my house: *Soul Brother.* I understand the words; but I feel, brother to what or to whom? I was once part of the flow, never thinking of myself as a presence. Then I looked in the mirror and decided to be free. All that my freedom has brought me is the knowledge that I have a face and have a body, that I must feed this body and clothe this body for a certain number of years. Then it will be over.

2 TELL ME WHO TO KILL

JUST LIKE MY BROTHER. He choose a bad morning to get married. Cold and wet, the little country parts between towns white rather than green, mist falling like rain, fields soaking, sometimes a cow standing up just like that. The little streams have a dirty milky colour and some of them are full of empty tins and other rubbish. Water everywhere, just like back home after a heavy shower in the rainy season, only the sky is not showing in the places where the water collect, and the sun is not coming out to heat up everything and steam it dry fast.

The train hot inside, the windows running with water, people and their clothes smelling. My old suit is smelling too. It is too big for me now, but it is the only suit I have and it is from the time of money. Oh my God. Just little bits of country between the towns, and sometimes I see a house far away, by itself, and I think how nice it would be to be there, to be watching the rain and the train in the early morning. Then that pass, and it is town again, and town again, and then the whole place is like one big town, everything brown, everything of brick or iron or rusty galvanize, like a big wet rubbish dump. And my heart drop and my stomach feel small.

Frank is looking at me, watching my face. Frank in his nice tweed jacket and grey flannel trousers. Tall, thin, going a little bald. But happy. Happy to be with me, happy when people look at us and see that he is with me. He is a good man, he is my friend. But inside he is puffed up with pride. No one is nice to me like Frank, but he is so happy to make himself small, bringing his knees together as though he is carrying a little box of cakes on them. He don't smile, but that is because he is so wise and happy. His old big shoes shining like a schoolteacher's shoes, and you could see that he shine them himself every evening, like a man saying his prayers and feeling good. He don't mean it, but he always make me feel sad and he always make me feel small, because I know I could never be as nice and neat as Frank and I could never be so wise and happy. But I know, oh God I know,

I lose everybody else, and the only friend I have in the world is Frank.

A boy writing on the wet window with his finger and the letters melting down. The boy is with his mother and he is all right. He know where they are going when the train stop. It is a moment I don't like at all, when the train stop and every-body scatter, when the ship dock and everybody take away their luggage. Everybody have their own luggage, and every-body's luggage so different. Everybody is brisk then, and happy, no time for talk, because they can see where they are going. Since I come to this country that is something I can't do. I can't see where I am going. I can only wait to see what is going to turn up.

I am going to my brother's wedding now. But I don't know what bus we will take when we get to the station, or what other train, what street we will walk down, what gate we will go through, and what door we will open into what room.

My brother. I remember a day like this, but with heat. The sky set black night and day, the rain always coming, beating on the galvanize roof, the ground turn to mud below the house, in the yard the water frothing yellow with mud, the pará-grass in the field at the back bending down with wet, everything damp and sticky, bare skin itching.

The cart is under the house and the donkey is in the pen at the back. The pen is wet and dirty with mud and manure and fresh grass mixed up with old grass, and the donkey is standing up quiet with a sugarsack on his back to prevent him catching cold. In the kitchen shed my mother is cooking, and the smoke from the wet wood thick and smelling. Everything will taste of smoke, but on a day like this you can't think of food. The mud and the heat and the smell make you want to throw up instead. My father is upstairs, in merino and drawers, rocking in the gallery, rubbing his hands on his arms. The smoke is not keeping away the mos-quitoes up there, but mosquitoes don't bite him. He is not think-ing of anything too much; he is just looking out at the black sky and the sugarcane fields and rocking. And in one of the rooms inside, below the old galvanize roof, my brother is lying on the floor with the ague.

It is a bare room, and the bare cedar boards have nothing on them except nails and some clothes and a calendar. You build a house and you have nothing to put in it. And my pretty brother is trembling with the ague, lying on the floor on a floursack spread on a sugarsack, with another floursack for counterpane. You can see the sickness on his little face. The fever is on him but he is not sweating. He can't understand what you say, and what he is saying is not making sense. He is saying that everything around him and inside him is heavy and smooth, very smooth.

It is as if he is going to die, and you think it is not right that someone so small and pretty should suffer so much, while someone like yourself should be so strong. He is so pretty. If he grow up he will be like a star-boy, like Errol Flim or Fairley Granger. The beauty in that room is like a wonder to me, and I can't bear the thought of losing it. I can't bear the thought of the bare room and the wet coming through the gaps in the boards and the black mud outside and the smell of the smoke and the mosquitoes and the night coming.

This is how I remember my brother, even afterwards, even when he grow up. Even after we sell the donkey-cart and start working the lorry and we pull down the old house and build a nice one, paint and everything. It is how I think of my brother, small and sick, suffering for me, and so pretty. I feel I could kill anyone who make him suffer. I don't care about myself. I have no life.

I know that it was in 1954 or 1955, some ordinary year, that my brother was sick, and from the weather I can tell you the month is January or December. But in my mind it happen so long ago I can't put a time to it. And just as I can't put a time to it, so in my mind I can't put a real place to it. I know where our house is and I know, oh my God, that if ever I go back I will get off the taxi at the junction and walk down the old Savannah Road. I know that road well; I know it in all sorts of weather. But what I see in my mind is in no place at all. Everything blot out except the rain and the night coming and the house and the mud and the field and the donkey and the smoke from the kitchen and my father in the gallery and my brother in the room on the floor.

And it is as though because you are frightened of something it is bound to come, as though because you are carrying danger with you danger is bound to come. And again it is like a dream. I see myself in this old English house, like something in *Rebecca* starring Laurence Oliver and Joan Fountain. It is an upstairs room with a lot of jalousies and fretwork. No weather. I am there with my brother, and we are strangers in the house. My brother is at college or school in England, pursuing his studies, and he is visiting this college friend and he is staying with the boy's family. And then in a corridor, just outside a door, something happen. A quarrel, a friendly argument, a scuffle. They are only playing, but the knife go in the boy, easy, and he drop without making a noise. I just see his face surprised, I don't see any blood, and I don't want to stoop to look. I see my brother opening his mouth to scream, but no scream coming. Nothing making noise. I feel fright – the gallows for him, just like that, and it was only an accident, it isn't true – and I know at that moment that the love and the danger I carry all my life burst. My life finish. It spoil, it spoil.

The worst part is still to come. We have to eat with the boy's parents. They don't know what happen. And both of us, my brother and me, we have to sit down and eat with them. And the body is in the house, in a chest, like in *Rope* with Fairley Granger. It is there at the beginning, it is there for ever, and everything else is only like a mockery. But we eat. My brother is trembling; he is not a good actor. The people we are eating with, I can't see their faces, I don't know what they look like.

They could be like any of the white people on this train. Like that woman with the boy writing on the wet window.

I can't help anybody now. My life spoil. I would like the train never to stop. But look, the buildings are getting higher and closer together and now they are right beside the tracks and you can see rooms and washing and other things hanging up in kitchens behind the wet windows. London. I am glad Frank is with me. He will look after me when the train stop. He will take me to the wedding house, wherever it is. My brother is getting married. And inside me is like lead.

When the train stop we let the others rush, and I calm down. No rain when we go outside, and it even look as if the sun is going to break through. Frank say we have a lot of time and we decide to walk a little. The streets dirty after the rain, the buildings black, old newspapers in the gutters. I follow Frank and he lead me to streets I know well. I wonder whether it is an accident or whether he know. He know everything.

And then I see the shop. Like a dirty box with a glass front. Now it is a jokes-shop, with little cards in the dusty window. Amuse your friends, frighten your friends. Card tricks, false false-teeth, solid glasses of Guinness, rubber spiders, itching powder, plastic dog-mess. It isn't much, but you wouldn't believe that once upon a time for a few months the place was mine.

'This is the place,' I tell Frank. 'The mistake of my life. This is where all my money went. Two thousand pounds. It take me five years to save that. In five months it went there.'

Two thousand pounds. Pounds don't sound like real money if you spend most of your life dealing in dollars and cents. But in ten years my father couldn't make two thousand pounds. How a man could revive after that? You can say: I will do it again, I will work again and save again. You can say that, but you know that when your courage break, it break.

Frank put his arm around my shoulders to take me away from the shop window. The owner, the new owner, the man with the lease, look at us. A yellow little bald fellow with a soft little paunch, and everything in his window already look as if it is collecting dust. Frank stiffen a little, the old pride puffing him up, and he is acting for the bald fellow and anybody else who is watching us.

I say, 'You white bitch.'

It is as though Frank love the obscene language. He get very tender and gentle, and because he is tender I start saying things I don't really feel.

'I am going to make a lot more money, Frank. I am going to make more money than you will ever make in your whole life, you white bitch. I will buy the tallest building here. I will buy the whole street.'

But even as I talk I know it is foolishness. I know that my life spoil and even I myself feel like laughing.

I don't want to be out in the street now. It isn't that I don't want people to see me; I don't want to see people. Frank tell me it is because they are white. I don't know, when Frank talk like that I feel he is challenging me to kill one of them.

I want to get off the street, to calm down. Frank take me to a café and we sit right at the back, facing the wall. He sit beside me. And he is talking to me. He talk about his own childhood, and I feel he is trying to show me that he too as a child had ague in a bare room. But he win through in life, he is in his city, he is now wise and strong. He don't know how jealous he is making me of him. I don't want to listen. I look at the flowers on the paper napkins and I lose myself in the lines. He can't see what is

locked up in my mind. He will never in a hundred years understand how ordinary the world was for me, with nothing good in
it, nothing to see except sugarcane and the pitch road, and how
from small I know I had no life.

Ordinary for me, but for my brother it wasn't going to be like
that. He was going to break away; he was going to be a professional man; I was going to see to that. For the rich and the
professional the world is not ordinary. I know, I see them.
Where you build a hut, they build a mansion; where you have
mud and a pará-grass field, they have a garden; when you kill
time on a Sunday, they have parties. We all come out of the
same pot, but some people move ahead and some people get left
behind. Some people get left behind so far they don't know and
they stop caring.

Like my father. He couldn't read and write and he didn't care.
He even joke about his illiteracy, slapping his fat arms and laughing. He say he is happy to leave that side of life to his younger
brother, who is a law clerk in the city. And whenever he meet
this brother, my father is always turning his own life into a story
and a joke, and he turn us his children into a joke too. But for all
the jokes he make, you could see that my father feel that he is
very wise, that it is he who pick up the bargain. My two older
sisters and my older brother are like that too. They learn just so
much in school; then – it was the way of the old days – they get
married, and my older brother start beating his wife and so on,
doing everything in the way people before him do, getting drunk
on a Friday and Saturday, wasting his money, without shame.

I was the fourth child and the second son. The world change
around me when I was growing up. I see people going away to
further their studies and coming back as big men. I know that
I miss out. I know how much I lose when I have to stop school,
and I decide that it wasn't going to be like that for my younger
brother. I feel I see things so much better than the rest of my
family; they always tell me I am very touchy. But I feel I become
like the head of the family. I get the ambition and the shame
for all of them. The ambition is like shame, and the shame is
like a secret, and it is always hurting. Even now, when it is all
over, it can start hurting again. Frank can never see what I see
in my mind.

* * *

A man used to live near us in a big two-storey house. The house was of concrete, with decorated concrete blocks, and it was in a lovely ochre colour with chocolate wood facings, everything so neat and nice it look like something to eat. I study this house every day and I think of it as the rich man's house, because the man was rich. He was rich, but once upon a time he was poor, like us, and the story was that he had a few acres of oil land in the south. A simple man, like my father, without too much education. But in my eyes the oil land and the luck and the money and the house make this man great.

I worship this man. Nothing extravagant about him; sometimes you could see him standing up on the road waiting for a bus or a taxi to go to town, and if you didn't know who he was you wouldn't notice him. I study everything about him, seeing luck and money in everything, in the hair he comb, in the shirt his hands button, in the shoes his hands lace up. He live alone in the house. His children married, and the story is that he don't get on with his family, that he is a man with a lot of worries. But to me even that is part of the greatness.

One time there was a wedding in the village, the old-fashioned all-night wedding, and the rich man lend his house. And on the wedding night I went in the house for the first time. The house that look so big from the outside is really very small inside. Downstairs is just concrete pillars, walls around open space. Upstairs is five small rooms, not counting galleries back and front. The lights dim, dim. It is what I remember most. That and the dead-rat smell. You feel dust everywhere, dust falling on you even while you walk. It isn't dust, it is the droppings from wood-lice, hard smooth tiny eggs of wood that roll below your hand if you put your hand down anywhere.

The drawing-room choke up with furniture, Morris suite and centre tables and everything else; but you feel that if you press too hard on anything it will crush. Just the furniture, nothing else in the drawing-room, no pictures or calendars even, nothing except for a pile of Christian magazines, Jehovah's Witness or something like that, things that the rest of us throw away but he the rich man keep, and he is not even a Christian. The place is like a tomb. It is as though nobody live there, as though the rich man don't know why he build the house.

And then one day somebody shoot the man. For money, for some family bad blood, nobody know. It is another country mystery. The black police nail up Five Hundred Dollars Reward posters everywhere, as though the village is suddenly like Dodge City or like something in *Jesse James*, with Henry Fonda and Tyrum Powers just around the corner.

Everybody wait for the drama. But no drama happen. The posters fade and tear, the police forget, the house remain. The ochre paint discolour, the galvanize roof rust and the rust run down the walls, and the damp run up fast from the ground like a bright green bush. The bright green get dark, it get black, real bush grow up in front of it. Mildew stain the house, the roof is all rust. The paint wash off the woodwork, the grain of the wood begin to show, the wood begin to get hollow, the soft parts melting away, until only the hard grain remain, like a skeleton. And all the time I live there the house just standing there like that.

I see now that the man I thought was a rich man wasn't rich at all. And from here, from this city which is like a country, I feel I could look down and see that whole village in the damp flat lands, the lumpy little pitch road, black between the green sugarcane, the ditches with the tall grass, the thatched huts, water in the yellow yards after rain, and the rusty roof of that one concrete house rotting.

You wonder how people get to a village like that, how that place become their home. But it is home, and on a sunny Sunday morning, nobody working, see everybody relaxing in their front yards, a few zinnias growing here and there, a few marigolds and old maid and coxcomb and lady's slipper and the usual hibiscus. The barber making his round, people sitting down below mango trees and getting their hair cut. And in my mind it is on a morning like this that I can see my father's younger brother coming up the pitch road on his bicycle.

My father's brother is living in the city. How he get there, how he get education when my father get none, how he get this job with the lawyer, all of this happen a long time ago, before I was born, and is now like a mystery. He is a Christian, or he take a Christian name, Stephen, as a mark of his progressiveness. My father does mock him behind his back for that name, but all of us are proud of Stephen and we well enjoy the little fame and respect he give us in the village.

It is a big thing when he come to visit us. The neighbours spreading the news in advance, my mother chasing and killing a chicken right away, my father getting out the rum bottle and glasses and water. Fête! And at the end, just before he leave, Stephen sharing out coppers to the children for the Sunday 4.30 matinée double.

Or so it used to be. I adore Stephen when I was small. And adoring him like this, I used to think that he live alone in the city, that we was his only family. But then I get let down. I realize that Stephen have his own family, that he have a whole heap of girl children, going to the Convent, and that he have his own son, a bright boy, a great student, and he worship this son. The boy is my own age too, or just a little older. Once or twice he come to see us. He is nice and quiet, not pulling any style on us, and you could see that in a special way my father is prouder of him than he is of me or my younger brother, that Stephen's son is what he expect, different, a bright boy and a future professional. My father don't give him coppers for a matinée. He send him a Shirley Temple fountain pen, a Mickey Mouse wristwatch.

Stephen never tell us when he is coming, and you wonder why a man like that would decide to leave his family on a Sunday morning to come and have a country fête with us. My father say that Stephen is glad to get away from that modern life sometimes, that Stephen is not happy with his Christian wife, and that Stephen, because of his progressiveness, is full of worries. I don't know what worries a man like Stephen could have. And if he have worries, they don't always show.

Stephen is a joker and a mocker. Even before he put his bicycle in the shade, even before he take off his hat and bicycle clips, even before he take the first shot of rum, Stephen start mocking. I don't know why he find our donkey so funny; it is as though he never see one before. He mock us because of the donkey; he mock us when the donkey die. Then when we buy the lorry and it get laid up for a few weeks below the house, blocks of wood below the axle, he mock us because of that. Everything we do is only like a mockery to Stephen, and my father encourage him by laughing.

Stephen mock me a lot too, in the beginning. 'When you marrying off this one?' he used to ask my father, even when I was small. My father always laugh and say, 'Next season. I got a nice girl for him.' But as I grow older I show I don't appreciate the humour, and Stephen stop mocking me.

He is not a bad or cruel man, Stephen. He is just a natural

joker, with all his so-called worries. Sometimes he mock himself. One time, when he bring his son to see us, he say, 'My son never yet tell a lie.' I ask the boy, 'It is true?' He say, 'No.' Stephen burst out laughing and say, 'My God, the influence of you people! The boy just tell his first lie.' This is Stephen, a little seriousness always below the mockery, and you feel that one reason he mock us is because he would like us to be a little more progressive.

Stephen is always asking my father what we are doing to educate my younger brother. 'The others are lost,' Stephen say. 'But you could still give this one a little education. Dayo, boy, you would like to take some studies?' And Dayo would rub his foot against his ankle and say, 'Yes, I would like to take some studies.' It was the beauty of the boy that attract Stephen, I feel. He used to say, 'I will take away Dayo with me.' – 'Yes,' my father would say, 'you take him away and give him some studies. In this school here he learning nothing at all. I don't know what teachers teaching these days.'

I always think it would be nice if Stephen could take an interest in Dayo and use his contacts to get Dayo in a good school in the city. But I know that Stephen is just talking, or rather, it is the rum and curry chicken talking, and I don't see how I can talk to him seriously about Dayo. If Stephen was a stranger it would have been different. But Stephen is family, and family is funny. I don't want to give Stephen or his son the idea that I am running them competition. Stephen would more than mock, if he feel that; he might even get vexed.

So I let Stephen talk. I know that he will drink and mock, that his eyes will get redder and redder until his worries begin to show on his face in truth, and that when the fête is over he will jump on his bicycle and ride off back to the city and his family.

I know that Stephen can't really take an interest in Dayo, because Stephen's whole mind and heart is full of his own son. For years Stephen talk of his son's further studies, and for years he save for these further studies; he don't keep it secret. Even when the time for these studies get close, when everything is fixed up with the university in Canada, Stephen don't relax. You begin to feel then that Stephen is more than ambitious for his son, that he is a little frightened too. He is like a man carrying something that could break and cut him. Even my father notice the difference, and he begin to say behind Stephen's back, 'My brother Stephen is going to get throw down by his son.' Like a happy man, my father. He educate none of his own children to throw him down.

Then one Sunday afternoon, some months before the boy leave, Stephen come. Without warning, as usual. This time he is not on a bicycle and he is not alone. He is in a motor-car and he is with his whole family. From the pará-grass field at the back of the house I see the car stop and I see all Stephen's girl children get out, and I remember the condition of our house. I race up in a foolish kind of way trying to sweep and straighten up. But my heart is failing me, because I can see the house as the girls will see it. And in the end, hearing the voices coming up the steps at the side, I pretend to be like my father, not caring, ready to make a joke of everything, letting people know that we have what we have, and that is that.

So they all come upstairs. And you could see the scorn in the face of Stephen's Christian wife and his Christian daughters. It would be much more bearable if they was ugly. But they are not ugly, and I feel that their scorn is right. I try to stay in the background. But then my mother, rubbing her dirty foot against her ankle, grin and pull up her veil over the top of her head, as though it is the only thing she have to do to make herself presentable, and she say, 'But, Stephen, you didn't give us warning. You had this boy' – and she point to me – 'running about trying to clean up the place.' And she laugh, as though she make a good joke.

The foolish woman didn't know what she was saying. I run out of the house to the pará-grass field at the back and then through the sugarcane, trying to fight down the shame and vexation.

I walk and walk, and I feel I would never like to go back to the house. But the day finish, I have to go back. The frogs croaking and singing in the canals and the ditches, the dim lights on in the house. Nobody miss me. Nobody care what they did say to me. Nobody ask where I went or what I do. Everybody in the house is just full of this piece of news. Dayo is going to live in the city with Stephen and his family. Stephen is going to send him to school or college and look after his studies. Stephen is going to make him a doctor, lawyer, anything. Everything settled.

It was like a dream. But it come at the wrong moment. I should be happy, but I feel that everything is now poisoned for me. Now that Dayo is about to go away, I begin to feel that I am carrying him inside me the way Stephen is carrying his own son, like something that might break and cut. And at the same time,

forgive me, a new feeling is in my heart. I am just waiting for my
father and mother, for Stephen and all Stephen's family, for all of
them who was there that day, I am just waiting for all of them to
die, to bury my shame with them. I hate them.

Even today I can hate them, when I should have more cause
to hate white people, to hate this café and this street and these
people who cripple me and spoil my life. But now the dead man
is me.

I used to have a vision of a big city. It wasn't like this, not streets
like this. I used to see a pretty park with high black iron railings
like spears, old thick trees growing out of the wide pavement,
rain falling the way it fall over Robert Taylor in *Waterloo Bridge*,
and the pavement covered with flat leaves of a perfect shape in
pretty colours, gold and red and crimson.

Maple leaves. Stephen's son send us one, not long after he went
to Montreal to pursue his higher studies. The envelope is long,
the stamp strange, and inside the envelope and his letter is this
pretty maple leaf, one leaf from the thousands on that pavement.
I handle the envelope and the leaf a lot, I study the stamp, and I
see Stephen's son walking on the pavement beside the black rail-
ing. It is very cold, and I see him stopping to blow his nose, looking down at the leaves and then thinking of us his cousins. He is
wearing an overcoat to keep out the cold and he have a briefcase
under his arm. That is how I think of him in Montreal, furthering
his studies, and happy among the maple leaves. And that is how
I want to see Dayo.

It was after Stephen's son went to Montreal that the jealousy
really did break out in Stephen's family against Dayo. They did
always scorn the boy. They used to make him sleep in the
drawing-room, and he had to make up a bed on the floor after
everybody else went to sleep. He didn't have a room to pursue
his studies in, like Stephen's son. He used to read his books in
the tiny front gallery of Stephen's tiny house. The gallery was
almost on the pavement, so that he could see everybody that
pass and they could see him. See him? They could reach out a
hand and turn the page of the book he was reading. Still, this
regular reading and studying he do in the gallery win him a
little fame and respect in the area, and I feel it was this little
respect that the poor boy start to pick up that make Stephen's

family vexed. They feel they are the only ones who should pursue studies.

Stephen's daughters especially take against the boy, when you would think they ought to have been proud of their handsome cousin. But no, like all poor people, they want to be the only ones to rise. It is the poor who always want to keep down the poor. So they feel that Dayo is lowering them. It wouldn't have surprised me to get a message one day from Stephen that Dayo was interfering and tampering with his daughters.

You can imagine how glad they all was when Dayo sit his various exams and fail. You can imagine how much that make their heart rejoice. The reason was the bad school Dayo was going to. He couldn't get into any of the good ones. Those schools always talk about a lack of background and grounding, and Dayo had to go to a private school where the teachers themselves was a set of dunces without any qualifications. But Stephen's daughters don't look at that.

You would think that Stephen, after all his grand charge about progressiveness, would stand up for Dayo and do something to give the boy a little help and courage. But Stephen himself, when his son went away, get very funny. He is not interested in anything at all; he is like a man in mourning. He is like a man expecting bad news, the thing that would break in his hands and cut him. His face get puffy, his hair get grey and coarse.

But the first bad news was mine. I come home one weekday, tired after my lorry work, and I find Dayo. He is well dressed, he is like a man on a visit. But he say he leave Stephen's house for good, he is not going back. He say, 'They try to make me a yardboy. They try to get me to run messages for them.' I could see how much he was suffering, and I could see that he was frightened we wouldn't believe him and would force him to go back.

It is what my father would like to do. He scratch his arms and rub his hand over the stiff grey hair on his chin, making that sound he does like, and he say, as though he know everything and is very wise, 'It is what you have to put up with.'

So poor Dayo could only turn to me. And when I look at his face, so sad and frightened, I feel my body get weak and trembling. The blood run up and down my veins, and my arms start hurting inside, as though inside them is wire and the wire is being pulled.

Dayo say, 'I got to go away. I got to leave. I feel that if I stay here those people are going to cripple me with their jealousy.'

I don't know what to say. I don't know the ropes, I don't have any contacts. Stephen is the man with the contacts, but now I can't ask Stephen anything.

'There is nothing for me to do here,' Dayo say.

'What about the oilfields?' I ask him.

'Oilfields, oilfields. The white people keep the best jobs for themselves. All you could do there is to become a bench-chemist.'

Bench-chemist, I never hear this word before, and it impress me to hear it. Stephen's family don't give Dayo any credit for learning, but I can see how much the boy improve in the two years and how he develop a new way of talking. He don't talk fast now, his voice is not going up and down, he use his hands a lot, and he is getting a nice little accent, so that sometimes he sound like a woman, the way educated people sound. I like his new way of talking, though it embarrasses me to look at him and think that he my brother is now a master of language. So now he start talking, and I let him talk, and as he talk he lose his sadness and fright.

Then I ask him, 'What you would study when you go away? Medicine, chartered accountancy, law?'

My mother jump in and say, 'I don't know, ever since Dayo small, I always feel I would like him to do dentistry.'

That is her intelligence, and you well know that she never think of dentistry or anything else for Dayo until that moment. We let her say what she have to say, and she go down to the kitchen, and Dayo begin to talk in his way. He don't give me a straight answer, he is working up to something, and at last it come. He say: 'Aeronautical engineering.'

This is a word, like bench-chemist, that I never hear before. It frighten me a little, but Dayo say they have a college in England where you just go and pay the fees. Anyway, so we agree. He was going to go away to further his studies in aeronautical engineering.

And as soon as we agree on that Dayo start behaving as though he is a prisoner on the run, as though he have a ship to catch, as though he couldn't stay another month on the island. It turn out in truth that he had a ship to catch. It turn out that he had some friends he did want to go to England with. So I run about here and there, raising money from this one and that one, signing my name on this paper and that paper, until the money side was settled.

Everything happen very fast, and I remember thinking, watching Dayo go aboard the ship with a smile, that it was one of those moments you can only properly think about afterwards. When the ship pull away and I see the oily water between the ship and the dock, my heart sink. I feel sick, I feel the whole thing was too easy, that something so easy cannot end well. And on top of all this is my grief for the boy, that slender boy in the new suit.

The grief work on me. In my mind I blame Stephen and his family for their jealousy. And, I couldn't help it, two or three days after Dayo leave I went to the city and went to Stephen's house.

It was a poky little old-fashioned wood house in a bad part of the city, and it shame me to think that once upon a time I used to look on Stephen as a big man. Now I see that in the city Stephen is not much, that all his hope and all his daughters' hope is in that son who is studying in Montreal. He is like the Prince to them. And in that little house, with no front-yard and next to no back-yard, they are living like Snow White and the seven dwarfs, with their little foreign pictures in their little drawing-room, and their little pieces of polished furniture. You feel you have to stoop, that if you take a normal step you will break something.

It was late afternoon when I went. Everybody home. Stephen rocking in the gallery. It surprise me to see him looking so old. The hair on his head really grey now, standing up short and stiff. Everybody is looking at me as though they feel I come to make trouble. I disappoint them. I kiss Stephen on his cheek and I kiss his wife. The girls pretend they don't see me, and that is all right by me.

They give me tea. Not in our crude country fashion, condensed milk and brown sugar and tea mixed up in one. No, man. Tea, milk, white sugar, everything separate. I pretend I am one of the seven dwarfs and I do everything they want me to do. Then, as I was expecting, they ask about Dayo.

I stir my tea with their little teaspoon and take a sip and I put the cup down and say, 'Oh, Dayo. He gone away. On the *Colombie*.'

Stephen is so surprised he stop rocking. Then he begin to smile. He look just like my father.

Stephen's wife, Miss Shameless Christian Short-Dress herself, she ask, 'And what he gone away for? To look for a work?'

I lift up the teacup and say, 'To pursue his higher studies.'

Stephen is vexed now. 'Higher studies? But he didn't even begin his lower studies.'

'That is an opinion,' I say, using some words I pick up from Dayo.

One of the girls, a real pretty and malicious little one, come out and ask, 'What he is going to study?'

'Aeronautical engineering.'

The shock show on Stephen's face, and I feel I could laugh. All of them are mad with jealousy now. All the girls come out and stand up around me in that little drawing-room as though I am the brown girl in the ring. I just drinking my tea out of their little teacup. On the walls they have all those pictures and photographs of foreign scenes, as though because they are Christian and so on, they must know about these things.

'Aeronautical engineering,' Stephen say. 'He would be better off piloting a taxi between the airport and the city.'

The girls giggle and Stephen's wife smile. Stephen is the mocker and joker again, the man in control, and it is all right again for his family. They get a little happier. I see that if I stay any longer I would have to start insulting them, so I get up and leave. As I leave I hear one of the girls laugh. I can't tell you how full my heart get with hate.

Next morning I wake up at four o'clock, and the hate is still with me. The hate eat me and eat me until the day break and I get up, and all that day the hate eating me while I am working, driving the lorry to and from the gravel pits.

In the afternoon, work over, the lorry parked below the house, I take a taxi and went back to the city, to Stephen's house. I didn't know what I was going to do. Half the time I was thinking that I would go and make friends with them again, that I would go and take Stephen's jokes and show that I could laugh at the jokes.

But that is the way of weakness and it would be foolish and wrong, because you cannot really joke with your enemy. When you find out who your enemy is, you must kill him before he kill you. And so with the other half of my mind I was thinking

I would go there and break everything in the house, swinging one of those drawing-room bentwood chairs from wall to wall, from jalousie to jalousie, in all those tiny rooms, through all that damn fretwork.

Then a strange thing happen. Perhaps it was because I did wake up so early that morning. The constipation that was with me all day suddenly stop, and by the time I reach Stephen's house all I want is a toilet.

So I rush in the house. Stephen rocking in the little gallery. But I didn't tell him anything. I didn't say good afternoon or anything to his wife and his daughters. I went straight through to their toilet and I stay there a long time, and I pull the chain and I wait until the cistern full again and I pull the chain again. Then I walk out and I walk through the house and I didn't tell anybody anything, and I walk out on the street, and the feeling come back to my arms, no more stretched wires inside them, and I walk and walk until my head cool down, and then I take taxi home, to the junction.

And next morning again I wake up in the darkness at four o'clock, but this time I am frightened. I only feel like crying and praying for forgiveness, and I begin to know something gone wrong with me, that my life and my mind not right. Even the hate break inside me. I can't feel the hate. I begin to feel lost. I think of Dayo lying sick on the floor in the old house and I think of him leaving on the white *Colombie*. And even when I get up in the morning I feel lost.

I expect punishment. I don't know how it is coming, but every day I wait for it. Every day I wait to hear from Dayo, but he don't write. I feel I would like to go back to Stephen's house, just go back and sit down and do nothing, not even talk. But I never go.

And then Stephen get news of his son. And the news is that Stephen's son gone foolish in Montreal. The further studies and his father too much for him, and in Montreal he is foolish, like those police dogs that get foolish, like pets, if you kill their handlers. Stephen get his bad news now! The Prince is not coming, and in that little house in the city the whole family mash up, in truth.

My father say, 'I always say that Stephen was going to get throw down by that boy.'

He feel he win. He do nothing; he just wait and win. But I

remember my own hate, the hate that make me sick, and I feel I kill all of them.

I think now of the maple leaf the boy send us in the airmail envelope with the strange stamp. Walking on the street with his overcoat and briefcase, when he was pursuing his studies. The street is still there, the rain fall on it a thousand times, the leaves still on the pavement beside the black railings. Now I feel I walk on that pavement myself, among the strange leaves. Strange leaves, strange flowers that sometimes I pick. I have paper; the paper have lines like a schoolchild's copybook, and a number; and Frank write my name in his own handwriting at the top on the dotted line. But I have nobody to write and send a leaf or a flower to.

The water black, the ship white, the lights blazing. And inside the ship, far below, everybody like prisoners already. The lights dim, everyone in their bunk. In the morning the water is blue, but you can't see land. You are just going where the ship is going, you will never be a free man again. The ship smelling, like vomit, like the back door of a restaurant. Night and day the ship is moving. The sea and sky lose colour, everything is grey.

I don't want the ship to stop, I don't want to touch land again. On the bunk below me is a jeweller fellow called Khan or Mohammed. He is wearing a hat all the time, all the time, and you would think he is wearing it for the joke. But he is not laughing, his face is small, and he is talking already of going back. I can't go back, I will have to stay. I don't know how I trap myself.

The land come nearer, and one morning through the rain you see it, more white than green, no colours there. The ship stop suddenly and it is very quiet, and there in the water below is a boat and some men in oilskins. You see them move but you can't hear them. And after all the days at sea everything in and around that little boat is very bright, as though a black-and-white picture suddenly turn Technicolor. The rocking water is deep and green, the oilskins very yellow, the faces of the people very pink.

The mystery land is theirs, the stranger is you. None of those houses in the rain there belong to you. You can't see yourself walking down those streets set down so flat on that cliff. But that is where you have to go, and as soon as everybody get down in the launch with their luggage the ship hoot. It is white and big and safe, it is saying goodbye, it is in a hurry to get away and to leave you behind. The Technicolor is over, the picture change. Now is only noise and rush and luggage, train and traffic. This is it, and already you are like a man in blinkers.

I tell myself I come to England to be with Dayo and to look after him, to keep him well while he is pursuing his studies. But I didn't see Dayo at the dock and I didn't see him at the railway station. He leave me alone. I do what I see other people do, and I manage. I find a job, I get some rooms in Paddington. I learn bus numbers and place names; I watch the season change from cold to warm. I manage, I am all right, but only because I feel it is not my life. I feel as I feel on the ship, that I lose that, that I throw that away.

Then, after all those weeks when he leave me guessing, Dayo write. He try to blame me; he say he had to write home to get my address. He is in another town. He write nothing about his aeronautical engineering, but he say he just finish one particular course of studies and he get a diploma, and now he want some help to move down to London to do some more studies.

I take the day off from the cigarette factory and draw out a few pounds from the post office and went up by train to the town where he was staying. It is always like this now. You are always taking trains and buses to strange places. You never know what sort of street you are going to find yourself in, what sort of house you will be knocking at.

The street is solid with little grey brick houses. Only a few steps from the gate of the house to the door, and the man who open the door get mad as soon as he hear my name. He is a small old man, his neck very loose in his collar, and I can't understand his accent too well. But I understand him to say that Dayo is owing him twelve pounds in rent, that Dayo run away without paying, and that he is not giving up Dayo's suitcase until he get his money. I begin to hate the little fellow and his mildewed house. Dirt shining on the walls, and when I see the little cubicle he is charging three pounds a week for, I had to control myself. You always have to control yourself now, I don't know for what reward.

In the cubicle I see Dayo's suitcase, still with the *Colombie* sticker. I pay and take it straightaway. I don't know where in this town Dayo can be, where he is hiding these last four weeks, but like a fool with this heavy suitcase, as though I just get off the ship myself, I walk up and down the streets, looking.

Even when I went back to the railway station I couldn't make up my mind to leave. The waiting-room empty, the seats cut up with long knife slashes that set your teeth on edge just to see them. I try to think of all the days that Dayo spend alone in this town, all the times he too see the day turn to evening, and he don't know who to turn to. And as the train take me back to London, I hate everything I see, houses, shops, traffic, all those settled people, those children playing games in fields.

At the station I wait again and take a bus and then another bus. Then there, outside my house, when I turn the corner with that heavy suitcase, I see Dayo, in the suit he went aboard the *Colombie* with.

He look as if he was waiting a long time, as if he nearly forget what he was waiting for. He is not thin; if anything, he is a little stouter. As soon as he see me he get sad, and the tears run to my eyes. When we go down to the basement we embrace and we sit down together on the sofa-bed. I am ashamed to notice it, but he is smelling, his clothes are dirty.

He put his head on my lap and I pat him like a baby, thinking of all those days he spend alone, without me. He knock his head on my knee and say, 'I don't have confidence, brother. I lose my confidence.' I look at his long hair that no barber cut for weeks, I see the inside of his dirty collar. I see his dirty shoes. Again and again he say, 'I don't have confidence, I don't have confidence.'

All the bad things I did want to say to him drop away. I rock him on my lap until I come to myself and see that it is dark, the street lamp on outside. I don't want him to do anything foolish because of false pride. I want to give him a way out. So I ask, 'You don't want to go through with your studies?' He don't answer. He only sob. I ask him again, 'You don't want to take any more studies?' He lift his head up and blow his nose and say, 'It is all right, brother. I like studies.' And I can tell he is happier, that he was only a little worried and lonely and down-couraged; and that it is going to be all right in truth.

In the kitchen, as soon as I turn on the light, cockroaches scatter everywhere, over dirty old stove and mash-up pot and pan. I bring out bread and milk and a tin of New Brunswick sardines.

It is full-moon night, and the old white woman upstairs start getting on the way she does always get on when the moon is full, shouting and fighting with her husband, screaming and cursing until one of them shut the other one outside.

I light a little fire, more firelighter and newspaper than coal, and Dayo and I sit and eat. I just regret the basement have no bath. But Dayo will go next day to the public baths, sixpence with the smooth old towel. Right now the little fire make the room more than warm, the damp dry out a little. The rat smell the food right away: I hear him scratching at the box I put over his hole. It is like living in a camp, in this basement. Not long after I move in I make a joke about putting a tiny lady's hand mirror right in the centre of the wall over the fireplace. Now Dayo is here to appreciate that joke.

We pull out the bed part of the sofa-bed and make it up. I even forget the smell, of dead rat and old dirt and gas and rust. Upstairs, the old woman shut her husband out. When I wake up in the night it is because the husband is either shouting from the pavement or banging on the door. In the morning all is calm. The monthly madness is over.

So, suddenly, the sadness and the fright pass, and the happy time come. The happy time come and it don't go away, and I start forgetting. Stephen and his family, my father and mother, the sugarcane and the mud and the rich man's rotting house, the ship at night and the mystery land in the morning, all of that I forget. It is far away, like another life; none of that can touch me again. And in that basement, with the old mad woman upstairs, I feel as the London months pass that I get back my life, living with Dayo alone, knowing nobody else.

I fix up the little back bedroom for Dayo, with a reading-light and everything, and he start taking some regular studies. He get back his confidence and it looks as though what he say is true, that he really like studies, because as fast as he finish one diploma he start another. In the new clothes I buy for him he is looking nice, even sharp. He develop his way of talking and he is looking good to me, like any professional. I know my own ignorance and I don't interfere with his studies. I let him go his own way and take his own time. I don't want anything to happen to him again. It is enough for me that he is there.

And you could say that I begin to like big-city life. At home,

where people treat you rough and generally get on as though
work is a crime and a punishment, I did always prefer to be my
own boss. But here I get to like the factory. Nobody watching
you; you lower nobody; nobody mock you. I like the nice sharp
tobacco smell, and I get to like the machine I mind, with the
cigarettes coming out in one long piece, so long and strong you
could skip with it. I never think work would be like this, that it
would make me feel good to think that the factory is always there
and I could always go to it on a morning.

Every Friday they give you a hundred free cigarettes. These
cigarettes have a special watermark, but those fellows from
Pakistan don't always appreciate this and some of them get catch.
A white fellow start walking out one day like a cowboy on high
heels. When they stop him they find his shoes stuff up with
tobacco. Things like this always happen. The factory is like a
school that you don't like at first but then you like more and more.

No hustling with the lorry, nobody beating you down all the
time, and you get your money in a little brown envelope, as
though you are some kind of civil servant or professional. Regular work, regular money. After some months I finish paying off
the money-lender at home, and then I even start saving a little
for myself. I am not keeping this money at home, as my father
used to do with his few cents. It is going straight in the post office;
I have my own little book. One day I find I have a hundred
pounds. Mine, not money I borrow. A hundred pounds. I feel
safe. I can't tell you how safe I feel. Whenever I think of it I close
my eyes and put my hand to my heart.

But it is so when you get too happy. You forget too much. That
hundred pounds make me forget myself. It give me ideas. It make
me forget why I am in London. I want to feel more than safe now.
I want to see that money grow, I want to see the clerks writing in
my book in their different handwriting every week. That
become like a craze with me. I know it is foolishness, and I don't
tell Dayo about it; but at the same time I enjoy the secret. And
it is because I want to see this money grow week after week that
I take a second job. I look around and I get a night work in a
restaurant kitchen.

So I start stunning myself with work, and my life become
one long work. I get up about six. By seven, Dayo still sleeping,
I leave for the cigarette factory. I come back about six to the

basement, sometimes Dayo there, sometimes he is not there. By eight I leave for the restaurant, and I come back about midnight or later. London for me is the bus rides, morning, evening, night, the factory, the restaurant kitchen, the basement. I know it is too much, but for me that is part of the pleasure. Like when you are sick and thin, you want to get thinner and thinner, just to see how thin you could get. Or like some fat people who don't like being fat but still they just want to see how fat they could get: they are always looking at their shadow, and that is like their secret hobby. So now I am always tired when I go to sleep and tired in the morning, but I like and enjoy the tiredness. That is like the secret too, like the money adding up, fifty, sixty pounds a month. And the tiredness does always go in the middle of the morning.

I feel Dayo would mock me if he get to find out what possess my mind. He don't say anything, but I know that he, as a student in London, can't really appreciate having his brother working in a restaurant kitchen. But as the months pass, as one year pass, and two years, as the life hold out and the money add up, I find the money making me strong. And because the money make me strong I can put up with anything. I don't mind what people say or how they watch me. When I didn't have money I used to hate the basement, and I used to daydream about buying nice clothes not only for Dayo but for me too. But now my clothes don't matter to me, and I even get a thrill to think that nobody seeing me in my working clothes, on that street, coming out of that basement, would believe that I have a thousand pounds in the post office, that I have twelve hundred, that I have fifteen.

I scarcely believe it myself. Life in London! This was what people say at home, to mean everything nice. I didn't look for it; it wasn't what I come for. But I feel that that life come now, and if I was frightened of anything it was that my strength wouldn't hold out, that Dayo would finish his studies and leave me alone in the basement, and that the life would end.

It is true. This was the happy time, when Dayo live in my basement and I work like a man in blinkers, when I have the factory to go to every morning and the restaurant every evening, when I can enjoy a Sunday the way I never enjoy a Sunday before. Sometimes I think of the first day, and those men in yellow oil-skins in the deep green water in the morning. But that to me is now like a memory from somewhere else, like something I make up.

Craziness. How a man could fool himself like that? Look at these streets now. Look at these things and people I never did see. They have their life too; the city is theirs. I don't know where I thought I was, behaving as though the city was a ghost city, working by itself, and that it is something I discover by myself. Frank will never understand. He will never see the city I see; he will never understand how I work like that.

He is only querying and probing me about foremen who insult me at the factory, about people who fight with me at the restaurant. He is forever worrying me with his discrimination inquiries. He is my friend, the only friend I have. I alone know how much he help me, from how far he bring me back. But he is digging me all the time because he prefer to see me weak. He like opening up manholes for me to fall in; he is anxious to push me down in the darkness.

His attitude, in the café and then at the bus stop and then in the bus, is: keep off, this man is weak, this man is under my protection. When he is like this he have the power to draw all the strength from me, he with his shining shoes and his nice tweed jacket. As though one time I couldn't go in a shop and buy twelve tweed jackets and pay in cash.

But now the money gone and everything gone and I only have this suit, and it is smelling. But everything does smell here. At home, at home, windows are always open and everything get clean in the open air. Here everything is locked up. Even on a bus no breeze does blow.

Somewhere in the city Dayo is getting married today. I don't know where he think he is.

I work and work and save and save and the money grow and grow, and when it reach two thousand pounds, I get stunned. I don't feel I can go on. I know the life have to stop sometime, that I can't go on with two jobs, that something have to happen. And now the thought of working and saving another thousand is too much for me. So I stop work altogether. I leave the cigarette factory, I leave the restaurant. I take out my two thousand from the post office and I decide to use it.

It is ignorance, it is madness. It is the madness the money itself bring on. The money make me feel strong. The money make me feel that money is easy. The money make me forget how hard money is to make, that it take me more than four years to save what I have. The money in my hand, two thousand pounds, make me forget that my father never get more than ten pounds a month for his donkey-cart work, that he bring all of us up on that ten pounds a month, and that ten by twelve is one hundred and twenty, that the money I have in my hand is the pay of my father for fifteen or sixteen years. The money make me feel that London is mine.

I take my money out and I do with it what I see people do at home. I buy a business. It is the madness working on me, the money madness. I don't know London and I know nothing about business, but I buy a business. In my mind I am only calculating like those people at home who buy one lorry and work that and buy a second lorry and buy another and another.

The business I had in mind was a little roti-and-curry shop. Not a restaurant, something more like a stall you get at a race-course, two or three little basins of curry on the counter on this side, a little pile of rotis or chapattis or dalpuris on that side. A lot of women at home do very well that way. The idea come to me just like that one day when I was still at the cigarette factory, and it never leave me. And because the idea come just like that, as though somebody give it to me, I feel it is right. Dayo wasn't too interested. He talk a lot in that way he have, talking and talking and leaving you guessing about what he mean. I don't know whether he is ashamed or whether he find the idea of a roti-shop in London too funny, a reminder of home and simple things. I let him talk.

The first shock I get was the price of properties. But I didn't get frightened and stop. No, the madness is on me, I can't pull back. I am behaving as though I have a train to catch and must spend my money first. And the strange thing is that as soon as that first piece of money go, for the lease for a few years of a rundown little place in that scruffy street, as soon as that piece of money actually leave my hand, I know it is foolishness and I feel that all the money gone, that I have nothing. I feel the business bust already. I feel I start to bleed, and I am like a man only look-ing to down-courage himself.

So in just four or five weeks the whole world change for me again. I am no longer strong and rich, not caring what people say or think. Now, suddenly, I am a pauper, and my shabbiness worry me, and I begin to pine for the little things I didn't give myself, like twelve-pound tweed jackets, which now, after I pay decorators, electricians and the catering company, I can't afford.

Then I run into prejudice and regulations. At home you can put up a table outside your house any time and start selling what you want. Here they have regulations. Those suspicious men in tweeds and flannels, some of them young, young fellows, are coming round with their forms and pressing me on every side. They are not leaving me any peace of mind at all. They are full of remarks, they don't smile, they like nothing I do. And I have to shop and cook and clean, and the area is not good and business is bad, and no amount of hard work and early rising will help.

I see I kill myself. The little courage that still remain with me wash away, and the secret vision I had of buying up London, the foolishness I always really know was foolishness, burst. Without my two thousand pounds in the post office, without my real cash, I was without my strength, like Samson without his hair.

When the men in flannels go, the young English louts come. I don't know what attract them to the place, why they pick on me. Half the time I can't understand what they say, but they are not people you can get on with at all. They only dress up and come to make trouble. Sometimes they eat and don't pay; sometimes they mash up plates and glasses and bend the cutlery. That become like their hobby, a lot of them against me alone. That is their bravery and education. And nobody on my side.

Before, in the days of the hard work, of the two jobs, in the days of money, this was the sort of thing that didn't bother me at all. But now everything is hurting. I can't bear the way those louts talk or laugh or dress, and I feel my heart getting full of hate again, as it used to be for Stephen and his family, that hate that make me sick.

Dayo should have helped me. He was my brother. He was the man I make the money for. He was the man I went aboard the ship for. But now he leave me alone. He is there with me in the basement; sometimes we still eat together on a Sunday; but his attitude is that what I do is my business alone, he have his own things to do. He is going his own way, pursuing his studies or doing whatever he is doing. Sometimes the light is on in his room when I come in; sometimes he come tiptoeing in afterwards; in the morning I always leave him sleeping. He is there. You can't forget him. And then my heart begin to set against him too.

I begin to hate the way he talk. I begin to look at him. Once he was the pretty boy, using Vaseline Hair Tonic and combing his hair like Fairley Granger. Now you could see the face becoming just a labourer's face, without even the hardness that my father's face get from work and sun. And when he start talking in that way he have – and he can start talking about anything: all you have to say is 'Dayo, give me a match' – he make me feel that something is wrong with him, that someone who is using words in this way is not right. He still have his accent, but he is like a man who have no control over his speech, as though it is the first time he talk that day, as though he have nobody in London to talk to.

So in these days I start worrying about Dayo. The roti-shop is always there to worry about, but that to me is in the past now. I do my hard work, I waste my money and my reward. I can't start again. I can't go back to the cigarette factory and those insulting illiterate girls and that long ride in the cold morning to the factory. That finish. Now I concentrate on Dayo, my brother. I watch his face, I watch the way he walk, the way he shave. He don't understand; he is just talking in his womanish way. I don't tell him anything. I don't even know what I think. I just look at him and study him.

I wake up early one morning with a wet-dream. It was the second wet-dream I had; the first happen when I was a boy. It leave me exhausted and dirty and ashamed. I want to go to Dayo and beg him to forgive me, because this, the thing that just happen to me, is something I never did think about for him. I feel I let him down, that I betray him in my heart, and I feel I would like to go to him and make up and talk as in the old days. I feel I must show him that I always love him.

I go in his little room at the back, the early back-yard light showing through the thin curtains, and I look at the boy with the labourer's face sleeping on the narrow iron bed. On the table, that I cover with red oilcloth for him, is the reading-lamp I fix up for him for his studies, and his big books, and the paperbacks he read for relaxation sometimes, and the little transistor radio he get me to buy for him so that he could listen to his pop music.

A labourer's face. But the sadness of the sleeping face hit me, and the smallness of the room, and the concrete wall outside the window, and that yard where no sun fall. And I wonder what it is leading to, what will happen to him and me, whether he will ever take that ship back and get off one bright morning and take a taxi to the junction and drive through places he know.

I notice the saucer he is using as an ashtray, and the expensive cigarettes. I notice the dirtiness of his finger-nails and hands, the fatness at the top of his arms. Once those arms was so strong. Once he used to walk so nice, I used to think like Fonda.

I stand and watch him in the cold room. He twist and turn, he open his eyes, he recognize me. He get frightened. He jump up. And how dirty the sheets he is sleeping in. How dirty.

He say, 'What happen?'

He talk without his accent. He look at me as though I come in the room to kill him. He say nothing else; he suddenly lose his way of talking. The labourer's face.

Sadness, but my sadness. It flow through my body like a fluid.

I say, 'What course of studies you are now pursuing, Dayo?'

The fright leave his face. He try to get vexed. Try. He say, 'Somebody make you a policeman or what?' He is not talking with his accent now, he is not going on and on. He is like a child again, back home.

I say, 'I just want to talk with you. You know I am busy with the shop. It is a long time since we talk seriously.'

He say, and as he talk he get back his accent, 'Well, since you ask, and you have every right to ask, I will tell you. It isn't easy to take studies in this place as you and other people believe. A lot of people come here with their own ideas and they think they will start taking studies—'

I had to stop him. 'What you are taking?'

'I am preparing myself for the modern world. I am taking a course in computer programming, if you want to know. Com-puter pro-gram-ming. I hope this meet with your approval and satisfaction.'

I lift up the pack of cigarettes from the table. I say, 'Expensive.'

He say, in his accent, 'I smoke good cigarettes.'

The labourer's face. The labourer's backchat. I feel that if I stay in that room I would hit him.

And yet I went to his room with love and shame.

The shame stay with me all day. In the evening, after a bad

time in the shop, more trouble with those white louts, my arms getting the feeling that there is stretched wire inside them, I travel back by the night bus. When I get off, a black dog with a collar round its neck start following me. The street lamps shining on the trees, those trees with the peeling bark that is a little bit like the bark of our guava trees. The pavements damp, footmarks in the thin black mud. The big dog is friendly. I know it is making a mistake and I try to chase it away. But it only look at me, wagging its tail, and as soon as I walk on it follow me again, really close, as though it want to feel me all the time.

It follow me and follow me, right down past the rubbish bins to the basement. You would think that it would know now that it make a mistake. But no, it slip inside as soon as I open the door and it run up and down the hall, happy, wagging its tail, leaving footmarks everywhere.

I look for Dayo in his room, and the dog look too. I just see the dirty bed when I switch on the light, the sheet gathered up in the centre, the sheet and the pillow brown with dirt, the saucer full of cigarette ends. Oh my God.

I am hungry, but I can't stand the thought of food. I make a little Ovaltine. When I start to drink, the dog come right up to me again, wagging its tail. And wagging its tail, it follow me to the hall. I open the door. The dog know now it make a mistake. It race up the steps, not looking back at me, and run away in the night. It leave me feeling lonely.

Later, lying down, I hear Dayo tiptoeing in and switching on his light.

And it was the next morning, leaving Dayo sleeping in his room, and taking the Underground to the market, it was then that I see the advertisement in the carriage: PREPARE YOURSELF FOR TOMORROW'S WORLD WITH A COURSE IN COMPUTER PROGRAMMING.

I understand. I am not surprised. But the hate fill my heart. I want to see his face get frightened again. I get off the train after a couple of stops. I walk about the platform, I don't know what I want to do. I smoke a couple of cigarettes, I let the trains pass. I feel people start looking at me. I cross over to the other platform, not many people waiting that side, and take the train back.

The smart labourer boy. He only smoke good cigarettes. Oh God. I see myself going down to the basement to that room with

the dirty sheets and the saucer with the expensive good cigarettes. I see myself lifting him out of that bed and hitting him on
that lying labourer's mouth.

But I can't bring myself to go down the basement steps. I stand
up for a long time looking down at the dustbins and the break-
down fence with two or three hedge plants that grow too big,
like little trees, nobody trimming them, the basement window
dull with dirt, scraps of wet-and-dried paper and other rubbish
scattered about the little garden where somehow a type of grass
is still growing.

The moon-mad white woman open the front door. Her face
wrinkled and yellow, and you get a glimpse of the blackness
behind her. The woman is dazed; the monthly madness tire her
out; you can see that every night she is fighting in her sleep. As
she bend down to take the milk, I see her yellow hair thin like a
baby's. She look at me and I can see that she recognize me but
she isn't sure. I nearly say good morning. It is the only thing we
say to one another after five years. But then I change my mind
and walk away fast to the corner. And I think: Oh my God, I am
glad I change my mind.

But I can't leave and go to the market. I can't face that now,
I feel I have to settle this thing first. I wait and wait at the corner,
I don't know what for. I don't know what I want to do. Until I
see Dayo stepping out, in his suit, with his books.

I know the bus stop he is going to. I turn left and walk to the
stop before. The bus come; I get on and find a seat on the right-
hand side. At the next stop Dayo is waiting. It is funny, studying
him like this, as though he is a stranger, and he not knowing that
you are studying him. You could see that he just throw some cold
water over his face this morning, that his shirt is dirty, that he is
not taking care of himself. He get on; he go upstairs; he does
smoke good cigarettes.

He get off at Oxford Circus, and at the traffic lights I get off
and follow him down Oxford Street through the crowds. At
the end of Oxford Street he buy a paper and go inside a Lyons.
I wait a good time. It is getting late now, the morning half gone.
I follow him down Great Russell Street, and now I can see that
he is idling in truth, looking at the window of the Indian food-
shop, the noticeboards outside the newsagent selling foreign
papers, crossing the road to look at the dusty books outside the
bookshop. A lot of Africans knocking around here, with jacket

and tie and briefcase; I don't know what good the studies they are taking will ever do them.

No more shops, only tall black iron railings beside the pavement, and then Dayo turn in the big open yard of the British Museum. A lot of foreign tourists here, in light tourist clothes. It is like a different city, and he is like a man among the tourists: watch him going up the wide steps with his suit and his books. But these people come for the day; they are happy, they have buses to take them back to their hotels; they have countries to go back to, they have houses. The sadness I feel make my heart seize.

He go inside. I know I have no more to see, but I decide to wait. I look at the tourists and walk about. I walk about the portico, the yard, and out in the street below the trees. One time I walk back nearly to Tottenham Court Road. The Indian restaurant is hot and smelling. It make me think of my own shop, the way I trap myself and throw away my life there. Lunchtime, I nearly forget. I run back to the Museum and I run straight up the steps through the tourists coming and going and I nearly run through the door. But then I see him outside, in the portico, sitting on a wood bench and smoking.

He still have the books with him, and he is sitting very sprawled. The hate rush in my heart, I want to punish him in public, I want a big thing right there in the open, in front of everybody. But then I catch sight of his face, and I stay behind the pillar and study him.

It isn't only the sadness of the face. It isn't only the way he is smoking, letting the cigarette hand drop from his mouth like a man who don't care. He is not sprawling to show off. He is like a man who break his back in truth. It is the face of a tired, foolish boy. It is the face of someone lost. It is the same face of the boy who wake up in the room and look at me with terror. And I feel that if anything happen now to frighten him that mouth will open in a scream.

The sun shining bright now. The grass green and level and pretty. You can see the edges of the lawn black and rich, like the first time you clear a piece of bush and you know anything will grow: you can feel the damp with your foot when you walk, you can see the seeds coming up, splitting and tiny, growing day after day. The school-girls sitting young and indecent on the concrete kerb in their short blue skirts, laughing and talking loud to get people to look at them. The buses come and go. The taxis come and turn, and men and women get out and get in. The whole world going on. And I feel outside it, seeing only my brother and myself in this place, among the pillars, me in my working clothes, he in his suit that is so cheap it can't hold a crease or a shape, smoking his cigarette. I would like him to smoke the best cigarettes in the world.

I don't want him to turn foolish like Stephen's son. I don't want that to happen. I want to go to him and embrace him and put my hand on his head and smell his body. I want to tell him that it is all right, that I will protect him, that he must take no more studies, that he is a free man. I would like him then to smile at me. But he wouldn't smile at me. If I go to him now I will frighten him and he will open his mouth to scream. This is what I do, this is what I bring on myself. I can't go to him. I can only stand behind the pillar and watch him.

He put out his cigarette. Then with his books he walk out through the gate between the big black railings. Lunchtime now, pub, sandwich, people coming out of offices, walking below the trees. He mingle with them. But he have nowhere to go. And after I watch him leave I feel that I too have nowhere to go, and that the life in London is over.

I have nowhere to go and I walk now, like Dayo, where the tourists walk. The roti-shop: that noose I put my neck in. I think how nice it would be if I could just leave it, leave it just like that. Let the curry from yesterday go stale and rotten and turn red like poison, let the dust fall from the ceiling and settle. Take Dayo home before he get foolish. If a man could do that, if a man could just leave a life that spoil.

To leave the basement with the moon-mad woman upstairs, to leave the windows that look out on nothing back and front. Night after night in the basement the rat scratch. One time, when I did take away the box to stop up the hole with Polyfilla, I see where the claws scratch and scratch in the dark. Something like white fur cover that part of the box. Let the rat come out. The life is over. I am like a man who is giving up. I come with nothing. I have nothing, I will leave with nothing.

All afternoon as I walk I feel like a free man. I scorn everything I see, and when I tire myself out with walking, and the afternoon gone, I still scorn. I scorn the bus, the conductor, the street.

I scorn the white boys who come in the shop in the evening.

They come to make trouble. But it is different tonight. I am fighting for nothing here. They are provoking me. But they give me strength. Samson get back his hair, he is strong. Nothing can touch him. He is going back on the ship, and no matter how black the water is at night, in the morning it will be blue. Just for a little bit more he must be strong, and he will leave. He will go away and let the dust fall and the rats come.

The glasses and the plates are breaking. The words and that laugh are everywhere. Let everything break. I will take Dayo on that ship with me, and his face will not be sad, his mouth will not open to scream. I am walking out, I will go now, the knife is in my hand. But then at the door I feel I want to bawl. I see Dayo's face again, I feel the strength run right out of me, my bones turning to wire in my arms. These people take my money, these people spoil my life. I close the door and turn the key, and I know then I turn around and I hear myself say, 'I am taking one of you today. Two of us going today.' I hear nothing else.

Then, always, in the quiet, I see the boy's face surprised. And it is strange, because he and Dayo are college friends and Dayo is staying with him in this old-fashioned wood house in England. It is an accident; they was only playing. But how easy the knife go in him, how easy he drop. I can't look down. Dayo look at me and open his mouth to bawl, but no scream coming. He want me to help him, his eyes jumping with fright, but I can't help him now. It is the gallows for him. I can't take that for him. I only know that inside me mash up, and that the love and danger I carry all this time break and cut, and my life finish. Nothing making noise now. The body is in the chest, like in *Rope*, but in this English house. Then the worst part always come: the quiet dark ride, and the sitting down at the dining-table with the boy's parents. Dayo is trembling; he is not a good actor; he will give himself away. It is like his body in that chest, it is like mine. I can't see what the house is like. I can't see the boy's parents. It is like a dream, when you can't move, and you want to wake up quick.

Then noise come back, and I know that something bad happen to my right eye. But I can't even move my hand to feel it.

Frank is sitting beside me on the bus now. I am on the inside, looking down the road. He is on the outside, pressing against me. We will go to another railway station and take a train; then we will take a bus again. And at the end, in some building, in some church, I will see my brother and the white girl he is going to marry. In these three years Dayo make his own way. He give up studies, he get a work.

I used to think of him going back to the basement that day and finding nobody there, and nobody coming home; and I used to think of that as the end of the world. But he do better without me; he don't need me. I lose him. I can't see the sort of life he get into, I can't see the people he is going to mix with now. Sometimes I think of him as a stranger, different from the man I did know. Sometimes I see him as he was, and feel that he is alone, like me.

The rain stop, the sun come out. In the train we go past the backs of tall houses. The brick grey; no paint here, except for the window frames, bright red and bright green. People living one on top of the other. All kinds of rubbish on top of the flat roofs over projecting back rooms, and sometimes a little plant in a pot inside, behind windows running with wet and steam. Everybody on his shelf, in his little place. But a man can leave everything, a man can just disappear. Somebody will come after him to clean up and clear away, and that new person will settle down there until his own time come.

When we come to the station it is as though we are out of London again. The station building small and low, the houses small and neat in red brick, the little chimneys smoking. The big advertisements in the station yard make you feel that everybody here is very happy, laughing below an umbrella in the shape of a house-roof, eating sausages and making funny faces, the whole family sitting down to eat together.

As we wait for the bus, for this last lap, my nervousness return. The street is wide, everything is clean, and I feel exposed. But Frank know me well. He edge up close, as though he want to protect me from the little cold wind that is blowing. The wind make Frank's face white and it lift a little of his thin hair, so that he look a little bit like a boy.

I see him playing as a boy in streets like this one. I don't know why, I see him with a dirty face and dirty clothes, like those children asking for a penny for the guy. And as I am thinking this, looking down at Frank's big shining shoes, a very little girl in very small jeans come right up to Frank and embrace his knees and ask for a penny. He say no, and she hit him on his leg and say, 'You *have* a penny.' She is a very young child; she don't know what she is doing, rubbing up against strangers; she don't even know what money is. But Frank's white face get very hard, and even after the girl go away Frank is nervous still. He is glad to get on the bus when it come.

Now on this last lap to the church I feel I am entering enemy territory. I can't see my brother living in this sort of place. I can't see him getting mixed up with these people. The streets wide, the trees without leaves, and everything is looking new. Even the church is looking new. It is of red brick; it don't have a fence or anything; it is just there, on the main road.

We stand up on the pavement and wait. The wind cold now, and I am nervous. But I feel Frank is even more nervous. A woman in a tweed suit come out of the church. She is about fifty and she have a nice face. She smile at us. And now Frank is shyer than me. I don't know whether the woman is my brother's mother-in-law or whether she is just someone who is helping out. You think of a wedding, you think of people waiting outside the church or hall or whatever it is. You don't think of it like this.

Some more people come out, not many, with one or two children. And they looking hard at me, like an enemy, these people who spoil my life.

Frank touch me on the arm. I am glad he touch me, but I shrug his hand away. I know it isn't true, but I tell myself he is on the other side, with those others, looking at me without looking at me. I know it isn't true about Frank because, look, he too is nervous. He want to be alone with me; he don't like being with his own people. It isn't like being on a bus or in a café, where he can be like a man saying: I protect this man with me. It is different here outside the church, with the two of us standing on the pavement on one side, and the other sad people standing on another side, the sun red like an orange, the trees hardly throwing a shadow, the grass wild all around the brick church.

A taxi stop. It is my brother. He have a thin white boy with him, and the two of them in suits. Taxi today, wedding day. No turban, no procession, no drums, no ceremony of welcome, no green arches, no lights in the wedding tent, no wedding songs. Just the taxi, the thin white boy with sharp shoes and short hair, smoking, and my brother with a white rose in his jacket. He is just the same. The ugly labourer's face, and he is talking to his friend, showing everybody he is very cool. I don't know why I did think he would get different in three years.

When he and his friend come to me I look at my brother's eyes and his big cheeks and the laughing mouth. It is a soft face and a frightened face. I hope nobody take it into their head one day to break that face up. The friend looking at me, smoking, squinting with the smoke, sly eyes in a rough thin face.

I can feel Frank stiffening and getting more nervous. But then the nice woman in the tweed suit come and start talking in her very brisk way. She is making a noise, breaking up the silence rather than talking, and she take my brother and his friend away and she start moving about among the people on the other side, always making this noise. She is a nice woman; she have this nice face; at this bad moment she is being very nice.

We go in the church and the nice lady make us sit on the right side. Nobody else there but Frank and me, and then the other people come in and sit on the left side, and the ugly church is so big it is as though nobody is there at all. It is the first time I am in a church and I don't like it. It is as though they are making me eat beef and pork. The flowers and the brass and the old smell and the body on the cross make me think of the dead. The funny taste is in my mouth, my old nausea, and I feel I would vomit if I swallow.

I look down, I do what Frank do, and all the time the taste is in my mouth. I don't look at my brother and the girl until it is all over. Then I see this girl in white, with her veil and flowers, like somebody dead, and her face is blank and broad and very white, the little make-up shining on cheeks and temples like wax. She is a stranger. I don't know how my brother allow himself to do this thing. It is not right. He is a lost man here. You can see it on everybody's face except the girl's.

Outside, the air is fresh. They take a lot of pictures, and still it is more like a funeral than a wedding. Then the nice lady make Frank and me get in the photographer's car. He is a businessman with worries, this photographer. With his gold-rimmed glasses and his little moustache, business is all he is talking about, and he is driving very fast, like one of our mad taxi drivers. He is talking about the jobs he have to do, about how he start in the photography business, his contacts with newspapers and so on, and even as he is driving he is digging in his breast pocket and turning round to smile and give us his card.

He drive us to a sort of restaurant and straightaway he is busy with his camera and he forget us. It is an old-fashioned building and you go inside a courtyard in the middle, galleries all around. A lot of crooked brown beams everywhere, like in some old British picture, and they take us into a crooked little room with some very crooked beams. In that room everybody gather again and get photographed. Everybody can fit in that small room, everybody at the wedding.

Some of the women crying, my brother looking tired and stunned, the girl looking tired. His wife. How quick a big thing like that settle, how quick a man spoil his life. Frank stick close to me, and when the time come for us to sit down he sit next to me. Nobody talking too much. You get more talk at a wake. Only the pretty waitress, so nice and neat in her white apron and black dress, is happy. She is outside it, and only she is behaving as though it is a wedding party.

No meat for me, and Frank say no meat for him either. He want to do everything like me now. The nice waitress bring us trout. The skin burn black and crispy at the top, and when I eat a piece of the fish it is raw and rotten, so that the church taste come back in my mouth, and I think of the dead again, and brass and flowers.

The waitress come in, her armpits smelling now, and ask if anybody want wine. She say she forgot to ask the first time. Nobody hear, nobody answer. She ask again; she say some people drink wine at wedding parties. Still nobody answer. And then an old man who never say anything before, he looking so sad, he lift his face up, he laugh and say, '*There's* your answer, miss.' And I feel he must be like Stephen, the wise and funny man of the family, and that people expect to laugh at what he say. And people laugh, and I feel I like that man.

I love them. They take my money, they spoil my life, they separate us. But you can't kill them. O God, show me the enemy. Once you find out who the enemy is, you can kill him. But these people here they confuse me. Who hurt me? Who spoil my life? Tell me who to beat back. I work four years to save my money, I work like a donkey night and day. My brother was to be the educated one, the nice one. And this is how it is ending, in this room, eating with these people. Tell me who to kill.

And now my brother come to me. He is going away with his wife, for good. He hold me by the hand, he look at me, tears come in his eyes, and he say, 'I love you.' It is true, it is like the time he cry and say he didn't have confidence. I know that he love me, that now it is true, but that it will not be true as soon as he go out of this room, that he will have to forget me. Because it was my idea after my trouble that nobody should know, that the message should go back home that I was dead. And for all this time I am the dead man.

I have my own place to go back to. Frank will take me there when this is over. And now that my brother leave me for good I forget his face already, and I only seeing the rain and the house and the mud, the field at the back with the pará-grass bending down with the rain, the donkey and the smoke from the kitchen, my father in the gallery and my brother in the room on the floor, and that boy opening his mouth to scream, like in *Rope*.

I WAS GOING TO Egypt, this time by air, and I broke my journey at Milan. I did so for business reasons. But it was Christmas week, not a time for business, and I had to stay in Milan over the holidays. The weather was bad, the hotel empty and desolate.

Returning through the rain to the hotel one evening, after a restaurant dinner, I saw two Chinese men in dark-blue suits come out of the hotel dining-room. Fellow Asiatics, the three of us, I thought, wanderers in industrial Europe. But they didn't glance at me. They had companions: three more Chinese came out of the dining-room, two young men in suits, a fresh-complexioned young woman in a flowered tunic and slacks. Then five more Chinese came out, healthy young men and women; then about a dozen. Then I couldn't count. Chinese poured out of the dining-room and swirled about the spacious carpeted lobby before moving in a slow, softly chattering mass up the steps.

There must have been about a hundred Chinese. It was minutes before the lobby emptied. The waiters, serving-napkins in hand, stood in the door of the dining-room and watched, like people able at last to acknowledge an astonishment. Two more Chinese came out of the dining-room; they were the last. They were both short, elderly men, wrinkled and stringy, with glasses. One of them held a fat wallet in his small hand, but awkwardly, as though the responsibility made him nervous. The waiters straightened up. Not attempting style, puzzling over the Italian notes, the old Chinese with the wallet tipped, thanked and shook hands with each waiter. Then both the Chinese bowed and got into the lift. And the hotel lobby was desolate again.

'They are the circus,' the dark-suited desk-clerk said. He was as awed as the waiters. '*Vengono dalla Cina rossa*. They come from Red China.'

I left Milan in snow. In Cairo, in the derelict cul-de-sac behind my hotel, children in dingy jibbahs, feeble from their day-long

Ramadan fasting, played football in the white, warm dust. In cafés, shabbier than I remembered, Greek and Lebanese businessmen in suits read the local French and English newspapers and talked with sullen excitement about the deals that might be made in Rhodesian tobacco, now that it was outlawed. The Museum was still haunted by Egyptian guides possessing only native knowledge. And on the other bank of the Nile there was a new Hilton hotel.

But Egypt still had her revolution. Street signs were now in Arabic alone; people in tobacco kiosks reacted sharply, as to an insult, when they were asked for *Egyptian* cigarettes; and in the railway station, when I went to get the train south, there was a reminder of the wars that had come with the revolution. Sunburnt soldiers, back from duty in Sinai, crouched and sprawled on the floor of the waiting-room. These men with shrunken faces were the guardians of the land and the revolution; but to Egyptians they were only common soldiers, peasants, objects of a disregard that was older and more rooted than the revolution.

All day the peasant land rolled past the windows of the train: the muddy river, the green fields, the desert, the black mud, the *shadouf*, the choked and crumbling flat-roofed towns the colour of dust: the Egypt of the school geography book. The sun set in a smoky sky; the land felt old. It was dark when I left the train at Luxor. Later that evening I went to the temple of Karnak. It was a good way of seeing it for the first time, in the darkness, separate from the distress of Egypt: those extravagant columns, ancient in ancient times, the work of men of this Nile Valley.

There was no coin in Egypt that year, only paper money. All foreign currencies went far; and Luxor, in recent imperial days a winter resort of some style, was accommodating itself to simpler tourists. At the Old Winter Palace Hotel, where fat Negro servants in long white gowns stood about in the corridors, they told me they were giving me the room they used to give the Aga Khan. It was an enormous room, overfurnished in a pleasing old-fashioned way. It had a balcony and a view of the Nile and low desert hills on the other bank.

In those hills were the tombs. Not all were of kings and not all were solemn. The ancient artist, recording the life of a lesser personage, sometimes recorded with a freer hand the pleasures of that life: the pleasures of the river, full of fish and birds, the pleasures of food and drink. The land had been studied, everything in it categorized, exalted into design. It was the special vision of men who knew no other land and saw what they had as rich and complete. The muddy Nile was only water: in the paintings, a blue-green chevron: recognizable, but remote, a river in fairyland.

It could be hot in the tombs. The guide, who was also sometimes the watchman, crouched and chattered in Arabic, earning his paper piastres, pointing out every symbol of the goddess Hathor, rubbing a grimy finger on the paintings he was meant to protect. Outside, after the darkness and the bright visions of the past, there was only rubbled white sand; the sunlight stunned; and sometimes there were beggar boys in jibbahs.

To me these boys, springing up expectantly out of rock and sand when men approached, were like a type of sand animal. But my driver knew some of them by name; when he shooed them away it was with a languid gesture which also contained a wave. He was a young man, the driver, of the desert himself, and once no doubt he had been a boy in a jibbah. But he had grown up differently. He wore trousers and shirt and was vain of his good looks. He was reliable and correct, without the frenzy of the desert guide. Somehow in the desert he had learned boredom. His thoughts were of Cairo and a real job. He was bored with the antiquities, the tourists and the tourist routine.

I was spending the whole of that day in the desert, and now it was time for lunch. I had a Winter Palace lunch-box, and I had seen somewhere in the desert the new government rest-house where tourists could sit at tables and eat their sandwiches and buy coffee. I thought the driver was taking me there. But we went by unfamiliar ways to a little oasis with palm trees and a large, dried-up timber hut. There were no cars, no minibuses, no tourists, only anxious Egyptian serving-people in rough clothes. I didn't want to stay. The driver seemed about to argue, but then he was only bored. He drove to the new rest-house, set me down and said he would come back for me later.

The rest-house was crowded. Sunglassed tourists, exploring their cardboard lunch-boxes, chattered in various European languages. I sat on the terrace at a table with two young Germans. A brisk middle-aged Egyptian in Arab dress moved among the tables and served coffee. He had a camel-whip at his waist, and I saw, but only slowly, that for some way around the rest-house the hummocked sand was alive with little desert children. The desert was clean, the air was clean; these children were very dirty.

The rest-house was out of bounds to them. When they came close, tempted by the offer of a sandwich or an apple, the man with the camel-whip gave a camel-frightening shout. Sometimes he ran out among them, beating the sand with his whip, and they skittered away, thin little sand-smoothed legs frantic below swinging jibbahs. There was no rebuke for the tourists who had offered the food; this was an Egyptian game with Egyptian rules.

It was hardly a disturbance. The young Germans at my table paid no attention. The English students inside the rest-house, behind glass, were talking competitively about Carter and Lord Carnarvon. But the middle-aged Italian group on the terrace, as they understood the rules of the game, became playful. They threw apples and made the children run far. Experimentally they broke up sandwiches and threw the pieces out on to the sand; and they got the children to come up quite close. Soon it was all action around the Italians; and the man with the camel-whip, like a man understanding what was required of him, energetic-ally patrolled that end of the terrace, shouting, beating the sand, earning his paper piastres.

A tall Italian in a cerise jersey stood up and took out his camera. He laid out food just below the terrace and the children came running. But this time, as though it had to be real for the camera, the camel-whip fell not on sand but on their backs, with louder, quicker camel-shouts. And still, among the tourists in the rest-house and among the Egyptian drivers standing about their cars and minibuses, there was no disturbance. Only the man with the whip and the children scrabbling in the sand were frantic. The Italians were cool. The man in the cerise jersey was opening another packet of sandwiches. A shorter, older man in a white suit had stood up and was adjusting his camera. More food was thrown out; the camel-whip continued to fall; the shouts of the man with the whip turned to resonant grunts.

Still the Germans at my table didn't notice; the students inside were still talking. I saw that my hand was trembling. I put down the sandwich I was eating on the metal table; it was my last decision. Lucidity, and anxiety, came to me only when I was almost on the man with the camel-whip. I was shouting. I took the whip away, threw it on the sand. He was astonished, relieved. I said, 'I will report this to Cairo.' He was frightened; he began to plead in Arabic. The children were puzzled; they ran off a little way and stood up to watch. The two Italians, fingering cameras, looked quite calm behind their sunglasses. The women in the party leaned back in their chairs to consider me.

I felt exposed, futile, and wanted only to be back at my table. When I got back I took up my sandwich. It had happened quickly; there had been no disturbance. The Germans stared at me. But I was indifferent to them now as I was indifferent to the Italian in the cerise jersey. The Italian women had stood up, the group was leaving; and he was ostentatiously shaking out lunch-boxes and sandwich wrappers on to the sand.

The children remained where they were. The man from whom I had taken the whip came to give me coffee and to plead again in Arabic and English. The coffee was free; it was his gift to me. But even while he was talking the children had begun to come closer. Soon they would be back, raking the sand for what they had seen the Italian throw out.

I didn't want to see that. The driver was waiting, leaning against the car door, his bare arms crossed. He had seen all that had happened. From him, an emancipated young man of the desert in belted trousers and sports shirt, with his thoughts of Cairo, I was expecting some gesture, some sign of approval. He smiled at me with the corners of his wide mouth, with his narrow eyes. He crushed his cigarette in the sand and slowly breathed out smoke through his lips; he sighed. But that was his way of smoking. I couldn't tell what he thought. He was as correct as before, he looked as bored.

Everywhere I went that afternoon I saw the pea-green Volks-wagen minibus of the Italian group. Everywhere I saw the cerise jersey. I learned to recognize the plump, squiffy, short-stepped walk that went with it, the dark glasses, the receding hairline, the little stiff swing of the arms. At the ferry I thought I had managed to escape; but the minibus arrived, the Italians got out. I thought we would separate on the Luxor bank. But they too were staying at the Winter Palace. The cerise jersey bobbed confidently through bowing Egyptian servants in the lobby, the bar, the grand dining-room with fresh flowers and intricately folded napkins. In Egypt that year there was only paper money.

I stayed for a day or two on the Luxor bank. Dutifully, I saw Karnak by moonlight. When I went back to the desert I was anxious to avoid the rest-house. The driver understood. Without any show of triumph he took me when the time came to the timber hut among the palm trees. They were doing more business that day. There were about four or five parked minibuses. Inside, the hut was dark, cool and uncluttered. A number of tables had been joined together; and at this central dining-board there were about forty or fifty Chinese, men and women, chattering softly. They were part of the circus I had seen in Milan.

The two elderly Chinese sat together at the end of the long table, next to a small, finely made lady who looked just a little too old to be an acrobat. I had missed her in the crowd in Milan. Again, when the time came to pay, the man with the fat wallet used his hands awkwardly. The lady spoke to the Egyptian waiter. He called the other waiters and they all formed a line. For each waiter the lady had a handshake and gifts, money, something in an envelope, a medal. The ragged waiters stood stiffly, with serious averted faces, like soldiers being decorated. Then all the Chinese rose and, chattering, laughing softly, shuffled out of the echoing hut with their relaxed, slightly splayed gait. They didn't look at me; they appeared scarcely to notice the hut. They were as cool and well-dressed in the desert, the men in suits, the girls in slacks, as they had been in the rain of Milan. So self-contained, so handsome and healthy, so silently content with one another: it was hard to think of them as sightseers.

The waiter, his face still tense with pleasure, showed the medal on his dirty striped jibbah. It had been turned out from a mould that had lost its sharpness; but the ill-defined face was no doubt Chinese and no doubt that of the leader. In the envelope were pretty coloured postcards of Chinese peonies.

Peonies, China! So many empires had come here. Not far from where we were was the colossus on whose shin the Emperor Hadrian had caused to be carved verses in praise of himself, to commemorate his visit. On the other bank, not far from the Winter Palace, was a stone with a rougher Roman inscription marking the southern limit of the Empire, defining an area of retreat. Now another, more remote empire was announcing itself. A medal, a postcard; and all that was asked in return was anger and a sense of injustice.

Perhaps that had been the only pure time, at the beginning, when the ancient artist, knowing no other land, had learned to look at his own and had seen it as complete. But it was hard, travelling back to Cairo, looking with my stranger's eye at the fields and the people who worked in them, the dusty towns, the agitated peasant crowds at railway stations, it was hard to believe that there had been such innocence. Perhaps that vision of the land, in which the Nile was only water, a blue-green chevron, had always been a fabrication, a cause for yearning, something for the tomb.

The air-conditioning in the coach didn't work well; but that might have been because the two Negro attendants, still with the habits of the village, preferred to sit before the open doors to chat. Sand and dust blew in all day; it was hot until the sun set and everything went black against the red sky. In the dimly lit waiting-room of Cairo station there were more sprawled soldiers from Sinai, peasants in bulky woollen uniforms going back on leave to their villages. Seventeen months later these men, or men like them, were to know total defeat in the desert; and news photographs taken from helicopters flying down low were to show them lost, trying to walk back home, casting long shadows on the sand.

August 1969–October 1970

CHINUA ACHEBE
The African Trilogy
Things Fall Apart

ISABEL ALLENDE
The House of the Spirits

ISAAC ASIMOV
Foundation
Foundation and Empire
Second Foundation
(in 1 vol.)

MARGARET ATWOOD
The Handmaid's Tale

GIORGIO BASSANI
The Garden of the Finzi-Continis

SIMONE DE BEAUVOIR
The Second Sex

SAMUEL BECKETT
Molloy, Malone Dies,
The Unnamable
(US only)

SAUL BELLOW
The Adventures of Augie March

JORGE LUIS BORGES
Ficciones

RAY BRADBURY
The Stories of Ray Bradbury

MIKHAIL BULGAKOV
The Master and Margarita

JAMES M. CAIN
The Postman Always Rings Twice
Double Indemnity
Mildred Pierce
Selected Stories
(1 vol. US only)

ITALO CALVINO
If on a winter's night a traveler

ALBERT CAMUS
The Outsider (UK)
The Stranger (US)
The Plague, The Fall,
Exile and the Kingdom,
and Selected Essays
(in 1 vol.)

WILLA CATHER
Death Comes for the Archbishop
(US only)
My Ántonia

RAYMOND CHANDLER
The novels (2 vols)
Collected Stories

G. K. CHESTERTON
The Everyman Chesterton

KATE CHOPIN
The Awakening

JOSEPH CONRAD
Heart of Darkness
Lord Jim
Nostromo
The Secret Agent
Typhoon and Other Stories
Under Western Eyes
Victory

ROALD DAHL
Collected Stories

JOAN DIDION
We Tell Ourselves Stories in
Order to Live (US only)

UMBERTO ECO
The Name of the Rose

WILLIAM FAULKNER
The Sound and the Fury
(UK only)

F. SCOTT FITZGERALD
The Great Gatsby
This Side of Paradise
(UK only)

PENELOPE FITZGERALD
The Bookshop
The Gate of Angels
The Blue Flower
(in 1 vol.)
Offshore
Human Voices
The Beginning of Spring
(in 1 vol.)

FORD MADOX FORD
The Good Soldier
Parade's End

RICHARD FORD
The Bascombe Novels

E. M. FORSTER
Howards End
A Passage to India

ANNE FRANK
The Diary of a Young Girl
(US only)

GEORGE MACDONALD
FRASER
Flashman
Flash for Freedom!
Flashman in the Great Game

KAHLIL GIBRAN
The Collected Works

GÜNTER GRASS
The Tin Drum

GRAHAM GREENE
Brighton Rock
The Human Factor

DASHIELL HAMMETT
The Maltese Falcon
The Thin Man
Red Harvest
(in 1 vol.)
The Dain Curse
The Glass Key
and Selected Stories
(in 1 vol.)

JAROSLAV HAŠEK
The Good Soldier Švejk

JOSEPH HELLER
Catch-22

ERNEST HEMINGWAY
A Farewell to Arms
The Collected Stories
(UK only)

MICHAEL HERR
Dispatches (US only)

PATRICIA HIGHSMITH
The Talented Mr. Ripley
Ripley Under Ground
Ripley's Game
(in 1 vol.)

JAMES JOYCE
Dubliners
A Portrait of the Artist as
a Young Man
Ulysses

FRANZ KAFKA
Collected Stories
The Castle
The Trial

MAXINE HONG KINGSTON
The Woman Warrior and
China Men
(US only)

RUDYARD KIPLING
Collected Stories
Kim

GIUSEPPE TOMASI DI
LAMPEDUSA
The Leopard

D. H. LAWRENCE
Collected Stories
The Rainbow
Sons and Lovers
Women in Love

DORIS LESSING
Stories

PRIMO LEVI
If This is a Man and The Truce
(UK only)
The Periodic Table

NAGUIB MAHFOUZ
The Cairo Trilogy
Three Novels of Ancient Egypt

THOMAS MANN
Buddenbrooks
Collected Stories (UK only)
Death in Venice and Other Stories
(US only)
Doctor Faustus
Joseph and His Brothers
The Magic Mountain

KATHERINE MANSFIELD
The Garden Party and Other
Stories

GABRIEL GARCÍA MÁRQUEZ
The General in His Labyrinth
Love in the Time of Cholera
One Hundred Years of Solitude

W. SOMERSET MAUGHAM
Collected Stories

CORMAC McCARTHY
The Border Trilogy

YUKIO MISHIMA
The Temple of the
Golden Pavilion

This book is set in BEMBO which was cut
by the punch-cutter Francesco Griffo
for the Venetian printer-publisher
Aldus Manutius in early 1495
and first used in a pamphlet
by a young scholar
named Pietro
Bembo.